RESCUING CROCKETT

Published 2023

Special Limited Edition Paperback ISBN: 978-1-959440-00-0

Hardcover ISBN: 978-1-959440-01-7

Paperback ISBN: 978-1-959440-02-4

Kindle ISBN: 978-1-959440-03-1

EPUB ISBN: 978-1-959440-04-8

Library of Congress Control Number: 2023908368

Published by Leonard Street Publishing

Denton, Texas

leonardstreetpublishing.com

For information and special orders, email contact@leonardstreetpublishing.com.

For Suzanne

Forever and always.

AUTHOR'S NOTES

This is a work of fiction.

I want to be clear: this novel is not suggesting an alternate theory of Texas history.

Real people, places, events, and situations from history provide authenticity, but they are used fictitiously. I attempted to be faithful to the historical record as long as that record fit the narrative of the novel. When it did not, I went my own way.

On the use of Texian:
Throughout the novel, I use "Texian" to refer to the White, Black, and Tejano people of Texas instead of "Texan." Texian was used to describe the people of the Republic of Texas at the time of the novel. By the 1850s, Texian was being replaced by Texan. A shame, really. But folks from the Republic period continued to call themselves Texians up to the turn of the century.

On the use of Spanish and English:

At times I use the Spanish courtesy titles "señor" and "señora," at other times their English equivalents. The difference? When characters are conversing in Spanish, dialogue is presented in English. Hence, the use of "Mr." or "sir" instead of "señor" and "Mrs." instead of "señora" in dialogue conducted in Spanish. When dialogue is conducted in English and a character employs a Spanish word, such as "señor," "señora," or "señorita," that is an intentional usage of a foreign-language term. In that context, the word is not translatable.

On the use of Madam or Madame:

Both terms appear in the novel. Madam is, like Miss or Mrs., a courtesy title. Madame is a formal, bestowed title.

A SILAS GRANT NOVEL

RESCUING CROCKETT

DAVID Z. PYKE

PROLOGUE

MARCH 6, 1836

THE MORNING WAS smoke and blood.

The captain slogged across torn, broken earth that writhed around him. Arms and legs moved and twitched without purpose, driven only by pain. Faces, scorched by the firing of their own muskets, lifted pleadingly for help, mouths too dry to form words.

The day's colors had turned hideous. Blue jackets, white trousers, and black shakos lay in red pools, all suffused in a sulfurous miasma that hung over the field littered with severed limbs.

The last sounds of battle had ended several minutes ago with a final volley of screams, sporadic gun shots, and steel blades sinking into flesh, leaving only the laments of the wounded, the jubilant calls of winged scavengers whirling over the coming feast, and the buzz of blowflies drawn to the fresh breeding ground.

The assault on the rebel-held fort had begun before dawn. Four columns totaling more than a thousand men. General Cós to the northwest corner. Colonel Duqué to north wall. Colonel Romero to the east wall at the cattle pen. Colonel Morales to the south wall and the palisade between the chapel and the south gate.

The artillery barrage that had lasted throughout the siege had been lifted the night before the assault, luring the exhausted defenders to sleep. In the silence an hour before sunrise, the columns crept forward undetected. But as they approached the walls, the attackers broke into shouts and cheers, rousing the defenders who quickly rushed to their positions and opened fire on the massed enemy. Rifles picked off targets and cannon gouged bloody holes in the attackers' ranks, repulsing the first two onslaughts and inflicting heavy casualties.

Among the wounded was Duqué, shot from his horse. General Castrillón took command of the remnants of Duqué's troops and again threw them at the north wall while Morales shifted away from the marksmen at the palisade and concentrated on the fort's southwest corner.

On the third attempt, the breakthroughs came. Using ladders, crowbars, and axes, the attackers climbed over or broke through the north wall. Cós's men swept right and breached the west wall, Romero stormed gun positions at the cattle pen, and Morales gained entry at the south wall. Bolstered by reinforcements, the attackers poured into the fort. The outcome was decided.

However, the attackers' promise that they would show no mercy and take no prisoners gave the surviving defenders no choice but to fight or flee. A few went over the walls and ran into the fields around the fort but were cut down by cavalry. Some retreated to the long barracks, firing through windows and loopholes before being killed to the last man in brutal hand-to-hand combat. Others made a last stand behind makeshift barricades in front of the chapel, where they were blasted by their own cannon wielded by the attackers and finished with bayonets.

The captain, a member of Duqué's Toluca Battalion, spent the battle on horseback, reporting to Castrillón after Duqué fell and delivering messages between Cós and Romero as they tried to coordinate their attacks. For an hour, the captain rode back and forth across the battlefield while under fire. He felt bullets zipping around him but never had the opportunity to fire a shot nor draw his sword.

Now the captain walked beside his sweat-soaked, stumbling mount. He took off his white, wide-brimmed hat and wiped his smallpox-scarred face with a bandana. His breathing had slowed but his heart still raged and his left hand trembled slightly. Just one hand, a trivial quiver, and he thought it odd.

When the carnage ended, when the shooting and stabbing finally subsided and a bugler sounded recall, the captain found himself by the west wall. He dismounted and headed to the north wall where his battalion had begun the morning and was so savagely cut to pieces.

He paused by a dead Toluca private and looked at the holes in the corpse's face—gaping mouth, stilled nostrils, staring eyes, and the terrible crater where a Texian bullet had blown off the top of his head. A spray of blood and brains was spread on the ground beneath him, and the captain imagined himself lying there.

The captain tried to clear his head and fight off the shock of the battle's aftermath. There was much to do.

While many were dead—too many to count at a glance—the majority of casualties were alive, yet no one was attending to them. Soldiers who escaped injury could offer paltry help to their fellows as they carried no bandages, no canteens, nothing that could provide aid, and the captain could see no medical personnel anywhere, leaving the wounded to fester in their misery.

"Corporal!" the captain called to a man kneeling over a dead comrade. The corporal had removed his shako, which now lay in the dirt. "Where are the surgeons?"

The corporal just shook his head without looking up.

"Corporal!" the captain yelled, advancing on the grieving man. "Corporal," he said, lowering his voice. "Look at me." He put his hand on the corporal's shoulder. That broke the man's reverie. With a shaking hand, the corporal located his shako and put it on before rising to meet the officer.

"Sir."

"Do you know where the surgeons are? Have you seen the surgeons?"

"No, sir. I have…" he trailed off. "I haven't seen any…" and he looked around at the mass of wounded, anger and disgust welling up. "Captain, where are the surgeons?"

"Corporal, stay with me," the captain said, trying to steady the man. "We're going to get organized and help our people." Not soldiers, not the men, our people. That struck a chord with the corporal. "Here's what I need you to do. Gather some men who are not injured or at least not too badly wounded and can walk." He waited to see if the words were sinking in.

"Yes, sir." The glaze in the corporal's eyes appeared to be lifting.

"I want you to look for Sergeant Alvarado and Lieutenant Heredia. Do you understand?"

"Sergeant Alvarado and Lieutenant Heredia, yes, sir."

"Whoever you find first, tell them to go into town and find civilian doctors or nurses or anyone who has bandages and can use them. Bring them here immediately. I don't care if they have to drag a doctor here at the point of a bayonet. Understood?"

"Yes, sir!"

"Good man. I'm going back to the camp and find the army surgeons." *Incompetent butchers though they are*, he thought. "I'll be back as soon as I can."

The corporal, freshened by purpose, spun, picked up his musket, and jogged away. The captain noticed the man wore sandals instead of proper soldiers' brogans. The army didn't even have enough shoes to go around.

The captain took another look around for Toluca officers, saw none, and turned toward the camp. He had only taken a few steps when the corporal called out.

"Captain!" The corporal was standing thirty yards away beside a small knot of soldiers, one of whom was kneeling. "Lieutenant Heredia!"

The captain jogged toward the group, putting his hand on the sword and scabbard on his left hip to prevent it from swinging as he ran.

The closer the captain got to the group, the more his heart sank. He could see three men, and none was the lieutenant. But the kneeling soldier stood and moved back, revealing a fourth man lying on the ground.

"No…no, no, no, no…"

The soldiers parted and the captain moved past them, paused for a moment, and knelt beside the man on his back.

"Captain," Lieutenant Heredia said, offering a smile on his clean-shaven, handsome face. He always had such a pleasant countenance.

"José," the captain said, breaking formality. "How are you?" It was a stupid question. He could see very well how Lieutenant Heredia was. He was shot in the chest, but the young officer was calm as ever.

"We did well," Heredia said. "The men made a valiant charge." His sword was still in his hand, as it was when he urged his platoon toward the walls. As it was when he was cut down. "You were right. The Texians are excellent marksmen."

"Rest easy, José. Help is on the way," the captain said, and turned to the ashen-faced enlisted men gathered around. "Corporal, take one man and go to our camp. Find a surgeon and get him here for the lieutenant as quickly as you can. If anyone questions you, tell them the surgeon is for Lieutenant Heredia."

The corporal paused. This wasn't shock any longer; the corporal just didn't want to abandon Heredia, who was regarded an honest, fair man, respected by the officers and beloved by the men. But he needed help and that moved the corporal to action. The corporal pointed to a short private with unkempt hair and mustache, who a moment before had been kneeling at Heredia's side, and the two of them dashed off toward the camp.

"Does anyone have some water?" the captain asked. No one did, so one of the privates was dispatched to find some. A few more soldiers had gathered around the fallen officer.

"I told you," Lieutenant Heredia said. "I told you I would not see my family again."

"You're not dead, not yet," the captain said, and addressed the group. "Has anyone seen Captain Macotela?"

"Yes," Heredia said. "He's dying, too."

"I saw Captain Macotela fall," confirmed one of the newcomers, a man the captain recognized as a private named Vega. Vega had been wounded in the right thigh and was using his empty musket as a crutch. "I think he was shot like me, from back there." Vega shook his fist at their own lines.

The captain nodded. Reserve companies had tried to provide support fire to suppress the Texians on the walls. It was a foolish waste of ammunition as the walls and their defenders were well out of range of the army's Brown Bess and India Pattern muskets. Worse, the terrified, poorly trained reserves had fired blindly into the smoke and darkness, and consequently into their own assault troops.

"Has anyone seen any surgeons?" the captain asked, then noticed Vega's injured leg. It was bandaged.

"Yes, sir," Vega said. "I saw an officer—I think it was Captain Huerta—run there." He pointed to a hidden door in the north wall, which had been forced open during the battle. "Huerta was with three men. When they got near the wall, there was more shooting inside the fort. Huerta told the others to wait while he went inside. One of the men with Huerta saw me. He said he was a doctor, and he put something on my leg. He said, 'This will hurt, but it will help,' and he bandaged my wound. Then Huerta returned and called to the doctor and led him into the fort."

"Who was this doctor?" the captain asked.

"He was civilian, I think. He was wearing a long, gray coat, not a uniform. I don't think he was Mexican. Huerta called him Dr. Thorn."

The captain glanced at the fort. "Did you see the doctor again?"

"No, sir," Vega said.

The captain straightened. "Vega, you and the others remain here with Lieutenant Heredia. I'm going into the fort to find this doctor. Keep an eye out for the corporal bringing help from the camp. I'll be back."

He leaned toward Heredia. "I'll be back, José. I promise. You stay still." Heredia nodded.

It was almost an hour before the captain returned. He was alone.

"No doctor, Captain?" Heredia said.

The captain shook his head. "There's been no surgeon from the camp?"

"No, sir," Vega said.

The corporal who had been dispatched to the camp returned a few minutes later, looking as dejected as the captain.

"I'm sorry, Lieutenant Heredia," the corporal said. "We looked in the camp and in the town. Captain, there are no surgeons for the men."

The captain's jaw fell open. "It can't be." He shook his head.

"They didn't even set up a field hospital!" the corporal shouted.

"Cheap bastards," Vega said.

"They won't spend a peso for us," a private muttered.

The captain did not chastise his soldiers for their insubordination. Many of these men had been pressed into service and provided minimal training. They had risked their lives—and too many had lost their lives—assaulting a fortified defensive position. It was unconscionable that surgeons and medical supplies were not standing by. But the generals had been holding back supplies since the army began the march north from Mexico and this was no different.

The captain would have to wait to give vent to his anger. "We're going to get organized, right now," he announced. Behind him, a column of nauseating, black smoke rose from beyond the fort. The bodies of the dead Texians were being burned.

By now, more than a dozen men of the Toluca Battalion had gathered, and the captain fixed his piercing eyes into their haggard, gunpowder-blackened faces. "I know you are exhausted. You've done everything anyone could expect. You are the bravest men in this army, and I'm proud of every one of you. But our friends are hurt, maybe dying. We must not fail them." Nods all around. Men stood a little straighter. "Corporal, assign what's left of your squad to bring water from the river and food from the camp. The rest of you, gather anything you can find to make bandages. Sheets, shirts, anything. We will give whatever help we can to our wounded comrades. Go."

Before Vega could get away, the captain grabbed him by the cross belts on his chest and pulled him closer. "Private, what is your Christian name?"

"Uh, Rafael, sir."

"Rafael, I need you to do something for me," the captain said. "I want you to ask around. Find out what you can about that doctor…"

"Thorn, sir."

"Dr. Thorn. Where did he come from and, more importantly, where did he go? Keep this quiet, Rafael, between us. Tell no one else. Understood?"

"Yes, sir."

"Help the others now, but stay off that leg as much as possible."

The remnants of the Toluca Battalion spent the rest of the day making the wounded as comfortable as circumstances allowed. But as the days passed, still no surgeons or medicine became available, and every day more of the wounded succumbed. As many men died in the next two weeks as were killed in the assault.

Heredia lasted longer than most. The young lieutenant accepted his fate bravely, but all who attended him knew he was in dreadful pain. Thirteen days after the battle, Heredia received the sacrament of the Eucharist and died surrounded by friends and comrades. Officers, including the captain, served as his pallbearers, and men wept openly at the funeral, which was held on Heredia's birthday.

Thirteen days of needless suffering and death left the captain with a fury he could barely contain and a hatred for the man he felt responsible.

And standing outside the ruins of a place in Texas called the Alamo, he swore revenge.

CHAPTER 1

1838

MEXICO CITY HAD waited anxiously for the arrival of the Spanish Minister Plenipotentiary, the first ambassador from Spain since Mexico won its independence in 1821, ending three hundred years of rule that dated back to Cortés's conquest of the Aztec Empire. However, it was not Ángel Calderón de la Barca, the forty-nine-year-old, balding, Argentine-born nobleman and diplomat, who was turning heads in Mexican social and political circles.

It was his wife.

Frances Calderón de la Barca, the former Frances Inglis of Edinburgh, Scotland, by way of New Brighton, New York, was luminous. Captivating eyes, a small mouth with full lips, flawless Scottish complexion, and rosy cheeks were perfectly framed by dark hair, not a strand of which was out of place. But Fanny was far more than beautiful, and woe to the man who underestimated her. The thirty-four-year-old, born into upper class comfort but plunged into family upheaval when her father went bankrupt and died, possessed a disarming charm but wielded a sharp wit and weapons-grade sarcasm.

Married just a year before Ángel was assigned this posting, the couple had been touring Mexico, getting to know its people, places, and customs, and this evening was the latest in their prodigious travels, which Fanny was chronicling.

The Calderón de la Barcas were guests at parties, receptions, soirées, banquets, dinners, lunches, and breakfasts. They attended concerts, plays, festivals, fêtes, and feasts; masses, posadas, consecrations, and funerals; bull fights and cockfights and gambling houses. They visited cities, towns, and villages; markets, inns, and taverns; museums, academies, and galleries; cathedrals, chapels, convents, monasteries, and missions; rancheros, farms, haciendas, and huts; forests, valleys, mountains, sandhills, orchards, gardens, lakes, rivers, and the bridges that crossed them. They met politicians and priests, monks and nuns, counts and countesses, bishops and beggars, presidents and peasants.

All the while, Fanny was having the same dazzling effect on Mexico that she had on Ángel, which was making his job as envoy much easier.

And she was absolutely slaying this room.

The room in question was the grand ballroom of the Prussian embassy in Mexico City, and the occasion was a reception and dinner in the Spanish ambassador's honor.

"Are you sure we're still in Mexico?" Fanny asked as she glanced about the ballroom, which would have been at home in any European capital and was decorated from floor to ceiling.

They walked across a parquet wood floor with an enormous inlaid starburst pattern in the center under a huge chandelier dripping with hundreds of crystals and hung from a ceiling that was covered with rose vines rendered in delicate gold leaf, and past intricate Viennese urns adorning white columns precisely spaced around the room. The walls were packed with dozens and dozens of gilt-framed paintings, all portraits.

"How many of the people in those paintings do you think are still alive?" Fanny asked.

"None, I should think," Ángel said.

A chamber ensemble played in a corner, the tempo rarely changing as the musicians churned out baroque adagios by Gluck, Handel, Bach, and Telemann.

Dining tables were dressed with Meissen vases and figurines, and the kitchen disgorged Reinhold Schlegelmilch bowls and platters heaped with local meat, fish, and vegetables but prepared in traditional Prussian style with vinegar, bay leaves, horseradish, juniper berries, caraway seeds, and mustard. Lots of mustard.

The minister's staff had erased every trace of Mexico from the Prussian embassy and done everything in its power to make the evening look, sound, smell, and taste like Berlin.

Fanny's implacable face revealed no judgment. But Ángel knew.

"You hate it, don't you, my dear?" he said.

The hint of a smile Fanny wore at such functions never faltered, and she nodded as one of the minister's staff hurried past. "It's a damned Prussian carbuncle," she said.

Ángel stifled a laugh. "Yes, I don't think the minister accepts that he's in Mexico."

Fanny paused. "What's his name?"

"Baron Heinrich Ernst Wilhelm Freiherr von Canitz und Dallwitz."

Fanny raised an eyebrow at the moniker. "And I thought you stuck me with a long name. Which part is his last name?"

"I'm believe its Freiherr, but he prefers the title, Canitz und Dallwitz."

"What do I call him?"

"Baron should suffice."

"Thank you, my love."

Ángel noticed the admiring looks from the multi-national ministerial assembly and nodded politely to each in turn. He was attired in his formal best: a black jacket with high, gilded collar, black trousers, and black shoes. A gold sash swooped over his right shoulder to his left hip while half a dozen fist-sized medals hung over his left breast—of which no one took the slightest notice.

All anyone saw was Fanny, resplendent in a French iridescent blue off-the-shoulder evening dress that ably showed off her figure and displayed her pale white shoulders, neck, and upper chest without ever threatening to expose any more than intended.

Ángel bore no jealousy of the attention paid his wife nor of the rather lecherous looks from other men. Whenever he walked with Fanny on his arm, Ángel wore a slight grin that seemed to say, "Enjoy the view gentlemen, but she's going home with me."

The ballroom murmured with a confounding of languages from both sides of the Atlantic, though heavy on German from the embassy staff. But in a crowd of international envoys, most of whom spoke three, four, or five languages, being understood was rarely an issue. French remained the language of diplomats, but in these unofficial settings, it was simply a matter of adapting to whoever you were addressing.

"And here they come," Ángel said as the Prussian minister, flanked by his wife and trailing a staff member and his wife, approached. The Calderón de la Barcas reinforced the sincerity of their counterfeit smiles and braced for impact.

The baron, Fanny saw, was quite the dandy. He advanced in a flourish of ruffles: a white cravat wrapped around his neck descended in waves down his white Regency shirt, which grudgingly disappeared under a dark jacket only to explode into view again in a burst of lace at the wrists.

"Ah, my dear Minister Calderón de la Barca," the baron said with an exaggerated bow. "How are you? I hope your journey has been pleasant."

"Very pleasant, Baron Freiherr von Canitz und Dallwitz," Ángel responded with a slight bow. "Very kind of you to ask. This is my wife, Frances Calderón de la Barca."

"Enchanted, Madame," the baron said, bowing and kissing Fanny's hand. "Welcome to Mexico City."

With that, the baron's wife stepped forward and embraced Fanny, who cordially returned the gesture.

"My dear, you look radiant," the baron's wife said. The baron, struck dumb by Fanny, had failed to introduce his wife.

"You're too kind," Fanny said.

The wife of the baron's staff member now stepped forward for her cursory embrace. Her poor husband remained at the back, forgotten by the baron.

"I am rejoiced to meet you, my dear," she said.

"And I you," Fanny said mechanically.

Fanny truly loved her husband, enjoyed their travels, and didn't mind the avalanche of events to which his job required attendance, but she found this kind of mandatory small talk and etiquette particularly tiresome. And very European. If she saw these women the next morning, they undoubtedly would inquire how she passed the night. Sigh.

"How have you found Mexico City, Madame Calderón de la Barca?" the baron asked while plumping one of his wrist ruffles. "Not too taxing, I hope."

You condescending fop, she thought.

"A noble, elegant city, sir," she said. "The Viga is one of the most impressive promenades I've ever seen. Today we saw the site of the great market at Tlatelolco."

"Ah, yes," the baron said. "I believe a convent chapel stands on the hill there now."

"Yes," Fanny said, and Ángel was struck by how much disapproval someone could voice in such a small word. "Where Cortés besieged the city. Before slaughtering the Aztecs and razing most of the city."

The baron shifted uncomfortably.

"I cannot help but wonder how beautiful ancient Tenochtitlan was," Fanny pressed. "The valley must have been so picturesque and fertile with its lakes and fine trees. Before Spanish settlers cut down the forests."

"Yes, trees…" the baron began. "Well…" he stumbled, looking for a way to change the subject but wary of what to say next.

"As you've done here, Baron," Fanny said, gesturing to the room. "This is the very picture of European style. Except for a few servants, you'd hardly know we were in Mexico. But that's the idea, isn't it?"

The baron swallowed behind a feeble smile. "Yes…well…uh…"

A few steps away, a pair of diplomatic dinner veterans watched with admiration as the exquisite Madame Calderón de la Barca tormented the squirming baron.

"Have you met the Spanish ambassador, Luis?" the tall, lean-faced American said.

"Yes," said the Mexican with heavily lidded eyes and dramatic muttonchop sideburns. "And his wife. I'm afraid the baron isn't up to dealing with her." Luis set aside a half-drained glass of champagne. "I suppose we should rescue him."

The duo made their way to the side of the floundering Prussian who was noticeably relieved at their intervention.

"Ah!" the baron said a bit too loudly. "Minister and Madame Calderón de la Barca, may I introduce Luis Gonzaga Cuevas, Mexico's Secretary of Foreign Affairs, and Powhatan Ellis, the Envoy Extraordinary and Minister Plenipotentiary from the United States."

Stiff bows and stately greetings all around.

"Madame Calderón de la Barca," Ellis said, "I believe we have a mutual friend in the United States. William Prescott."

"Indeed!" Fanny beamed at the mention. "Mr. Prescott is a treasured friend. He introduced me to my husband." She gave Ángel's arm a gentle squeeze.

Ellis turned to the Spaniard. "Then you, sir, owe Mr. Prescott quite a debt." Ángel nodded in agreement.

"What affairs occupy you in Mexico, Mr. Ellis?" the baron asked, eliciting a sigh from Ellis and a chuckle from Cuevas.

"Chasing a wild goose, sir, a wild goose," Ellis said. "It seems an American, convicted of a crime in Mexico and doing hard labor in a mine in Guadalajara, concocted the story that he is Davy Crockett."

"Davy Crockett?" Ángel said. "The American frontiersman?"

"And former member of the United States House of Representatives."

"Did he not die in Texas?" Ángel said.

"At the Alamo in 1836," Ellis said. "Absolute nonsense that he could still be alive two years later. But this prisoner managed to get a letter to a Mr. William White, who delivered the letter to Crockett's son, John, who requested an investigation from the US government. I received orders from Secretary of State Forsyth to look into the matter."

Cuevas chuckled again at the fool's errand foisted upon his friend.

"And?" Fanny said.

"I traveled to Guadalajara—a distance of some five hundred miles—and spoke to this prisoner. Bad luck for him. I served with David Crockett when he was a congressman and I was a senator. First, this brigand in the mine looked nothing like Crockett. The prisoner was several inches shorter and had a flat nose and blond hair. David was tall, with a long nose and brown hair.

"Further, Crockett preferred to be called David. The prisoner didn't know this. The prisoner was also rather foul mouthed, which Crockett was not. This imposter couldn't even tell me how many brothers and sisters he had, or his wife Elizabeth's maiden name."

"You knew Crockett well," Fanny said.

Ellis nodded. "He is remembered for his humor and charm, but I think of him as a man who fought for the rights of settlers to not have their lands taken from them. He was a decent, caring man. I do miss him."

"What of the fate of the impersonator?" the baron asked.

"I left him in his well-deserved privation. Unfortunately, the rumor of Crockett's possible survival has spread to Texas. I'm dispatching my report to Washington tomorrow, and I hope it will dispel these wild stories."

"Good that you put an end to such torture for his family," the baron said, taking a glass of champagne from a passing server. The other members of the group took glasses as well and toasted one another's health.

"Luis," Ellis said to his Mexican colleague who found the goose chase so amusing. "Why don't you tell everyone what you've been dealing with?"

Cuevas shot the American a sideways glare. He had hoped for a brief respite this evening from the conflict that had so completely occupied him of late.

"Trying to prevent a war," he said.

"A war?" Fanny said. She could scarcely believe she had found interesting conversation this evening.

"Oh, but do tell them what the war is about," Ellis said.

Cuevas took a sip of champagne, sighed, and lifted his head. "A pastry shop."

"A pastry shop," the baron nodded. Everyone in Mexico City's diplomatic circles had heard the story.

"A pastry shop," Cuevas confirmed. "It seems a French pastry chef, a Monsieur..."

"Remontel," the baron assisted.

"...Remontel claims his pastry shop in Mexico City was damaged by Mexican soldiers."

"Vandalized and looted, he alleges," the baron said.

"He demanded reparations of 60,000 pesos. The entire shop was worth less than 1,000 pesos, so my government denied the claim. Remontel appealed to the French king, and now France is demanding 600,000 pesos. If payment is not made, France threatens military action."

"Do you think they would actually go to such lengths?" Fanny said. "How much would it cost to conduct such an operation?"

"Sometimes these things become a matter of principle, my dear," the baron said, though Fanny suspected other motives at work.

"Regardless of expense or rationale, a French fleet under command of Admiral Baudin is setting up a blockade of Mexican ports on the Gulf Coast as we speak," Cuevas said. "No ship can sail in or out without risk of being fired upon."

"Are we able to send messages to the United States?" Fanny asked. "We've been able to do so via ship. Overland would take weeks."

"Perhaps months," Ellis said.

"I don't know," Cuevas said. "To be honest, I'm not sure what the Mexican navy can do against French *Océan* and *Tonnant* class warships."

"Those *Océan* ships possess more than one hundred guns," Ángel said.

"And *Tonnant* class have eighty," Ellis said. "Considerable firepower."

"You gentlemen know your ships," Fanny said.

"Part of the job, Madame," Ellis said, impressed with the lady and a bit jealous of the Spaniard. Fanny detected the sentiment and smiled at the American. He might be useful if things got out of hand.

"Any such confrontation would be bloody," Cuevas said. "I've been trying to negotiate with the French to settle the dispute and call off this foolishness before someone gets hurt."

"My sincerest best wishes to you, sir," the baron said and raised his glass. "To your success, Minister Cuevas."

With that, conversation turned more trivial, and the baron led the party to the reception's lone concession to the host nation: tables displaying local flowers, fruits, and delicacies. At the end of the second table, next to a platter of dulces, was a large sketchbook tied with a red ribbon.

"Madame Calderón de la Barca, with your permission I should like to show these works," the baron said, and Fanny nodded her approval. "The madame was kind enough to share these," the baron said to Cuevas and Ellis.

The baron untied the ribbon and carefully opened the sketchbook's cover. The large binder held several loose sheets of drawing paper. The baron spread the first few sketches for the group to view. An impressed silence fell over the audience.

"These are splendid," Cuevas finally said. "Are you the artist, Madame Calderón de la Barca?"

"Oh, no. I have no such skill. I have been writing about our experiences. These wonderful works were created by a traveling companion, Mrs. Ward. She is gifted with graphite pencil."

Cuevas eased a sketch from the stack. "This is Puente Nacional Bridge, is it not?"

"It is. And this," she said, reaching for another drawing, "is it not perfect in every detail?"

Fanny slid forward a depiction of the interior of an Indian hut. As she did, a sketch beneath was partially revealed. A portion of a portrait peered out. A long nose. An eye. An eye that struck Ellis as familiar.

Ellis studied the eye and nose.

It does rather resemble…

Ellis suppressed the urge to shove the other artwork aside.

Of course not, his mind told him. *You're mistaken. Not possible.*

Ellis casually stretched out a hand that he was surprised to see was shaking. He put a fingertip to the hut sketch and moved it ever so slightly aside. The face's other eye emerged and Ellis felt the blood drain from his head. His heart beat faster and his mouth went dry. His head spun and he fought off light-headedness that threatened to buckle his knees.

He exhaled and swallowed hard, and was sure everyone heard him, but the group's preoccupation with other drawings was unabated.

Now he could see a long sideburn and a hint of a grin that formed dimples at the corners of a full mouth. Dark hair—though the artist had suggested that the subject was graying—parted in the middle. *Longer hair*, Ellis thought, *than when last seen.*

When last seen? It's not possible.

But those eyes. Those eyes. Those damned sparkling eyes.

The baron droned on and Madame Calderón de la Barca responded with something about all of Mrs. Ward's sketches were something or other, but the conversation had faded into the muttering of the background noise. Blurry, as if the sound was being strangled in his ears. Ellis felt blood pumping loudly in his neck, and if at this moment someone called his name, he would not hear them.

Because Powhatan Ellis was looking at the face of a ghost. Undeniably, no matter how hard his mind denied it.

The ghost of the Gentleman from the Cane.

It's not possible!

Ellis composed himself and feigned interest in the conversation, flashing his best ambassadorial facade. But he could not move from this table. Would not be moved. Not yet.

His patience paid off when the baron directed Madame Calderón de la Barca's attention to a family across the room.

Ellis pretended to focus his attention to the platter of dulces and turned away from the baron holding court.

"Have you met the contessa?" Ellis heard the Prussian ask. "She is of the finest society…" and something about educating her daughters, as the dreary Baron guided Madame Calderón de la Barca and her husband off, Cuevas trailing with his hands clasped behind his back, to meet the contessa of the finest society. The baron's staff member and wife had long since been forgotten and drifted elsewhere in the ballroom.

Having manufactured a few moments unobserved, Ellis moved quickly. While his right hand picked up a dulce, he carefully took the edge of the ghost sketch with his left and slid it toward his greatcoat. Setting the sweetmeat onto a small plate—he might be committing theft but was not so discourteously ill-mannered as to touch and replace food on an open buffet!—he unbuttoned the greatcoat with his right hand and passed the sketch with his left into his coat, gently folding the sheet before stashing his loot in an inner pocket.

The American—rather pleased with himself and thinking he might have made a decent cutpurse had politics not worked out—picked up his plate of dulce and shuffled the remaining sketches to hide the gap left by Mrs. Ward's now-stolen art, and turned back to the ballroom.

And came face to face with a waiter carrying a tray of fruit and staring straight at him with a look that Ellis guiltily read as accusation.

Ellis's years in Congress and on the bench as a judge kicked in, and he met the waiter's gaze head on. He raised his chin, exuded his well-honed air of privilege and superiority, and returned fire with the piercing look employed to debase and cast down opponents on the floor of the United States Senate.

The waiter, thoroughly unimpressed and simply confused by the tall American's demeanor, merely shrugged, set the tray on the table, and continued on his rounds.

"Are you well, Powhatan?" It was Cuevas, who had noticed Ellis's absence and, relocating him, detected the sudden pallor in his face.

"Oh, yes, thank you, Luis. Fine, fine. A bit tired, I think."

"A thousand-mile round trip will do that."

"Yes, I'm sure that's it. Would you be so kind as to make my apologies to our host and the ambassador and his wife?" Ellis couldn't face Madame Calderón de la Barca now, feeling certain she would sense his crime immediately. "I think it best that I get some rest."

"Of course, my friend," Luis said. "I hope you're feeling better in the morning."

"I'm sure I shall. Thank you, Luis. Good evening."

Cuevas bowed and took his leave, and Ellis leisurely rushed from the ballroom. The American's mind swam. He missed the exit, circled back to the hall's main doors, and somehow found his waiting carriage. He wouldn't realize until the next day that he left behind his top hat and overcoat.

With a clatter of hooves, the carriage sped Ellis to the former American embassy, which closed in 1836 after Texas gained its independence but acted now as offices for Ellis and a small staff. He stumbled upstairs to his apartment, lit a candle, sat in his favorite wing-back, brown-leather armchair, and pulled the sketch from his coat.

He gazed at the drawing, rested his chin on his hand, and curled his fingers over his mouth. The room's only sound was the ticking of an Eli Terry mahogany clock on a bookshelf.

Then the thought struck him.

Where was this made!

He had no idea of the source of the evidence. The ambassador had walked out of the Prussian embassy without ascertaining where the sketch had been drawn and, consequently, where the ghost might be found.

Was I so liquored by the champagne or just too stunned to think clearly?

Praying for a reprieve, Ellis inspected the sketch from top to bottom, edge to edge. No indication of place or date. He flipped it over, expecting to find the revelatory legend on the back. Nothing. He went over it again, front and back. And again. Still nothing.

He slumped back into his armchair.

He thought of returning to the ballroom but the reception would almost certainly be finished by now. And if it was not, what would he say?

Excuse me, Madame Calderón de la Barca, could you tell me where Mrs. Ward found the subject of this sketch I just stole?

Ellis considered his options.

For the moment, the origin of the sketch could wait. The Spanish ambassador was some months into his two-year posting to Mexico, and he and his wife were busy touring the country. They could be found again. And even if Mrs. Ward wanted to leave on her own, she couldn't. With Admiral Baudin's fleet blockading

Mexican ports, France had effectively locked the exit and Ellis was the only man in Mexico who had a key.

What he needed now was to determine if what he was seeing was even remotely possible. After all, Ellis told himself, he hadn't seen the man in years. It was almost certainly an epically wild goose chase.

Almost certainly.

Ellis dispelled the thought of forgetting the matter. He could laugh about it later. Confirmation was required. He needed someone else to examine the sketch. Someone familiar with the ghost who had been in his presence more recently than Ellis. Someone who could conduct a discreet investigation. Who could be trusted to keep the affair secret. And who would not relent until the issue was resolved.

This much was certain: If this was possible, the situation must be remedied. American ambitions made that clear.

Ellis set the sketch aside, crossed to his desk, and spent the next few hours contemplating possible courses. He settled on a plan and prepared carefully worded correspondences and orders, some under his signature and seal, others of a more deniable variety.

Before dawn, Ellis, still dressed in his evening attire, was ready to put his scheme into motion.

Because one way or another, the ghost had to be removed from the game.

CHAPTER 2

THE SUN WAS beginning to ignite a purple, pink, and orange glow atop Mexico City's skyline, hinting at the dawn still half an hour away, when Ellis, running on adrenaline, emerged from his office the morning after the reception at the Prussian embassy. It would be several hours before he allowed the lack of sleep to catch up to him.

Ellis walked briskly through dark hallways past silent offices. Staff would not be at their posts for some time. He stepped out the building's back door into an alley filled with long, deep shadows.

Behind the shuttered legation was a stable where Ellis's carriage from the previous evening was parked. Next to the carriage were stalls for horses available to office staff. A man was brushing a bay mare, its reddish-brown coat looking black in the dim light.

"I've got a job for you, Hiram," Ellis said, skipping pleasantries as he entered the stable.

The man kept brushing the mare but was listening.

"This is top priority," Ellis said. "Anything else you're working on can wait. You'll be gone a month, maybe longer. I hope that doesn't cause difficulty for your enterprise, but it can't be helped."

"Overland or Veracruz?"

"Veracruz. You'll be sailing to Texas."

"A few stops on the way should take care of any issues."

Ellis glanced around the alley and the connecting street half a block away. No one was in sight. "Let's go inside. I have some packages for you to deliver."

In the candlelight of Ellis's office, the man was almost as indistinct as he had been in the stable. But that was one of Hiram's gifts. He was a human chameleon.

Hiram Brown was of average height and weight. He didn't look young or old, and Ellis had no idea of Brown's age. He was ethnically androgynous. His facial features, dark hair, and complexion could pass for Anglo, Hispanic, or Indigenous without causing doubt or second glance. He modified his facial hair for different situations and adjusted his posture to make himself shorter or taller. He affected a variety of regional and ethnic accents, raised or deepened the pitch of his voice, and spoke English, Spanish, and French as if they were his primary language. Brown could blend into a crowd of peasants or mix seamlessly into a formal occasion.

Ellis didn't even know the man's real name—though he'd bet it was not Brown—or where he was from.

If you weren't looking for Hiram Brown, you'd never see him.

He didn't bother to remove his sombrero as he took a seat in Ellis's office.

"These," Ellis began, "are what you are to deliver." The American minister showed Brown a package bound with heavy twine and sealed with wax. Alongside was a stack of six folios. "When you get to Houston, give these to la Branche." He indicated the package and a very official looking folio containing Ellis's report to US Secretary of State John Forsyth on the imposter in the Mexican mine with instructions for its safe delivery to Washington. "Give this to Dubois," Ellis said, handing Brown another folio.

"This," Ellis indicated a folio addressed to *Watchman*, "should get you past the French blockade. These are for your other captains." These last two were addressed to *Comanche* and *Fanny Butler*.

"Finally, give this to Captain Hunter." Ellis handed Brown an unaddressed folio. "Contact him through the Collector of Customs."

Ellis sat back. "Now, let me explain what this is about."

In government affairs, particularly those concerning intelligence or military matters, the overriding instinct was to provide field agents only those details absolutely necessary to complete the task at hand. In this situation, Brown could have delivered his assigned packages without knowing what was within or the reason for his mission. It could be argued that Brown's need-to-know ended at the names and locations of the intended recipients.

When it came to Brown, however, Powhatan Ellis's instinct was to tell him everything. Hiram wasn't a simple courier. He was a partner in Ellis's larger operations in Mexico. He was not only utterly trustworthy, he was remarkably resourceful. The more Brown knew, the more capable he was of performing a task and making critical decisions when a situation changed. Ellis knew this situation was bound to change again and again.

That was Hiram Brown's other gift: he was the most utilitarian human being Ellis had ever known. If there was a job Brown could not perform, Ellis had yet to find it. He'd never asked Brown for muscle work, certainly not to kill, but believed him capable of taking life.

Ellis finished relating the events of the previous evening and revealed the contents of the packages and the purpose of each meeting Brown was to undertake.

Brown was not easily impressed or surprised. This morning he was both.

"You really think this is possible?" he said.

"Frankly, no. I think it highly unlikely. If I hadn't seen that sketch myself…" Ellis took a deep breath. He'd passed the evening trying to convince himself this was a waste of time, even as he made these arrangements. "But if there's a chance, no matter how remote, we can't ignore it."

"I understand why."

"If this became public, at best we'd be subject to embarrassment and scorn. At worst…"

"Blackmail," Brown finished. "Or clamors for war with Mexico."

Ellis nodded. "Good luck, Hiram. Report to me as soon as you return. If there is any validity to this, you will have further involvement."

Brown gathered up the packages and folios and was on the road less than an hour later.

It was more than two hundred miles to Veracruz, a difficult journey of at least seven days without changing horses. Brown would need a strong mount to get there in a week.

But he did not start the trip on one of the fine horses in the legation stable. Instead, dressed in simple cotton shirt and pants, serape, sombrero, and cowhide boots, Brown walked out of Mexico City leading a mule laden with empty barrels, a bedroll, and meager provisions. To all the world just a poor peasant returning to his village.

The chameleon moving invisibly.

Hidden beneath the barrels and bedroll were saddle bags with Ellis's precious packages. Tucked inside the bedroll was Brown's favored defense, a double-barreled shotgun.

Brown's first stop was Mexico City's ceaselessly stinking streets in the flood-plagued slums to contact his network of spies within the city.

He didn't have to look for them. They always found him.

"Ichtaca," said the boy who suddenly materialized at Brown's elbow. "We need money."

"Coyotl," Brown greeted, calling the boy by the Aztec name he had adopted. Brown didn't know the boy's real name. Or if he even had a given name. "You are well?"

"We need money."

"I have money. You are well?"

"I will be better with more money, Ichtaca." Coyotl, barefoot and in rags, was always the businessman even at eleven years of age, though he looked older. Life down here was short and brutal.

Their arrangement was simple: Brown gave money to Coyotl, and Coyotl gave money to the Quauhtli, a battalion of street orphans that Coyotl led. In return, the Quauhtli gathered information throughout the city and fed it to Brown.

Quauhtli was an Aztec name that meant "eagle." Eagles were ancient Aztec elite warriors, but Brown thought the name also appropriate for the ability of these homeless children to drift through the city. They were unnoticed, disregarded, neglected. Guttersnipe to most. But they saw everything and reported what they saw to Brown, who they called Ichtaca, an Aztec name that meant "secret."

Coyotl led Brown into a particularly filthy, unoccupied alley. Brown slid open a false bottom on one of the barrels, retrieved a small bag of copper coins, and handed it to Coyotl.

"There is extra today," Brown said. "I will be gone for some time, at least a month. We will meet again when I return. I will have a new job for the Quauhtli."

Coyotl grinned at the prospect of more money, and turned to leave.

"Wait," Brown said. He dug deeply into the hidden compartment and produced another bag. "Give these to the healing woman. These are medicines." He pulled from the bag glass bottles of pills and liquids: morphine, quinine, chloral hydrate, diastase. "She will know what to do with them. But in exchange, tell her to treat Yaretzi. Right away. Today, you understand?"

"Ichtaca—"

"I want you to take Yaretzi to the healing woman today." He pressed more coins into Coyotl's hand.

"Ichtaca—"

"If the healing woman wants coin, give her coin. I will get you more money—"

"Ichtaca," Coyotl said, raising his voice. "Yaretzi is dead."

He said it so casually. The boy had seen so much suffering. He was not betraying indifference. He was numb. Just numb.

So much death.

"The tabardillo," Coyotl said. "It was the tabardillo."

Brown's surprise quickly gave way to grief. He blinked slowly and turned away, lowering his head and removing his sombrero before crushing it in a white-knuckled fist.

In all their meetings and all their dealings, Coyotl had never seen emotion on Brown's face. Except when he was around Yaretzi.

Six years old. Yaretzi was born in squalor and abandoned to misery, yet she was an angel. Her smile. Her voice. Her laugh. Such joy in such blight.

Brown choked back tears. The tabardillo was a type of typhus that swept through crowded, unsanitary areas in Mexico, like the city's slums. Brown knew the girl was sick but he'd prayed it was not too late.

A loving little angel. Gone.

"I will take these to the healing woman," Coyotl said, and turned and vanished into the morning crowd filling the street.

✫

Brown made a dozen stops before reaching Veracruz.

The Quauhtli was one part of Brown's "enterprise," as Ellis dubbed it, an undertaking that was the agent's most important contribution to the United States government—intelligence gathering.

Since beginning to assemble the enterprise three years earlier, Brown, bankrolled by the US government, had developed a collaborative relationship with hundreds of members of Mexico's lowest socioeconomic classes. Predominantly Indigenous, they were homeless like the Quauhtli, or indebted labor to haciendas, or scratched out a living on their own fields. They were beset by poverty, by disease, by taxes from the church, by fees for marriage and baptisms, and by exorbitant prices at hacienda stores.

Outside the cities, Brown had developed a market for small quantities of rarer goods, which the Indigenous peons could supply.

While the haciendas were producing wool from herds of sheep, some villages harvested raw materials from mulberry silkworms to produce fine silk.

While the haciendas curbed no-longer profitable silver mining, peons scraped turquoise, amethyst, and silver from the mines, and other villages provided craftsmen who turned those materials into jewelry.

Still other villages made mezcal, tequila, and pulque from agave.

The quantity from any one village was small and the cost of getting it to market was high, but Brown was able to aggregate a profitable amount of silk, jewelry, and alcohol to fill small merchant ships and take the goods to Texas and New Orleans. And since the merchandise never appeared in Mexican markets, it didn't cut into the haciendas' profits so was ignored. At least, so far.

The merchant ships' captains were happy because they made more money off the exotic goods than from cotton or corn. The shipments from villages to port were moved by Mexican carters to whom Brown provided start-up funding, and they were protected by a cartel of local bandits whom Brown paid off with a cut of the proceeds and with information on Mexican troop movements and the activity of rival gangs—information gathered by the Quauhtli and peons.

Brown, meanwhile, funneled his portion of the profits back into the network, providing money and medicine throughout his territory, which stretched several leagues west of Mexico City, east to Veracruz, and north to the Texas border. From this he harvested a wealth of knowledge on north and central Mexico—its roads, geography, economy, villages, and military capacity. And what Brown knew, Ellis and the US government knew.

Two hours after leaving the Quauhtli, Brown sold the mule and barrels, purchased a roan stallion at a small ranch outside the city, changed clothes, and was climbing east out of the Valley of Mexico.

Two days later he reached the Rio Frio, thirteen leagues from the city, and the terrain changed into hills wooded with oak, pine, and cedar.

Brown made contact at the villages of Rio Prieto, Nopaluca, Acagete, and Amosoque, confirming their goods were being transported and inquiring of problems. He dined at their inns and spent money in their shops, and they welcomed him as one of their own. At Ventilla, the locals treated him to one of his favorites, a custard made from chirimoya fruit.

Outside Perote, Brown stopped at a dilapidated flea-trap of a tavern.

"Is he here?" Brown asked a tortillera grinding corn on a metate under the shade of a thatched awning on the side of the tavern.

The tortillera nodded and turned toward the inn's door. "Salvator!" she turned back to the visitor. "You are well, Mr. Brown?" she asked.

"I am. And you?"

"Better for the new metate. Thank you."

"I suppose even a stone bowl wears out. How long had you been using the old one?"

"All my life. My mother used it all her life. My grandmother, all her life. And my daughters would have used it if Salvator had not dropped it and cracked it." She shook her head and bent back to work. "I will have fresh tortillas for you. You are staying tonight?"

"Of course. Where else?"

The tavern keeper appeared at the door.

"Don't interrupt her," Salvator said. "She is behind in her work."

"What would you know of work?" the tortillera said. "You just drink pulque all day."

Brown and Salvator grinned and stepped inside.

Salvator had never been a bandit, which Brown thought was a shame as he looked the part. He had narrow eyes, a perpetual scowl, and a thin scar on his left cheek. The scowl was because business was never as good as he wished, and the scar was due to his wife when she caught him with another woman.

The evening turned cold, and Brown and Salvator chased the chill with warm wine, sat around a table in the back of the tavern, and spoke well into the night.

"Lancers are patrolling the road between here and Las Vigas," Salvator said. "Let your friends know."

Brown nodded but just stared into his cup of wine.

"What troubles you?"

Brown looked up, finished the wine, and slowly set the cup on the table. "A girl. Six years old."

"One of the orphans? Dead?"

Brown said nothing, his vacant eyes pointed toward the empty cup.

"Videl," Salvator said, causing Brown to look up at the sound of a name he rarely heard anymore. "You cannot solve all of Mexico's ills."

Brown poured more wine and lifted the cup but paused at his lips. "I can try."

He slept fitfully that night, and before either the sun or Salvator had risen, he was back on the road.

Beyond the village of Las Vigas, the road became steep and Brown entered an alien landscape. The Mal Pais was two leagues of ancient, massive lava flows where only a few fir trees hacked out a living among the black rock. The area was also renowned as a haven for bandits who preyed on travelers. Fortunately for Brown, the outlaws in question were part of the enterprise, and they hailed and welcomed him, inviting him to lunch where Brown passed on Salvator's information about the lancers.

The land turned scenic again as he descended through areas bursting with flowers of scarlet, purple, white, and pink. He reached the town of Xalapa, home to several English merchants who did business in the port but preferred this scenery and clean air to the environment around the Veracruz. He stayed at an inn with brick floors, and the next morning he enjoyed a breakfast of eggs, chicken, coffee, and excellent bread with fresh butter.

At La Calera, the sea finally came into view, and he continued to descend to the coast. Crossing the Puente Nacional Bridge marked the home stretch, and after riding through Tolomé and Santa Fé, the terrain grew rough, the air thick, and the countryside bleak. A few hours later, he pulled into the port of Veracruz and went straight to the docks.

✴

"You tryin' to get me killed!" Levi Jones roared. "You want my boat sunk!"

"Captain, please—"

Jones stepped within a few inches of Hiram Brown's face and pointed out to sea. "You tellin' me to sail out there into those guns, you damned right I'm gonna kick!"

The captain of the merchant brig *Watchman* returned to stomping about the deck, circling Brown. Jones scratched at his scraggly beard and mustache, and his left hand fiddled with a hole in his blue tailcoat which had once been part of a military uniform but was now threadbare and missing two brass buttons.

"Ain't no one gettin' outta this damned port," Jones said.

"Them French ships got us bottled up tight, Mr. Brown," *Watchman's* first mate said.

"And how long are you prepared to stay here?" Brown asked the seven-man crew that had gathered behind their captain. "You're prepared to remain in port for how long? Weeks? Months? Do you want to spend months in Veracruz? The French are not leaving any time soon."

"Months is better 'n dead," a crewman said.

"Months and we might be dead," the first mate said as he watched a group of large black buzzards that the locals called sopilotes wheeling over the city. "We been here too long already. I don't want yellow fever."

A wave of agreement flashed through the crew.

"I am certain I can get you and your ship past the French blockade," Brown said.

"I'm glad you're all chirk about it," Jones said. "But I don't much care what you think. What we supposed to fight them French cannon with, a damned Arkansas toothpick?" Jones put his hand to the hilt of the long knife he wore constantly in a scabbard on his left hip. It was Jones's idea of intimidation, but Brown had never seen the captain draw the blade.

"Captain Jones," Brown began, then turned to the rest of the crew. "All of you, listen to me. There will be no battle. Our passage through the French blockade has been arranged. I have papers—" and he extracted the folio addressed to *Watchman*, "—to get this ship past the French. If you do exactly as I instruct, we'll get out of here and you'll be back making money. You have a ship full of cargo and customers waiting."

Nervous looks rolled across the faces of the crew.

"You sure?" the first mate asked. The crew went still awaiting a response.

"Absolutely," Brown said. "I'll be standing out front when we meet the French. If there's any shooting, I'll be the first one shot."

The crew looked at Brown, then at one another.

"I'm for it," the first mate said. "Captain?"

Jones stared at Brown and took a long, deep breath. "Ah, hell. I reckon."

Watchman put Veracruz behind it in full daylight, as Brown wanted no suggestion that the ship was trying to slip out in the dark.

Jones and his seven-man crew steered carefully through the dangerous rocky waters, past the black and red stone walls of the island fort of San Juan de Ulna and beneath the fort's cannon. The crew could see Mexican gunners on the walls, the looks on their faces incredulous, undoubtedly expecting a disastrous outcome for *Watchman*.

Once *Watchman* was past the shoals, French warships began looming on the horizon. They had not yet reacted to the small merchant brig but everyone on *Watchman* knew the French detected anything that moved from the port.

Brown stepped to the ship's prow.

"Slow and easy, Captain Jones," he called. "Do not change course. No matter what happens, do not change course. Do nothing that could be regarded as evasive maneuvers."

"Don't tell me how to run my boat," Jones muttered and pulled his frayed captain's cap low over his eyes.

Watchman was flying just enough canvas to move but did not have all its sails set, and she wallowed toward the blockade.

"They may fire a warning shot," Brown called. "Do not panic. Do not change course."

"Ain't deef," Jones said. "Heard first time."

At this crawling speed, it took half an hour for *Watchman* to come within range of the French guns, which was exactly what Brown wanted. No indication, not so much as a hint that the little brig was trying to sprint past the French. It would have been an absurd, suicidal attempt, as *Watchman's* top speed was below that of the French capital ships.

Once *Watchman* reached the extreme range of the French gunners, the nearest ship moved and closed rapidly. Though still at their stations, Jones's crew watched in terror as the French approached.

"Jesus," Jones let escape as he viewed the Frenchman through a spyglass. "I think that's *Montebello*." He swallowed hard.

"*Océan* class?" Brown asked.

Jones drew in a long, rattling breath. "Yes," he wheezed. "Carries 124 guns. I hear they added carronades to her quarterdeck."

"What…what…" a towheaded young crewman stammered, his lungs hammering short, panicked breaths. "What's a carronade?"

"Short, smoothbore gun," the first mate said. "Like a damned shotgun. One round would send us all to hell."

As *Montebello* closed, her massive size became evident. The shortest of her three masts was taller than *Watchman*'s main mast. She was more than twice as long as the merchantman, and her crew numbered more than a thousand, including a contingent of marines. The crew of each of her largest cannon was twice that of *Watchman*'s entire complement.

One of *Montebello*'s cannon fired.

Thunder and an enormous plume of smoke rose amidship of the Frenchman and a cannon ball screamed through the air, flying well over *Watchman*'s bow and splashing harmlessly into the Gulf of Mexico.

Watchman's crew instinctively crouched for cover.

"They gonna sink us!" the towheaded crewman shrieked.

"A warning shot," Brown said. "Captain, heave to and run up your American flag."

The crew, inspired by the hope of staying alive, didn't wait for orders from Jones and moved quickly, lowering sails while the first mate raised an American flag from the mainmast.

"Now what?" the towheaded crewman said.

"We wait," Brown said.

Montebello's towering bow bore down on *Watchman* before the great French ship of the line turned to port, heaved to, and settled in parallel to *Watchman*'s starboard side. Marines with long guns could be seen on deck taking aim at the merchantman as it gently bobbed. The frigate's starboard gun ports were open, their menacing cannon muzzles visible.

From this range, a volley from *Montebello's* eighteen-pound upper deck guns would rip off the tops of *Watchman's* masts. A volley from her twenty-four-pound middle deck cannon would shred canvas and splinter masts. But a volley from the lower deck, where sat colossal thirty-six-pound cannon—the largest guns on the sea and among the largest on the planet—would eviscerate *Watchman* and reduce her to kindling.

Brown knew *Montebello* was unlikely to waste such powder and ball on such an insignificant target. If necessary, the French would disable *Watchman* with a few precise rounds, and board and capture the small prize. Perhaps slaughter the crew with rifle and musket fire from the upper deck, which would truly be shooting fish in a barrel.

A French officer appeared high on *Montebello's* quarterdeck. "Return to port or you will be fired upon!" he called in Spanish, then repeated the warning in English.

Brown strode to the end of the prow. "Sir, I am a representative of the United States government," he responded in French. He knew he wasn't speaking directly with the captain but had no doubt the captain could hear. "This is an American vessel, and we have permission from the government of France to pass through your blockade. I possess documents to that effect."

The French officer considered this, turned to have a brief conversation with an unseen person—almost certainly the captain—and issued orders. Several crew members quickly prepared a longboat. The officer climbed down from the quarterdeck and joined a handful of marines and crewmen boarding the boat, which was lowered into the water. The longboat moved alongside *Watchman*, and the brig's crew put a rope ladder over its side.

Four marines boarded *Watchman* first, their muskets at the ready but not aimed, followed by the officer and one crewman carrying a bulky bag. Brown approached the Frenchmen, bowed, and advanced and shook hands with the officer. They spoke for several minutes in a fashion that seemed formal but cordial.

"They know each other?" the first mate said.

"Don't know," Jones said. "Somethin' odd here."

Brown presented the officer with a document which the Frenchman studied. The officer nodded his satisfaction and handed the paper back to Brown. Finally, the French crewman handed the bag to Brown.

The conversation concluded, Brown shook hands again with the officer, who turned and gave a brief salute to Jones before ordering his men back to the longboat. A few minutes later, they were returning to *Montebello*.

"Don't that beat all," the first mate said.

"Captain," Brown approached the stunned Jones. "Please run this up beneath your American flag," and Brown handed over the bag, "and we can be underway. Your destination is Texas, the port of Velasco."

The crew didn't budge. The only sound was the creaking of the ship's ropes and timbers and the lapping of the Gulf of Mexico against its hull. Brown waited patiently for the shock to pass. Finally, the captain and first mate opened the bag and hauled out a French flag. Jones nodded and the first mate moved to the mainmast.

"Once we're well north of the Mexican coast, you can lower those flags," Brown said. "After this voyage is complete, you may return to Veracruz if you wish but do not attempt to sail to any other Mexican port until this matter between France and Mexico is resolved. If you are within sight of Mexico or any French ship, fly the American flag with the French flag immediately beneath it. If you are challenged by a French ship, heave to, await their boarding party, and show them this."

Brown handed Jones the folio that minutes earlier had been presented to the *Montebello* officer. Inside was a very official looking letter with an extremely impressive signature. The letter was in French.

Jones shook his head. "What does it say? Who is this def... def-au..."

"Deffaudis. Baron Antoine-Louis Deffaudis. He is the French ambassador to Mexico. That letter gives you permission to sail in and out of the port of Veracruz and instructs any French ship to not sink your boat," Brown said. "I'd, uh, I'd hang on to that if I were you."

Jones threw Brown a questioning, doubt-riddled look. He stared at the letter, then looked up at the French banner now flying beneath *Watchman*'s own American flag. "How'd you get the French to let us pass? How'd you fix this?"

Brown ignored the questions.

"At your convenience, Captain. Take us to Texas."

CHAPTER 3

"A PASTRY SHOP?" Silas Grant said.

Sam McCulloch nodded as he walked alongside Silas at the head of a column of Texians.

"Seriously? They're going to war over a pastry shop?"

"That's the story," Henry Karnes said. "I reckon there's more to it, but that's why we're here." Karnes was a few steps ahead of Grant and McCulloch, and a line of two hundred men trailed behind them.

"The French have blockaded Mexico's ports," Sam said, "so the Mexicans are landing cargo in Texas and smuggling it across the border. Sam Houston doesn't want to give the French an excuse to blockade our ports."

"We're here to stop the smugglin'," Henry said, "without startin' a war with Mexico." Henry angled left and led the column through a field of tall, yellow Indiangrass dotted with pink coneflowers, brilliant goldenrod, and purple blazing star.

"Hmm," Silas considered. "Fight smugglers without getting into a fight. A puzzle worthy of a Philadelphia lawyer."

"That's why we brought you, Silas," Henry said.

"Because he's smarter than you?" Sam said.

"Now, I didn't say that. But, yes," and Henry returned his attention to picking a path through the brush of the coastal plain for the Texian militia dispatched in response to reports from a nearby trading post of unusual activity at Corpus Christi Bay.

The militia transitioned from the grassy field into a thicket of live oak, persimmon, hackberry, and well-armed mesquite, every man watchful of thorns. Sam tugged his gray, full-length frock coat to keep it from snagging on the brush.

"Don't know why you wear that thing," Henry said.

"I like the pockets," Sam said.

"Well, can't argue with pockets."

The roughly round Corpus Christi Bay lay on the southern coast of Texas, and from it two smaller bays protruded, one west and one south. The militia had ridden around to the southern side of Corpus Christi Bay and crossed and followed Oso Creek east until they reached the base of Oso Bay, a narrow, meandering cove that emptied off the southern edge of the larger harbor.

The trading post indicated that smugglers were operating on Encinal Peninsula, which was bordered by Oso Bay to the west and the Gulf of Mexico to the east. The only land access to the peninsula was from the south, past mudflats where red and white spoonbills were feeding. The Texians had dismounted a mile from the entrance to the peninsula and proceeded on foot, leaving a handful of men to guard the horses.

"Gator on the left!" Henry called, pointing to an alligator lying still, quiet, and virtually invisible in the tall saltgrass of the mudflats. As they edged away from the beast, the Texians aimed an array of single-shot, muzzle-loading flintlock and percussion firearms—Charleville, Brown Bess, and Escopeta muskets; Pennsylvania, Kentucky, and Baker rifles; and US Model 1816, British horse, and Spanish pistols—in the creature's direction.

"What a monster," Silas said, hefting his Hawken .50-caliber long rifle. "How big is that thing?"

"Looks like a twelve-footer," a tall young man with a round face and blue tailcoat said. "Never seen a gator before?"

"Just pictures. We don't have anything like that back home."

"Where's home?"

"Texas now, Brazos Valley. My family's from Missouri. We don't have alligators there. By the way, my name's Silas Grant."

"Nice to meet you, Silas. I'm Frank Ogden," he said with a thick Southern accent. "From Alabama."

"Do they have alligators there?"

"Sure. I knowed a fella back home kilt by a gator. They jus' sit there, waitin' for a meal to get close and careless, then jump out real quick. Big surprise."

"I've heard stories of Jim Bowie wrestling gators. Could that be true?"

"Don't know," Ogden said. "A fella'd have be crazy as a loon to jump on a gator. Mind, gators are good eatin'. Jus' tricky gettin' 'em in the pan."

"I can imagine," Silas said. "How long have you been in Texas?"

"Four years. Since I was fourteen. You?"

"Six years. We moved down here in '32, when I was ten years old."

The militia pushed a little further east before turning north into the peninsula, which was six miles long and two to three miles wide. If the smugglers were here as reported, they'd be on the Gulf side, so the Texians marched parallel to and a few hundred yards from the coastline.

"You know them fellas?" Ogden said to Silas, indicating McCulloch and Karnes.

"Sure."

"Really? I heard of 'em."

Few in Texas had not heard of Samuel McCulloch Jr. and Henry Wax Karnes, because Texians do love their legends. And though many Texians were not above exaggerating their involvement in the Texas Revolution and its tragedies and triumphs, the lies and boasts disappeared when in the presence of genuine Texas heroes, and that description covered McCulloch and Karnes.

"Henry," Silas said, "fought at Concepcion and the siege of Béxar."

"And Rocky Creek," Henry called.

"And at San Jacinto as a captain of the cavalry corps. Scouted the Mexican army before the battle and routed the Mexican cavalry during the fight."

"Oh, I like the sound of that," Henry said, removing his broad-brimmed, straw hat and revealing a pale, youthful face. He mopped his brow and ran a hand through his thick, red hair. "Sam, you hear how I routed the cavalry?"

"And got locked up," Sam said, stepping over a fallen, rotted log.

"But escaped!" Henry countered.

"He went to Matamoros," Silas explained to the enthralled Ogden, "to arrange for the release of Texian prisoners, but the Mexican authorities put him in jail."

"But escaped!" Henry reiterated.

"Sam was with the Matagorda Volunteers, the Texians who took Presidio La Bahia in '35. When the Texians stormed the fort, he was the first man through the wall."

"Here it comes," Henry said.

"The first man into the fort," Sam confirmed, "and the first Texian in the Revolution to be wounded," and he rubbed his right shoulder.

"In other words, the first man to not keep his fool head down," Henry said, earning a dirty look from McCulloch's dark eyes that glared out from bushy eyebrows and magnificent muttonchop sideburns. Karnes just smiled in return.

Ogden, however, was suitably impressed. "You fellas must be old hands at this game."

"Watch who you're callin' old," Henry said. "I'm twenty-five. He's the old one."

"Don't set much by him, Alabama," Sam said. "I'm just twenty-seven."

"You just look old," Henry said.

"Don't mind them," Silas said. "They just like to sound mean."

"How you know these fellas?" Ogden asked.

"In the war, during the Runaway Scrape. We were running like everyone else. My family was at the army's camp at Groce's Landing."

A few minutes later, Karnes held up a hand and the column stopped. Everyone instinctively crouched and went quiet. Henry moved toward the noise that no one else had heard, disappearing silently into the brush.

"Make sure your long guns are primed and loaded," Sam said. "But keep your fingers off the triggers. Pass it down."

The command carried down the line of militia, followed by the soft clicking of muskets and rifles being double checked. Ogden nervously inspected his plains long rifle while Silas confirmed his Hawken was ready.

Neither had ever fired at a man.

The Texians waited on their haunches and knees, sweating far more than called for by the weather. They couldn't see more than thirty yards into the undergrowth.

Finally, after twenty minutes that felt like two hours, Karnes reappeared. "They're down on the beach, alright. Unloadin' barrels and boxes from a ship offshore."

"How many?" Sam asked.

"At least two hundred."

"Then it's a fair fight," Ogden said. "And they don't know we're here."

"But we don't want a fight," Silas said.

"Anyone got any ideas?" Sam asked.

Silas was thinking about the gator in the tall grass. Waiting for a meal to get careless.

"Is there cover near their position?" he asked.

"Yeah," Henry said. "A little tree line 250 yards from the waterline. A few feet higher than the beach. Real nice spot for an ambush, and they got no guards on their perimeter."

Silas considered the situation a moment more. "I may have an idea."

Karnes led the Texians slowly through the brush, line-abreast. They took their time so as to not scatter the men all over the peninsula. Three hundred yards from the gulf, Henry again raised his hand, a gesture that somehow managed to filter down the line. At Karnes's direction, the Texians crawled the final fifty yards to the edge of the trees.

And there were the smugglers, busily unloading a longboat as they shuttled cargo from an old double-masted merchant brig. The beach was piling up with contraband. Several wagons had been backed onto the beach, and the smugglers had just begun loading the barrels.

Karnes pulled a nine-inch brass spyglass from a coat pocket and extended the tube to its full two feet, and nudged it forward through the scrub, careful to avoid sunlight glinting off its glass lens.

"See any uniforms, any insignia?" Sam asked.

"No, nothin'. Looks like Whites and Mexicans. Mostly White men." He trained the glass on the boat. "They got cannon on that ship. Two. I'd guess twelve pounders."

"Don't care to mess with artillery," Sam said. "Can you see any brands on the horses?"

Karnes turned his attention to the southern end of beach where the smugglers' remuda was being guarded by three vaqueros. "I can see old Placido Benvides's brand. A few others I don't recognize."

"You thinkin' these skunks work for this Ben-vides?" said a muleskinner whose curiosity had compelled him to crawl forward. He operated a mule team out of Goliad but left it behind for the opportunity to join this hastily assembled adventure.

"No," Silas said. "Placido Benevides fought for Texas in the Revolution."

"How you know? You jus' a button," the muleskinner said. "Maybe this Ben-vides is ramrod of this boodle."

Karnes glared over his shoulder and threw a go-to-hell look at the muleskinner.

McCulloch leaned down until the muleskinner could feel Sam's breath on his nose, "This 'button' was riding scout for Sam Houston in '36. This 'button' made bullets and repaired long guns in the army's camp at Groce's. Helped get the army across the Brazos on the way to San Jacinto. So you might give this 'button' a little respect."

The muleskinner swallowed and sank back. "Didn't mean no offense."

McCulloch leaned back and Karnes resumed his surveillance.

"Placido rode in the Revolution with my uncle, Dr. Grant," Silas said, and the muleskinner nodded. Dr. James Grant was well-known for his bravery in the war, exploits that cost him his life in battle with Mexican troops.

"Placido died a year ago," Silas said to the muleskinner, who nodded but chose to say no more before he slunk back to his position on the militia's firing line.

"These hombres likely stole some of Placido's horses," Henry said. "They got long guns, but they're stacked among those barrels."

"What're you thinking, Silas?" Sam asked.

"Frank, can we borrow your blue coat, please?"

Ogden peeled off the tailcoat and handed it to Silas.

"Think that could pass for a French officer's coat?" Silas asked.

"French?" Ogden said.

"I think I see where you're going," Sam said.

Silas carefully set down his Hawken rifle and took off his wide-brimmed flop hat, uncovering straight, sandy hair which he pushed back from his forehead. He looked doubtfully at the tailcoat needed for the subterfuge.

"It may not fit, but that coat matches your eyes, anyway," Henry kidded.

"Funny. Wish it matched my height."

Silas tried on the coat and it swallowed him. The sleeves covered his hands and the coat hung off his lean, muscular five-foot seven-inch frame down to the knees of his butternut trousers. He pulled off the coat and handed it toward Sam.

"Not me, button."

"Why not? Oh," Silas closed his eyes in exasperation at his oversight. "Yeah."

"Because I'm Black," Sam said. "You ever meet a Black French officer?"

"I never met any French officer, but I take your point," Silas said, and put the coat on again. Sam helped him roll up the sleeves, and another Texian handed up a belt. Silas wrapped it around the coat at his waist.

"We need a few more touches," Sam said. "A hat and cross belts. Anybody got a sword?"

One of the Texians offered a top hat, which from a distance might pass as a tall helmet. Sam enhanced the ruse with a seagull feather stuck in its crown.

"I suppose that's a plume?" Silas said, putting on the hat.

"What else would it be?"

A pair of white sashes were wrapped diagonally across Silas's chest to became cross belts, and a white-haired Texian named Zeb volunteered an old sword.

Henry removed the red bandana from around his neck, cut it in half with his Bowie knife, and handed the pieces to Sam.

"Ah, yes," Sam said, folding and arranging the pieces on Silas's shoulders.

"What's that supposed to be?"

"Epaulettes."

Silas sighed. He must look a sight. "How do you know a French officer has red epaulettes?"

"I don't and I bet those smugglers don't either."

"You bet?"

"Yeah. Bet your life." McCulloch admired his handiwork. "Yeah. That should work fine. From a distance. Now, Captain Grant– "

"Colonel Grant. What do I say to them?"

"Uh, anybody speak French?" Sam asked.

No response.

"Yeah," Silas conceded. "My mother taught me."

"Just the man for the job. Now when I say, you step out where they can see you. Not too far. Then tell them to lay down their arms and leave."

McCulloch turned to the Texian militia. "We're not trying to kill them. We just want to scare them off. We'll put fire on them, under the command of our French captain."

"Colonel," Silas corrected.

For the first time in his life, Silas Grant walked into a gun fight. And for the first time in his life, he felt the very real possibility that he might die in the next few minutes. He felt like his legs were shaking but was surprised to see they were not. He lifted the battered sword and was amazed that his hands were not trembling.

"Ready when you are, Colonel," Sam said. The militia pushed two-hundred gun barrels through the brush.

Silas walked forward a few feet, squeezing through the scrub until he emerged from the trees and was just visible to the beach.

"Attention!" he yelled. "Partez immédiatement! C'est le territoire Français!"

The startled smugglers stopped their work and looked at the figure at the tree line, glanced at one another, then back to the tree line. Confused faces stared at the Frenchman who had suddenly appeared.

"What did you say?" Sam said.

"I told them to leave, that this is French territory."

Several smugglers picked up long guns they'd leaned against the barrels. Silas couldn't tell if they were muskets or rifles. If they were muskets, at this range he was safe from a solitary shooter. Unless that shooter got very, very lucky.

A marksman with a rifle, however, was a different story.

"Sam!" Silas hissed over his shoulder. "They're getting ready to shoot!"

"Tell them again." Sam turned to the Texians. "Get ready to fire."

Silas turned back to the beach and puffed up his chest.

"Dépose tes armes!" Silas shouted, doing his best to sound menacing. "C'est le territoire Français!"

More smugglers grabbed guns. Now they were bringing their guns to bear on the tree line. More specifically, at the only Frenchman they could see.

Three shots rang out from the beach and slapped into the trees above Silas's head. He couldn't tell how close. Close enough.

Silas lifted his sword.

"Tirer!" he screamed and brought the blade down to emphasize the command.

Nothing happened. Dead still. The smugglers stared and the Texians waited.

"That means shoot!" Silas demanded, his face flaring in anger, and he pointed the sword at the smugglers.

"Fire!" Sam bellowed.

An enfilade of faux-French gunfire raked the beach. Bullets buzzed through the camp, splattering into sand, sea, and barrels and sending nearby curious seagulls on the wing. The beach disappeared in a cloud of acrid smoke, but Silas could see that the volley had plucked a few smugglers from their feet. They went down screaming.

"Recharger!" Silas said. "Recharger!"

The Texians guessed the meaning of the command and rapidly reloaded.

A second volley, however, was not necessary. The smugglers, believing they were facing a battalion of French soldiers, fled. They piled into wagons, leapt onto horses, or took to their feet and bolted for the southern exit of Encinal Peninsula, hell bent for the Rio Grande and Matamoros, 130 miles to the south.

The Texians gave the smugglers time to gather their wounded and clear the beach, and Karnes and a handful of men followed—from a safe distance—for a few miles. Once certain the area was clear, the Texians emerged from the brush and advanced on the beach.

Four smugglers lay dead.

"It's flour!" one of the Texians proclaimed, examining the trickle from a hole in the side of one of the barrels. "Should be fine once we sift the bullets out."

McCulloch opened a crate. "Mechanical gear of some kind." He read the label on the contraband crate. "Steamboat engine parts. We'll need wagons to haul this off the beach."

Several of the smugglers' wagons had been taken in their escape, but those not harnessed to horses had been left.

"Frank, take a few volunteers. Go back to where we left the horses and bring them here," Sam said. "Get the muleskinner to help."

"We've also got a ship," Silas said, pointing his sword to the smuggler's cargo vessel still sitting at anchor.

"Yeah, we might load this stuff back on board and sail it up the coast instead of hauling it around the bay." McCulloch smiled at Silas. "Not bad for your first day as an officer, Colonel."

"Yeah, not bad."

Silas returned the battered sword to its owner, removed his disguise and found his own gear in the tree line before joining a dozen Texians to take one of the smugglers' longboats to the merchant ship. Just two smugglers remained aboard, and they immediately surrendered.

With the Texians' deceit exposed, the militia couldn't release the prisoners to flee with their comrades south. They were bound and kept on the ship, to be delivered to the capital for interrogation and imprisonment. It might be a while before they saw home again, Silas reasoned.

The Texians dispatched riders to Copano, forty miles up the coast, for a crew to sail the Mexican prize to a friendly port. Some of the militia headed home but a large contingent stayed to guard the contraband and captured ship.

For the next few days, the Texians camped on the beach. Unlike the careless smugglers, the Texians posted guards around the perimeter, especially at the south end of the peninsula. They hunted, fished, and gathered turkey eggs to make biscuits from the liberated flour.

"I got a hankerin' for gator," Frank said. "Silas, you up for some huntin'?"

"Absolutely," he said.

The Texian named Zeb, same height as Silas but old enough to be his grandfather, had organized the camp's hunting parties, so he assembled a small group to join the gator hunt. Frank and Silas led the party toward the marshes.

"Silas, can I ask somethin'?" Frank said once they were away from the Texian camp.

"Of course."

"About Mr. McCulloch. I didn't know he was a Black fella. He a slave?"

"A slave? No, he's a freeman."

"How's that? I mean, I knowed lots of Black fellas in Alabama—"

"Look, Sam's a freeman," Silas said. "His father's White. I never met his mother. I think she died before his family moved to Texas. Sam was born in South Carolina and grew up in Alabama, and his sisters Jane, Harriet, and Mahaly were born there. The family also adopted a boy named Uldy, who used to be a slave. But they're all free. Their father saw to that."

"Sam's a good man," Zeb said.

"His wife Mary is a very nice lady," Silas said.

"You met her?" Frank asked.

"Sure. My family was at their wedding."

"Tell him the rest," Zeb said with a crooked grin and guttural laugh. "I wanna see this."

"Sam's wife is White," Silas said.

Ogden stopped in his tracks and Zeb slammed into the back of him.

"His wife is White?" Frank said. "A Black fella married to a White woman? Is that...well, is that...that ain't legal, is it?"

"I don't know," Silas said, "but I wouldn't try to break them up or throw him in jail."

"Lot of Texians, Sam Houston on down, wouldn't cotton to it," Zeb said, and the rest of the hunting party nodded their agreement.

"I'll be," Frank said. "You get to know someone, huh?"

The hunting party resumed their march.

"Back in Alabama," Silas said, "did you work with slaves?"

"Sure," Frank said. "My pa 'n me, we worked on farms, plantations. Worked with mule teams and carters. There was always slaves 'round those jobs."

"No, I mean, did you own slaves?"

"My pa and me? Nah. We's poor as Job's turkey."

"You and your pa, do you have a farm?"

Frank sighed. "We did. Saved ever' dime, moved here, bought a nice little place. My pa took sick 'n died, and Comanches burned the farm."

"I am sorry to hear that."

"I went after them Comanches. I was all wrathy. I got lucky."

"Lucky?" Silas said. "You caught them?"

"Lucky I didn't catch 'em. I don't want to think what they'd done to me if I caught 'em."

"I have no doubt."

"You sure talk like a book," Frank observed. "Where you get that?"

"My mother was a teacher. She taught us well."

"She sure did."

The hunt was a success, and the party brought back a pair of gators to add to the camp's menu. The Texians dined on gator and frog, on blue crab and shrimp, on striped mullet and snapper, on turkey, armadillo, wild boar, and white-tailed deer, and there was not a variety of critter that Ogden could not turn into a feast.

"Well," Frank asked upon serving the alligator, "what'd you think?"

"Not near as tough as gator I've had before," Sam said. "Good."

"Thank you, Mr. McCulloch," Ogden beamed. "Silas?"

"It's really good," Silas said, finishing off his plate. "Tastes a bit like chicken."

Several days later, a ship from the Republic of Texas navy, a schooner named *Brutus*, appeared at the mouth of Corpus Christi Bay and lay in next to the smugglers' ship. They transferred sailors to take charge of the captured boat and brought an end to the Texians' excursion. Emotional farewells trickled throughout the fellowship as they broke camp.

"I hope we see each other again," Frank said as he joined the remainder of the militia for the long ride home.

"I hope so, too," Silas said.

President Houston had ordered Henry and Sam to sail back on the captured boat to reach the capital faster, and they invited Silas to join them.

However, *Brutus*'s professional sailors identified a serious problem with the smugglers' ship, which they insisted had to be addressed before she set sail.

"She's got no name," *Brutus*'s captain pointed out.

There was no name on her stern, and no nameplate or markings of any kind could be found. The prisoners didn't know the name, as the smugglers had wiped, chipped, and sanded away any identifying information, reasoning that anonymity was best for their line of work.

"That's a caution right there," one of *Brutus*'s crew said. "Bad luck to sail a ship with no name."

So before weighing anchor and heading for Galveston, a name was painted on the brig's stern and a brief ceremony was held. Using a bottle of rum from *Brutus's* stores, the ship was christened: *Grant's Bluff.*

An hour later, the two ships set sail.

CHAPTER 4

FIVE DAYS AFTER departing Veracruz, *Watchman* reached the Texas port of Velasco, which lay between the bays of Matagorda and Galveston, sixty miles south of Houston. Since Texas gained its independence, the port had grown rapidly with the installation of facilities and warehouses by a pair of Galveston businessmen, and Jones was prepared to sell his cargo here rather than the more southerly ports he normally frequented.

"With your permission, I'll make arrangements for buyers to come to your ship to purchase your cargo," Brown said.

"Please," Jones said. The tension on the ship had eased as *Watchman* put distance between itself and the French warships.

"The buyers' names are Mr. Williams and Mr. McKinney, and I think you'll find they pay top prices. Their representatives should be here shortly.

"However," Brown added, and his tenor darkened and his eyes narrowed, "there is a condition to the use of that letter and that flag. As long as the French blockade is in effect, when it comes to Mexican ports, you're working for me."

"Now wait—"

"You sail in and out of Veracruz only. Approach any other Mexican port and you will be fired upon. You can dock at any Texas port. Galveston, Isabel, Linnville, Copano. You can sail to New Orleans. Your choice. But as concerns Mexico, you are strictly limited to Veracruz. Further, you are prohibited from carrying cargo to Mexico, and the only cargo you ship out of Veracruz is that provided by my agents, with whom you are well-acquainted."

Jones moved his hand to his knife, though Brown could tell the captain did not have the intent to draw it.

"And don't think for a moment that my agents in Mexico won't know of any tricks on your part.

"But don't worry," Brown tempered his tone. "Your merchant colleagues on *Comanche* and *Fanny Butler* will have the same arrangement and the same restrictions."

"Goddamn it, Brown—"

"You are not, of course, required to remain in my service. You can sail between other American ports on the Gulf or compete with the trans-Atlantic trade on the United States Eastern Seaboard. Again, your choice."

Jones, jaw clenched and teeth grinding, was torn between the profits he was making and the dictates of Brown, which he chafed against on basic principle. It was no choice at all, however. *Watchman* would not see the revenue from the heavily competitive American markets that it was getting from Veracruz, even with these constraints.

"The French won't be here forever, Brown."

"Very true, Captain," Hiram said as he threw his saddlebags over his shoulder, hefted his shotgun, and stepped onto the gangplank toward the dock. "But for the foreseeable future, I can arrange for American warships to patrol your shipping lanes as well. And American cannon will kill you just as surely as French. Good day."

After alerting the clerks at the Velasco warehouses to the cargo aboard *Watchman*, Brown bought a horse and rode north out of town. He camped at dusk on the far side of wetlands filled with herons, egrets, ducks, and dozens of other birds nesting in the salt marshes, having moved in after the great flocks of geese migrated north from their Texas winter encampment.

Brown hadn't been in Texas for more than a year and he had never been to Houston, which was barely a year old. The clerks at the Velasco port provided excellent directions and advised him to stay east of the Brazos River. His path wound through marshes, swamps, oxbow lakes, numerous creek and tributary crossings, and dense forests of oak, hickory, cypress, and pecan trees that grew along the waters. Most of the trip was conducted in shade, and mosquitoes buzzing in the damp air were constant companions.

He reached Houston two days later.

In four months, Houston had exploded from a population of twelve to more than fifteen hundred and was the seventh capital of Republic of Texas. Knowing little of the town, Brown headed to where it had first sprung to life—Allen's Landing, a dock with warehouses on the southern bank of Buffalo Bayou and the hub of Houston business activity. A helpful freight handler took a moment from unloading cargo off the steamboat *Laura* to provide directions to the capital.

Brown, however, began to doubt that the freight handler had understood what he was looking for.

The directions led Brown through a gauntlet of wretched saloons, inns, brothels, dram shops, grog shops, and doggeries, all pulsing to an alcohol-fueled cacophony of music, laughter, shouts, and occasional gunshots. He passed a lawman and an undertaker removing the latest victim of the city's street violence.

As impressive as Allen's Landing was, the rest of the town struck Brown as possessing an extremely interim attitude. Simple one-story, one-room wood-frame buildings with unpainted clapboard siding lined the main street. No proud facades, few windows, and timber graying in the humid coastal air. The blood-soaked red-light district was built fast to cash in on the rapidly evolving town before the city matured and moved on.

At the end of this corridor of adult entertainment, Brown located the capital building of the Republic of Texas.

Facing a large plaza and surrounded by blocks of single-story offices, the capital was unfinished and rising slowly. Government administrators mingled uncomfortably with construction workers who, as they swung lumber and buckets and tools, took no notice of the pencil pushers and were indifferent to injuring the men for whom they worked. Rumors of an impending exodus to a new capital in the center of the republic were rampant, undoubtedly undermining progress. Why finish a building that probably wouldn't be needed much longer?

Brown's multiple requests for assistance went ignored until an obnoxious clerk named Thompson overcame his irritation at the interruption and grudgingly directed Hiram to a recently finished block of offices housing various dignitaries.

After knocking on a few doors, Brown located the office of the American chargé d'affaires to the Republic, Alcée la Branche, whose very presence in Texas had been a point of major consternation in Mexico and led to the closing of the US legation in Mexico City.

Like Ellis, la Branche was an Andrew Jackson appointee, which Brown found amusing since a growing cadre of Jacksonians were being engaged in the matter of the ghost who had been a vocal opponent of President Jackson.

Brown presented himself in a somewhat road-weary condition, but la Branche's initial hesitation vanished with the mention of Ellis's name.

"Please, Mr. Brown, come in. I apologize for the state of my office," la Branche said, ushering the visitor into a room reeking of fresh lumber. A diploma from the Université de Sorreze and a pair of paintings leaned in a corner and waited to be hung on bare walls.

"Please forgive my appearance," Brown said. "I'm two weeks at sea and on horse, and have not had an opportunity to clean up."

"Oh, don't mention it, sir. I'm afraid that's how everyone looks in Houston."

Ellis had briefed Brown on la Branche, who was originally from New Orleans and educated in France. That presented an opportunity for Brown to increase the privacy of their meeting by holding their discussion in French.

The formalities concluded, la Branche sat at his desk and offered the room's only other chair to Brown, who took it gratefully, and set down the saddlebags he'd guarded so closely since leaving Ellis's office.

"What can I do for Mr. Ellis?"

Brown drew from his saddlebags the folio with Ellis's report for Washington. "First, he requests you deliver this to Secretary of State Forsyth. It's the report on the matter of the prisoner in the mine."

"It'll be on its way in the morning," la Branche said as he took possession of the report. "Nothing to the rumor, I suppose?"

"Nothing at all. Mr. Ellis would also appreciate if you could notify John Crockett of the investigation's result."

"Certainly. Anything else?"

"I'm afraid so," Brown said. "And in light of that report to Secretary Forsyth, the irony of this situation is breathtaking." Brown handed over the package and sat back.

La Branche dove into the documents, reading intently and periodically glancing from the correspondence to the sketch. At one point, he looked up incredulously at Brown, received no reaction, and returned to his reading. The ambassador's prodigious facial hair—a long mustache over a goatee that fell below his collar—made it difficult to be sure but Brown believed la Branche's mouth was hanging open through much of his examination. When he finished, la Branche looked up, eyes wide, eyebrows raised.

He stared at Brown, searching for some hint that this was a joke. "This is serious?" he said, his mustache fluttering as he spoke.

"Quite serious," Brown said. "The look on your face mirrors what I saw on Mr. Ellis when I last spoke to him."

"Incredible. Simply incredible." La Branche leaned back in his chair and templed his fingers at his chin. "Fascinating. The repercussions are…well…" He stopped, caught up in a web of possibilities. Finally, his eyes refocused on his guest. "What's the next step?"

"Mr. Ellis requires someone to look at that sketch and confirm his suspicions. Someone with close, personal knowledge of the subject."

La Branche thought for moment. "They'd need to be told nothing. Nothing at all, at least initially. Given no hint or suggestion of who this might be or what this is about. Let them reach their own opinion, independently and impartially."

"Agreed. If this person comes to the same conclusion as Mr. Ellis, we'd like them to discreetly investigate in Texas while I conduct inquiries in Mexico."

La Branche considered the problem. "I know who to ask."

★

While la Branche began preparing for Ellis's requested investigation, Brown visited an office three doors down from la Branche's.

Hiram knocked on the door and a stuffed shirt of a man with a tall forehead, full beard, and deep-set eyes answered.

"Good day, sir," Brown said in French. "My name is Hiram Brown. I bring a message from Powhatan Ellis. From Mexico."

The man bowed. "I am Jean Pierre Isidore Alphonse Dubois de Saligny, representative of the government of France. Please, Mr. Brown, come in."

CHAPTER 5

THIS WAS THE third time Silas had been to Houston, a city that grew noticeably larger with each visit. He was always struck by its clamor and commotion, its pace and progress, its spirit and stamina. He also came away with the sense that the city's wisdom, courage, and honor walked hand in hand with its ignorance, corruption, and greed.

"Are we done here?" he asked and slapped at a mosquito as Karnes and McCulloch descended from the capital following their debriefing with President Sam Houston on the engagement at Corpus Christi Bay.

"Almost," Henry said.

"What did the president say?"

"He is well satisfied with our actions, especially with your quick thinking," Sam said. "No smugglers, no French blockade, no war with Mexico."

"I suppose he couldn't thank me in person."

"Oh, far too busy, far too busy," Sam said.

"Fine. Can we leave?"

"Almost," Henry said.

"We've been asked to escort a pair of diplomats to San Antonio," Sam explained. "Make sure they don't get lost or bushwhacked or scalped."

"Mr. McCulloch! Mr. Karnes!" said a clerk pursuing from the capital building. "I have the details on the gentlemen in your care. Mr. la Branche and Mr. Brown will meet you here in the plaza first thing tomorrow morning. We will have horses and provisions for the four of you."

"Five, Mr. Thompson," Sam said.

"Hello, Algernon," Silas called.

"Oh, Silas," Thompson said. "Hello. Sorry, I didn't see you. You're going with them?"

"Yes, he is," Henry said.

Thompson hesitated, calculating the additional expense. "Very well. We will provide horses and provisions for five."

"We'll be here," Sam said. "Thank you, Mr. Thompson."

"How's your family, Silas?" Thompson asked.

"They're well, thanks. Do you ever get up to the Brazos Valley anymore?"

"I'm afraid not. Much too busy here." Thompson dashed off.

Silas nodded at the retreating clerk. "Glad to hear it."

"You have a problem with that fella?" Henry asked.

"No. I've known him a couple of years. We just have a… mutual…interest."

"Ah," Sam said. "This mutual interest wouldn't by chance have red hair and green eyes?"

"Possibly."

Much to Henry's disappointment, the Texians avoided Houston's disreputable areas.

Instead, they spent the evening at the respectable Half-Way Inn, a two-story structure with unpainted siding and a double-door entryway bracketed by tall pillars. The inn boasted a paneled dining room in a large central hall with a mirror behind the bar and hunting trophies on the walls. Bedrooms were upstairs on either side of the main hall.

They enjoyed a supper of steak, potatoes, apple pie, and biscuits with butter, dining—for the first time in a month—at a table with proper cutlery and china.

After dinner, Karnes and McCulloch enjoyed cigars and whiskey while Silas, having no taste for either vice, joined a card game with several capital clerks. Three hours later, he returned to Karnes and McCulloch, who had been joined in conversation by the captain and first mate of the *Laura*, the steamboat tied at Allen's Landing.

"Had enough?" Henry asked Silas.

"No, but they have."

Henry looked past Silas to see anguished countenances attesting to destitute pockets.

"I believe those gentlemen just got paid," the first mate chuckled. "Going to be a long dry spell for them," he said and lifted a glass of whiskey in toast to Silas for cleaning the clerks, who the merchant crews found annoying and useless.

"Silas, would you have anything—or anyone—in mind for that money?" Sam asked.

"Possibly."

They spoke and drank and smoked for another hour before calling it a night. The captain and mate returned to the *Laura*, and Silas, Henry, and Sam retired to upstairs guest rooms where they slept—for the first time in a month—in beds with proper linen and pillows. Each took his own room, billing all charges to the Republic.

The next morning, they assembled in the dining room for a breakfast of eggs, bacon, ham, biscuits, and coffee before walking to the plaza fronting the capital building and arriving at dawn.

"Everyone ready?" Sam said.

"Yeah," Henry said. "All we need are two greenhorns. And horses. And provisions. Dang, I hate it when people are late."

"Who are these diplomats?" Silas asked.

"Don't know," Sam said. "We were told they've been running around Houston a few days and now need to get to San Antonio."

Thirty minutes later, Brown and la Branche arrived and introductions were made, but it was another hour before the horses and provisions were delivered.

"No wonder nothin' gets done in this town," Henry said. "Check everything, fellas."

McCulloch, Karnes, and Silas examined their horses' legs, ribs, skin, coat, face, and hooves. They confirmed the tack: blanket, saddle, stirrups, straps, bridle, and reins; saddle bags, rifle scabbards, and bedrolls.

"Whose cookie on this trip?" Henry asked. "Silas?"

"Fine. I wish Frank Ogden was with us."

"Yeah, that fella's a fine dough-belly."

"Don't worry," Sam said. "There'll be plenty of stops along the way where we can eat. You won't have to cook every night."

Karnes checked the mule provided to haul provisions while Silas confirmed its load. Flour, lard, coffee, sugar, beans, bacon, hardtack, salt, and pepper. Silas was pleased that someone had included dried fruit as well. Pots, pans, Dutch oven, cooking spoons, tin plates, forks, and knives, as well as an oilcloth on which to serve the spread. Every horse was equipped with two canteens with extra canteens on the pack mule.

"Whiskey?" Henry hoped.

"Sorry, you're dry this trip," Silas said.

"Dang it."

Brown had finished checking his horse and was inspecting la Branche's mount. More than knowing his way around a horse, the Texians detected an air of extreme competence about Brown.

"Monsieur la Branche may be a highbrow," Silas said to Karnes and McCulloch, "but I don't believe this Mr. Brown is a diplomat."

"That's a man who can find his own way to San Antonio," Sam said.

"Bet he could track a bee in a blizzard," Henry said.

"Why do they need us?" Silas said.

"Ready, gentlemen?" la Branche said.

They rode cautiously at first, Brown and the Texians watching la Branche to make sure he was steady on his horse. McCulloch was not, however, worried about la Branche's riding ability. He was anticipating an attack that would almost certainly come in the next two or three days and against which the escort had no defense.

A few hours out of Houston, the party left behind the low-lying marshes, swamps, and mosquitoes. On the second day, after an uneventful crossing of the Brazos River, they plunged into the sprawling central Texas prairie. Ahead was day after day of vast grasslands of dense little bluestem, waves of grama grass, thick buffalograss, low-lying tumblegrass, and yellow-flowering snakeweed extending to an impossibly distant horizon under a towering cerulean sky. They passed forests of live oak, post oak, and mesquite, and even the Texian veterans were dazzled by oceans of bluebonnets.

All of which relentlessly, mercilessly assaulted Alcée la Branche.

"Oh, Lord," la Branche moaned.

He wheezed and sneezed and sniffled. His eyes watered and turned red. He scratched. His scalp crawled. He repeatedly pulled a handkerchief from a coat pocket and dabbed and wiped and blew his nose.

"I'm afraid it takes some getting used to, Mr. la Branche," Silas said.

"Oh, Lord," la Branche cried. "Is there anything to help?"

"I'm afraid not, sir," Silas said. "I had a rough time my first year in Texas." He gritted his teeth and knew immediately it was the wrong thing to say.

"First year? Year? Oh, Lord."

Karnes was trying to keep from laughing. He looked to his right and saw Brown struggling with the same impulse.

"It will calm down," Sam said. "We'll get you some water so you can wash."

The chargé d'affaires looked through blurry eyes at Brown, who was having no problems.

"Why are your immune?" la Branche accused.

"I've spent plenty of time in the spring in Texas," Brown said.

"Oh, Lord."

In deference to the struggling la Branche, they cut the day short and stayed in San Felipe de Austin, but they set out again at first light.

On the third day, a storm blew in fast, hit hard, then was gone, but light pelting rain continued most of the afternoon. The Texians, accustomed to these rapid weather changes and storms, were able to warn everyone into oilcloth great coats to ward off the rain.

While traveling in the rain was miserable and slow, it did have the benefit of washing the air and therefore providing la Branche a respite from his sneezing and itching. Wary of spending the night in mud, they made camp when they spotted high ground near the end of the day.

By the fourth day, la Branche was either acclimating or toughening quickly, and the group was able to pick up the pace. They crossed the Colorado River at Beeson's Ford before small talk and uncomfortable silence gave way to more substantial and personal questioning.

"I understand you are gentlemen of some renown," la Branche said. "You were all involved in the war for independence?"

"Henry and I were in the fighting," Sam said, "and young Silas was with the army during the retreat that led to San Jacinto."

"Excellent. You see, in addition to your skills in getting Mr. Brown and me safely to San Antonio, that's why President Houston suggested your presence. Chronicling the war and learning about Texas is the purpose of my mission."

"Mission?"

"Yes. There's a great deal of interest in Texas back east. We are…" He glanced at Brown. "…endeavoring to set the record straight on a few matters. Meeting with veterans such as you is indispensable to that cause. Tracing lineages. Some back in the States are making claims to land in Texas based on alleged relations, especially to those who died at the Alamo. We're attempting to track who was who."

"Hmm."

"Did any of you know the men in the Alamo?"

"Both of them did," Silas said.

"You knew Bowie, Crockett, Travis?"

"Knowed Jim Bowie and Crockett," Henry said. "Met Travis and some of the other fellas. We both knowed old Isaac."

"Knew Isaac before the war," Sam said. "He was one of the reinforcements from Gonzales. The men folks have taken to calling the Immortal 32."

"Immortal 32?" la Branche asked.

"Them fellas in the Alamo was surrounded by thousands of Mexican soldados," Henry said. "I promise, that ain't what they signed up for. They had chances to slip out of there and run like a Nueces steer but they didn't. They was brave as any, and they stayed and fought and gave the Mexicans hell. But they was trapped.

"Now them fellas from Gonzales, they was not trapped. They knowed what they was ridin' to, and they rode to it anyway. Facin' thousands of Mexicans is what they signed up for."

"Like Leonidas and his three hundred Spartans," la Branche admired. "Epic."

"It does bring to mind Thermopylae," Silas agreed.

"Isaac Millsaps was one of those men," Sam said. "Left behind a blind wife and seven children."

"Good, Lord."

"The Texian army was at Gonzales. When the Alamo fell, the army high-tailed it east," Sam said. "But in the confusion, Isaac's family got left behind."

"Sam Houston sent me and a couple other fellas to fetch 'em," Henry said.

La Branche turned to Silas. "You know your classics, I see. I am impressed that you know the story of Leonidas. Admirable."

"Oh, he do have book learnin'," Henry said.

"We're working on his Texian education," Sam said. "But he's coming along nicely."

"Ah, well, the practical is as important as the classroom," la Branche said. "This Mr. Millsaps. I presume he is dead?"

"Old Isaac died in the Alamo. But not Jacob."

"Jacob?'

"Jacob Millsaps, Isaac's younger brother," Sam said. "He was in and out of the Alamo during the siege. Helped get messages out and reinforcements in through the Mexican lines. He rode out with Crockett late in the siege to lead a group of men into the Alamo. Jacob delivered messages to Sam Houston, and was on his way back to the Alamo when the final attack came. Jacob knew those men well."

"Is he still alive?"

"Yes, sir," Silas said. "He lives in Gonzales, helps take care of his brother's family."

"Please excuse my ignorance of Texas geography, but where is Gonzales?"

"It's on our way to San Antonio," Silas said.

"Perhaps we could speak with Mr. Millsaps."

"You're welcome to try," Henry said. "Jacob tends to get his bristles up when folks ask about the war and his brother."

"Why?"

"Some in his family blame him for Isaac's death. Say Isaac wouldn't been there if'n Jacob hadn't got him involved in the war."

"Truth is, Isaac was just as passionate as Jacob," Sam said. "Jacob tried to keep Isaac with his wife and children. But old Isaac answered Travis's call."

"Then why—"

"Because Isaac is dead," Sam said, "and Jacob's alive. So he's blamed."

☆

La Branche had no expectations of what he would find at Gonzales, located on the Guadalupe River at the confluence of the San Marcos

River. He knew the first shots of the Texas Revolution were fired here in a skirmish dubbed the Battle of Gonzales, in which Mexican troops tried to reclaim a cannon loaned to the settlers for defense against Indians. The Texians refused, telling the Mexicans to "come and take it."

The Mexicans did not take the cannon, but the town did not survive the war.

A few days after the fall of the Alamo, the Texian army burned Gonzales to deny it to the Mexicans, and thus began the Runaway Scrape, the long retreat that ended in victory at San Jacinto.

In the two years since, the town's resurrection had been agonizingly slow, and most of its former residents had yet to return.

The Texians, la Branche, and Brown rode past heaps of debris cleared from the fire-ravaged town to an area nearer the river where new construction had begun. A handful of one-room log cabins had been built along what could generously be called a road. A wagon sat empty behind the cabins, next to a corral that held half a dozen horses.

Across from the cabins was a dog-run house with a stone chimney and a broad porch beneath a peaked roof. A woman sat in a rocking chair on the porch, a few children at her feet. The children retreated behind the woman at the newcomers' approach, but the woman's gaze did not meet the riders' or follow them as they rode past.

A lanky, six-foot tall figure appeared from one of the cabins, carrying tools and heading for a construction site where a handful of men were working. His bearded face was shaded by a black, wide-brimmed hat with a white band about its crown. He wore a linsey shirt, brown trousers, and brogans. He paused at the riders' approach.

"Jacob," Henry said.

"Henry. Sam," Millsaps responded. He tilted his head. "Is that Silas with you?"

"Yes, sir," Silas said. "Good to see you again."

"How's things?" Sam said.

"Slow. We've built some cabins so folks have places to live. This," he gestured to a building that was beginning to take shape from a pile of lumber, "is to be a post office. Hope to have it open next year. What brings you out here?"

"We're escortin' these gents to San Antonio," Henry said. "This here is Alcée la Branche. He's the ambassador to Texas from the United States."

"Mr. la Branche," Millsaps said.

"Mr. Millsaps," la Branche said. "This is my associate, Hiram Brown."

Brown and Millsaps simply nodded at one another.

"Jacob, Mr. la Branche would like to speak with you," Sam said.

"We're busy here. Got a lot of work to do."

McCulloch considered the problem. "Make a deal with you. You come inside and speak with me and Mr. la Branche, and Henry and Silas will help with the work."

Henry and Silas turned their heads in Sam's direction.

"Fair enough. Here you go, Henry," and Millsaps offered Karnes a hammer.

Henry stared at Sam.

"I'd help," Sam said, "but, you know, my shoulder."

"Yeah, I know, first man through the wall." Henry took the hammer and dismounted. "Come on, Silas. We been hornswoggled."

"I'll help, too," Brown said. The testimony he needed to hear would come in San Antonio.

Millsaps led McCulloch and la Branche into one of the log cabins. It was cool and dark inside. The floor was dirt, and the only furnishings were a single chair and a narrow bed against the back wall.

Jacob removed his hat, sat on the bed, and gestured la Branche to the chair. Sam, without alternative, leaned against the log wall that had been chinked with thick Texas clay.

"I've never seen a hat like that, Mr. Millsaps," la Branche said. "Very practical and stylish. May I ask where someone might acquire a hat like that?"

"Sure," Jacob said. "Kill a Mexican lancer. Then take his hat."

To his credit, la Branche did not fluster or ruffle. He returned Millsaps' glare with a slight grin, and moved on.

"As I explained to Mr. McCulloch, Mr. Brown and I are conducting investigations into claims made by citizens of the United States concerning land in Texas owned or granted to veterans of the war, in particular the men who died at the Alamo. We'd like you to join us in San Antonio to help with this. Mr. McCulloch and Mr. Karnes are assisting us."

"What sort of claims?"

"As I say, on land owned by veterans who died in the war."

"Why is the United States government getting involved? Wouldn't the Republic of Texas judge any claims?"

"Yes, Mr. Millsaps. The US government is simply trying to cooperate with Texas to keep claimants from needlessly cluttering Texas courts."

Jacob glanced at Sam.

"I don't know any more about this than you do, Jacob," Sam said. "Sam Houston just asked Henry and me to take these gentlemen to San Antonio."

"You can't vouch for this claim business?"

"No."

"I really don't see how I could help," Jacob said. "To be honest, I'm not sure what you're up to, Mr. la Branche."

"As I said—"

"I heard what you said. I just don't believe you." Millsaps crossed his arms, leaned back against the wall behind the bed, and considered la Branche for a long moment. Finally, he sat up.

"I'll come with you on one condition. The Republic of Texas granted $200 a year for ten years to Mary. That's my brother's widow. You might have seen her out on her porch. Paid her $100 so far. She couldn't afford the tax on the land that she and Isaac owned so she had to sell. I want you to talk to Sam Houston and those damned clerks of his."

"I'm happy to speak with President Houston, but I can't promise anything," la Branche said. "Frankly, I don't know how much the Republic's budget can afford to pay."

"Not money, Mr. la Branche," Jacob said. "Land. I want Texas to grant Mary the land owed to any other veteran." He pointed at McCulloch. "Same as they done for Sam, same as they done for Henry."

"Can't you obtain land in the same manner, Mr. Millsaps? You're a veteran of the war."

"I don't want it for me. It's for Mary. They grant it to me, I transfer to her, and I guarantee some no-account son of a bitch will find a way to take it from her. They'll claim taxes or come up with some other way to cheat her. I want Sam Houston to grant it to her, in her name and those of her children, so no one can take it. You promise me to do that, to do your best to do that, and I'll come with you to San Antonio."

"You have my word, Mr. Millsaps," la Branche said. "I will bring all pressure that I and the United States government can mount upon President Houston and the Republic of Texas to provide her with land and repay the debt owed to your sister-in-law."

Millsaps stood and shook hands with la Branche.

"All right."

★

On the seventh day of the journey west, the six-man party crossed the Salado River and reached San Antonio in early afternoon. Approaching from the east, the first thing they saw was the Alamo.

No one said a word. All was unearthly still.

La Branche felt the ethereal power of the old Spanish mission and fort. Sam, Henry, and Silas had been here many times, and Brown had been here once, but they, too, felt the ghosts of the hundreds who died.

Much of the stone walls and interior buildings had been destroyed by the Mexican army after the Alamo's capture in 1836, a condition that only heightened the haunted aspect.

They approached from the back of the chapel, its walls twenty-three feet tall and three feet thick. Rode past the palisade, the cut trees that the defenders had laid in front long gone. Rode past the spot where the mission's main gate on the south wall once stood. The gate and the trench and sally port around the gate were also gone. Continued to the west wall, the fort's longest wall but torn down. Reached the north wall, where so many Mexicans had fallen but a breach had been made. That wall, too, had been destroyed.

They dismounted and walked inside, past the still-standing long barracks where intense hand-to-hand fighting took place, to the area in front of the chapel.

"This," Karnes said, breaking the silence and startling la Branche, "is where we think it ended."

La Branche gazed at the carved columns on either side of the chapel's entrance, but his attention was drawn to the chapel's rough, flat, broken roofline. "Was it damaged in the battle?"

McCulloch shook his head. "The chapel's roof collapsed long ago. It's looked like that as long as I can remember."

La Branche wanted to enter the chapel but couldn't bring himself to move. "How many died here?" he whispered.

"Texians, we think around two hundred," Henry said. "Mexicans, probably more. Lot of their wounded died in the days after the battle. They lost maybe two or three times as many."

"As many as eight hundred dead between the two sides?" la Branche said. Karnes nodded.

"A lot of brave men died here in the main plaza," Sam said.

"Right here?" la Branche said, looking at the ground as if he were standing in blood. Finally, he looked up. "Were any of the defenders born in Texas?"

"Sure," Henry said. "The Tejanos."

"Tejanos?"

"Folks of Mexican birth or heritage who live in Texas," Sam explained. "At least eight Tejano defenders were born in Texas, some here in San Antonio."

"And the bodies of the Texians were burned?"

"Yes, sir," Henry said. "Juan Seguin come out here last year, gathered up what ashes and remains he could find, and give 'em a proper burial."

The group suddenly realized that Millsaps was not with them. They looked toward the city, past the rubble of the ruined west wall, and saw a single rider waiting at the bridge over the San Antonio River and into the city.

"He don't come in here," Henry said.

It was a somber day, and everyone felt a hangover from the visit to the Alamo.

McCulloch and Karnes secured lodging at Señora Candelaria's inn on the Calle del Calabozo, Millsaps drifted off to visit friends while Silas performed a mission of a personal nature in the Plaza de las Islas and the market in the Military Plaza.

It was agreed everyone would meet at the inn for dinner, which was much anticipated for Señora Candelaria's reputation as a splendid cook.

Brown and la Branche, meanwhile, attended to the purpose of this trip and headed for the Casa Reales, the government house.

Passing through the front door, they found themselves in the main room. A cluster of offices were at the back. The hall was large, white, and extremely spartan, built without aesthetics in mind. A clerk sat at a desk immediately inside the front entry, and la Branche and Brown asked to speak with the Chief Justice of Bexar County.

"May I say who is calling?"

"My name is la Branche. I believe the Chief Justice is expecting me."

The clerk excused himself, crossed the hall, and disappeared into one of the offices. He returned a moment later and escorted la Branche and Brown to the office.

"Good day, gentlemen," the Chief Justice rose from his desk and extended a hand. "I am Erasmo Seguin."

"I am Alcée la Branche," the diplomat said, accepting the proffered handshake. "This is my associate, Hiram Brown."

"Welcome, gentlemen. Mr. Neill and Mr. Alsbury have arrived and are guests in my home. We can hold your meetings here tomorrow. I have reserved the building and arranged for my staff to be off the premises."

"Excellent," la Branche said. "The United States government appreciates your help."

"Very well, gentlemen. Well, if there is nothing else, we will see you in the morning."

✭

"I love this town," Silas said as he, Sam, Henry, and Jacob emerged into a bright San Antonio morning, the streets quickly coming alive. The plaza was a daily iridescent festival.

Women moved through the streets in huipils adorned with floral embroidery and ribbon, and in rebozos dyed red, blue, green, yellow, orange, or purple. Rainbows danced on the hems of their skirts.

Men strolled in white tailored pants held by wide belts, their shoulders covered by capes with bright geometric patterns.

It was as if the city couldn't decide on one color, so it took them all.

The quartet had enjoyed a breakfast of eggs on corn tostadas topped with ranchero sauce, served with bacon and warm tortillas with honey.

"What'd Señora Candelaria call that?" Henry asked.

"Huevos rancheros," Silas said.

"They really know how to cook here," Jacob said.

"I do love this town," Silas said.

From Señora Candelaria's inn, they walked through San Antonio's plaza, which was divided in two parts, strung end to end, and nestled in the huge arc of the San Antonio River. The western half, the Plaza de Armas, was dominated by the stone edifice of the Cathedral de San Fernando while further east the Plaza de las Islas was home to the hub of city government.

"Where's la Branche?" Henry said.

"Brown left a note," Sam said. "Said to meet at Casa Reales. I guess they'll turn up."

"Does anyone know what this is about?" Jacob said. "I don't believe la Branche's nonsense."

"Not a word of it," Henry said as the group reached the government building. Henry pushed open the door. "I can't figure—"

A few steps inside the door stood three men, and the two groups gawked at one another.

"I'll be damned," Henry said, his face breaking into a smile. "All creation's here."

"J.C.? Juan? Horace?" Sam said.

"Jacob? Sam? Henry? How you boys been?" Horace Alsbury whooped.

Silas had met, spoken with, dined with, traveled with, and knew well all the men in the room, yet even he was starstruck at the reunion of a legendary Texian brotherhood. Six heroes of the Texas Revolution surged together in a fervor of joyful hellos, vigorous handshakes, and back-slapping embraces. Silas wondered the last time all six had been in the same place.

Even Jacob Millsaps looked happy to be here.

They didn't notice when la Branche and Brown entered the room from the back offices led by Erasmo Seguin.

"Good morning, my friends," Erasmo said. "It is very good to see you again."

"Erasmo! Good to see you!" everyone said. More hugs and back slaps. Everyone still all smiles.

"You all know one another," Erasmo said. "But for the benefit of our guests, Mr. la Branche and Mr. Brown, who we can thank for this gathering, I should make introductions.

"Horace Alsbury, who fought in the siege of Béxar in 1835, rode from the Alamo as a messenger, fought at San Jacinto, and followed and monitored the Mexican army as it retreated from Texas." A clean-shaven, thin-faced man in a black suit with a Palmetto straw hat bowed.

"Henry Wax Karnes, who fought at the Battle of Concepcion and the siege of Béxar, led a patrol of five men to defeat twenty Mexican soldiers at Rocky Creek, and was second-in-command of the Texian cavalry at San Jacinto." Henry, wearing a linsey shirt with the sleeves rolled up, wool pants, and brogans, waved his straw hat to the room.

"James Clinton Neill, who fired the first cannon shot in the Revolution at Gonzales, played a critical role in the capture of Béxar, was temporary commander of the Alamo, and commanded the Twin Sisters cannon at San Jacinto." A tall man with mutton-chop sideburns and wearing a top hat and checkered vest and pants took a tentative step forward, aided by a cane. "J.C. was rather seriously wounded in the hip at San Jacinto," Erasmo added.

"Jacob Millsaps, who stormed the Mexican defenses in the taking of Béxar in 1835, carried messages from and guided rein-forcements into the Alamo, and fought at San Jacinto." Jacob didn't acknowledge the introduction, just stood impatiently with his hands in the pockets of his knee-length brown coat.

"My son, Juan Seguin, who carried messages from William Travis in the Alamo to Sam Houston, scouted for Sam Houston's army, fought at San Jacinto, formally accepted the surrender of the Mexican forces in the Alamo, and returned to the Alamo to bury the remains of the defenders. He is now a senator in the Republic of Texas legislature." Juan resembled his father. He was very handsome, with black hair and wide-set eyes. This morning he wore a suit.

"And my friend Samuel McCulloch Jr. who was—"

"—the first man through the wall at Goliad," the crowd finished for Erasmo. Sam swept his white hat across his chest and bowed, displaying a receding hairline and causing his long frock coat to billow around him.

"Mr. Alcée la Branche, the United States chargé d'affaires to Texas, has brought us together. The gentleman with him is Hiram Brown." Erasmo paused and looked at la Branche. "And I'm afraid that's all I know. So, Mr. la Branche, how can we help you?"

"Gentlemen," la Branche said. "Thank you for coming. I can say unequivocally that you are precisely who we need."

"Wait a minute," Henry said. "Just wait." The curious nature of the meeting had suddenly hit. Neill lived in Harrisburg, near Houston. Alsbury at Calaveras Ranch near Goliad. "Not that I ain't happy to see you, J.C., but how'd you and Horace end up here?"

"I was just thinking the same about you," J.C. said. "How'd you and Sam end up so far from home? And with Jacob?"

"We just got back from chasing off smugglers on the coast," Sam said. "About a week ago, President Houston asked us to escort Mr. la Branche and Mr. Brown to San Antonio, and we picked up Jacob on the way." Sam turned to la Branche. "Now that I think of it, you knew about Jacob. You intended us to bring him to this shindig all along."

"Ten days ago, I got a visit from Mr. Brown and Mr. la Branche," J.C. said, "asking me to come to San Antonio and collect Horace from his ranch. Said something about land claims—"

"Gentlemen," la Branche interjected. "I apologize for the deception. Please believe that it was necessary. San Antonio seemed a logical place for this meeting, as the Seguins were here and Mr. Alsbury and Mr. Millsaps were close by. I sincerely appreciate those who have traveled long distances. Our business today will be brief, but I assure you it is of utmost importance, and I feel certain that each of you will find this matter of great interest. You are here because of your special knowledge of the question at hand. Frankly, very few men could address this issue. In fact, there is probably no one else to whom we could turn. I promise you, before we are finished today, you will know all.

"I'm afraid I must ask one more indulgence of you," la Branche said. "I apologize but it is absolutely necessary. I need all of you to wait in Erasmo Seguin's office."

Grumbles all around.

"We will call each of you one by one," la Branche said over the murmur of objections. "You will not be kept waiting long. But I cannot stress this enough: do not discuss what you see with anyone until we gather again shortly in this room."

Shrugs and sighs and exasperation gave way to a well-we're-here resignation, and the Texians followed Erasmo to his office.

"Do you want me to leave?" said Silas, overlooked and standing off to the side.

"Oh, dear, my boy," la Branche said. "I am so sorry. It might be best if you—"

"He can be trusted," Sam called from the doorway of the office. "Whatever this is about, he can be trusted." Then McCulloch stepped into the office and closed the door.

La Branche looked to Brown, who considered Silas a moment.

"Actually, you could help us, if you don't mind," Brown said.

Silas was happy to assist and delighted he would not miss whatever was about to happen, the anticipation of which was excruciating.

They instructed Silas to go to Erasmo's office and lead the Texians out one at a time; and after each was finished, lead them to the empty office next to Erasmo's.

One by one, the Texians were led out—Karnes, Alsbury, Neill, McCulloch, Millsaps, Juan, and finally Erasmo Seguin. Each sat at a table in front of la Branche and Brown.

"Please, tell me if you can identify the individual in this picture," was the only instruction la Branche gave before showing Mrs. Ward's sketch. The Texians asked questions, to which no answers were given.

The certainty of responses ranged from "it looks like…" to "I think it looks like…" to "it sure looks like…" to "that's definitely…" But every Texian's identification of the face in the sketch was the same.

David Crockett.

Erasmo, the final witness, remained still and stunned in the chair. When Silas opened the door to the spare office to retrieve the other Texians, not one made a sound. They filed out and gathered around Erasmo.

"Here is what we know," Brown took charge. "A few weeks ago, Powhatan Ellis, the American Envoy Extraordinary and Minister Plenipotentiary to Mexico, attended a reception in Mexico City for the Spanish ambassador and his wife. The ambassador and his wife, along with a traveling companion, have been touring Mexico. At this reception was a set of sketches that this companion, Mrs. Ward, had drawn. The sketch you just viewed was among them. Mr. Ellis, who served in Congress with Crockett and knew him well, recognized his face just as you have, and he stole the sketch."

"Are you saying—" J.C. began.

Brown nodded. "This sketch was drawn this year."

"This year?" J.C. said.

Brown nodded.

"This year? This year as in 1838?"

Brown nodded again, incurring blank stares from the Texians.

"We believe no one else at that reception saw this sketch, and that the Spanish ambassador, his wife, and Mrs. Ward have no inkling as to what this suggests."

"Suggests?" Horace said. "It suggests…" He put his hand to his mouth. "I can't say it."

"That David Crockett…is alive," the deathly pale Erasmo Seguin said.

"That's impossible," Jacob said.

"I'd have said so before I saw that," Juan pointed to the sketch. "I buried those bones and ashes. It just seems…"

"Unthinkable," Brown said. "That's why Mr. Ellis sent me from Mexico City, to have someone confirm or deny his suspicion. You knew Crockett more recently than Mr. Ellis, and you have viewed the evidence and reached the same conclusion. In light of this, I can tell you that Mr. Ellis is determined to learn the truth of this matter."

"How?"

"I'm returning to Mexico," Brown said. "I will determine the circumstances in which this sketch was made. In the meantime, we would like you gentlemen to make some discreet investigations here in Texas. Find out what happened at the Alamo and if it is possible that Crockett is alive."

The Texians looked at one another.

"I don't see what choice we have," Sam said. He looked at the other Texians.

"We keep this quiet," Horace said. "Mention it to no one. No friends, no family, no one."

"Agreed," J.C. said.

"What do we tell folks?" Henry said. "If we're askin' about Crockett, what's our story?"

"Dispelling rumors," J.C. said. "We've all heard that foolishness about Crockett in a Mexican mine." He looked at Brown. "That rumor is foolishness, isn't it?"

"It is," Brown said. "Mr. Ellis investigated it personally. That story is false."

"There's our cover story," J.C. said. "If cover is needed, we're gathering information to put that scurrilous rumor to rest and bring peace to the Crockett family."

"I hate to mention money, but this could get expensive," J.C. said. "Traveling all over Texas, horses, provisions, being away from our homes and farms and businesses."

"The United States government is prepared, covertly and off the books, to fund this investigation," la Branche said, "as well as whatever further action it necessitates."

"I don't believe this!" Jacob erupted. He walked away from the group, then spun back on them. "Do any of you believe this? Do any of you believe that David Crockett would surrender?"

"Jacob," Erasmo said, trying to lower the tension. "There is no dishonor in surrender when there is no hope. We fight for what we believe, but we are not expected to come home bearing our shield or on it."

"I understand that, Erasmo," Jacob said, regaining his composure. "There is no dishonor in surrender. But Santa Anna did not offer surrender. I heard the Mexicans play the Degüello and saw their blood-red flag. I just don't believe David Crockett would try to save his own neck while everyone else was being killed."

An intense hush filled the hall.

"The Mexicans were not accepting surrender," J.C. reasoned, rubbing his temples while thinking out loud. "Why, in the heat of battle, in the middle of that bloodlust, take one man prisoner while everyone else is killed?"

"And why keep him alive all this time?" Henry said.

"Look at a map."

All heads turned. "What did you say, Silas?" Sam said.

"Look at a map," Silas repeated. "Half of the North American continent, from Texas to the Pacific Ocean. Nuevo Mexico, California. That land belonged to Spain. Now it belongs to Mexico, and the United States wants it. Isn't that so, Mr. la Branche?"

La Branche remained silent.

"And Mexico has long known the Americans covet that territory," Silas said. "If Crockett is alive, Mexico could be holding him as a bargaining chip."

"A hostage," Juan said.

Silas nodded. "To deter American action against Mexico or drive up the price if Mexico decided to sell. Or am I wrong, Mr. la Branche?"

The chargé d'affaires hesitated. He cleared his throat. "What you describe is…possible."

"That's why you're here," Juan said. "The Americans need Crockett out of the way."

Millsaps stared at the floor. "I still don't believe it." Another silence.

Finally, Jacob sighed and lifted his head. "But, if there's any chance this is true, any chance at all, we've got to know."

"And if it's true," J.C. said, "then what?"

Millsap looked around the room. His eyes challenged every Texian. None flinched. None looked away.

"We go get him."

CHAPTER 6

"FELLAS," HENRY SAID, "my head's so buffaloed right now, I don't know what to think."

The confrontation with the unimaginable was just an hour old. Each of the Texians had studied, scrutinized, and poured over the sketch, but their attempts to dissuade themselves of the evidence of their eyes failed again and again.

After the other Texians had finished, Silas took a turn with the drawing. To his surprise—and considerable pride—he found himself welcomed into this sudden fellowship, a full partner in whatever was to come. The sixteen-year-old wondered what he could contribute to these battle veterans, but today he could offer a dispassionate eye in the search for clues.

"Are you discovering anything?" Brown asked.

"I'm just thinking about the drawing itself," Silas said. "Mrs. Ward didn't include anything in the background, like you see in many portraits. Nothing to identify time or place. His clothing is not defined, but the details in his face are remarkable. The artist was completely focused on her subject. He must have made quite an impression on her. Even months later, there's a good chance she would remember him."

"And perhaps remember where she saw him," Brown said. "I'm returning to Mexico."

With the examination of the sketch complete, it was agreed that Brown take the drawing to show Mrs. Ward and pinpoint its origin. Within minutes, Brown was packed and ready to leave, but as he headed toward the door, he nudged la Branche.

"What? Oh, yes," la Branche stood and addressed the Texians. "I'll let you speak among yourselves. I'll walk Mr. Brown out, then I'll be at Señora Candelaria's inn."

"Gentlemen, I've enjoyed meeting you," Brown said. "I appreciate your hospitality and cooperation, and I know Mr. Ellis would agree. I hope we meet again under less stressful conditions." Brown and la Branche departed.

The Texians collectively exhaled. Those who were standing took seats. Those who were seated stood and stretched.

"We are all rather overwhelmed in the wake of this incredible revelation," Erasmo said. "I doubt any of us are thinking clearly. I suggest we adjourn and meet tonight at my home. We will dine and make plans."

The Texians said little as they drifted out of Casa Reales and stumbled into town. The sun was high and the day clear and bright but they took in none of it.

Karnes found his way to a watering hole but discovered he had no desire for drink, which surprised him as he was certain he was up for a good bout of elbow bending. He sat awhile at a table, a forlorn beer in front of him, before wandering back into the streets.

His fellows drifted through town on their own, bumping into one another and gathering in twos and threes, speaking little and avoiding any mention of the sketch or Mexico.

And certainly not the name Crockett.

*

Sunset ambushed the Texians.

Even those with watches had lost track of time when they noticed dusk's approach and headed for Erasmo Seguin's house in the Plaza de las Islas.

It was a simple but elegant white adobe house. The front door opened into a modest living room with a fireplace and an impressive wood mantel. A large dining area held a long table and chairs. There was a well-equipped kitchen and a hall leading to the bedrooms. The fireplace was cold but heat from the kitchen warmed the house nicely.

The Texians gathered around the dining table, and Erasmo, his wife Maria, and son Juan served a meal of cabrito, frijoles, tortillas, onions, and nopalitos. Their guests had arrived without appetite, but the aroma of garlic and chilis quickly remedied that condition.

"I do love this town," Silas said, soaking up his dinner's remnants with a tortilla.

"You enjoy Tejano cuisine?" Señora Seguin said.

"Yes, ma'am. I enjoy everything about San Antonio."

"Maybe we'll make a Béxareño of you," Juan said.

As the meal finished, Silas and Henry helped clear away dishes and cutlery. Cigars, whiskey, and coffee were brought out, along with a platter of tortillas and a bowl of pink jam.

"Is that what I hope it is?" Henry said, pausing as he was about to pour a whiskey.

"Prickly pear jam," Señora Seguin said. "I think you'll enjoy this, Silas."

"Thank you, Señora," Silas said, and everyone joined in thanking her for the superb supper.

"Very well," Horace began, "where do we start?"

"We're obviously not depending solely on the sketch and waiting for Hiram Brown to locate the artist," J.C. said. "We talk to folks who might have seen something. Might not even know they saw something. I'm thinking about survivors from the Alamo and Mexican soldiers who were there. Perhaps they'll give us clues to follow. Figure out if Crockett could have survived, how they could have gotten him out of the Alamo, and where they would have taken him."

"I was among those who followed the retreating Mexican army, and I was in their camp," Horace said. "We never saw any prisoners. Course, it was two thousand, three thousand men, strung out over miles so we couldn't see everything."

"There were no Texian prisoners among the Mexican forces that surrendered to us at the Alamo after San Jacinto," Juan said. "We know their forces were scattered in multiple locations when Santa Anna ordered them back to Mexico. We need to know about their movements, their lines of march."

"Two years later, a blind man could follow the march of the main body of the army," Sam said, lighting a cigar. "They left a lot of gear and goods scattered on their retreat south."

"I suggest we start with the witnesses, the survivors, the rumors," Erasmo said.

"Many of the survivors are still in San Antonio," Juan said. "Yorba, Esparza, Ruiz, perhaps others. My father and I will speak with them. I don't know of any former Mexican soldiers in Texas, though almost certainly some were left behind, either injured or deserted."

"What about the Texians who ran the prison camps after San Jacinto?" Silas asked between bites of tortilla smeared with the sweet, tart jam. "They might have spoken with the prisoners."

"What's that fella's name?" Henry searched. "George... somethin'."

"Dolson," J.C. said. "George Dolson. He was the interpreter at the Galveston camp."

"Mexican officers were held there," Juan said between sips of coffee.

"All right, I'll go to Galveston and talk to Dolson," J.C. said.

"Your leg up to it?" Henry asked.

"I appreciate the concern but I can ride just fine, Henry," J.C. said. "As long as I don't have to walk there, I'm good."

"I'll speak with Juana," Horace said in little more than a whisper, his hands nervously turning a glass of whiskey.

"Horace—" Erasmo began.

"I know. She's been through so much. More than most folk see in a lifetime. But she was in the Alamo until the finish. We need to know what she saw." His gaze drifted away and he went quiet. His friends waited for him. "Two years now, we've never spoken about what she went through. She doesn't speak of it to anyone. Maybe it's time."

"Very well, my friend," Erasmo said.

"Anyone know where we can find Joe?" Jacob said. "I doubt anyone alive saw the fighting like he did."

"I heard he was sent back to William Travis's estate near Columbia," Juan said.

"Naw, he run off last year," Henry said, savoring a spoonful of prickly pear jam. "Borrowed a pair of brush horses and was hell-for-leather. Last I heard, he was workin' somewhere north of here. Joe worked hisself 'til Travis was in the grave, got shot for his trouble, and they kept him a slave."

"I might know where to find Joe," Sam said. "I'll talk to him."

"We should take a look at Groce's Landing, too," Horace said. "Everybody was camped there. Refugees from all over Texas and the entire army. Some of them still live in the area."

"Lots of construction going on," Sam said. "Lot of folks from the camp in '36 are rebuilding the ferry and putting up new buildings. Good chance to catch some rumors."

"Silas, you were at the camp as long as anyone. You feel like going?" Horace said.

"Sure," Silas said. "My family isn't far from there, so I can use a visit home as good reason to be there."

"Good," J.C. said. "Now—"

"You know what else," Sam jabbed the air with his cigar, "or I should say, who else isn't far—"

"Don't," Silas cut him off, shook his head, and wagged a finger. "Don't say it."

"Say what?" Sam faked innocence, hands out placatingly.

"Aw, Silas, he weren't gonna say nothin' about someone with red hair and green eyes," Henry deadpanned.

"You guys are hilarious."

"Why do you think he's been shopping all over town?" Juan said.

Silas cocked his head and looked at the younger Seguin. "How do you—"

"Please, señor, this is my town," Juan said. Silas leaned back and grinned.

"Well...I...don't know what any of that's about, but you've got a fine excuse to go," J.C. said. "So...go."

Neill had been scribbling notes on the leads each of the Texians would follow, notes he would burn when this meeting was concluded. He read through the list.

"Juan and Erasmo will talk to Alamo survivors here in San Antonio. Horace is going to speak with Juana. Sam's going to find Joe. I'm going to talk to Dolson in Galveston. Silas is going to Groce's Landing." He looked around the room. "What else?"

Neill knew perfectly well what else but didn't feel like forcing it on the two unspoken-for members of the group or mentioning one name in particular in front of Horace.

A very heavy silence descended and hovered over the table.

"Oh, hell," Jacob finally spoke up. "We got to talk to her."

"Aw, no, Jacob," Henry said.

"It's all right," Jacob responded. "I'll do it."

"Brave man, Jacob," Sam said.

"You're speaking of Susanna Dickinson, I assume?" Erasmo said. "Thank you, Jacob. It may be unpleasant but, I agree, necessary."

At the other end of the table, Horace grimaced at the mention of Dickinson.

"I'll ride with you," Henry said. "Then we'll go south and talk to Elizabeth Powell. The Mexican army was at her place after San Jacinto. Maybe she heard or saw somethin'."

"Deal," Jacob said, and helped himself to a whiskey.

"And perhaps you, Jacob, and J.C. can escort Mr. la Branche to Houston before you continue with your investigations," Erasmo said. "From Houston, he will be better positioned to receive messages from Mexico and use his couriers to relay them to us."

"Do we trust him?" Silas asked.

"No," Erasmo said. "I believe Mr. la Branche to be honorable, but his loyalty lies elsewhere. It is possible that our interests and his could diverge. I suggest we report our findings only among ourselves. We'll decide what to tell Mr. la Branche. We make use of him but don't confide in him. Not yet."

Everyone agreed.

"When do we meet again?" Sam said.

"J.C.'s got furthest to go," Henry said. "At least fifteen days round trip."

"Then I suggest we reconvene in three weeks," the elder Seguin said. "And to keep our investigation confidential, we meet at my ranch southeast of town."

"Very well," J.C. said. "We meet again in three weeks at Casa Blanca."

✷

It was getting late when the Texians returned to Señora Candelaria's inn.

Silas had reached his room and was about to remove his brogans when he heard a knock at the door. He opened it to find a chagrinned-looking Sam McCulloch.

"Can I talk to you for a moment?" Sam asked.

"Of course. Come in."

"I need to ask a favor," Sam said once the door was closed behind him.

"Sure, Sam, whatever you need."

"It's a big favor, so, hear me out before you agree. I, uh, well, do you have any of that poker money left? The money you won from the clerks in Houston? I apologize for joking with you about that and about—"

"It's all right," Silas said. "I know you didn't mean anything. Yeah, I got a little left. I've finished...acquiring what I need."

"I hate to ask—"

"You don't have to ask," Silas said. "You can have it. I, uh, don't have much left."

"Got what you needed?"

"I sure hope so," Silas said. "I don't know what I'm doing, but the ladies in the market were really helpful. You want to see what I got?"

"Yeah, I'm curious."

Silas pulled packages from under his bed and laid out the goods purchased across San Antonio.

"What do you think?"

"I'm impressed," Sam said, closely examining the treasures. "I'm really impressed. You have done extremely well. Someone with red hair and green eyes is going to be very happy."

"You think so?"

"Silas, I don't think you need this stuff. I think she really likes you." He took a closer look at one item in particular. "But this definitely will not hurt."

Silas had forty dollars, which he happily offered to Sam, though McCulloch told him to keep five dollars for traveling money. "With what I already have, this should be enough. Thank you. I'll pay you back."

"Do you mind me asking what this is for?"

Sam hesitated. "You might not want to know."

Silas nodded. "Knowing where you're headed and who you're seeking, I suspect I already do."

"You good with that?"

"I am. Very much. I wish you success."

Sam headed for the door but turned to face Silas. He started to shake the boy's hand, but instead the two embraced.

"Thank you, Silas. And good luck to you."

Four days after obtaining the confirmation from the Texians in San Antonio, Hiram Brown reached Copano Bay, the primary base of operations for the merchant brigs *Watchman*, *Comanche*, and *Fanny Butler*. He found *Fanny Butler* in port and provided the same information and document to her captain he had delivered to Levi Jones of *Watchman*.

Brown sailed on *Fanny Butler* to New Orleans. He met with Captain H.D. Hunter of the schooner *Woodbury*, explained the situation, and provided him with the final folio prepared by Powhatan Ellis weeks earlier. The next day, Brown sailed on *Woodbury* for Veracruz.

Unfortunately, Brown missed *Comanche* at Copano. She sailed a day earlier for Mexico without the document needed to pass the blockade and without knowledge of the situation in the gulf.

Comanche entered the blockade zone and a French warship moved to intercept. *Comanche*'s captain decided to outrun the Frenchman.

The massive French ship easily ran her down. *Comanche* took evasive action when a warning shot flew over her bow. The brig's crew sealed their fate when they fired their own guns, a pair of twelve-pound cannon. Rifle fire from French marines took out the gunners, and a volley of thirty-six-pound cannon balls tore into the merchant ship's hull.

Comanche was blown out of the water and everyone aboard was killed.

CHAPTER 7

THE BOY CAME to Campo Santo every morning to place fresh flowers, picked from the banks of San Pedro Creek, on his father's grave.

Every day he replaced the flowers he laid the day before and tried not to repeat the same colors two days in a row, which was easy in spring and summer.

Even in winter, he could find something. He could recall only one time in his life when snow fell, but that was when he was much younger and the snow didn't last long. It had not snowed in the two years since he began his treks to Campo Santo, and it was never cold enough to keep him from his daily devotion.

In the cold months, he just had to search longer for something to decorate the grave, even if it was just a sprig of red berries from a leafless possomhaw bush. Sometimes he ventured beyond the creek to the fields where no one lived anymore. No one had lived around the cemetery during his life, but he knew people once did. Their houses had been washed away in a flood, and he sometimes played with his brothers and sister in the old ruins.

On this fine spring day, the morning was mild and the afternoon would be warm, so Enrique Esparza was quite comfortable barefoot. He had perfectly serviceable sandals but preferred going without, and his mother had long since given up trying to keep his feet covered. The same went for his brothers and sister.

Juan Seguin also often visited Campo Santo, which was roughly a thousand feet northwest of the Plaza de Armas and the cathedral. The city's Catholic priests had sanctified the walled cemetery, and thirty years later it was filled with wooden crosses. Juan had attended many funerals here, though he had known few of the interred as well as he had known Enrique's father, Gregorio Esparza.

This, however, was not a random visit to an old friend's grave.

Seguin preferred to spare the boy this conversation, but Enrique's mother never spoke of what happened in the Alamo, and Juan needed to know what the Esparzas saw.

"Good morning, Enrique," Juan said as he approached the boy, who had just placed red corn poppies on his father's grave.

"Good morning," Enrique said.

"Would you like to be alone with your father? I can return later." Juan always asked when he met Enrique in Campo Santo, but the answer was always the same.

"No, please stay. I like having you here," the ten-year-old said. "I know my father was your friend."

"Yes, he was, and I miss him very much." Juan placed daisies on the grave, next to Enrique's poppies. "He was a very brave man." Enrique needed to hear that. It was important to a man's family—perhaps more so to a man's son than to his wife—to know he died well.

They stood quietly awhile. A hawk glided over a field to the west of the cemetery, herons stalked breakfast in the nearby creek, and all around the air was alive with the songs of vireos, sparrows, chickadees, wrens, and cardinals, though the territorial cardinals had a habit of harassing and driving away their neighbors.

Enrique's feet and the hems of his trousers were damp with dew and mud, as were Seguin's tall black boots.

"Your father would be very proud that you honor him so well," Juan said.

The boy just looked at the grave marker. "Do you think I could be a soldier like him?"

"You can be anything you want. Isn't there anything else you would like to be?"

"No. I want to fight like he did." Enrique's jaw was set, his fists clenched. "I will protect my family as he did."

"Do you remember how your father protected your family?"

"Oh, yes. My father was going to take our family away, but when Santa Anna came, he said he would go to the fort. My mother said we would all go to the fort. Later, my father asked her to leave but she refused to go, and she said that if my father stayed we would stay. I wanted to stay, too."

"Were you afraid?"

"No." Enrique hesitated. "Yes. A little. I heard the men say that Santa Anna would kill anyone who surrendered, so they would all die fighting."

God, Juan thought, *to ask such of a child.*

Now I am asking more.

"Do you remember the men called Travis, Bowie, and Crockett?"

"I heard the names Travis and Bowie but I did not know them. I remember the tall man, Crockett. At night, he would share the fire with us. He spoke to us. He was a very nice man. You knew Crockett, didn't you?"

"Yes, he was my friend, like your father. Do you…" Juan paused. He bit his lip and hated what he was doing but had to ask. "Do you remember the last day? The battle?"

"I remember. We heard the guns and shouting, and we woke up. My father grabbed his rifle and went to fight. The shooting went on and on. Then a Mexican soldier came into our room and pointed a gun at my mother. He said the Americans had money and he wanted to know where it was. My mother didn't know, and I thought he was going to stab her with his long knife. But another Mexican soldier came in and told the other man not to hurt us. When all the fighting was over, they let us leave. They gave us a few coins and a blanket."

"You did not see your father or Crockett again?"

"I never saw my father again," Enrique said. Juan saw the boy was crying. "I saw my uncle after the fighting was over. He was with the Mexican army, and he came to find my father, to bury him. My uncle said my father died in the fighting."

"I am sorry, Enrique. Would you like to walk back to town? I will buy you a treat."

"Yes, please!"

They turned to leave.

"I did see the tall man, Crockett," Enrique said. "When my father ran out to fight, I followed him but by mother called me back. But I saw Crockett."

"Where? Where did you see him?"

"Between the big gates and the chapel. He was with his men."

Between the big gates and the chapel. That would put him at the south end of the compound, probably at the palisade which the Tennesseans defended. They started back to town, and Juan took Enrique to a bakery and let him choose anything he wanted.

"It makes me sad," Enrique said as they approached the Esparzas' house.

"What makes you sad?"

Enrique stopped and looked at Seguin. "That no one remembers my father. Everyone talks about Bowie and Crockett and Travis. My father was as brave as any of them. But no one remembers."

"Don't worry, Enrique. I promise, your father will not be forgotten."

★

While Juan Seguin was speaking to the humble, honest Enrique Esparza, Erasmo Seguin was dealing with Francisco Antonio Ruiz.

Who was not so humble.

Seguin and Ruiz had each held the position of alcalde in San Antonio and each still held significant political power, Seguin as chief justice of the county and Ruiz as a city alderman. But Erasmo was twenty years senior and possessed greater social position, and so was someone whose approval Ruiz sought.

That gave Erasmo an opening to question Ruiz, who had been alcalde during the siege of the Alamo and therefore in communication with Santa Anna. It was known that Ruiz was brought to the battlefield after the fighting.

Erasmo found him at Casa Reales.

"Good day, Don Pancho," Erasmo said. "May I speak with you about your memories of the Alamo—"

And with that, Ruiz was off and running. Seguin might have been chief justice but Ruiz was holding court now.

"Of course!" Ruiz said. "I saw much of the battle, more than most. More, I daresay, than some who were in the fighting. Santa Anna had me and others, oh, Don Ramon Músquiz and Don Refugio de la Garza, brought to the battlefield to see the attack and identify the leaders of the defenders. Our party even came under fire from Mexican dragoons!"

If that was the case, the Mexican dragoons would have been firing back toward their own lines. As unlikely as that was, Erasmo could sympathize with the dragoons. He wouldn't mind taking a shot at Ruiz.

"Don Pancho—"

"I saw the devastation. Take the Toluca Battalion. Of its eight hundred men, only 130 were left alive."

That would be 670 dead in one battalion. Quite a feat, considering the entire Mexican army didn't suffer that many killed at the Alamo.

"Don Pancho—"

"We were taken to the fort. We found Travis on the north battery, shot in the forehead. Bowie was found dead in his bed in a room on the south wall. He had been very sick, you see, and was bedridden."

"What of Crockett?"

"We found Colonel Crockett toward the west in a small fort opposite the city."

What?

"A small fort opposite the city, you say?"

"That's right. Did you know the Mexicans suffered sixteen hundred dead! The flower of Santa Anna's army!"

No, they didn't, you puffed up, overblown—

"The Mexican generals marveled at the gallantry of the defenders!"

"I don't understand," Erasmo persevered. "You found Crockett toward the west in a small fort opposite the city? Was he inside or outside the Alamo?"

"Yes!" Ruiz shouted. "The generals were astonished at the resistance."

"But about Crockett," Erasmo tried again. "Did you find him inside or outside of the Alamo?"

"Exactly! Did you know that Santa Anna put me in charge of the dead Mexican soldiers? We put them in carts to take them to the cemetery."

"I see, Don Pancho. But could you tell me exactly where you found Crockett—"

"There were too many dead soldiers to bury, so I had some thrown into the river."

"I am well aware of how you disposed of the Mexican corpses," Erasmo said. "They clogged the river and rotted for days until a group of townspeople extricated them so they could float down river. I pray for those poor men, and those who lived down river."

"Yes, well, the matter it was resolved, was it not?"

Erasmo sighed, trying not to show too much contempt for Ruiz. Erasmo had reached his own point of capitulation and stood to take his leave. "Thank you for your time, Don Pancho."

"Certainly, Erasmo, certainly. Delighted to speak anytime!"

"Why are you asking me about this, Juan?" Eulalia Yorba trembled. "I don't like to talk about…that day. I don't like to think about it."

"I hate to ask you," Juan Seguin said. "I know the memories are terrible."

"So very terrible. I will never forget that day. I don't think I can ever forget. There was so much…" She started to sob and buried her face in the hands.

It had been three days since Juan spoke with Enrique in Campo Santo, and he had been trying to talk to Eulalia ever since. She lived life at a frantic pace, dealing with feeding and caring for her children, making repairs to her home, and helping the church, and it left little time during the day to sit still.

But today a soaking rain had sequestered her in her house, and Seguin ventured into the downpour to speak for a few minutes in a corner of the kitchen in her small home east of the San Antonio River. Yorba's children were playing elsewhere in the house.

Finally, she lowered her hands and crossed them on the lap of her loose-fitting white dress with green and red collar and sleeves.

Juan sat in front of her. "Eulalia, we have known each other for many years. I have the utmost respect for you. I would not ask you about this if it was not important. I wish I could explain more, but please believe me. This is very important."

Eulalia Yorba was thirty-seven years old, a mother, and a dedicated member of San Fernando Cathedral's congregation. Juan remembered her when she moved to San Antonio as a joyful person who laughed and smiled and enjoyed the town's fandangos. Now she rarely revealed her emotions and devoted her days to her children or the church, where she worked with San Antonio's pastors, especially Father José Antonio Valdez, who owned a home near Eulalia south of the Alamo.

Yorba wanted nothing to do with the Revolution. But on March 6, 1836, she was in the wrong place at the wrong time and found herself dragged into the aftermath of a bloodbath.

She took a deep breath and tried to still her shaking hands.

"The morning of the battle," she began. "I had no food in the house. My children were hungry, and we had not been able to get food because of the war and the soldiers. I went to Father Valdez's house to see if he had anything to spare."

"Then the battle started," Juan said.

"Yes. Looking out of Father Valdez's window, we could see the smoke at the fort. The guns kept firing and firing, and we could hear men shouting and screaming. The Mexicans were on the top of the walls and we knew the men in the Alamo were doomed. Father Valdez pulled me away from the window.

"At nine o'clock, a Mexican colonel came to Father Valdez's house and asked us to come to the Alamo to help the wounded. It was such a dreadful sight. The stones of the church were spattered with blood, and pools of blood were everywhere. We had to step over the bodies. I can still see the corpses in my mind. It was horrible…"

"Don't talk about it anymore, Eulalia," Juan said. "I just need to ask a question. Did you see David Crockett?"

"Crockett?"

"Yes, Colonel Crockett."

"I think so. I was washing the face of a dying man. Next to him was a tall man, about fifty years old. I think it was Crockett. His coat and woolen shirt were soaked with blood so you could not see the color. He must have been shot or stabbed by a bayonet in the chest."

"Do you know where you saw him?"

"We came in the main gate and looked for bandages in the hospital, and he was nearby. He must have been in the plaza."

"In the plaza?" Juan said.

"Yes, I think so."

"Thank you, Eulalia. That is very helpful."

"Is that all?" she said, more of a prayer than a question.

"Yes, Eulalia, that is all. Are you alright?"

She breathed deeply, exhaled in halting fashion, and wiped the tears from her cheeks. "Yes, Juan, I am well. Better, I think. I have held that in for so long. I could not speak to anyone, not even Father Valdez. Why does it help to speak of such things?"

"I don't know, Eulalia, but it does. I fought at San Jacinto. I saw so many dead men. I killed men. It is not an easy thing to kill a man, and their deaths still haunt me. But I spoke with my father, and that helped. We think we must hide our pain, but I think it helps to tell someone. I don't know why it helps, but sometimes it does.

"I will never ask you about that day again," he added. "But if you ever need to talk about it, I will listen."

"Thank you, Juan. God bless you."

At least fourteen people who were in the Alamo at the time of the final attack survived. Six were children. Six were women.

Seven of the survivors—two women, one man, and four children—remained in San Antonio after the war. The lone male, Brigido Guerrero, deserted the Mexican army early in the war and joined the Texian ranks. Upon seeing that the Alamo would fall, he locked himself in a jail cell in the Alamo and convinced the Mexican troops after the battle that he had been held prisoner. He saw nothing of the battle's conclusion from his self-imposed incarceration.

Of all of the survivors, no one was making more of their Alamo notoriety than María Andrea Castañón Villanueva. Married to Candelario Villanueva, she was better known in San Antonio as Señora Candelaria, although most English speakers called her Madam Candelaria.

While the rest of the city's Alamo survivors avoided speaking of their experiences, such was not the case with Señora Candelaria. Instead, she turned her celebrity status into a cottage industry. She would speak to anyone who wished to listen, and her stories combined with her remarkable cooking skills to fuel the success of her inn, which was frequented by all manner of San Antonio society.

In later years, right up to her death in 1899, Señora Candelaria would even pose for tourists' photographs—for a small fee.

It wasn't that she was a bad person. To the contrary, throughout her life she would be known for her charity, for organizing dances at the former Spanish Governor's Palace, and later for caring for more than twenty orphaned children.

The problem Erasmo Seguin faced was figuring out which of Señora Candelaria's Alamo stories to believe.

"Why do you care, Seguin?" Señora Candelaria argued as she bustled about her inn's kitchen, preparing the evening dinner. She bore a scar on her chin, a mark left by a Mexican bayonet as soldiers killed the helpless Jim Bowie, who Señora Candelaria had been tending.

"I just want to know what happened, Señora Candelaria. What you saw," Erasmo said. "You may have heard the rumors of David Crockett being held in a mine in Mexico."

"Yes, I have heard. Nonsense. He's dead. Dead with the rest."

"I certainly believe that as well. But I, my son, and some associates are trying to establish exactly how and where he died to quash these rumors and bring peace to his family."

"You'd also bring an end to my story telling," she said, tasting a pot of spicy bean soup. She turned on Erasmo and jabbed at him with her soup ladle. "You tell everyone what happened and no one will come to my inn to hear my stories."

"Señora Candelaria, we are not going to publish a report or tell the newspapers. We just want to tell the Crockett family."

"And they'll tell the newspapers. You think they don't like publicity?"

"We just want to bring peace to them," Erasmo pleaded.

"So, what does it matter? Tell them what you want. Better, tell them whatever you think they want. Yes, tell them what they want to hear. That's what I do to those who want to hear stories of the Alamo.

"Crockett was among the first to fall while advancing from the church, slowly and with great deliberation, until a volley caused him to fall forward on his face, dead. No, they wouldn't like that one.

"You could tell them he was grand and terrible," and she gestured with her arms in practiced performance, "battling Mexican infantry until his rifle was empty, swinging his rifle like a club until he was bayoneted and fell upon a heap of dead enemies. That one's good.

"But I would tell them my personal favorite," she said, extending her hands out in a wait-until-you-hear-this theatrical flourish. "He died in front of the entrance to the church, rifle in hand, the last man in the Alamo to die. Yes, the last man to die. The family would like that best. Trust me, all the Whites love that story.

"Now get out of my kitchen. I have dinner to cook."

CHAPTER 8

IT WAS A three-day ride north from San Antonio to the village of Waterloo.

Calling Waterloo a village was generous. Although the area of fertile land and plentiful game invited much greater settlement, only four families had settled on the north bank of the Colorado River hard by Shoal Creek to the west.

There was, however, good reason for the lack of development. Two miles west of Shoal Creek, above a bend in the Colorado River, the landscape rose rapidly to breathtaking limestone cliffs that overlooked tiny Waterloo and marked the eastern rim of a geological area known as the Balcones Escarpment.

It was also the eastern boundary of the Comancheria, the domain of the Comanches, the greatest mounted warriors in the world.

Living in Waterloo was, therefore, quite literally living on the edge.

"Pardon me," Sam McCulloch called to a man tending to buffalo hides outside a cabin near the bank of Shoal Creek, two hundred yards from the Colorado. "Are you Mr. Harrell?"

"Yep," Harrell said. "You with the scouts?"

"No, sir," Sam said. "I'm looking for someone and was told you know the area better than anyone."

"Should. First one here three years ago."

"I wondered if you could help me."

"Maybe. If you're lookin' for the scouts and surveyors, they left a few days ago. Might still be trompin' in the hills, but I ain't seen 'em today."

"Surveyors, sir?"

"Yep. Plannin' the new capital, or so they say."

"Capital of Texas? Are there that many folks here?"

"Naw," Harrell said. "Sounds like a lot more'll be comin' soon."

"There's no one else?"

"There's some fellas come up with the surveyors. Camped over yonder," said Harrell and pointed east. "They been cuttin' trees. Don't hear 'em now, but you can see where they are."

Sam looked east and saw smoke beginning to rise from the forest. "Thank you, sir," Sam said and turned his horse toward the smoke.

A hundred yards from the cabin, the smell of wood smoke began to build, pleasant at first but intensifying the further east he went. Sam tied a bandana across his face.

A mile from the cabin, Sam emerged into a forest of stumps. Recently felled trees were stacked on the far side of the clearing while stumps were being uprooted, heaped, and burned. At least twenty men were dragging stumps and shattered tree limbs to the flames of multiple fires.

The crew was a mix of White, Tejano, and Black, but it was difficult to tell them apart. Their faces were covered with bandanas and coated with sweat, dirt, and ash.

Sam hailed a man tossing branches onto the nearest bonfire. The man straightened and Sam could hear his spine pop. "Talk to

Quitman," the worker said and pointed to a White man several yards away barking instructions to other workers.

Sam approached but waited for Quitman to finish hectoring his crew.

"Afternoon," Sam said. "Excuse me, sir, are you Mr. Quitman?"

The man pulled down the bandana covering his mouth and nose. "Yeah," he said. Quitman was deeply tanned and well-muscled from heavy labor. He was a couple of inches shorter than Sam and had a full beard and mustache clotted with soot and cinders. "You lookin' for work?"

"No, sir. I'm looking for someone. I heard he might be up this way. Named Joe."

Quitman's face went stern. "Why you lookin' for 'im. Who you with?"

"I'm not with anyone and I'm not looking for trouble. I just need to speak with him."

"You ain't with them gawddamn lawyers? From the estate?"

"Estate?"

"Yeah, dead Travis's estate. Them lawyers, what do you call them…"

"Executors?"

"Yeah, them."

"No, sir. You have my word. I am not working for the estate of William Barret Travis."

"I paid good money to rent that slave. They want 'im back early. Probably got a job that'll pay better, but he's stayin' 'til I get my money's worth." Quitman looked sideways at Sam, a look McCulloch had seen before from White men. "Say, you ain't—"

"No, sir. Freeman. Got the paper to prove it," Sam said, swallowing the anger that such questions always stirred. A White man's assumption that a Black man was a slave never failed to infuriate

Sam. That a Black man couldn't show that anger without provoking hostility and maybe getting shot or hanged made it worse.

"The executors do that often?" Sam said, trying to move the conversation along.

"Often enough," Quitman shrugged. "They got debts, and they're hard up for money."

"I'm not looking to take Joe back. I just need to speak with him for a few minutes."

"I didn't rent 'im so you could talk to 'im. He got work to do and so do I."

"All right, how much did you pay for him?"

"Why?"

"Just answer the question. Might be a profit in it for you."

"Got 'im two months for sixty dollars," Quitman said.

You lying cracker, Sam thought. No way he paid that much for just two months, unless he was an idiot. Which was entirely possible.

"A dollar a day?"

"Plus cost of food and water and haulin' 'im up here. And fallin' behind my schedule."

"All right." Sam leaned over the horn of his saddle toward Quitman. "I'll pay you three dollars to talk to him. That's more than a day's worth, and all I want to do is talk to him for a little while." Sam pulled coins from his pocket. "Deal?"

"Yeah, all right," Quitman grunted and took the money. "Get off your horse and follow me, and keep your hands where I can see 'em."

Sam did as instructed and followed Quitman into the middle of the clearing where the smoke was stifling. He drew glances from other crew members, but they quickly lost interest.

"You working for the surveyors?" Sam asked. "Mr. Harrell said you came up with them."

"Judge Waller hired me," Quitman said. "He's layin' out the new town."

"For the new capital?"

"That's what I'm told. Hey, Joe!" Quitman yelled, and a man by one of the fires turned in response. "This fella wants to talk at you. It's all right."

"Who?" Joe called.

"It's Sam McCulloch, Joe," Sam said and removed his hat and bandana. Joe peered through the smoke, nodded, and pointed to a spot away from the fire.

"Make it quick," Quitman spat.

McCulloch very much wanted to tell Quitman that he had paid for a day and he would take as much of that day as he damned well pleased. But he didn't. He swallowed the retort and ignored the comment.

Joe stopped about fifty yards from the fires, at the edge of the clearing where a little breeze brushed away the smothering stench.

"McCulloch," Joe said. It was a joyless greeting.

"Joe." Sam extended his hand and Joe shook it. The men stood eye to eye, both a little over five feet ten.

"Water?" Sam offered his canteen.

"Yeah," and Joe took a drink, pulled a bandana from a back pocket, poured water onto it, and wiped his face. The bandana came away caked with ash. Joe took off his battered straw hat and turned the canteen over his face and close-cropped black hair, letting the cool water run down his high forehead, long nose, and strong jaw line before dripping off his chin.

He opened his heavily lidded blue-gray eyes and handed the canteen back to Sam.

Like Sam, Joe was mulatto, but Joe's skin was darker. Sam's White ancestry traced to his father, while Joe's to his grandfather.

Sam was five years older than Joe, yet Joe looked the older of the two. Such was a life of whips and chains.

Joe was born in Kentucky, one of seven children to a slave woman named Elizabeth, who was the illegitimate daughter of a slave mother and a White father: Daniel Boone.

That relation to fame—for no one in the United States was better known than the legendary explorer and frontiersman—counted nothing for Elizabeth and her family. By the time Joe was a toddler, the family was sold away from Boone and his kin. At age nine, Joe watched his mother whipped. Before Joe was twenty, the family had been sold and rented and traded and shuttled across country, scattered from one White master to another. One by one, the family was torn apart.

It had been nine years since Joe had seen his brothers. Six years since Joe had seen his baby sister Elizabeth. Four years since he had seen his mother. All vanished among America's vast living dead.

"Why are you here?" Joe said.

"Me and some others are tracking down rumors from the war, from the Alamo," Sam explained. "We're talking to as many survivors as we can."

"Why should I care?"

"No reason. No reason at all."

Joe considered Sam. The seconds drifted by and Sam feared Joe was about to walk away, but finally he sat and leaned back against a stump. Sam took a seat cross-legged.

"What do you want to know?" Joe said, willing to offer disinterested assistance in exchange for a break in the work.

"I just need to know what you saw. I don't care about the stories you told at Washington-on-the-Brazos and how heroic everyone was. I just need to know what you saw that last morning."

Joe shrugged.

"We were sleeping. I shared a room with Mr. Travis. He bought me from a man named Cummings for $500. Mr. Travis was an arrogant cuss, but he treated me about as well as a White man treats a slave. Bastard said he was fighting oppression, yet here he was owning slaves."

"Don't make much sense."

"Never met a White man who did.

"When the Mexicans attacked," Joe continued, "Mr. Travis grabbed his shotgun and sword and ran to the walls. He told me to follow, so I grabbed a rifle and followed. We got up on the north wall, next to a cannon. It was dark and hard to see, but you could make out all these Mexican soldiers swarming to the walls. Mr. Travis leaned over the wall and fired his shotgun into the Mexicans. I fired my rifle. The Mexicans shot back and hit Mr. Travis in the head. He was one of the first to die.

"He was brave, and I know White folk think he died well, but I don't know he was any too smart. When the siege began, the Mexicans demanded unconditional surrender. He answered with a cannon shot. Bold and brave, but foolish. Anyway, he looked good and died a hero.

"After he was dead, I ran to one of the rooms, I guess on the east side of the plaza. A Mexican kicked in the door and asked if there were any negroes. I know the Mexicans don't hold with slavery. I was back in the shadows, so I stepped forward. That's the first time Black skin saved my ass.

"Of course, those Mexicans were all riled. They'd been killing and watching their friends get killed. Those Texians were outnumbered but they fought like wildcats. The Mexicans' blood was up, and one of them shot me in the side and another tried to bayonet me, but just nicked me in the other side. An officer told them to stop, and he took me out of there.

"I never seen so much blood in my life," Joe said. "Men dead and dying. Mexicans stabbing Texians, making sure they were dead. They took me to the general, Santa Anna, and he asked questions. They told me to identify Mr. Travis, and I done that. They weren't too interested in keeping me, and I got away without any trouble. I ended up in Gonzales, and went along on the retreat. I guess that's when I met you."

"I was healing up," Sam said. "Got shot some time earlier."

"How's your shoulder?"

"Tolerable."

"That's good. Anyway, that bunch at Washington-on-the-Brazos…"

"The commission?"

"Yeah. They asked me questions and I told stories. You know what they called me? Travis's negro." Joe sighed. "I told them what they wanted to hear. How brave all them Texians were. No lie, they were that. White and Tejano. So were those Mexican boys. Lot of them got killed. Don't think that bothered Santa Anna much.

"I told stories and told them again and again. I bet that's the first time any those White folk actually listened to a Black man. Actually looked a Black man in the eye. Patted me on the back. Said what a fine fellow I was. 'You're a fine, brave fellow, Joe!' Then they shipped my Black ass back to Mr. Travis's estate. Back to being a slave. A fine fellow. Few months later, this fine fellow was shoveling out horse stalls at a tavern."

"Not much of a thank you."

"Yeah, not much."

"That last morning," Sam asked. "Did you see Crockett?"

"Sure. He was running to the walls, same as everyone. He left the Alamo twice at least. Last time, he and that tall fellow, the one whose brother come from Gonzales…"

"Jacob Millsaps."

"Yeah, him. Crockett and him, maybe another, too. They went out a few days before the attack to bring more men in and take messages out. I think that fellow Millsaps took the messages. Mr. Travis was a fine one for writing letters. He was asking for help, but I think he really just wanted to have all these letters out. 'Victory or death,' he wrote. He wanted everyone to know how heroic he was.

"But Crockett, he could have run." Joe paused. "But he came back and brought them others. Day before the attack, he came back. I don't think he cared about being a hero, but I don't think he could run, either. Just couldn't bring himself to leave. Crockett was always talking to the others, encouraging. That last morning, he was urging the men to fight. He was in his long buckskin coat so everyone could see him. He cheered them fellows plenty, right up to the end. Poor Mr. Travis, he wasn't much for lifting spirits. He wanted to be the brave, heroic leader. He was that, I guess."

"Where did you see Crockett last?"

"Over by the palisade. Next to the church. That's where things ended, right where Crockett and his boys was the last time I seen. There was a loophole in the wall of the room where I was. I could see the Mexicans drag the Texians' big cannon down there. The Mexicans blasted them, and I saw an officer, I think a general, tall as us, walking that direction."

"What makes you think he was a general?"

"He had this fancy uniform with a red and blue jacket, all covered in brass and gold, and a tall, fancy hat. He was a sight. After they brought me out, I saw the tall general again, standing in the middle of those Texians' bodies. That's about all I know."

McCulloch nodded and smiled. "Thanks, Joe. I appreciate the help."

"That all you need?"

"That's all."

"All right. Thanks for the water." Joe stood to return to the fires.

"One more thing, though," Sam said, and Joe stopped. "You think about running again?"

Joe laughed. "Every damn day, Sam. In Missouri, I ran with my mother, got as far as Illinois before they caught us. I ran last year but they caught me again."

"Maybe I can help. You feel like trying again?"

Joe looked hard at Sam to see if he was serious. "Sure. I got a plan this time."

"Good," Sam said, looking carefully over Joe's shoulder to make sure no one was close enough to hear. "Do they chain you at night?"

"No. They figure there's no place to go out here."

"You think you can slip away tonight?"

"Shouldn't be a problem."

"Is there a place we can meet, someplace we can both find in the dark?"

"I know a place, but you won't need to find it in the dark. You get gone now. They might watch you awhile, but no more than a mile or two before they turn back. About five miles east of here, the river bends northeast, just before it makes a big loop south. There's a spot where a creek joins the river. There's a big sand bar in the river. You can't miss it. You head there now. Camp on the north side of the river next to that creek. Don't make a fire. I'll find you."

McCulloch rode east parallel to the Colorado River, alert to anyone who might be following. He thought someone shadowed him for a couple of miles but felt sure they gave up before he reached the spot designated by Joe.

He rode a few of miles beyond that point to a secluded location where he had left supplies, retrieved the gear, and doubled back to the meeting place next to the creek.

The sandbar and creek were just as Joe said. Sam hobbled his horse out of sight back in the trees and settled down to wait.

He had dozed off when, long after midnight, he heard someone approaching. He sat up and put his hand to the butt of his pistol.

"It's me, Sam."

"Come on in," Sam said and stood. The half-moon offered just enough light for the two men to see each other's faces.

"Thank you for this," Joe said.

"Shoulda done it long ago."

"You're not going to get in trouble?"

"Not if they don't find us and not if you don't say anything if you're caught," Sam said.

"I won't."

"I know. Where you headed?"

"Alabama."

Even in the meager light, Joe could see the shock on Sam McCulloch's face. Sam just stood, his mouth open, staring in disbelief.

"Alabama!" he almost shouted. "Are you crazy? They got slave patrols all over. These Texians, some have slaves, but Alabama's the real thing."

"I know."

"And you gotta go through Mississippi and Louisiana."

"I know."

"Why not Mexico? They don't allow slavery. They got laws against it."

"I know, Sam."

"Why you want to go so far? That's got to be five hundred, six hundred miles!" Sam said, struggling to keep his voice low.

Joe offered a conciliatory smile. "Sam, what would I do in Mexico? Where would I go?"

"Well—"

"Listen to me. I don't speak Spanish. I got no special skills. There's nothing for me there but scraping out a living. I got a plan. Mr. Travis's brother, Nicholas, is in Alabama. I think Mr. Travis's children are there, too. Mr. Travis talked about his brother. He's a decent man."

"A slave owner?"

"Yes, he is. But that means there might be a place for me. A place I can live for a long time and not be sold to some bastard with a whip. I can tell him about his brother."

"I'm sure he's heard that his brother is dead," Sam pointed out.

"Sure he knows. But he doesn't know how he died. I can tell him about how Mr. Travis lived and how he died. I've seen how these White men like to hear those stories, how much it means to them, even when the story comes from a stranger. I'm betting his brother would want to hear that and maybe let me stay. Maybe give me a place to call home. I never had that, Sam. You got a home. You married?"

"Yes. We're starting a family."

"See? A family and a home. That's what I want. That's all I ever wanted. Even if it's not my family, maybe in a way it can be my family. And my home."

Sam considered what Joe said and nodded. "You know how to get there?"

"I've been planning. I know where I'm going. Concecuh County. Place called Sparta. Nicholas Travis has a farm there. That's where I'm going."

"I think it'll take a miracle for you get there, but maybe you're due a miracle."

McCulloch disappeared into the trees, and reappeared a moment later leading two horses. He handed Joe the reins to a brown gelding.

"It's a calm, steady horse. It's only got a blanket. I thought a saddle might attract attention. Should help you get clear of Texas. After that…"

"After that I'll leave the horse. I'll travel by night, stay off the roads."

Sam nodded and handed Joe a bag. "Got a change of clothes and some good shoes in there. A coat, too. Nothing fancy, but something that doesn't smell like sawdust and smoke." He handed Joe another bag. "Some dried meat, dried fruit, nuts, and pemmican. A canteen and a knife. And here's twelve dollars. It's all that's left after I bought your gear. Might be helpful."

"This is…this is mighty generous, Sam. You must have spent, I don't know, a lot. I don't know what to say."

"I had help. Took up a collection from the Texians I'm working with."

"They know what you're up to?"

"Every one of them."

"Please thank them for me."

Sam packed his bedroll and gear, and Joe helped clear all signs that they had been there. They walked their horses until the sun rose, mounted, and rode east.

They rode for four days, figuring Sam's standing as a free-man would provide the cover needed if Joe was questioned, but they avoided settlements and other travelers. When they reached McCulloch's home in the northern part of the Brazos Valley, Joe about fell over when he was introduced to Sam's wife, Mary.

"You married a White woman!" Joe said to Sam later. "And they ain't come for you?"

Joe stayed with the McCullochs for three days, rested, ate well, and enjoyed the company. It was the only happy time of his life in Texas. Then it was time to go.

Sam and his wife invited Joe to stay but they knew he wouldn't. Texas was too risky. His mind was set and he wanted to get started. Five hundred miles was a long way to travel.

The next morning, after some teary farewells, Joe headed east.

CHAPTER 9

EVEN BY EARLY nineteenth-century standards, when life expectancy was less than forty years, the volume of tragedy visited upon Juana Alsbury was astonishing.

Her mother died when she was seventeen. Within a year, her father remarried and abandoned Juana and her sister, Gertrudis.

Her aunt and uncle, who adopted Juana and Gertrudis after their father's desertion, died of cholera. Her cousin Ursula, who Juana regarded as a sister, died in the same epidemic.

She married Alejo Perez Ramigio, but their first child, a daughter, died in infancy.

While Juana was pregnant with their second child, Alejo died in another cholera outbreak.

By the time Juana was twenty-two years old, six of her closest family members were dead.

And that was before she found herself trapped inside the Alamo on March 6, 1836, when the widower of her beloved cousin was bayoneted in his sickbed, when hundreds were maimed and killed in battle, and when she narrowly escaped with her life and that of her infant son.

If she needed any more reason to feel the world was out to get her, the father who abandoned her died three months after the fall of the Alamo.

Juana Navarro Alsbury, the former Juana Navarro Ramigio nee Juana Navarro, had every right to be an embittered woman. That she was not was testament to her remarkable spirit.

That resiliency, however, was again tested in the months after the Texas Revolution, when Whites falsely accused her of betraying the Alamo defenders and she was falsely accused by those loyal to Mexico of siding against her own people. A pariah to both sides of the conflict, she left her hometown of San Antonio.

Horace had known Juana and the Navarro family for years and had known her charm and beauty. That youthful grace had worn thin by the time she married Horace in January 1836, and it was almost invisible now. But she still had her son, Alejo Jr., now three years old, and she still had Horace, and every day Juana fought the bitterness in her soul.

That, Horace felt, was all anyone could ask.

"Good morning, my dear," Horace said as he walked into the dining room. It was two days since his return from San Antonio. "How are you?" he asked and kissed his wife.

"I am well, Horace," she said. Juana had risen before her husband without disturbing him, as was her habit. "Breakfast is ready."

"And how are you, Alejo?" he asked his stepson, already at the table and enjoying a bowl of cinnamon-laden avena. Horace kissed Alejo on the forehead.

They joined Alejo at the dining table for a meal of eggs, bacon, potatoes, and cheese, accompanied by a pot of hot tea.

Horace had deliberately and cautiously not compelled his wife into a discussion about the business in San Antonio and the subject about which he wanted to question her. He knew she would initiate conversation when she was ready.

"Who did you meet in San Antonio?" she asked.

"Erasmo and Juan Seguin," Horace said. "They send their regards. Also J.C. Neill, of course. You saw him when he stopped by to request my presence. And Henry Karnes, Sam McCulloch, Jacob Millsaps, and Silas Grant."

"I don't know Silas Grant."

"Oh, he's a young man we met during the war, during the retreat. He was in camp with us at Groce's Landing."

"How old?"

"I believe he's sixteen."

"What part is he playing in your business?" she pressed.

"He's helping us considerably. He helped Jacob and Henry deal with smugglers down on the Gulf Coast. Out-foxed the bunch and drove them off with minimal violence. Yes, a young man of considerable promise."

"That is what you and your friends are doing with him. What is he doing with you?"

"I suppose he's learning to be a Texian."

"I see. What was the nature of the business with your associates?"

Horace swallowed a mouthful of potatoes and dabbed his lips with a napkin. "It has been brought to our attention that rumors are spreading about David Crockett. Apparently, an American criminal serving time in a mine in Guadalajara claimed to be Crockett. We have been asked to investigate the claim on this side of the border with the intention of quelling the rumor." He stabbed a bit of egg.

"How?"

"We're talking to those who witnessed the events at the Alamo, to construct a more complete picture of exactly what happened. Meanwhile, a representative of the United States is addressing the rumor in Mexico by investigating the imposter. I believe he's traveling to the mine," he explained, omitting the fact that such mission had already been undertaken.

He also knew this was already conjuring painful memories for his wife, who went very quiet. Horace continued eating.

"Finish your breakfast, Alejo," he said.

Finally, Juana found her voice.

"Are you going to speak with that…woman?"

"No, my love, I most certainly am not," Horace said. "I will not speak to her, nor will I speak her name, as I have sworn."

She nodded.

"Are your friends going to speak to her?"

"Yes. It is not by choice. But it was felt that, in order to properly investigate the matter, it is necessary. It was with great reluctance that Jacob agreed to see her."

"Reluctance?"

"Great reluctance. I believe he and all my fellows share our estimation of her character."

"Very well. Please tell him I appreciate his sacrifice."

Juana said nothing else and Horace did not pursue further, but he felt the door had been opened. For the moment, Juana needed to heal from even thinking of Susanna Dickinson.

Dickinson had been the source of accusations that Juana passed secrets to the Mexican army and that she fled the Alamo prior to the final assault. Whether Dickinson deliberately spread malicious lies or misunderstood events that took place prior to the fall of the Alamo, the fact was she did not attempt to discover the truth before making her allegations.

The truth was that two days before the final assault, Colonel Travis asked Juana to act as an emissary to Santa Anna and attempt to negotiate an honorable surrender for the beleaguered defenders.

Santa Anna, however, had no interest in surrender. If the rebels' resolve was weakening, all the more reason to attack. He wanted to take the Alamo in a grand, bloody spectacle and send a message throughout Texas.

Concerning Juana's escape from the Alamo, that came in the same manner as Enrique Esparza and Joe and Dickinson herself. She was spared when a Mexican officer interceded during the fighting. Manuel Perez, a Mexican officer and the brother of Juana's late husband, escorted Juana, her son, and her sister out of the Alamo to the home of her father, who still lived in San Antonio and was a member of Santa Anna's staff. Fortuitous as Perez's assistance was, it may have fueled the subsequent unfounded rumors.

Accused of simultaneous treason to the Texians and to Mexico and with no way to disprove the conspiracy theories save for the impossibly contradictory nature of the charges, Juana and Horace quit San Antonio for their Calaveras Ranch outside of Goliad.

Horace and Juana spoke minimally the rest of the day. Just brief, casual bits of conversation. "Lunch is ready." And, "Would you like more tea?"

Then she took Horace by surprise.

"Do you have any questions for me?" Juana asked in a timid voice.

"If you wish."

"I believe I am prepared."

They took seats in the living room and faced one another. Alejo had long since been put to bed.

"Why don't you tell me—"

"Why did you leave me there?" she suddenly asked. Her face was a mask of anger, repressed for two years and now barely contained. "You left me there. You left me there."

Horace swallowed hard. "I know."

"Why?" she shot back.

"I was asked to go to East Texas for reinforcements. I left you with Jim Bowie because the Mexican army had not yet arrived, and I thought I could get back and take you to safety. I should have done that first. I should have seen to your safety first. I should have done that first, and I regret...my actions. I don't blame Jim for taking you inside the Alamo when the Mexicans took the city. He had no choice. The Mexicans arrived sooner than I anticipated."

Horace lowered his eyes. "And I could not reach you." His voice cracked. "I failed you, my love. I am so very sorry. I failed you."

The only sound in the room was the ticking of a wall clock, rhythmically ticking off the seconds that moved like hours, like days, like years. Like two unspoken years, measuring a silence that had weighed down on Horace and Juana Navarro through two years in exile.

"Horace," Juana said. "Horace, please, look at me. Horace, I forgive you. I forgive you, my love."

Horace looked up, tears in his eyes. Juana had never seen Horace cry.

"I forgive you," she said.

Horace collected himself. He managed a smile. "Thank you, my love," he croaked. They reached out a hand, touched one another's fingers, and clasped hands. They smiled.

Horace wiped his eyes. "I think that's enough for both of us. Perhaps we should retire for the evening."

"No," Juana stopped him. "No, I need to finish. I need to tell you what I saw. I don't think it will be of any use to you, but I feel that I need to tell you. I need to tell you."

"If you are sure. Whenever you are ready."

Juana sat back and folded her hands in her lap, a pose Horace had seen many times. Her eyes glazed. She was no longer seeing the room and could no longer see Horace or hear the clock's ticking. Her eyes fluttered.

"When the attack came, Gertrudis and I and Alejo were in our room. We didn't know what time it was, but suddenly we heard terrible noise and knew the final battle had begun. We huddled in the back of the room. We could hear bullets striking the other side of the wall, and we were terrified the battle would come right through the wall.

"I don't know how long the fighting lasted. It seemed hours but I know it was not. We could hear fighting in the plaza, and we knew the Mexicans were inside the walls and it would be over soon. That was the worst part. We could hear men dying on the other side of the door."

Suddenly she was back in the room. "You were at San Jacinto?"

"Yes. I fought with Henry Karnes's company."

"Did you...kill men?"

"Yes."

"Was it..."

"Terrible," Horace said.

"I am sorry for you, my love." And she was gone again, not seeing the room. Seeing the other room. The room in the Alamo where she and her son and her sister huddled with the sounds of battle roaring around them.

"Finally, soldiers opened the door and came into our room. Their faces were...I can't describe it. They were in a state of such rage and, I suppose, bloodlust. I've never seen anyone like that. God willing, I never will again.

"After the soldiers entered the room, they killed two Texians…I saw them die. The first was one of Jim Bowie's men. He rushed in to protect us and they shot him. He had visited Jim while I tended to him. I wish I knew his name. I'm sure I heard it, but I don't remember. A moment later, a young Tejano ran into the room. I think he was seeking refuge. They bayoneted him…I can hear him…" She blinked. Her breathing quickened.

"My dear, perhaps we should stop," Horace tried to interject but Juana kept going.

"They saw Gertrudis and me, and they seemed to calm. I suppose, even in their state, they did not see women and a child as a threat. They saw my trunk and broke it open. They took the watches several officers gave me to hold. They took Colonel Travis's watch. It was very nice. I wish I had been able to save that watch. I would like to have provided it to his family…"

She had edged forward in her chair and now sat back and composed herself, unfolding her hands which had been clinched so hard that the knuckles were white. She breathed slowly, raised her chin, and calmly folded her hands in her lap again.

"After that, an officer entered the room and sent the soldiers outside. There was still shooting, though not as much as earlier. The officer was angry that his men were looting while their fellows were risking their lives. He told us to stay in the room. I think they forgot about us after that. The shooting had stopped, but we dared not leave the room. Gertrudis opened the door to let the soldiers know we were no threat, but a soldier threatened her and she retreated, and we agreed we would wait until they came for us.

"Finally, Manuel found us. Manuel Perez, Alejo's brother, my brother-in-law. We were so relieved. He led us out into the plaza. We hesitated at the door, but he assured us we would not be harmed. The sun was up and it was so bright, it took a moment to adjust our eyes. There was still much activity. The Mexicans were making sure all the Texians were dead. Stabbing and stabbing and stabbing…"

She had tensed again. The veins stood out on her neck and her jaw tightened. Horace wanted to stop her but didn't know how. She had come this far and needed to finish.

"An officer and three men ran into the plaza from the north wall. I remember the officer because he was so tall. Taller than anyone else. He had a shako with a tall red plume. One of the men with him was not in uniform. I think he was not Mexican. The tall officer pointed the man toward the area near the church, and he followed the officer's directions. Manuel hurried us out, and we walked toward the south gate. We had to step over bodies but we stepped in blood because there was so much and…we could not avoid the blood…I covered Alejo's eyes. I could feel damp on the hem of my dress and on my shoes and I knew it was blood but we didn't stop and I could hear splashing through the puddles. Then we were outside."

Juana's ragged breathing began to slow as she left the Alamo in her mind. She blinked rapidly.

"Then Manuel took us to my father's home."

Slowly, Juana's body began to unwind. The veins and her jaw relaxed and her hands unclenched, though Horace could see the pain her hands were causing.

"That is all. I have nothing more to say. Thank you, Horace, I think this—"

"What I told you earlier was not completely true," Horace blurted out. The words rushed out of him before he could stop them, but he didn't want to stop them. He needed her to know.

"I will not lie to you," he said. "I will tell you all, but you must swear to tell no one. Not ever. Please swear to me. Please promise me or I cannot tell you."

"I promise."

"You must never tell anyone. You must swear. If you swear it, I believe this secret will be safe with you. But you must swear it. Swear it now."

"I swear it. I swear it, Horace. I swear it."

"You will find this difficult to hear, but…there is evidence that David Crockett…may not be dead," Horace said, and Juana gasped and her eyes went wide and she was sure she had not heard him correctly.

"The evidence is compelling but not definite," he said. "The men with whom I met are spreading throughout Texas to investigate. Someone we met in San Antonio is investigating in Mexico. I don't know what will come of this, but we are agreed that we must learn the truth."

They fell back into silence. Only the clock. Tick, tick, tick, tick, tick…

"If he is alive," Juana finally said, "you must find him. Do whatever you must. I will be waiting for you here. And I will never tell a living soul."

CHAPTER 10

HENRY KARNES, JACOB Millsaps, J.C. Neill, and Silas Grant rode east on their respective tasks, with Alcée la Branche in tow.

The American diplomat held up better on this crossing of the central Texas prairie, but the seven-day trip took eight after a line of thunderstorms roared in. It was the kind of storm that generates tornados, so the Texians sought protection in Columbus, a small village on the Colorado River. A family allowed them to shelter in their cabin.

The heart of the storm neared and extinguished the daylight. Lightning danced on the horizon, backed up by crashes of thunder, and the seconds between the flash and the furor shrank.

"Does this happen often—" la Branche started to say when the dark was suddenly lit in every direction and the cabin was shaken by a blinding, deafening burst of lightning and thunder in the same instant. La Branche jumped. So did the Texians.

"That was close," one of them said, but la Branche couldn't tell who.

"Is this just a springtime occurrence?" la Branche asked.

"Yep," Henry said. "And summer. And fall. Not often in winter."

"Happens a few times a year," J.C. said.

"You fellows are used to this, I guess."

"Sort of," J.C. said. "As long as you're in a nice, dry place."

"And there ain't a tornado tearin' your roof off," Henry added.

"So, no, not really," Jacob said. "We just know to respect it and take cover."

"Like we're doing now," Silas said.

Rain sheeting sideways emptied roads all over East Texas, and winds ripped up trees and destroyed several cabins. But in typical Texas fashion, the worst of the storm struck hard and then was gone.

The next morning the sun was out and a fair wind helped dry things, so the Texians were back on the road. Silas left the group, turning northeast toward Groce's Landing while his friends continued east.

"I'll see you in a couple of weeks," Silas called.

"All right, well, be careful out here alone," Henry said.

Three days later, la Branche was delivered to Houston, which he welcomed. He'd had enough travel and excitement. Millsaps and Karnes headed for Harrisburg.

Neill, meanwhile, turned southeast, and two days later he reached Galveston Island and began his search for George Dolson.

Like Crockett and Sam Houston, J.C. Neill was from Tennessee, and like his fellow Tennesseans, he fought in the Creek War. He moved his family to Texas in 1831 and joined the Texian militia in the early days of the conflict that would lead to the Texas Revolution.

As one of the few militiamen experienced with cannon, he was commissioned an artillery officer with the rank of captain and was in charge of the Texian cannon at the Battle of Gonzales and the

Siege of Béxar. His actions earned him the rank of lieutenant colonel, and he held together the undermanned garrison of the Alamo.

Serious illnesses in his family, however, compelled Neill to leave and hand over command to William Travis in early February, before the Mexican army's arrival. Neill was on his way back, carrying medicine for the garrison, when the fort fell. Neill joined the army in the Runaway Scrape and commanded the Twin Sisters—a pair of six-pound cannon donated to Texas by concerned citizens in Cincinnati, Ohio—at San Jacinto. In an artillery exchange with the Mexicans the day before the Battle of San Jacinto, Neill and his gun crews drove off an enemy probe, but Neill was wounded in the hip by Mexican grapeshot.

Awarded a league of land in Harrisburg for his service in the war, Neill was planning to run for the position of general with the militia next year. He mused that service in this Crockett matter would be a significant benefit to his political career.

Too bad no one would ever know of it.

Neill's hip was getting sore as he wandered through Galveston and questioned those in the town and at the port's docks. The problem was Dolson didn't seem to be in any one place at any specific time, but J.C. was advised of the haunts where he was likely to be at some point during the day. Neill staked out one of those locations, a saloon.

"What'll you have?" the bartender asked.

"Beer," J.C. said. The place was less than half full.

"Thank you," J.C. said, accepting the mug and paying for the beer. "Do you know a fellow named George Dolson? I'm told he's a regular customer."

"What do want with him?" the bartender said, suddenly concerned about any trouble. More accurately, concerned about any trouble starting in his saloon.

"I just need to speak with him," J.C. said.

"He'll likely be in sometime. Usually later in the afternoon. Who's asking?"

"James Clinton Neill."

That caught the bartender's attention. "Yes, sir, Colonel Neill. I'll, uh, let George know you're here when he shows up."

"Thank you very much. Could you tell me what he looks like?"

The bartender provided enough information to identify Dolson, and Neill collected his beer and stationed himself at a table with a view to the saloon's door.

Two hours, two beers, and a dozen customers later, a man matching Dolson's description appeared. He was neat and tidy in a three-piece suit, a blue tie, tall black boots, and a watch chain. The characteristic that matched the bartender's description was his hair: balding on top with a thick but well-groomed chin-curtain beard.

Dolson paused in the doorway, advanced on the bar, and ordered a bottle. Neill held his place. The bartender whispered something to Dolson, causing him to look over his shoulder. Dolson approached Neill, who rose in response.

"Colonel Neill? I understand you're looking for me. I'm George Dolson."

"A pleasure to meet you, Mr. Dolson," J.C. said. "Or do you prefer Sergeant Dolson?"

"No, no. I am a soldier no more. I'm in business, trying to make an honest dollar. Now, how can I help you, sir?"

"Do you have a few minutes to speak, in private?"

"Certainly. Let's adjourn to one of the tables in the back."

Dolson led J.C. to an empty table in a corner of the saloon, away from the handful of other patrons.

George Dolson came to Galveston Island to work in the prisoner-of-war camp following the Texians' victory at San Jacinto. He stayed for the opportunities.

Galveston was the primary seaport in Texas, established by Mexico in 1825 but seized by the Texians during the Revolution. It became home to the Republic's navy and took a turn as one of the seven temporary capitals of the Republic. It was also an engine of massive economic growth, driving the explosive expansion of Houston a few miles inland up Buffalo Bayou.

In short, there was money to be made here, and Dolson wanted his share.

"You appear to be prospering, Mr. Dolson," J.C. said. "I hope business is good."

"Tolerable, sir. It's a matter of recognizing needs and providing for them. Something I learned in my time here after the war."

"How so?"

"We were constantly short. Short of rations, short of provisions, short of men. The prisoners were brought here, and it was left to Colonel Morgan, his staff, and me to work out the details of the internment. We were constantly scrambling for supplies of beeves, corn, beans, and, of course, medical supplies. Those supplies were inconsistent at best, so we tried to anticipate needs to timely address them."

Of Santa Anna's thirteen hundred men at San Jacinto, almost half were killed. What had been nine hundred Texians in retreat a few days earlier had become a victorious army in possession of several hundred prisoners—more than two hundred of them wounded—for which they had little capacity and no plan.

As an island regularly serviced by shipping and located just forty miles from the San Jacinto battlefield, Galveston made sense as the location of the internment camp for captured Mexican soldiers. And as a sergeant in the Texas army who spoke English and Spanish, Dolson made sense as an interpreter for the interrogations and interviews that camp commander Colonel James Morgan was to conduct.

But the first concern was feeding and sheltering the prisoners and the Texian garrison.

"We were overwhelmed at first," Dolson said. "We didn't have near enough men or supplies to handle so many prisoners, so we were going to ship some to Liberty."

"That would be the camp northeast of here, at William Hardin's plantation," J.C. recalled.

"Exactly. But we couldn't because we didn't have enough men to provide escort. We didn't even have enough to fully garrison the island. Eventually we transferred sixty prisoners, mostly officers, to Hardin's property. I understand people in that region have taken to calling it Mexican Hill."

"And you were here for the duration of the camp's operation?"

"I was here until the parole of the last soldado."

"Excellent. That is why I've come to speak with you," J.C. said. "You see, I am working with some veterans of the war chasing rumors concerning some events at the Alamo."

"You are referring, I presume, to the Crockett rumor?"

Neill felt his heart skip a beat. "The story about the mine?" he said.

"Crockett languishing in a Mexican mine, yes. Utter nonsense."

"Precisely," J.C. said, mentally exhaling. "This rumor has reached the attention of the Crockett family, and we're trying to put an end to this falsehood once and for all."

"Admirable on your part, sir, admirable. Please, how can I be of assistance?"

"Was there ever any mention by the prisoners of Crockett?"

"Oh, there were some wild, wooly tales," Dolson said. "To hear it, David Crockett could literally whip his weight in wildcats. One Mexican soldier said Crockett killed eight before he was killed by a sword blow. Another said Crockett stood inside a door and stabbed with a knife every Mexican who tried to enter the room, and used his gun as a club before he was killed by a volley of muskets. Another told of Crockett parrying bayonet thrusts with a knife and killing several Mexicans before he fell."

"I suppose the greater your foe, the greater your glory. But you were involved with the interrogation of officers, correct?"

"Yes. I was Colonel Morgan's interpreter."

"Was there ever any mention of Crockett in those formal interviews?"

Now it was Dolson's turn to squirm. He looked around to see that no one was within hearing distance. When he spoke again, he lowered his voice to a whisper, leaned over the table, and edged forward to allow Neill to hear.

"Um…I reveal this to you in strictest confidence, Colonel."

"I completely understand. This goes no further."

"I was present to take the statement of a Mexican officer, Colonel Juan Almonte. It was just me, Colonel Morgan, and Almonte in Colonel Morgan's quarters. Almonte stated that six Texians were captured in the Alamo by General Castrillón. He said one of the men was Crockett. Castrillón promised to save the prisoners and escorted them to Santa Anna. Almonte stated that he saw Crockett. Castrillón presented the prisoners to Santa Anna, who reprimanded Castrillón, saying, and I have never forgotten these words and I doubt I ever will. 'Who has given you orders to take prisoners? I do not want to see those men living. Shoot them.' Almonte said that several men around Santa Anna executed the prisoners immediately."

"Good, Lord," J.C. said. "And there is no way to verify the story since General Castrillón was killed at San Jacinto."

"One thing, though, that made me question the statement," Dolson said. "Almonte went on to describe the executioners in such lurid terms, 'hell-hounds of the tyrant,' as to be overly dramatic. I felt he was trying to convince us of his sincerity and of his own innocence. Maybe he feared we might shoot him.

"But here's what was really strange. After the last Mexican prisoners had been sent home and this camp and Liberty were closed, I spoke with Dr. George Patrick. He was at the Liberty camp. Dr. Patrick said that General Martín Perfecto de Cós—"

"The commander of Béxar before we captured the city."

"The same. Dr. Patrick said that General Cós told him that he, General Cós, captured Crockett, and that Crockett was the only such prisoner. Cós said he brought Crockett before Santa Anna, and when Santa Anna ordered his execution, Crockett attacked Santa Anna with a knife, but a Mexican soldier killed Crockett with a bayonet thrust."

"Those stories seem rather at odds with one another. Tell me, Mr. Dolson, do you believe any part of these stories?"

"Colonel, I had my doubts about Almonte. But after hearing Cós's fanciful account, well, Dr. Patrick, Colonel Morgan, and I were of the same opinion. And, please, forgive my language, sir, for I do not use such lightly or in polite company. But frankly, we think the pricks were just trying to make us mad."

CHAPTER 11

HARRISBURG WAS A Texas phoenix.

It began as a settlement established by John Harris on the bank of Buffalo Bayou near the northern tip of Galveston Bay. It was not named by a grateful populace in honor of its founder but rather *by* its founder in his own honor.

Harris expected it to be a lucrative location and his vision proved true. Twenty-five years later the railroads brought a surge of commerce, and ninety years later Buffalo Bayou was widened to become the Houston Ship Channel, one of the busiest seaports in the world.

Harrisburg was the third of seven temporary capitals of Texas. But during the Texas Revolution, the scorched-earth defense of the retreating Texians, the incendiary campaign of the advancing Santa Anna army, and the vindictive reprisals of the withdrawing Mexican forces left towns, villages, ranches, and farms in ruins. Five days before his defeat at San Jacinto, Santa Anna burned Harrisburg, destroying everything save one house.

By 1838, Harrisburg was resurgent. New building projects, financed by investors from as far away as Boston who could see the town's commercial possibilities, got Harrisburg back on its feet. It was formally incorporated a year after its destruction, and its population was expected to exceed one thousand within a year.

"Not bad for a burned-down ghost town," Jacob Millsaps said as he and Henry Karnes rode down Harrisburg's main thoroughfare.

They rode down a main street busy with construction workers and crewmen on shore leave from ships anchored in Galveston Bay.

"Any idea where we find Dickinson?" Jacob asked.

"I hear tell she's got herself a boardin' house," Henry said. "You know where she learned how to run it?" Millsaps shook his head. "She lived in the Mansion House last year."

"Pamela Mann taught her?"

"Yep."

"It'll probably be the loudest place in town."

One of Houston's less reputable businesses was Pamela Mann's Mansion House, a blood-on-the-floor hotel and restaurant frequented by diverse elements of Houston society. Mann, who had harangued Sam Houston for the return of her oxen that his Texian army borrowed to pull its artillery to San Jacinto, faced her own troubles with law enforcement. She was accused of a variety of crimes of moral turpitude, including counterfeiting, assault, and theft. Such was the character of Susanna Dickinson's instructor.

The Texians followed the street's din to a shabby inn in the middle of town. There were blood stains on the walls and floor that no one bothered to clean. One splatter pattern was fresh—so much so that the owner of the blood was still slumped beneath it.

"Lookin' for Sue Dickinson," Henry hollered to a scar-faced bartender. The barman just shook his head and pointed on up the street.

Two blocks further on, they came upon another boarding house, this one strangely quiet. Its front porch was clean. Its doors were hung straight and swung true. Its windows were glass paned with no cracks or bullet holes.

And on the second-floor balcony, a neatly painted wood sign proclaimed the inn's name.

ALAMO HOUSE

"You been around her much?" Jacob said.

"Not much," Henry said.

"She can be sweet as molasses one moment, and like all possessed the next. We'll have to tread careful."

They dismounted, tied their horses to the railing out front, and stepped inside.

The place was near full. Only a handful of chairs sat empty, and the clientele sat at tables or stood at the bar drinking beer and whiskey.

All heads turned at the newcomers, who were covered in trail dust. Henry removed his hat to swat the dust from his arms but stopped as his eyes adjusted to the saloon's low light. Every man in the place was dressed in his Sunday best: suit and tie and polished shoes, and every hat had been removed and sat neatly on the tables.

Henry shoved his hat back on his head.

Jacob and Henry moved farther inside, where they could see walls covered with items from the Revolution. Drawings of Jim Bowie, William Travis, and David Crockett adorned one wall. On the opposite were a Mexican soldier's jacket with a blood-stained bullet hole, a bicorn hat, a shako, and a crossed pair of Brown Bess muskets with bayonets attached.

The bar's patrons conversed in hushed tones in an eerie, almost reverent stillness. Like a church service that got lost and wandered in.

"You sure she learned from Pamela Mann?" Jacob said.

Millsaps and Karnes approached the bar, and the crowd parted to give them space.

Behind the bar was a drawing of a woman with dark, braided hair that fell to her shoulders, a thin mouth, and wide-set eyes, wearing a dark dress with a broach at the neck. Next to it was a drawing of a man with blue eyes, a narrow mouth, black hair swept across a high forehead, and long sideburns. He wore a brown jacket over a white shirt with a cravat at his neck. Under each was a small, engraved plate with the subject's name.

SUSANNA DICKINSON. ALMERON DICKINSON.

"It's a good likeness of Almeron," Jacob said.

"Mmm, looks just like him," Henry agreed.

"Did you gentlemen know Mr. Dickinson?" the bartender said. Every ear in the place was tuned to the conversation.

"I met him," Henry said. "Didn't know him well. Jacob here knew him better."

"You did, sir?" the bartender inquired.

"Knew him from San Antonio. Had dinner with him and Sue in the Músquiz house."

"Then drinks are on the house, gentlemen. Oh, first round only, of course," and the bartender produced a bottle and filled two shot glasses with dark whiskey.

"Very kind," Jacob said. He leaned toward the bartender and lowered his voice. "Is Mrs. Dickinson available?"

"Oh, no sir. She does not mix with strangers in the bar," the bartender said with slight indignation. "No, sir. She's much too fine a lady for that."

"Meant nothing by it," Jacob said. "We're old acquaintances."

A tall man with a bowler hat under his arm and a pistol tucked in his belt walked up behind Karnes and Millsaps, flanked by two more well-dressed, well-armed men. Henry and Jacob detected their approach.

"You say you know Mrs. Dickinson?" the owner of the bowler hat said.

Jacob did not turn. He took a sip of whiskey, tasting hints of vanilla, cedar, and tobacco. It was excellent malt whiskey. "Not that it's any of your concern," he said.

"We're making it our concern," one of the bowler hat's seconds said.

"You don't belong," the other second said, looking dismissively at Jacob and Henry's road-worn condition.

"Fellas, we just dropped in for a drink and to say hello," Henry said.

"Just drop out. This is more a private club, and you're not welcome."

"A private club?" Henry scoffed. "Since when do folk need an invitation to drink in a dang groggery?"

Every head in the place lifted at this remark, dismay on every face.

"This, sir, is no groggery," the bowler hat said. "This is the fine establishment of Mrs. Dickinson, and you will show respect to the lady and watch your tongue. The way you speak is a sin to Crockett."

And then it hit Jacob and Henry. This wasn't a church service that got lost. This *was* a church, and these were worshipers of the mistress of the Alamo.

"What would you know of Crockett?" Jacob said, turning to face the bowler hat and rising to his full six-foot height. His anger rose as well.

Henry removed his straw hat, uncovering his head of red hair and his smirking face.

One of the bowler hat's seconds squinted at Henry. His eyes went wide and the anger drained out of his face, replaced by recognition. He stepped back, leaving the bowler hat's side. The bowler hat didn't notice the desertion, but the other second did, and he stepped back and whispered with the man trying to make his way back to his table. The other second whipped his head around at the two interlopers, and both seconds melted into the congregation.

The bowler hat began to wither under Jacob's glare but decided to go all in.

"Were you in the war? We were. All of us. All veterans."

"You were, huh?" Henry said.

"And I don't remember seeing you at San Jacinto," the bowler hat said.

Neither Jacob nor Henry could possibly identify all nine hundred Texians on the field on April 21, 1836. But had every man who claimed to have been at San Jacinto actually been present, Sam Houston's forces would have outnumbered the Mexicans ten to one.

"Funny," Jacob said. "I was thinking the same about you."

"And just who the hell are you?"

"Name's Millsaps."

In the pantheon of heroes of the Texas Revolution, the highest level is reserved for Sam Houston, William Travis, Jim Bowie, and David Crockett. Not far behind, however, are the Immortal 32, the men from Gonzales who answered Travis's call. Perhaps best known of the thirty-two was Isaac Millsaps. The place in Texas legend of Isaac's wife Mary rivaled even that of Susanna Dickinson.

And this was Isaac Millsaps's brother, Jacob. Who led the Immortal 32 through the Mexican forces into the Alamo. Who dared to ride through the Mexican siege again for additional reinforcements. Who rode with Mirabeau Lamar's calvary at San Jacinto.

The bowler hat looked to Henry, afraid to ask.

"Karnes," Henry answered.

"Henry Karnes?" the bowler hat croaked. "Henry Wax Karnes?"

Henry Wax Karnes! Who rode with Deaf Smith to learn the fate of the Alamo. Who was Mirabeau Lamar's second-in-command of the Texian cavalry at San Jacinto. Henry Wax Karnes!

The bowler hat felt the blood drain from his head. His left knee fluttered and he rocked ever so slightly back on his heels, and what moisture remained in his mouth evaporated to leave only cotton. He wanted to hide, to fade into the crowd, to disappear forever. An Alamo acolyte no more. Now shamed. Heretic. Apostate.

"I, uh…" the bowler hat trailed off, waiting for help from his fellows that did not come, leaving silence hanging in the former acolyte's throat. The crowd's demeanor had changed, as if a blue norther had rolled in and chilled their flesh. Hostility had been replaced with respect bordering on worship.

"It was a big battlefield," Henry said. "Guess you couldn't see ever'one."

"Lot of smoke," Jacob said.

"Yes," the bowler hat swallowed. "Lot of smoke."

"I don't want to talk about it," Susanna Dickinson said.

After Henry and Jacob won over Dickinson's devotees, the bartender went upstairs and announced their presence to his mistress, and she agreed to see them. But by the time the bartender had escorted Karnes and Millsaps up, her mood had darkened.

They found her in an overstuffed chair in her room on the second floor of the boarding house. The walls reflected nothing of the saloon downstairs, no mention at all of the Alamo or the Revolution or Texas. Plain, pale blue curtains hung over the window and a plain, pale blue coverlet lay over the bed. A wall clock ticked too loudly in one corner.

Her face was thinner than Jacob remembered. There were lines on her forehead and circles beneath her eyes. Her hair was graying and her mouth was turned down at the corners.

She looked as though the life had been drained from her.

"I don't want to talk about it," she repeated.

"Since when?" Jacob said. "You've done nothing but talk about the Alamo."

"And you're friends with that Alsbury, aren't you?" she raged at Henry. "He and his traitorous wife. That bitch betrayed us!"

"She didn't betray a thing," Henry said. "Travis sent her out to talk with Santa Anna, to arrange a surrender."

Dickinson shook her head violently. "Travis wouldn't surrender. None of them would."

"But Santa Anna wouldn't listen."

"No, no, no, no, no—"

"Mrs. Dickinson, Mrs. Alsbury told the Mexicans nothin'," Henry said. "She was as scared as you."

"Why? She wasn't even in the Alamo when the attack came."

"Yes, Sue, she was," Jacob said. "And she's hurting just like you. But she wants none of your fame. None of it. She's been chased out of San Antonio. All she wants is a measure of peace. But this isn't about her. We just want to know what you saw."

"We just need to ask one question," Henry said.

"I'm not talking to you," she snarled. "Either of you."

Jacob knelt beside Susanna. "Sue, please, just listen to me for a moment, and we'll leave," Jacob said, as softly as he could. "You keep telling that story about Travis drawing a line in the sand. That's fine. You keep telling all your stories. By, God, you earned it. You earned every bit of attention you get, and every bit of love and devotion folks give you. Your husband was killed, and you went through hell. But you kept your daughter safe. You kept your head and you kept her alive. We got no argument with you, Sue. We're not here to hurt you."

Susanna Dickinson, scarred and scared and surviving on stories of glories, real and imagined, began to weep. Jacob clasped her right hand with both of his hands. Henry knelt on the other side of Dickinson's chair and took her left hand. The three of them stayed like that for as long as Sue wanted. As long as she needed. As long as it took to cry herself out.

"What do you want to know?" she finally said.

Henry nodded and Jacob lifted Sue's face.

"We need to know what you saw of Crockett. After the battle. A Mexican officer told you, 'If you wish to save your life, follow me.' Yes?"

Dickinson nodded. The Texians knew this because Sue had repeated it many times.

"You left the chapel. Where was Crockett?"

"Why? Why do you ask?" she flared.

"Because rumors are out there," Jacob said. "Hurtful, awful rumors about David. Rumors about him being in a mine in Mexico. Rumors that he must have surrendered. You know he wouldn't surrender."

"No, he wouldn't. He absolutely wouldn't."

"Those rumors have gotten back to the Crockett family. It's causing them pain, Sue. We want to stop that pain. That's all we're trying to do."

Dickinson smiled beneath tear-streaked cheeks. "You're such a good man, Jacob. Are you taking care of Isaac's dear wife?"

"I am, Sue. We built her a new house. Remember how her old house got burned down? We built a new one for her and her children. Henry here is helping me. Some others, too. We got to help each other. We're all hurt. I know you're hurt, too. Help me, Sue, to heal the Crockett family. Please?"

Dickinson collected herself and wiped her tears with a handkerchief. Her voice was suddenly strong. "I saw him when I walked out, Jacob. He was near the palisade, lying amid the other Texians. The Mexicans used a cannon, one of our own. I saw Crockett lying there. The cannon ball must have hit him, because one of his legs was terribly twisted and mutilated, almost torn off. There was blood everywhere. He was dead, Jacob. That cannon ball took his leg."

"And he was near the palisade."

"Yes."

Jacob stood and kissed Susanna's forehead. "Thank you, Sue."

"Thank you, Mrs. Dickinson," Henry said. "It was a pleasure seein' you. You take care."

Susanna smiled sweetly, and was still smiling when Millsaps and Karnes departed.

CHAPTER 12

A DAY OUT of Harrisburg, Henry picked up the trail he was looking for.

"This is where they started?" Jacob said.

"Yep, this is where the Mexican retreat began," Henry said. "General Filisola's army was camped here when the end came for Santa Anna."

The lead units of the Mexican army that were not with Santa Anna had reached as far north as Fort Bend, an isolated, ramshackle blockhouse on the Brazos River built in 1822 for protection against Indian raids. The fort wasn't much, described by one of its builders as a "little log shanty," but its location at a ford across the Brazos had attracted a small settlement.

"I didn't know they were this close," Jacob said. "I mean, I knew the rest of the Mexican army wasn't far, but, Lord, they were just a day away, maybe two."

"Fifteen hundred men," Henry said. "Thirty miles from our nine hundred at San Jacinto. And us half scattered and fresh off a fight. Few days later, General Urrea arrived here. The Mexicans musta had three thousand men by then."

"Thank goodness they obeyed Santa Anna's orders and didn't march on us. If they had, what you think we would have done?"

"I wonder," Henry mused. "If the Mexicans attacked, would we have shot or hanged Santa Anna, or the other prisoners? Can't say what old Sam woulda done. Just glad we didn't have to make that choice."

"What are we looking for?"

"We're gonna track the Mexican retreat. Should take us to Madam Powell's. Maybe we find sign of a smaller outfit, maybe a company or just a platoon, comin' from San Antonio."

"Escorting a certain prisoner to Mexico. It's a plain trail, all right. Two years gone and it's still clear."

"Three thousand men leave a hell of a footprint, don't they?"

Though two years had begun to hide the path of the retreating Mexican army, Karnes and Millsaps had no difficulty following the scar left by a long column of men, horses, and wagons as it headed home.

The area was a mix of prairie and woodland, teaming with game, and the Texians snacked on wild berries. They hunted for a couple of hours and came away with a good-sized deer, which they draped over the back of a pack mule they purchased in Harrisburg.

Near the end of their second day out of Harrisburg, they arrived at Madam Powell's, which, in 1836, was a dog-run house and a series of outbuildings, including a kitchen and guest rooms, located near San Bernard River and Turkey Creek. It was run by Elizabeth Powell, a widow who came to Texas in 1828, along with four of her adult children and was a stopping place for travelers going to or coming from the Gulf Coast.

"Hello, Henry!" a pretty, smiling young woman called as the Texians drew up.

"Ellen!" Henry said and dismounted. He gave the girl a hug, and she returned it with a kiss. "How are you?"

"Best as can be. We make do."

"Got a cabin up, I see."

"Better than nothing," Ellen Powell said.

Nothing was what the Mexican army left the Powells.

The Mexican retreat came through the Powells' land. The Mexicans camped one night, assembled an officers' meeting that evening, and at first light began their long walk to Mexico. After partaking of Madam Powell's hospitality, Mexican troops set fire to every building and left the family homeless. There was no strategic or sound military reason to burn the place.

"We was up in Harrisburg and thought we'd stop by, if'n that's all right," Henry said.

"You know you're always welcome, Henry. And your friend."

"Sorry we don't have much to offer," said Ellen's sister, emerging from the one-room log cabin. "Hello, Henry!"

"Elizabeth!" Henry welcomed and got another hug and kiss. "Ladies, this my friend, Jacob Millsaps. Jacob, this is Ellen and Elizabeth Powell."

"Very nice to meet you both," Jacob said.

"And I'm sure their mother is around someplace."

"She's with the boys working on the new kitchen," Elizabeth said.

"How's it coming?" Henry said.

"Making progress," Ellen said. "We had to sell twenty-five acres to Samuel Damon. He's building a sawmill, and he gave us some lumber to help us start over."

"The Mexicans burned everything?" Jacob asked.

"Everything," Elizabeth said.

"Why they do that?" Jacob said.

"They did it for spite!" Madam Powell hollered as she walked up, wiping her hands on a worn apron. She was flanked by her sons. "So good to see you, Henry," Madam Powell said, and Karnes got another hug and kiss.

"Hello, fellas," Henry said, turning to the Powell boys. "Joseph, Samuel, how are you?"

"Tired," one of the boys said, but Millsaps wasn't sure if it was Joseph or Samuel.

"You staying the night?" Madam Powell said. "We don't have much, but you're welcome to what we got."

"We didn't come to dinner empty handed," Henry said. "We brung meat." He led the Powells to the pack mule and the deer carcass.

"Oh, thank you, Henry, Jacob!" Madam Powell said. "I've been hungry for venison. Boys, get this meat taken care of. We'll get a fire going, and we'll have us a fine supper."

And so they did. Madam Powell, even without a functioning kitchen, did wonders with the venison. Henry and Jacob had purchased coffee, sugar, and flour which they presented to the Powells, and dinner was accompanied by vegetables from the Powells' stores. Henry also brought a bottle, and everyone passed the whiskey around, no glasses needed.

"Did the Republic ever pay you for your losses?" Jacob asked.

"Hell, no," Madam Powell said. "We put in a claim, one of the first to file. They never answered, just ignored us."

"The whole Mexican army camped here?" Jacob asked.

"Oh, they were coming and going," Madam Powell said.

"Santa Anna came through chasing you fellas," Ellen said. "Then General Filisola, on his way to Old Fort. General Urrea's forces followed a few days later."

"Ever see any smaller units?" Jacob said.

"Company size or maybe just a platoon?" Henry added.

"On their own?" Madam Powell said. "No. But the Mexicans got strung out, and lots of stragglers dragged through here for a couple of days."

"But no smaller, independent outfits," Jacob pressed.

"I don't think so."

"No one comin' in from the west?" Henry asked.

"Don't believe so," Madam Powell said, and her family agreed. The whiskey was taking the edge off the Powells, so they didn't bother to ask the reason for the questions.

It was a rare festive evening for the Powells, for whom every day had been a struggle for two years. Finally, the evening wore down.

"We have no beds for you," Madam Powell said. "All I've got is a couple of tents. We slept in them while we were building the cabin. You're welcome to use them, though I'm ashamed to say it. Never turned anyone away from my house here or in New Orleans."

"You'll be back on top," Henry said. "We'll try to get back out this way again, maybe bring some help and get you a proper house built."

"That would be wonderful. Good night, boys."

"Good night, Madam Powell," Jacob said. "We'll see you in the morning."

One of the Powell boys, Jacob still wasn't sure which, brought out the tents and helped set them up. He muttered a good night and returned to the cabin.

"You know these folks well," Jacob said. "You come out here often?"

"Not often enough. I'm just a friend of the family," Henry said. "Good night, Jacob."

Millsaps settled into his tent for some much-needed rest. Fortunately, he found sleeping outdoors invigorating and restful.

Unfortunately, he was unlikely to enjoy a quiet, undisturbed night. Not long after turning in, he heard voices coming from Henry's tent—Henry's voice and a woman's voice. Jacob wondered which of the Powell daughters Karnes was bedding.

Then he realized he was actually hearing Henry and two female voices.

"Friend of the family, indeed," Jacob muttered.

★

"Why in hell did them damned fools march down here?" Henry asked.

"There was a perfectly good road on higher ground just a few miles west," Jacob said. "They must not had decent maps, or sent out patrols."

Karnes and Millsaps had followed the trail of the retreat for days. The Mexican army had marched west for a day, doubled back, and marched northwest toward the Atascocita Road, which headed west before curving south all the way to the border. But they quickly abandoned that route and turned south off the Atascocita, taking a lower-lying, less-traveled but more direct road to Victoria and Goliad.

Like the Mexicans they were tracing, Karnes and Millsaps slogged through low-lying roads and paths that would become swamps when the rains came.

And in late April and early May of 1836, the rains did come. The day the Mexican army left Madam Powell's, heavy rains descended and continued for days. Mules foundered in the mud. Wagons and cannon became mired, and soldiers wasted time hauling them out. Much of the army's goods were stranded or discarded.

The route was strewn with buttons, bullets, unit insignias, bayonets, powder horns, shakos, and cross belts. The Texians found a creek laden with rusting muskets that soldiers had simply tossed down. There was loot from across Texas: nails and ceramics, cups and plates, forks and knives and spoons, bedding, candlesticks, music boxes—an assortment that could be found on almost any farm. Much of the debris had been scavenged in the two years hence, but some would remain for more than a century.

And there were the dead. Two years on, they were just skeletal remains clad in ragged bits of uniform, and all had provided a meal to wildlife, so many of the remains were scattered. But many of the wounded, suffering in deplorable conditions, fell out of the march or were left by the side of the road to die. The Mexicans stumbled through thickets of trees and streams where men became lost or got separated from their battalions, companies, and platoons.

Henry and Jacob paused to bury the human remains they found in a common grave.

Six days of hard travel brought the Texians to Goliad. It took the Mexican army a month and an unknown number of dead to cover the same distance. Nowhere did the Texians find any sign of a smaller column joining the march from the west.

"If troops brought Crockett from San Antonio, they must have come down the road to Goliad," Jacob said.

"And joined here to head south to Mexico. Course, maybe they left the Alamo early. Before San Jacinto. Road woulda been clear. With Mexican troops all over the area—"

"—from Urrea's army that held the Gulf Coast—"

"—folks would have kept off these roads. Too dangerous. And travelin' by themselves, it would've been easy to keep their secret."

"If there was a secret to keep," Jacob said.

"Partner, I think we got ever'thing from this trip we're gonna get."

"You sure got everything you could get at Madam Powell's. Not much you didn't have. I was surprised you could walk the next day."

Henry just smiled, both at Jacob's comment and the memory of the night in the tent with the Powell girls.

After days on the trail and nights under the stars, Millsaps and Karnes rested for two days in Goliad, eating well and sleeping in beds with clean sheets. Then they headed north to Erasmo Seguin's Calaveras Ranch outside of San Antonio.

CHAPTER 13

SILAS GRANT RODE home.

Home was the Brazos River Valley and surrounding area—forty miles west to the Colorado River and a day's ride east to the piney woods, north to the Old San Antonio Road and south to the Atascosito Road.

It was a mix of dark-soiled blackland prairies, rolling hills of post oak savannah, and hardwood-forested bottomlands.

It was veined with rivers and creeks and streams. It was thick with oak, hickory, elm, walnut, post oak, sugarberry, pecan, mesquite and pine. It abounded with grasslands that supported wildlife and settlers' livestock.

Its people grew corn and beans and squash, rice and cotton, wheat and oats. There were peas and potatoes, beets and cucumbers, radishes and tomatoes, pumpkins and peppers. There were cantaloupes and watermelons, apples and apricots, blackberries and blueberries. And peaches. Oh, the peaches. Nectar of the gods. Ambrosia that made summer's heat bearable.

Its winters were mild and in spring it exploded with wildflowers.

The Brazos Valley was the kind of place that attracted folks—Indian, Hispanic, White, Black, and all variations thereof. Among those who felt its pull was a man named Stephen F. Austin, who founded the first Anglo-American settlement in Texas.

That settlement, in turn, attracted a young blacksmith named Duncan Grant, born in Scotland and migrated to Missouri, who moved his family to Texas. Newly minted as a master of his trade, he saw an opportunity to start his own blacksmith, farrier, and wheelwright business.

For Duncan's oldest son, Silas, Texas had been the most exciting place imaginable to grow into adulthood, and that excitement reached a fever pitch when the Texas Revolution began. Texians declared independence from Mexico at a place called Washington-on-the-Brazos, just a few miles from his family's house and smithy.

It had been a few months since Silas had been back, and he welcomed this trip.

The sights and aromas of the Brazos Valley enveloped him, but his ears told him he was home. Proximity to his father's blacksmith shop was announced by the sharp clanks and rings of hammer, anvil, and hot metal. He reined in a few feet from the smithy.

"I could use some new shoes for this old horse," Silas called to the broad-shouldered blacksmith's back.

"I only work for paying customers," Duncan said without turning, "not deadbeats looking for a handout."

"I tell you what, why don't we play cards for it?" Silas said, dismounting.

Duncan turned and narrowed his brown eyes. "You look to me like the kind who would cheat."

"I'm as honest as the father who taught me."

"That's what I'm afraid of," Duncan said. "Good to see you, son. How you been keeping?"

"I'm well," Silas said, and he and his father hugged. Silas was frustrated to find he was still two inches shorter than his father, as he had been for more than a year. "And you? How's the shoulder?"

"Not bad," Duncan said. "Acts up now and again but nothing that slows my work. Dr. Labadie passed through not long ago and took a look. Said it healed well."

"I guess he did a good job on you and Sam."

"He got a lot of practice digging out bullets and patching holes. McCulloch got shot in the same place as me."

"I recall. You were hit in the right shoulder while capturing San Antonio back in '35 alongside old Ben Milam."

"I've told that story before, huh?"

"Once or twice."

"How is Sam? Seen him recently?"

"He's good. He gripes from time to time about his shoulder. Like you."

"Wait until you get shot. Speaking of strong shoulders, you feel like putting yours into a bellows for while?"

"You may be surprised to hear this, but I'd like that."

Funny thing, Silas thought, he really was looking forward to working around fire and iron. He had risen to apprentice level under his father and could imagine himself with his own smithy someday. There was something comforting about creating something useful or beautiful—or both—out a cold lump of metal.

Silas devoted the rest of the afternoon working alongside his father and the evening in his family home, talking with his younger brother (who was growing rapidly and wouldn't be his little brother much longer), doting on his golden-haired little sister, helping his eternally patient mother in the kitchen and reveling in her cooking, and regaling the family with the story of his adventure with the smugglers on the Gulf Coast.

Texas had been one long adventure for Silas. He had been allowed, much to his mother's consternation, to accompany his father when Duncan joined the Texian fight against Mexico and participated in the siege of Béxar that saw the Texians take San Antonio and the Alamo. Silas drove a wagon of wounded—which included his father—to Gonzales, where they were recuperating when the Alamo fell. Silas found himself caught up in the Runaway Scrape, chased by the Mexican army all the way back to the Brazos Valley, where he was among the refugees camped with the Texian army at Groce's Landing, a ferry across the Brazos River, and on the sprawling grounds of Leonard Groce's Bernardo Plantation.

Silas looked for any way he could help. With his background in smithing, he assisted repairing firearms and mounting the Texians' cannon—the Twin Sisters—to be hauled to San Jacinto. He rode with Seguin, Karnes, and Millsaps scouting west toward the Mexicans and east toward San Jacinto, though he was desperately disappointed at being left behind when the army marched toward its showdown with Santa Anna.

As much as the experience matured him, it also grew in him a burning anger that would stay with him for the rest of his life.

In his zeal to help, Silas volunteered for the important if tedious task of melting lead pipes and making bullets. That meant working alongside Bernardo Plantation's slaves. He quickly came to respect and befriend these men and women of color, and those relationships developed in him a rage over the plantation lifestyle, its dependence on slavery, and its disgraceful treatment of fellow human beings.

"I don't understand," he had said to his father. "Why treat people like that? Shackled and whipped. What gives Groce or any man the right?"

"There's no right," his father said. "Slavery is what comes of people convincing themselves they're better than others. Belief in your own superiority breeds intolerance, cruelty, and evil."

In a world at war, Silas grew up fast. That did not, however, mean life in the Brazos Valley during the Texas Revolution was all toil and strife and conflict. Silas became friends with Sam McCulloch, who was convalescing in the camp, and with Sam's family. He met future presidents of Texas Sam Houston and Mirabeau Lamar. He got to know and learn from Henry Karnes, Juan Seguin, Jacob Millsaps, Horace Alsbury, and James Clinton Neill.

Mostly, though, there was Emily.

Emily Perry was the younger sister of James Perry. After the death of her father, Emily lived with her brother and his wife, and the family moved from New York to Texas in 1836. They took up residence in the Brazos Valley, and Silas and Emily, both fourteen years old, became friends in the last moments of childhood.

Emily had the same effect on Silas as she did on every man who saw her. She simply took his breath away. Each time he looked at her, Silas had to remind himself not to stare.

She had green eyes which exuded warmth and friendliness or contempt and scorn with equal intensity. Her red hair shimmered to the middle of her back and was frequently tied with combs and decorated with wildflowers. She had a narrow waist and slender figure, and her skin was smooth and flawless. Her mouth curled ever so slightly at the corners, giving her full lips a hint of a grin. When she smiled, she smiled with her entire face, her lips and cheeks and eyes aglow.

Emily was exquisite. Stunning. Easily the most beautiful woman Silas had ever seen.

Silas was not alone in that opinion. But Emily had a remarkable defense against relentless advances and marriage proposals. She was extremely intelligent, well-read, witty, determined, and self-reliant with an independent streak—all of which discouraged many admirers. That suited her fine, for any man who was intimidated by a strong, smart woman was a man in whom she had no interest.

Silas, on the other hand, found all those qualities attractive. Actually, he found everything about Emily attractive and could find no fault in her.

What Silas didn't know—what he hoped and dreamed and prayed but couldn't bring himself to believe—was that Emily was as fond of him as he was of her, and she didn't mind if he stared. In Silas, she saw a handsome young man who was smart and funny, sweet and kind, resourceful and honest and not a bit threatened by her strength and intelligence. He was everything she wanted.

Inexorably, Emily and Silas drew closer. But at fourteen years old in the middle of a war, neither knew what to do about it.

With the Mexican army bearing down on the Texians, the Grants and the Perrys wound up at the refugee camp at Groce's Landing, where the army prepared for its final stand against Santa Anna. However, the families had a falling out over support of Sam Houston. James Perry disliked Houston, criticized his every decision, and took offense at others who disagreed with his estimation. The Grants, meanwhile, supported and believed in Houston.

Their disagreement did not affect Silas and Emily, and the families did not forbid their friendship. Which was wise, as neither of them would have acceded to such an ultimatum nor obeyed any prohibition.

And again, Emily and Silas drew closer.

After the war, Silas spent time with McCulloch, Millsaps, Seguin, and Karnes, continuing to hone his frontier skills while keeping up with work in his father's smithy and his schoolwork directed by his mother.

And though Silas was frequently away, Emily was always in his heart.

✫

"Silas Grant!" Leonard Groce bellowed. "How have you been?"

"I'm well, Mr. Groce," Silas said as he curbed his horse on the east bank of the Brazos at the base of the bluff upon which sat Bernardo Plantation's main house. It was an impressive structure, one and a half stories tall with two rooms and a hall upstairs, four rooms and a large gallery downstairs, and two sandstone chimneys. In back was the kitchen, a doctor's office, and a hall for entertaining. Surrounding this opulence was the slaves' world: the overseer's house, a kitchen, rows of squat shacks, and vast fields of cotton.

Silas didn't like to be near the big house for everything it represented, but, unfortunately, he needed the master of the plantation now.

"How are things here?" Silas asked.

"We're rebuilding," Groce said. "Lots of work to do, and not many hands available. With so much destroyed during the war, everyone is rebuilding their farms and houses. What brings you back?"

"Visiting my folks. No matter how long I'm away, I always come back to the Brazos. It's home."

"I understand how you feel. If you have some time, we could sure use some help with our construction. We're concentrating on the ferry and a new school."

"Sure, Mr. Groce. But if I'm going to be working here, is there any place close where I can stay?"

"The house is full, and so is the guest house, but there's a new cabin for the foreman we're going to hire," Groce said and pointed to a small house of unfinished wood. "It's got a wood floor and a window with curtains, and we just chinked the walls. It has a bed, a chair, and a table. I think there's a washstand, too."

"That's more than enough."

"Good. I tell you what, why don't we just barter for it? The room in exchange for work?"

With little choice, Silas nodded agreement.

"Excellent," Groce said. "I'll have clean linen delivered, and candles so you don't stumble around in the dark."

Silas had told his folks he planned to stay at the Landing for a few days, hoping to be recruited for the work crews. Those crews included several Texas Revolution veterans, and Silas listened to their gossip and rumors, sparked conversations, turned their discussions in directions of his interest, and learned everything he could.

The Alamo rumors flew.

That first day, after packing his gear into the foreman's cabin that was thick with the smell of fresh-cut lumber, Silas worked on the pier on the west side of the Brazos River to replace the one destroyed by the retreating Texian army. For much of the day, he was hip deep in the river and wrangling big timbers into place.

The next day, he was sent with a small crew to help finish a new schoolhouse which was already in use. Silas was helping saw lumber for a wall when he heard a familiar voice coming from the school. At that moment, children bolted from the classroom, hurtling outside to play and leaving their teacher alone in the doorway.

Emily.

Silas just stood there, staring and struggling to find his voice.

"Hello, Emily," he finally said, unable to contain a smile.

"Silas?" she said, unwilling to hide a smile. "How...how are you?"

"I'm good," he said, walking toward her. "You?"

"I'm well," she said, taking a few steps forward. "The students keep me busy."

"I bet. Chasing school kids sounds like work. I didn't know you were teaching."

"If you were around more, you'd know all sorts of things," she gently chided. "I enjoy teaching. It gives me something to do."

"I hear your brother moved back to New York."

"Yes, he's entering the ministry. He's been assigned to a parish in Burlington."

Silas shifted his feet. "I'm glad you stayed. Where are you living?"

"With the Carters. Do you know them?"

"Richard Carter? Wife and daughter, I believe."

"Yes, they're very nice," she said. "Very nice."

"That's nice."

"How are your folks?"

"They're good. They're...good."

"That's good."

Awkward silence followed.

"Damn it, Silas!" Emily lunged forward, thumped her fists on Silas's chest, grabbed handfuls of his linsey shirt, pulled him close, and threw her arms around him. "I missed you. I didn't go with my brother because..."

"I've thought about you so much," Silas said, wrapping his arms around Emily. "I knew I was coming back to see you. I just had to take care of some things, but I was always coming back. I never stopped thinking about you."

"Really?"

"Really."

They fell into another long silence. Somehow not so awkward. Emily was only an inch shorter than Silas and their eyes easily locked into one another's.

Slowly and for the first time, they kissed. It began soft and shy and innocent, but it carried two years of anticipation and longing, and the passion of that first kiss grew. And it lasted. And lasted. And lasted. Finally, their lips reluctantly parted, and Emily rested her head against Silas's shoulder. He put a hand gently at the back of her neck and touched her hair. His other hand was on the small of her back, and he closed his eyes. He had dreamed about this very moment so many times. Of holding Emily. Of the smell of her hair. Of the touch of her hands on his back. Of the taste of her lips.

★

Emily and Silas filled the rest of the day talking. Not awkward I-have-no-idea-what-to-say teenage conversation. They talked about what they wanted to do with their lives. What they hoped for. What might be next.

About the possibility of a life together.

As dusk approached, Silas walked Emily to the Carters' house and was invited to dinner. After supper, Emily and Silas sat on the Carters' front porch and held hands and kissed again and again before Silas, in his gentlemanly best, saw Emily back inside and returned to his cabin.

That evening, he made plans. Or tried to. He had brought the packages from San Antonio and stashed them under the bed, and now he thought of how he'd give them to Emily. She had her own room at the Carters so she had a place to put them, but he struggled with scenarios for the gift giving and was still wrestling with the question when he fell asleep.

Silas rose early the next day, cleaned up at the cabin's washstand, threw out the dirty water, and told himself to get more water later before he headed for breakfast with the work crew and joined the building of the pier on the east shore of the Brazos.

The day was hot and the work demanding, but they finished the job. His muscles ached as he returned to his cabin, the dilemma of the gift-giving temporarily forgotten.

He wanted to find Emily. It was getting late in the afternoon and he didn't know if school was already out, but he wanted to find her.

Unfortunately, he was a mess—a sweaty, grimy mess—and could not possibly call on Emily like this. But a wash and a change of clothes would solve that.

He unbuttoned his shirt and tried to remove it, but the linsey was pasted to his back, and instead of slipping off, it peeled away like a layer of skin. Without bending down, he pushed his brogans off his feet, planting his toes at the heel of each shoe and shoving. He didn't know how much his feet hurt until they were free.

He unbuttoned and took off his trousers, removed his drawers, and tossed the dirty clothes aside. Stripped naked, he stretched. Arched his back. Flexed his toes. Better.

Now, a quick wash. Silas turned to the washstand. The basin was empty. He had told himself that morning to fetch more water and would have sworn that he had, but he had so much on his mind that he must have overlooked it. He picked up the pitcher on the table. Also empty. No water, no soap, no towels. He sighed and leaned his hands on the washstand.

He was about to put his pants on and go in search of soap and water when he looked in the washstand's mirror.

Behind him, standing in the cabin doorway.

Emily.

She's here. What do I do? Where are my pants? What do I do? I can't believe she's here!

Silas hesitated a moment, then turned and faced Emily. They looked at each other. She blushed. He blushed. But she did not look away and he did not cover himself.

She was carrying a pitcher of water, a bar of soap, and a washcloth. A towel was draped over her shoulder.

Standing naked before Emily, with her eyes on him, Silas began to arouse. Couldn't fight it. Wouldn't if he could.

Emily let slip a tiny grin. She reached back and closed the door, then walked to the washstand and filled the basin. She dipped the washcloth in the water and began to wipe the Texas dust from Silas's face, neck, and shoulders. His eyes never left her.

Neither uttered a word nor made a sound.

Drops of water rolled down Silas's torso, carving paths in the grime. She dipped the cloth again and continued wiping his arms and chest. Then his legs. Her arm brushed his erection.

Still, they said nothing.

A few drops of water splashed her sleeves and her skirt, and she paused and looked at her blouse, her mind wrestling with the choice before her. She looked at Silas, stepped back, and moved across the cabin to the room's lone chair against the far wall.

Emily slipped off her shoes and slid them under the chair. With her back turned to Silas, she unbuttoned her flower-print blouse, took it off, and draped it on the chair. She slid off her blue, three-quarter-length skirt.

Clad only in a white, knee-length linen chemise decorated with delicate lace around the neck and arms and tied at her breasts with a thin, blue silk ribbon, Emily stepped within arm's reach of Silas, her mind firmly set on her course of action.

Silas took a slow, deep breath. His course, too, was set.

Silas reached out carefully, as if any sudden movement might break the spell. He took hold of the end of the ribbon, and with a gentle tug, the ribbon untied and the top of the chemise fell open, just slightly.

He exhaled.

She unbuttoned the chemise, allowing it to fall open. Emily reached across to her left shoulder, slipped a finger under the lace strap, and the chemise fell away. Now she, too, was naked.

And in this moment, Silas Grant knew that this was the most beautiful sight he would ever behold.

They stood before one another, smiles broadening, arousal complete.

In unison, they moved forward and their lips met, long and soft, then harder and harder, until they pressed themselves tightly against one another. His hands at her hips, hers on his back, and they stood in that embrace. The world disappeared. Time vanished. Nothing else mattered.

They turned and walked to the narrow bed and lay next to one another, still kissing, hands exploring. Silas's lips moved gradually across Emily's cheeks, her forehead, behind her ears, and ever so slowly down her neck. He reveled in Emily, immersed himself in every moment and every inch of her.

Silas kissed his way down Emily's chest and lingered on her breasts. Finally, he kissed down her belly to her thighs.

"Um," Emily hesitated, "do you think it's all right?"

Silas paused. Neither had ever done anything like this, had no instructions, no plan, no clue what they were supposed to do.

Silas had received versions of "the talk" from his mother and father. At the time, it seemed reasonably comprehensive. At this moment, though, it seemed wholly inadequate.

Emily had been too young for discussions of sex before her mother and father died, and her brother had certainly never broached the subject. Fortunately, Emily was a very clever young woman.

But right now, Silas and Emily were running purely on instinct.

"I don't ever want us to do anything you're not comfortable with, especially just because you think I want you to," Silas said. "You say stop, we stop."

Emily smiled in response. "I didn't say stop."

Silas nodded. He kissed his way down her thighs, lowered his face into the red hair between the curves of her trim hips, and took her with his lips and tongue.

He took his time. Experimenting. Mapping reactions. Learning her. Emily gasped and her entire body shuddered when she reached orgasm for the first time in her life. Then the second. Then the third. Then she lost count.

When they were both ready, Silas stood, gazed at Emily, and felt intoxicated by her. She reached for him, and they eased themselves together. Carefully. Gradually. Gently. They sucked in their breath and their hearts raced. A moment of exquisite panic. She arched her back and dug her fingers into his arms. His body tensed. They remembered to exhale and the panic faded. They felt warm. Breathed deeply. Relaxed. Their eyes locked and they smiled at each other, a slightly embarrassed, tremendously elated smile. He waited, she nodded, and he slowly began to move.

Their first time was perfect. Perfect. In every conceivable way, perfect.

The second time was even better.

Few words had been exchanged from the time Emily stepped into the cabin until she undressed, but the rest of the night was a running conversation. Questions explored and answers discovered. Needs and desires, what felt good, what felt really good, and numerous requests to do that again please.

When they finally rose from the bed, they moved to the basin and washed each other, smiling, kissing, giggling, kissing, caressing, and kissing again and again and again.

Silas sank back onto the bed in exhausted satisfaction, but he did not close his eyes. He never wanted to sleep again, never wanted his eyes to leave Emily. He had not stopped looking at her since she appeared—what, two, three hours ago? The approaching sundown was glowing through the cabin's curtained window when she arrived, but the room was now deep in half-moon night.

Emily sat on the edge of the bed, let her eyes roam over her lover, and traced her fingers down his body. She kissed Silas, long and deep, then her lips and tongue were dancing across his forehead and cheeks, down his neck, lingered on his chest, moved down his belly, burning lower and lower, burning away the exhaustion, bringing him back.

Then she straddled him and took him inside her.

And the night kept getting better.

When they finally came up for air, they sat and talked, still naked, still reveling in one another in the moonlight, still kissing and caressing.

And Silas suddenly realized his dilemma was solved.

He leapt to his feet, startling Emily.

"What?"

"I have something for you," he said, crossed the room, and lit a candle in a pewter holder on the cabin's small table.

"I think you already gave me something," she said.

"No…well…yes…but…something else," he said, setting the candle on the corner of the washstand. "More than one something, actually."

He knelt beside the bed, realized where he was, and took the opportunity to kiss her thighs before refocusing and remembering what he was doing. He reached under the bed.

He paused and considered. Which one first. Uh…yes. He produced a small box and handed it to Emily.

"What is it?" she said before opening it.

Nestled in the box was a silver bracelet, enameled in robin's egg blue with a delicate floral pattern that glimmered in the candlelight. Her eyes went wide.

"It's the most beautiful thing anyone has ever given me," she said.

Silas smiled but wondered if he should have held this gift until last. Too late now.

She put on the bracelet, and much to Silas's relief, it fit perfectly. He had described Emily to the women in the market in San Antonio, and they knew it would fit.

It was spectacular against her pale skin.

She pulled his face close and kissed him. "I'm never taking this off," Emily said.

"Never?"

"Well…"

"Next."

Next was a package wrapped in paper and tied with string. Silas set it in Emily's lap, allowing his hands to linger on her legs and slide up her thighs. She looked at the paper, pulled her hair back over an ear—a small gesture but one that always made Silas feel contented—and untied the string and carefully opened the wrapping.

"Oh, my. Silas, where did you get this?"

"San Antonio."

It was a rebozo, a Mexican shawl made of emerald-green silk with tassels at each end.

"I don't know how you wear one of those," he said.

"I do," Emily said, unfolding the rebozo.

She stood, wrapped it around her red hair, around her shoulders, and down the sides of her naked body.

"I'm never taking this off," Emily said.

"Never?" and Silas slid his hands up her hips and kissed her belly.

She smiled, turned, and looked at herself in the washstand mirror. "I can't believe this. It's so gorgeous."

"It's very pretty," he said. "You're gorgeous."

They kissed again. And again.

"Next," Silas said. Emily sat at end of the bed as Silas dug into the treasure chamber.

"Next? Oh, my, what…"

Silas pulled from under the bed a much larger package, heavy, wrapped protectively in layers of paper. It had traveled far and Silas prayed for its contents, which he had not seen since he left San Antonio. As he lifted it, he listened for any telltale sounds of damage, but heard none. He set it on the bed and sat opposite Emily.

Still wearing her first two gifts, she untied the string and tore away the paper, layer after layer. She stopped and looked at Silas.

"Do you like it?" he asked.

"Do I…Silas…oh, my."

"I never even heard of a dressing case. But I thought you'd like it. I hope you like it."

"Like it? Oh, my sweet darling, I'd be horrible if I didn't love it."

The dressing case was made of rosewood and was approximately a foot square, slightly wider than it was tall or deep. The case's exterior was engraved with flowers and vines. It's corners, latches, and hinges were brass. She opened the lid to reveal five cut-glass bottles, Silas guessed for perfumes and what else he didn't know. Each bottle had a silver lid and silver around the base. The bottles, wrapped in cloth, had survived the trip from San Antonio.

On the inside of the lid was a beveled mirror with a silver gilt frame. The cut-glass bottles took up a row across the full width of the back of the case. In front of the bottles were two sections, each half the width of the box. They folded out to the sides, revealing small drawers lined with blue velvet and containing silver boxes, hand-held mirrors, hairbrushes, scented soaps, scissors, a mother-of-pearl pen knife. There were vanity tools, many of which Silas had no idea of their purpose. There was a ribbon threader, a glove-buttoning hook, and a crochet hook. There was a pencil and pencil case, a medicine spoon, a needle case.

"This is too much, Silas."

"I guess I can take it back."

"Don't you dare!"

They leaned forward and kissed, carefully with the dressing case between them. Silas wondered how to put the case back together, but Emily figured it out easily.

"One more," Silas said, carefully moving the dressing case onto the cabin table.

"Another?"

"Just one more, Emily."

"I didn't get you anything."

"I wouldn't say that," Silas said, and Emily blushed.

He withdrew from under the bed a rectangular box, six inches wide, four inches deep, and three inches tall. It, too, was wrapped in packing paper, which Silas removed to reveal flowered giftwrap. The flowers on the paper reminded Silas of the flowers Emily liked to wear in her hair.

He handed Emily the box. She took it, her hands shaking. She bit her lower lip, which also never failed to make Silas's heart skip, removed the giftwrap, and slowly opened the box. Her eyes grew wide, and she pushed the rebozo back from her head.

"This one," Silas said, "is my favorite." He lifted from the box a hair comb. Slender tendrils of silver flowed out in all directions, like the stems of Texas wildflowers. At the tips of some of stems were tiny pearls. At the tips of others were small, brilliant emeralds.

"I thought of you the moment I saw it," he said. "The emeralds made me think of your eyes."

Tears were welling in those emerald green eyes. "You remembered the color of my eyes."

"Emily, I memorized your face long ago."

She held herself together long enough for Silas to put the comb in her hair, just the way the ladies in the market had shown him.

Perfect.

Emily rushed to the mirror over the washstand. She put her hand over her mouth, and the tears flowed. Silas stood behind Emily, wrapped his arms around her, and kissed her neck.

"You are too good," she said. "Much, much too good for me."

"There is no such thing," he whispered in her ear. "Nothing is too good for you."

Emily separated herself from Silas and walked across the room. She removed the rebozo, folded it neatly, and set it on the chair with her clothes. She removed the bangle from her wrist and set it atop the rebozo. The emerald hair comb she kept on.

Then she took Silas by the hand and led him back to the bed.

And the night just kept getting better.

At some point, the lovers slept. He on his back, she on top of him, his arms around her, hers curled on his chest.

When they woke, Silas put on pants and went to find food. Instead of the plantation house's kitchen, he headed for the slaves' kitchen, where he was welcomed and hugged. He gave a brief, very tasteful recap of the previous evening, the details of which the cooks were able to guess. There was a what-took-you-so-long attitude, and the cooks provided biscuits, butter, honey, bacon, cheese, a pot of coffee, and plates, cups, napkins, and cutlery. He offered payment and they declined. He persisted and they refused. He insisted and they finally accepted and shooed him back to Emily.

"Oh, I can't believe all this," Emily said after the splendid meal. She was looking at her gifts and looking at Silas, who she had ordered out of his pants as soon as he set down the food for a nude breakfast in bed. "I've never been this happy."

Silas was remembering last night, when he was certain that seeing Emily standing naked before him was the most beautiful sight he would ever behold. This morning he realized he was wrong. She was more beautiful today, and in this moment, he understood that Emily would be even more beautiful tomorrow, and she would be so for the rest of their tomorrows.

She was on the verge of tears again. "I just..." And then she was crying.

"I really hope those are good tears."

"They are," she said, laughing and crying at the same time. "This has all been so wonderful."

They kissed again, and Silas realized he could not get enough of Emily's lips. Not ever.

"How did you manage to do this?" she asked. "This must have cost—"

"No, no," Silas cut her off. "Don't concern yourself about that. This was really important, and I just figured out how to make it happen."

She grabbed his face and kissed him, and set those green eyes on him. "Tell me how."

Silas realized she was going to get the story out of him and there was nothing he could do about it. "If you really want to know…" Silas lowered his eyes, then looked back up. "Henry and I robbed a bank."

Silas looked as serious as he could be, and Emily could detect no mirth in his tone. She just stared at him in shock.

"You didn't."

"Of course, I didn't."

Those green eyes narrowed.

"Just a little joke," he said.

"How!"

"I've been saving up for this for months," Silas said, which made her smile sweetly. "I had set some money aside, but what gave me the…resources…was cards."

"Cards?"

"I won at poker. See, my father taught me and my brother to play poker. He's going to teach Katie, my little sister. He says it's a good skill to have. Helps you read people and teaches you to think. You learn how to bluff."

"I think you learned to bluff a little too well."

"Sorry."

"I forgive you," she said. "With whom were you playing cards?"

"A crowd of government clerks in Houston. They figured some teenage kid was an easy mark. I laid on the innocent babe-in-the-woods act. They'd just been paid."

"Ouch. Long, dry month for them."

"That's just what someone else said."

"Was Algernon one of them?" Algernon Thompson had shown interest in Emily, as had just about every male between fourteen and seventy in the Brazos Valley. Emily's older brother, James, was a friend of Algernon and actively promoted the idea of their marriage.

But Emily found Algernon caustic and arrogant, and she wasn't about to marry someone just because her brother wanted her to.

"No," Silas said. "He wasn't in the game. I didn't want his money. Not for this."

"That's sweet. But next time, you have my permission to take every cent he has."

"Yes, ma'am. I'll remember that."

Silas and Emily had the next three days together. Three days that transformed a rough-walled, shabby little shack into Shangri-la, a paradise never to be dimmed in memory by the years. One afternoon, they stole down to a secluded stream, bathed together, and made love on the stream's bank, though they had to bathe again afterward to clean off the sand.

They dined at the Carters' house again. Silas transported Emily's gifts to their home, and they were greatly impressed.

They dined at Silas's parents' home and had a fine evening. Though there was never a word spoken about Emily and Silas's much more intimate and serious relationship, it was obvious, and Silas's mother and father were delighted. Younger brother Thomas feigned disinterest but was smitten with Emily, and little sister Katie was instantly drawn to Emily and spent the evening in her lap until bedtime, Katie's objections to which were cut short by Silas.

"You get ready for bed, Katie, and I'll tuck you in," he said. "And sing to you."

"About the moon and stars?" Katie brightened.

"From meadows magically rise," Silas said. Katie kissed Emily's cheek, then put out her arms and let her big brother carry her off to bed.

"Nighty night," Katie called to her parents, Thomas, and Emily.

"The moon and stars?" Emily said.

"It's called 'The Evening Song.' It's one of Katie's favorites," Duncan said.

"But she only wants Silas to sing it to her," Alice said, and a moment later Silas's voice drifted in from the bedroom.

"The moon is risen, beaming,
The golden stars are gleaming
So brightly in the skies;
The hushed, black woods are dreaming,
The mists, like phantoms seeming,
From meadows magically rise."

Every night Silas and Emily returned to the bare little cabin—the scent of its fresh-cut lumber now an aphrodisiac—and made love and slept in each other's arms on the narrow straw-stuffed mattress. They spoke of the future which they felt sure they would share, although the reality of the immediate future began to creep in. Silas would be leaving again, soon.

On their last night together, Emily cried after they made love, and Silas held her until the sun came up.

"Look at you," Sam McCulloch said as he reined in his horse at the cabin. Silas had saddled his horse, packed his bedroll and goods, and was holding Emily.

"Good morning, Sam," Silas said, still holding Emily. "You know Emily, don't you?"

"Of course. Good morning to you, Emily Perry. You look wonderful."

"Thank you, Mr. McCulloch."

"Please, call me Sam."

"Did you find what you were looking for?" Silas asked.

"Everything went well. Got us some answers. Everything good here?"

Silas looked at Emily. "Could not be better."

"You ready to head back?"

Silas sighed but nodded, still looking at Emily.

"I am truly sorry to take him away," Sam said. "But he'll be back."

Emily tore her eyes from Silas and fixed them on Sam, and Sam saw those sensational green eyes flash sternly.

"I want him back," she said. "I don't know what's going on. I understand it's something important, maybe dangerous. But I want him back. You hear me, Sam? You bring him home."

"Yes, ma'am," Sam said. No smile, no grin, no humor. Completely serious. "I'll give you two a moment. Take as much time as you need. It was very nice seeing you again, Emily." Sam turned his horse and rode off a bit.

"I don't know what you and he and probably some others are up to," she said. "I'm not going to ask. But you come back to me, Silas Grant. You come back to me."

They hugged, more urgently than they had in the days prior, each squeezing their eyes shut throughout the embrace. She kissed him, deep and hard, and started to turn away but Silas caught her arm.

"I'll be back. I promise. I will be back."

Emily tried to pull away but Silas held her gently and cradled her face in his hands.

"Know this: I am yours, Emily Perry. In every way, all that I am is yours. For me, there is no one else. Never has been, never will be."

Emily was crying. Without bothering to wipe away the tears, Silas kissed her as tenderly as he could. Emily buried her face in Silas's chest and hugged him tightly.

Silas lifted her face, his lips less than an inch from hers. "I love you, Emily. I love you, and I always will."

"I love you, Silas." She touched his cheek and they kissed.

Silas climbed into the saddle. He leaned down and kissed Emily again, and she turned and ran. Silas watched her go a moment, then followed Sam toward San Antonio.

CHAPTER 14

AS THE SAN Antonio River slid south out of the largest city in Texas, its passage turned southeast and twisted, wriggled, and zigzagged through ranch and farm country.

On a hill overlooking this contorted course, thirty miles from the Alamo, sat a large, white stone house, the sight of which told travelers that their journey from the Gulf Coast to San Antonio was almost complete. Whether dignitaries, diplomats, or carters hauling freight, all were welcome to pause and partake of Don Erasmo Seguin's hospitality at Casa Blanca.

Three weeks after adjourning their meeting at Erasmo's home in San Antonio, the Texians arrived at Casa Blanca on Seguin's nine-thousand-acre ranch. J.C. Neill arrived first from Galveston, followed a few hours later by Jacob Millsaps, Henry Karnes, and Horace Alsbury, who Millsaps and Karnes picked up from his ranch on the road from Goliad. The next day, Silas Grant and Sam McCulloch pulled in from the Brazos Valley.

The Texians settled into guest rooms in the massive hacienda. After weeks and a combined two thousand miles in the saddle, the Texians were tired, dusty, hungry, and very thirsty, and it was suggested they wait until morning for their information-sharing meeting. Curiosity, however, drove them to meet immediately.

They conceded, happily, to first sit down to dinner. Everyone headed to their rooms, cleaned off the Texas dirt, changed into clean clothes, and gathered in the hacienda's spacious dining room for a banquet. The Casa Blanca kitchen staff served venison and chicken and rabbit, chile guisado and tamales, onions and tomatoes and squash and beans, and warm tortillas, and the diners feasted on the Tejano cuisine.

After dinner, the Texians sipped tequila and smoked cigars—except Silas.

"You do not drink?" Erasmo asked.

"I mean no offense, Señor Seguin," Silas said. "I just don't care for the taste of alcohol."

"No offense taken."

"Try this, Silas," Señora Seguin said and offered a glass of a red beverage. "It's called agua fresca."

"Fresh water?"

"Yes, but sweetened with sugar and the juice of many fruits."

"Thank you," he said, and took a sip. "Oh, that's wonderful." Silas took another long drink. "I need a canteen of this for the next long ride."

"Uh, Señora Seguin, could I please get one of those?" Jacob asked.

The Señora had a pitcher of agua fresca and glasses brought to the dining room. "I'll leave you gentlemen to your deliberations."

"Please, Maria, you do not need to leave," Erasmo said. "Gentlemen, do you object to my wife remaining with us?"

There was no objection. Señora Seguin went to the sideboard, poured herself a glass of tequila, and headed toward a seat next to her husband. She paused at Silas's shoulder and leaned down to his ear.

"Emily is a lovely girl," she said.

Silas turned toward the Señora. "How did you know?" he said, but she just smiled and took her seat. Silas snapped his head toward Sam, who was looking at the ceiling.

"What have we learned?" Erasmo opened. "I'm not sure how we begin. Perhaps we should each report what we uncovered and go from there."

"I'll start," J.C. said. "I spoke with George Dolson, who was interpreter for prisoner interrogations in Galveston. He recounted the testimony of two senior Mexican officers who were in the Alamo. These officers told similar stories, that Crockett was captured and executed. However, the stories directly contradict one another in significant details, and the discrepancies are impossible to resolve. Dolson questioned their motives. I believe we can eliminate their testimony."

Juan Seguin spoke next. "I spoke to witnesses who were in the Alamo either during or immediately after the battle. Young Enrique Esparza said he saw Crockett, with whom he was familiar, at the beginning of the battle at the south end of the Alamo, between the gate and the chapel. That would put him in the vicinity of the palisade."

"The area the Tennesseans were defending," Erasmo said.

"However, Eulalia Yorba, who entered the Alamo after the battle's conclusion, thinks she saw Crockett dead in the plaza."

"The witnesses in town I spoke with peddle in exaggerations and wild stories," Erasmo said. "No substance at all."

"Don Pancho Ruiz and Señora Candelaria?" Juan said.

"Yes," Erasmo sighed.

"Speaking of wild rumors," Silas said. "The Brazos Valley is awash in them. The story of Crockett in the mine has folks all in a lather. Everyone is convinced he died, but there is no consensus on how or where. Crockett died by sword, by gunshot, by bayonet, by lance. Crockett died at the gate, at the chapel, on the north wall, in the plaza. There were some spirited arguments. The main thing I came away with, no one believes he surrendered, and no one believes he's alive."

"Just useless tales," Sam said.

"One thing, though," Silas added. "Since everyone believes him dead, if he is alive, it may be possible for him to re-enter the world under a new identity."

"I think Mr. la Branche and Mr. Ellis would appreciate that," Erasmo said.

"Now, Silas," Henry jumped in. "Is that truly all you learned?"

Silas looked at Henry, who was smirking contentedly, and at Sam, who was again transfixed by the dining-room ceiling. An involuntary smile slowly spread across Silas's face.

"No," Silas said. "I also learned that Emily Perry is in love with me."

The room exploded in applause and the Texians slapped Silas on the back. Silas blushed but did not mind.

"Yeah, they are definitely in love," Sam said. "I saw them together. And, by the way," Sam paused and pointed around the room, "if we don't get Silas back to Emily in one piece, we might as well not come home. There'll be no place in Texas any of us could hide."

"So?" Henry pressed. "You gonna marry her?"

Silas nodded. "If she'll have me. Someday, when I can support her. Yes. I'm very much in love with her."

More applause and back slaps.

"Dang, Silas won the heart of the prettiest girl in Texas," Henry said.

"Congratulations, Silas," Horace said.

"I'm very happy for you," Juan said. "I have not had the pleasure of meeting Señorita Perry. While I have no doubt she is quite lovely, do all of you truly believe she is the prettiest girl in Texas?"

"Oh, yes," Sam, Henry, J.C., and Horace testified in unison. "Lord, yes," Henry added.

"Really?" Juan said.

"Yes, indeed," Señora Seguin said, which was accompanied by vigorous head nods all around. Juan raised an eyebrow.

"Now that we've embarrassed Silas," J.C. said, "can we move on?"

"Sure," a grinning Sam said. His face turned serious. "I found Joe, up where they're planning the new capital at Waterloo. Joe's still a slave. He was rented out to a crew cutting trees. He told me he saw Crockett near the palisade, next to the chapel. He said Crockett was in his buckskin coat. Joe was in the Alamo through the whole siege, and being around Travis, he would have known Crockett well."

"That sounds like dependable information," Erasmo said.

"I agree," Sam said. "And I don't think he felt he had anything to gain by telling me. Immediately after the battle, he told stories that might have been embellished, but it got him nothing. I think he was truthful."

Horace was next. "Juana didn't see Crockett. She was in her quarters during the battle. Afterward, and was escorted out by her brother-in-law. I don't believe she saw anything of use to us. But it was good to talk about it. We...cleared the air. I think we're both better for it."

"That is good, my friend," Erasmo said. "Gentlemen, what of Mrs. Dickinson?"

"Once Jacob got her to calm down, I think she give us the truth," Henry said.

"Susanna said that when the Mexicans walked her out of the chapel, she saw Crockett," Jacob said. "He was at the palisade, and his leg was badly maimed. She thought maybe a cannon ball hit him. His leg was almost blown off."

"We also visited Madam Powell," Henry said. "The Powells never seen a column come from the west to join the rest of the army. We traced the Mexican retreat and couldn't find sign of a smaller unit comin' from San Antonio. We followed the trail all the way to Goliad. If they snuck Crockett out, I'm bettin' they come from San Antonio down El Camino Real to Goliad."

The reports were complete. As he had at the planning meeting, J.C. was taking notes. "What have we got?" he said. "Three witnesses, who seem to be reliable, saw Crockett at the palisade, two before the fight, one after. We also have a reliable witness, Señora Yorba, who said Crockett was in the plaza."

"Juan, do you think Señora Yorba met Crockett?" Silas asked.

Juan looked at his father. "It is possible she saw him in town before the Mexicans arrived," Erasmo said.

"But she was not in the fort during the siege," Juan added.

"I wonder how she identified him," Silas said. "Was she identifying Crockett or someone who fit his description?"

"She said the dead man she saw was tall, about fifty years old, wearing a coat and woolen shirt," Juan said.

"Wait," Silas said. "Sam, didn't you say Joe saw Crockett wearing buckskin?"

"That's right, he did," Sam confirmed.

"How many men of that age were in the Alamo?" Silas asked.

"A few," Juan said. "You know, now that I think of it, Crockett didn't look his age."

"No, looked younger," Henry said.

"Possible she saw someone else," J.C. said.

"An older man, tall, in a coat and woolen shirt," Jacob said. "That might have been…"

"No, Jacob," Juan said. "Your brother wasn't that old, was he?"

"No. But he looked older. Looked older than Crockett." He stopped, thought for a moment. "I think she saw my brother."

The Texians fell quiet.

"Did she say how he died?" Jacob said, almost a whisper.

"She said he was shot in the chest," Juan recounted. "From what she said, it sounds like he died quickly."

Jacob closed his eyes, nodded.

"I am sorry, Jacob," Henry said, putting his hand on his friend's shoulder.

"So…what does this all mean?" Jacob said.

"I think…" Silas began, thinking out loud. "We've got all these different stories. But when we cull out the questionable testimony, a single, dependable account of Crockett takes shape. We have multiple witnesses who put him at the palisade."

"Where his men were stationed," Horace said. "Everything we know of the battle points to the last of the defenders making a final stand next to the chapel at the palisade. It's certainly reasonable that Crockett would have been there."

"Especially since we have no consistent account of him being anywhere else," J.C. said.

"Something else Joe mentioned," Sam said. "After Travis died, Joe hid in a room. Through a loophole, he saw the Mexicans dragging that big eighteen-pound cannon in the direction of the chapel and the palisade. He heard that cannon fire."

"Which backs up Dickinson's story," Jacob said.

"How long could someone survive with that kind of injury?" Silas asked.

"I've heard of fellas lose an arm or leg and live," Henry said.

"But he would have needed medical attention quickly," said Horace, who had some medical training. "Stopping blood loss would be critical."

"How could he have received such care?" Erasmo said. "We heard stories that the Mexican army lacked treatment for the wounded."

"Jacob and me saw the result followin' the Mexican retreat," Henry said. "Their wounded died all along the road."

"We know of no surgeons in the Alamo after the battle," Erasmo said.

Horace sat up. "Perhaps we do. Juana said, after she and her sister were brought out of their room, she saw a tall officer wearing a shako with a red plume and three other men headed toward the chapel. They could have just as easily been headed toward the palisade. And one of them was not in uniform. She didn't think he was Mexican."

"Perhaps a civilian doctor?" J.C. suggested. "Did any go missing from the town?"

"No," Erasmo said. "I think our physicians hid themselves away."

"Very wise," Jacob said.

"No, wait," Henry said, and closed his eyes. "Wait…wait… when I was in Matamoros to get our prisoners free…"

"And got locked up." Sam couldn't resist.

"But escaped! After I got locked up, the Texians I talked to said somethin' 'bout a doctor got captured down south…dang it, can't remember the name…uh…Burn or Torn…"

"Thorn?" Juan said.

"That's it! Thorn," Henry said.

"I recall a Dr. Thorn captured by Urrea's troops," Juan said.

"Anybody ever hear of him again?" Silas asked.

No one had.

"Something else Joe said," Sam recalled. "He saw a general headed toward the south end of the Alamo. He thought he was a general because of his fancy uniform and fancy hat. When Joe was brought out, he saw that general standing in the middle of those Tennessee boys."

"Why would a general be making sure everyone was dead?" J.C. said. "He'd leave that to the enlisted men. Let them do the dirty work. So, why?"

"Unless…" Silas said. "Unless he was taking charge of…"

From the beginning, this entire ridiculous, unthinkable premise had been impossible.

Until it was possible.

CHAPTER 15

NONE OF THE Texians slept well the night after the meeting at Casa Blanca.

When this adventure began, Silas found the imaginings difficult to quell. The possibility of rescuing the legendary David Crockett was the stuff of boyhood dreams. But now those childish thoughts of glory had been pushed aside by the reality of Emily, who was his life's dream. When he closed his eyes, he did not see Crockett or the Alamo. He only saw Emily and her green eyes and loving smile.

But for the Revolution veterans, the revelations were disturbing. Disquieting. Millsaps, Karnes, Alsbury, Juan Seguin, and Neill had been at Alamo during its capture in December 1835 or in the days leading up to its fall, and they and McCulloch had left friends within the fortress walls. Fellow Texians who died on that horrible Sunday morning, and these discoveries were ripping each man's guilty conscious from the graveyard of their memories.

There was no cause for that guilt, save that they were alive and their friends were dead. But this episode offered a tantalizing chance to clear some of that guilt by bringing just one of those friends back. And each man seized on that chance.

★

The Texians awoke the next morning energized to continue the investigation. At first light, Juan prepared to lead them to the Alamo and from there to follow the road south to Goliad.

"What are we looking for?" Silas asked. He reasoned that any traces of the passing of a small column of soldiers and wagons would long since have vanished.

"We're lookin'," Henry said as he climbed in the saddle, "for whatever we can find." His back ached and his backside protested as he settled onto a sorrel gelding. "Dang it. I was kinda hopin' for a few days without seein' a horse."

"Everybody ready?" J.C. called.

"I suggest we follow Cibolo Creek north for any signs of the Mexican army's passage," Juan said. "Turn west to San Antonio and follow El Camino Real from the Alamo to Goliad."

"Any chance they would have taken a different route?" Silas asked. "Maybe get off the road and go due south for Mexico?"

"Doubtful," Horace said. "That would be rough going in this country, and the road would be less traumatic for a wounded man. Besides, they didn't need to hide. They owned the road."

The ride north and then west was quiet and uneventful, giving up no clues, and they pulled into San Antonio at dusk, riding silently past the darkening Alamo. After dinner, they split up for the night, some staying in Juan Seguin's home, the rest at Señora Candelaria's inn.

The next day, the Texians rose early, slipped out of town, crossed the bridge over the San Antonio River onto the Calle de la Alameda, turned north, walked their mounts into the Alamo's plaza, and there gathered in the pre-dawn where Crockett and his fellows once stood. The chapel stood to their left, the timbers and barricades of the palisade long since gone.

A few minutes later, the dawn blazed red and orange, lighting up clouds over the chapel. At an unspoken command, the Texians mounted and headed south.

Their path paralleled the course of the San Antonio River southeast toward Goliad through South Texas brush country. The road was edged with thorns. Mesquite was everywhere, entangled with great colonies of cactus and fields of grasses, ready to reclaim the rutted path if the passage of humans ceased.

They made their way slowly, examining every road and path. They found burned farms, ransacked houses, and deserted cabins. A handful of new farms had gone up further off the road, as if an extra hundred yards would protect them from future raiders.

They inquired at every farm, every cabin, every house. They spoke to every traveler they met, but no one knew anything or they simply refused to speak, ducking inside cabins or hurrying away.

"Lot of fear around here," Silas said.

"Bandits have been in the area," Horace said. "Army deserters who decided not to go back to Mexico."

Each evening, they carefully cleared a camp site, choosing not to impose on the frightened farmers who were barely eking out a living.

Late morning of the fourth day, near the confluence of the San Antonio River and Cleto Creek, they came upon a farm being worked by a Tejano man, his wife, and two boys. The man was Silas's height, with broad shoulders and a thin mustache. His posture showed the strain of years of hard work in the Texas heat. His shirt and pants were homemade of cotton. He wore a sombrero, a worn pair of brogans, and a dirty bandana about his neck. A pair of pigs rooted near the farm's cabin, and further back sat a chicken coop. Several hens scratched in the yard.

"Good morning, sir," Juan called in Spanish. "I apologize for the interruption. Could we speak to you for a moment?"

"A moment," the man allowed.

"My name is Juan Seguin. I am a senator in the Republic of Texas legislature. My friends and I are looking into the damages caused by the Mexican army two years ago."

"A little late for that," the farmer said.

"May I ask your name, sir?"

The farmer eyed them warily. "Sotero."

"It is very nice to meet you, sir." Juan noticed a pair of wooden crosses a short distance from the cabin.

"You want to know of damages?" Sotero walked to the graves and stared down at them. "The Mexican army stole from us. They stole when they marched north and they stole when the crawled south. They took our food, our animals. They destroyed our crops. My youngest child, our daughter, died in her mother's arms. A soldier threw my wife aside to get at a basket of corn. The baby hit her head. For a basket of corn. We would have given them the corn."

He looked up at Juan, grief and anger competing in his eyes. "My eldest son tried to protect his mother. The soldiers bayoneted him. His mother and I saw him die. My children are buried here."

Horace removed his hat, bowed his head, and said a prayer. The other Texians uncovered as well, as did Sotero.

"I am very sorry for your loss," Juan said when Horace had finished.

"Were they with the army or renegades?" Jacob asked. "We've heard of renegade Mexican soldiers raiding farms and ranches."

"The army stole from us. The outlaw soldiers murdered my children."

"I am very sorry, Sotero. There is no way the Republic can possibly compensate for such loss. But here," and Juan handed Sotero a small bag of money. "Fifty dollars from the Republic of Texas." The money was not from the Republic of Texas but from the Seguins' own pockets. Juan brought money in case it was needed to encourage witnesses to talk. This seemed like a better use. "I know it is not much, but perhaps it will help feed your family."

"Thank you, Mr. Seguin," Sotero said. "I know of your family. You are honorable people. Thank you."

"Are there many farmers in the area?" Horace asked.

"A few. We get by. There are Tejanos and Whites. We get along. We trade with each other. Eggs, corn, beans, flour, sugar, meat. Meat is very scarce."

"I saw signs of javelina about a mile back," Henry said. "Silas, Sam, you feel like doing a little huntin' for these folks?"

"Be a pleasure," Sam answered, and Henry, Sam, and Silas rode back up the road.

"May we ask a few questions?" Juan said, and Sotero nodded. "When did the Mexican army pass through here?"

"The last of them came through in the summer two years ago. A general, I believe his name was Andrade, led them."

"I met Andrade," Juan said. "He was in command when we took the surrender of the Alamo, after San Jacinto." Juan turned back to Sotero. "Did any other soldiers come through?"

"No, Andrade's men were the last. There was some before, but not many."

"Before? Before Andrade?"

"Yes, but only a small group. Maybe ten men."

"Any officers?" Juan asked.

"Yes, there was an officer. A very fine officer. I don't know his name but he was very, very tall, taller than any Mexican I have ever seen. He wore a tall soldier's hat. I don't know what it is called…"

"A shako?" Juan said.

"Yes, a shako. The tall officer had a shako with a high red plume."

"That fits the description of the officer Juana saw," Horace said.

"Why do you remember this officer, Sotero?" Juan asked.

"Because he told his men not to steal from us, and he was very polite. The others, coming north, going south, no one else did that. The other officers, the generals, they told their men to take what they want. This fine officer did not do that. He just asked for water, and he gave me five pesos for the water. But the water was not for him. He gave it to the man with them."

"What man?" Juan asked.

"The man in the wagon. He was not Mexican. He got out of the wagon, and there was blood on his clothes. He thanked me for the water and got back in the wagon."

"Was anyone else in the wagon?"

"I could not see. It had a roof and the sides were covered with canvas."

"And this wagon was accompanied by this tall officer and ten soldiers?"

"Yes."

"Have you seen any other Mexican soldiers?" Horace asked.

"No, no others. Well, just one. He was with Andrade's men, but he quit. He was limping from a wound, and he just stopped, sat by the road, and let the others go. The others did not say anything to him. They just walked on while he sat over there." Sotero pointed to a shady copse on the other side of the road.

"Do you know what happened to him?" Juan said.

"Oh, yes. He asked if we could give him something to eat. He said he was starving. I was afraid to say no in case he might hurt my family, but he said he would work on our farm. He stayed here for a few months. Now he lives on an abandoned farm not far from here."

"Where?"

"Why? What do you want with him?"

"Just to talk," Juan said. "He is not our enemy."

Sotero considered this for a moment. "His farm is two miles over there," and Sotero pointed west. "A little further south, there is a path off the road to his farm. We see each other from time to time and help each other. He is a good man."

The remaining Texians passed the rest of the day helping on the farm, repairing the chicken coop and the cabin's crooked front door, cutting back brush to make room to plant more corn, and continuing to speak with Sotero for additional information.

They heard distant, sporadic gunshots, causing Sotero's wife to panic. Juan assured her it was their friends hunting, but the Texians kept their weapons close in case he was wrong.

Three hours after their departure, the hunting party returned with three javelinas, field dressed and ready for the cookfire or to be smoked and dried. The idea of javelina jerky sounded horrid, but Juan imagined it sounded much better to those with no meat at all.

"Nice work, Henry," Juan said.

"I got one of 'em," he said.

"Good work, Sam!" Juan said, but Sam just grunted a response.

"Dang it, Silas got two," Henry said.

"I'm blasting away without hitting a thing, and sharpshooter Grant here got two of the critters," Sam complained.

"I just got lucky," Silas said.

"Yeah, well, the way I hear, you been gettin' lucky a lot lately," Henry said.

Silas just smiled and carried one of the carcasses to a cookfire that Jacob had started.

Sotero was delighted, and the Texians helped prepare what for his family was a feast. The Texians ate sparingly, reserving most of the meat for Sotero and his kin.

That evening, after Sotero and his family had gone to bed with full bellies for the first time in months, the Texians gathered around the fire and reported to Henry, Sam, and Silas what Sotero had said.

"Sounds like Sotero saw the same officer and civilian that Juana saw," J.C. said.

"God almighty, that sure sounds like what we been lookin' for," Henry said. "I can't believe this. Fellas, is this really true?"

Jacob shook his head. "It's getting hard to disbelieve."

"We should reach Goliad tomorrow," Juan said. "But first, we visit this Mexican soldier and hear what he has to say."

"Did Sotero tell you this man's name?" Silas asked.

"Yeah," Horace said. "Said his name is Rafael Vega."

CHAPTER 16

HIRAM BROWN DROPPED his saddle bags on the floor and dropped himself into a chair, the same chair from which he had been launched on his odyssey forty-six days ago.

Forty-six days on the road or at sea, from Mexico City to Veracruz, Houston, San Antonio, Copano Bay, and New Orleans, and back to Veracruz and Mexico City. All he wanted now was his own bed. But first, he had to report to the Envoy Extraordinary and Minister Plenipotentiary of the United States.

"I don't think I've ever seen you so tired," Powhatan Ellis said.

"I don't think I've ever been so tired," Brown said.

"Well?"

"Your suspicions are confirmed."

Ellis sighed and fell back into the depths of his brown-leather armchair, slipping deeply into the embrace of the chair's wingbacks. "I was hoping you would tell me how foolish I was. In the time you were away, I had convinced myself I was wrong."

"I am the bearer of bad news. Confirmed not by one, but by seven Texians."

"Seven? How many people did you bring into this?"

"Mr. la Branche and I agree that all of these men are trust-worthy. I'm not concerned about leaks. Regardless, no one would believe such a story."

"Unless they show the sketch."

"They wouldn't. And they can't," Brown reached into the saddle bags and fished out the sketch. "The point is, seven men who knew Crockett, more recently than you, independently identified the man in the sketch as Crockett."

"Independently?"

"We had them view the sketch one at a time."

"With no prompting—"

"None."

"No suggestions of who this was—"

"None."

Ellis leaned on his left elbow and rested his chin in his hand. He stayed that way for three seconds before pushing himself up. "Very well. We must determine the provenance of that sketch. That means finding the artist, this Mrs. Ward."

"She's still in country?"

"Nowhere else for her to go."

"Do you know where she is?"

"Not at the moment, but I should be able to find out. The Calderón de la Barcas are still sight-seeing Mexico, with occasional returns to Mexico City. Give me a day or two to learn where they and Mrs. Ward are, and you go see them. Talk to Ward. Show her the sketch and find out all you can. What steps are our friends in Texas taking?"

"They're investigating what might have transpired two years ago," Brown said. "Hopefully they'll learn if there is any substance beyond this," and he held the sketch aloft, "rather paper-thin proof we have now. They're resourceful men. I have confidence in them.

The other question is, what do we do if he's alive and we determine his location? I assume you've given thought to a resolution."

"I've thought of damned little else since you left."

"If I may," Brown said, "I believe the Texians could be useful. Any actions they take in Mexico would afford us deniability. If they fail, if they're killed or captured, they are rogues or agents of a foreign government and not affiliated with the United States. Texians have gotten themselves into trouble in Mexico before. It would not reflect on us."

"Are they capable?"

"Quite."

"And the French?"

"I spoke with Dubois, the ambassador to Texas, when I was in Houston. While they don't know the details of the situation, they will allow access to Veracruz and will look the other way as long as we don't interfere with their operations."

"Very well," Ellis said. "Once we learn where Crockett is, you return to Texas with that information. We can use *Woodbury* to transport you and the Texians."

"It is standing by as we speak, anchored outside Veracruz."

"Good."

"And if the Texians fail?"

"We deny all knowledge of their actions. We deny all knowledge of them."

"And Crockett?"

Ellis shook his head. This kind of cloak-and-dagger adventurism was not normally part of his portfolio, but Washington would regard it as his responsibility. He felt trapped, squeezed into a corner with only one way out.

"That will be where you come in," Ellis said. "We need him out of Mexico. Or dead."

It took a couple of days for Ellis to learn the travel plans of the Spanish Minister Plenipotentiary and his wife. The minister did not yet have a legation or embassy; rather he was representing Spain by traveling the country. While Mexico wasn't ready to forgive and forget three hundred years of conquest and subjugation, the gracious minister and his charming wife had endeared themselves to the Mexican people.

"Powhatan," Luis Cuevas greeted Ellis at the office of the Mexican Secretary of Foreign Affairs. "I was told you need assistance. Nothing serious, I hope."

"No, Luis," Ellis said. "I apologize in advance but I wasn't sure where to turn. You remember Madame Calderón de la Barca, don't you?"

"A difficult woman to forget."

"Indeed. She asked about sending correspondence to the United States. The blockade has cut off the packet ships which handle such deliveries. I have a ship that the French are allowing passage through the blockade for humanitarian purposes, and I wish to extend the service to Madame Calderón de la Barca. Problem is, I don't know where she and her husband are. I can send one of my assistants to meet her, pick up her correspondence, and deliver it to Veracruz."

"I believe I can help you," Cuevas said. "The minister is keeping my office informed of their travels. Let me check their schedule for the next few days."

It had rained the night before, and Real del Monte was exploding in greenery and blossoms the morning Hiram Brown arrived.

With the Spanish minister's travel plans in hand, it was simple for Brown to intercept the minister and his wife. It was just a matter of selecting a location for the meeting, and a scenic setting, Ellis hoped, would ensure that Mrs. Ward and her sketch pad would be present.

Real del Monte, Brown mused, qualified as scenic.

It was a two-day ride northeast from Mexico City to the mountain mining town that was one of the wealthiest in Mexico. It was also one of the least Mexican cities in Mexico.

The Spanish discovered gold and silver in the sixteenth century, but by the eighteenth century, production was down due to flooding in the mines. By the time the Spanish were kicked out of Mexico, mining in the region was down to a trickle of its former prodigious levels. So the Mexicans brought in experts—Cornish miners from England.

Possessing state-of-the-art technology and led by Cornish miner Francis Rule, the imports revived the mines and brought production back to full. Money flowed, not least of all to Rule, and the town took on a decidedly English style.

Brown headed for Rule's house, where the minister and his wife were being received at a small morning reception and to which Ellis had gained an invitation.

The Rule house sat high on the mountain slope with a view of the city and the valley below. A fire crackled in large fireplace. Rule and his wife had rolled out an English breakfast of eggs, toast, bacon, grilled tomatoes, and sausages but with some Mexican touches, including a cream cheese with a sweet chili sauce, garlic, chopped red chiles, and green onions.

Brown, sharp but uncomfortable in suit and tie and polished shoes, mingled and listened but heard nothing of substance, nor had he been able to identify Mrs. Ward.

Well-fed, the group left the house to visit the mining operation. The city's upper streets, which the English had cut through a forest of oak and pine, were filled with a mix of Indigenous and European residents, and Madame Calderón de la Barca stopped the tour when she spotted a redheaded man with a Scottish brogue and began speaking with her kinsman.

While the minister's wife was occupied, Brown noticed a handsome woman, about fifty years old, in a brightly colored dress with lace at the collar. She had a sketchpad and was taking advantage of the pause in the procession to draw Real del Monte's church.

The group started to move again and eventually gathered around a ladder leading into the narrow entrance to a mine shaft, which Madame Calderón de la Barca was disappointed to learn was off limits to the tour.

"This mine we call Delores," Rule explained to the group. "The miners wear a tallow candle on a cap on their heads…"

It sounded like Rule was launching into a long, prepared speech, and the artist quickly lost interest and returned to sketching the church. Brown approached her.

"That's very impressive," Brown said to the woman. "You have talent."

"Oh, thank you," she said, slightly startled. "It's an old habit. I see something interesting and I just want to draw it. Places, people, anything."

"You are American?"

"Yes! You sound like you are as well."

"Where are you from?" Brown asked.

"Philadelphia originally. Now I live in New York."

"We're practically neighbors! I'm from Boston."

"Oh, how nice to meet a fellow Yank. This trip has been wonderful, but I miss home."

"I understand. I've been here two years," Brown lied.

"I couldn't stand being away that long."

"Part of my job, I'm afraid. I'm special assistant to Powhatan Ellis."

"Oh, yes, the American minister. My name is Mrs. Edith Ward."

"A pleasure to meet you, Mrs. Ward. I'm Hiram Brown."

"It's so nice to meet you, Mr. Brown."

"The style of your art reminds me of a picture Minister Ellis admired." Brown pretended to study Mrs. Ward's sketch. "Yes, your technique is an exact match. Are you by chance traveling with the Calderón de la Barcas?"

"Why, yes I am. Fanny and I are old friends."

"I believe it's you I came to find. You see…this is rather embarrassing…Minister Ellis so admired one of your sketches that he accidentally took it from a display at the Prussian minister's reception for the Calderón de la Barcas. I believe it's yours."

Brown pulled the sketch from his coat pocket.

"Yes, that is my work!"

"The minister offers his sincere apologies. He was admiring it when he took ill at the reception. He put on his coat to leave and apparently the sketch got caught up in his coat. He recently found it and asked me to find the artist. I've been looking for days."

"Oh, my," Mrs. Ward said. "Such a fuss over a sketch. Please, tell the minister to keep it. I'm delighted he so enjoyed it."

Which was precisely what Brown had expected. This was going well. Now just one more bit of information and he was home.

"Thank you, that's very kind. One question, though. Can you tell me anything about this sketch? Mr. Ellis wondered where you found this subject."

"Oh, dear…" Mrs. Ward stammered. "I have such a dreadful memory. I'm afraid I don't remember. I remember the gentleman.

Such a nice man, but I can't remember where I saw him. We've traveled so much, you see."

Damn, Brown thought.

"I quite understand. The thing is, this looks very much like an old friend of Mr. Ellis, and the minister desperately wants to find him. He's a dear friend, and it would mean the world to him to know where you made this sketch."

"Oh, dear, I just...I just can't remember...I..." Mrs. Ward paused. "I know."

Brown's hopes soared.

"Fanny keeps a journal of our travels," Mrs. Ward said. "If you let me keep the sketch, perhaps I can look at the journal and figure out where I saw him."

"Uh, well, certainly," Brown said and hesitantly handed over the sketch which he had protected with his life for almost two months.

"I promise to return it to Mr. Ellis."

"Mrs. Ward, you are very kind. Thank you. This means the world to the minister."

"How can I contact you?" Mrs. Ward asked.

"You can contact myself or Minister Ellis at the United States legation in Mexico City. Just send a message and we'll meet you any place that is convenient."

"Thank you, Mr. Brown. It was so nice meeting you, but I should get back to the group."

"A delight meeting you. I hope you enjoy the rest of your visit."

Brown bowed and departed. The meeting had gone so well but had come up just short of the goal. Still, there was a chance to get the answer they needed.

CHAPTER 17

SOTERO'S DIRECTIONS WERE good. Two miles down the road to Goliad, the Texians found a path leading through the brush to the west. It was narrow but freshly traveled, and footprints in the path suggested a lone mule led by a man on foot.

"How we handlin' this?" Henry asked. "Seven armed Texians go ridin' in there, he's like to get spooked, him bein' a Mexican soldado."

"He might think we're hunting him," Jacob agreed. "Maybe think we're here to chase him off his land. Or hang him."

"I'll go in alone," Juan said. "Perhaps he will be less intimidated by a kinsman."

"And if he's armed?" Jacob said.

"How 'bout the rest of us circle round the place?" Henry said. "Jacob and me go 'round to the right, Silas and Sam to the left. J.C. and Horace, you back up Juan. Juan, give us half an hour to get in position. You go in, slow. Ever'one stay out of sight but stay close. If there's any trouble, we'll come in fast."

Juan, J.C., and Horace got off the road and hid back in the trees in case Vega appeared while the rest of the Texians surrounded the farm. Thirty minutes later, the trio started down the mule path, then Alsbury and Neill laid back while Seguin proceeded alone. After a short distance, Juan decided to dismount. An approaching stranger would be less threatening on foot than mounted.

He hoped.

The mule path meandered through mesquite and cactus which had not been cleared well off the trail's edges. Intentionally, Juan figured. It was slowing him and would certainly impede any raiders while also preventing an unobstructed view ahead.

Juan had walked a mile when the dense scrub finally started to thin, and he could just make out a clearing ahead with a jacal. It was about as ramshackle a home as you could find. Walls of mesquite and oak branches plastered with mud, with rocks around the base and a thatched roof on top. A door of lashed-together oak branches was held in place with leather hinges, and a loop of rope served as a door handle.

Patches of corn, beans, and squash were on either side of the jacal, and a handful of chickens wandered in the front yard. A mule was tied up in front of the jacal. A man suddenly appeared from behind the jacal, walking without alarm from one field to the other and carrying a hoe over his shoulder. The man limped. He was dressed in simple cotton pants and shirt, a sash for a belt, a sombrero, and sandals.

"Rafael!" The man stopped. "Sotero sent me," Juan called in Spanish. "May I come in?"

Vega took the hoe off his shoulder and held in both hands. "Slowly," he commanded.

Seguin walked his horse from the mule path into the clearing in front of the jacal. He walked with his hands out and raised, his horse's reins in one and the other empty. Once he was in the clearing, he stopped.

"Sotero sent you?" Vega said. "Why? Who are you and what do you want?"

"My name is Juan Seguin. Sotero said you might be able to help me."

"Help you?" Vega spat. "How can I help you? Look at this place. Look at me." He removed his sombrero. He had dark, lank hair and dark eyes. He looked twenty years older than he probably was. "How can I help a rich man like you. Why would I help a rich man like you?"

"If you know me and my family, you know—"

"I don't know you. But I can see you are rich by your fine horse and fine saddle, and your fine clothes and fine boots. But, yes," he nodded, "I recognize your name. Are you Texians still hunting Mexicans? Still avenging your dead friends? If you wish to kill me, I cannot stop you. Call your friends. I know they're out there. Call them and kill me. Shoot me or hang me. There is a tree over there," and Vega pointed behind Seguin. "It has a fine limb to hang a Mexican."

"Rafael, I am not hunting you. My friends and I are not here to kill you."

"Bring them in and let's see. You may still decide to hang me." Vega put the business end of the hoe on the ground, leaned on the handle, and waited.

"J.C., Horace!" Juan called over his shoulder. "Sam, Henry, come on in."

Juan stayed back out of range of Vega's hoe while the rest of the Texians entered the clearing from all sides. They were careful not to trample Vega's crops.

The Texians ringed Vega.

"Not hunting, eh?" Vega snarled. "Looks like you're hunting."

"Gentlemen, please," Juan said. "Dismount and join me." The Texians did as asked and gathered around Juan. "Rafael, we are not going to hang you."

"We was just bein' cautious," Henry said.

"It's a good time to be cautious, is it not?" Vega said. "All sorts of bad men are about. You say you need my help and are not going to hang me." Vega narrowed his eyes. "I'm not sure I believe you. I think you may hang me, but perhaps you will disappoint me."

"You sound like you want to die," Jacob said.

"Almost everyone I know is dead. My friends in the Toluca Battalion are dead. Or maimed. The rest walked a thousand miles home. Many of them died on the way, and to return to what? To fight for men who despise us? The fighting goes on. Did you know that? In Mexico, they are still fighting. General against general. Men like Santa Anna and Urrea. No more. I'm done killing. I sold my musket and uniform to buy a few chickens and some seeds. I made a chair and a bed. That is all I need. I stay here, but I know you Texians will come soon enough to chase me off this land. Or hang me. Either way, you will take my land. If not you, others who look like you."

"I understand you not wanting to kill," Jacob said. "But why join the army?"

"Join? I didn't join." Vega laughed. "Few of us joined. We were forced into the army. Taken from our homes, given a rifle and bayonet, and told to march on empty bellies."

"The Mexican army took plenty of food from all over Texas," Henry said.

"Yes, the Mexican *army* took food," Vega said. "But Mexican soldiers did not eat the food. That went to the officers, into their bellies and onto their wagons and mules. Our officers were gathering goods to create their own colonies in Texas. Officers like that bastard Huerta, pretending to be kind and a gentleman, but he is a cruel, evil man. And that coward Ramirez pocketed money that was supposed to buy us food and medicine. They *sold* food to us. They transported crackers and rice and salt in sacks. In gunny sacks! The rain came and the sacks got wet and the food rotted. Can you imagine carrying crackers in gunny sacks?"

Vega shook his head and tossed down the hoe, which clanged on the rocky ground. A chicken squawked in alarm.

"Huerta, Ramirez, Tornel, Pavón. They are all santanistas. Loyal to their president no matter what. But what could we soldiers do? We were hundreds of miles from home. To leave would have meant being shot. So," Vega shrugged, "we marched. We marched and we fought. We killed you and you killed us. For what?"

"Were all the officers bad?"

"No," Vega said, and slowly shook his head. "Not all. Lieutenant Heredia was a very good man. Captain Macotela. But they're dead. I was running to help Captain Macotela when I was shot in the leg," Vega laughed. "I don't know who shot me, if it was the Texians in the fort or our reserves behind us. It was dark, and they were firing blindly into the smoke. Can you imagine? We were charging the walls and our own army was shooting into us from behind. I could not walk. I fired my musket into the air and waited for the battle to end. But no help came for the wounded. No surgeons. We just lay there and suffered. Heredia, that poor boy. It took him two weeks to die."

"You got shot?" Jacob said. "We heard there were no doctors for the soldiers. How'd you keep your leg?"

"Ah, I was lucky. When the battle was done, wounded were everywhere, shot or hit by cannon fire. No one to help us. Then Captain Huerta showed up with two of his loyal men. They had another man with them, not Mexican, not in uniform. They were taking him to the fort. There was more shooting from inside, so Huerta told the man to wait while he went inside to see what was happening. And while this man waited, he saw me."

Vega looked down. "Me, out of all the wounded. He put something on my leg and bandaged the wound. Huerta came back and took the man away. Out of all the wounded, just me. Why? Tell me, please. You were in the war, were you not?"

Seguin, Millsaps, Neill, Alsbury, Karnes, and McCulloch all nodded. Silas stood silently. Vega approached Silas.

"Why?" Vega asked Silas. "You are too young to have fought. Can you tell me? Why am I alive and the others are dead?"

"I wish I could, sir," Silas said. "I truly wish I could."

Vega studied Silas. "You have not killed. I can see it." Vega looked at the other Texians. "They have killed." He turned back to Silas. "Do you want to kill a man?"

"No, sir."

"Good. Good. Because blood does not wash away. Once you kill, you are a killer always. Ask your friends. My friends are dead. My friends in the Toluca Battalion. Lieutenant Heredia. Captain Macotela. All dead. My friends died. But not me. Why?"

"Ain't no reason," Henry said. "Ain't no way for a man to know why he lives and another dies with bullets flyin' around. I wish I could say why I'm alive and some other fella's dead. We just go on, live as best we can."

"We're lucky and someone else is not? That is..." Vega looked away. "That is a hard thing." He turned back to Silas. "Why? Why are you here with these killers?"

"They're good men," Silas said. "We're trying to help someone each of these men knew and called friend. He's lost, and we're trying to find him."

"You do not know this man you seek?"

"No, sir. But I know these men. They're my friends."

"What is your reason?"

"My reason, sir?"

"Yes, your reason. Your reason for..." Vega shook his head. "I have no reason. No reason for anything. Please, tell me you have a reason for what you are doing."

Silas didn't hesitate. "There is someone I love very much. She's more important than anyone or anything, and we're going to have a life together. You ask my reason, well, she is my reason."

Vega's brow relaxed, and his anger and frustration abated. "What is her name?"

"Emily."

Vega's anger flooded back. "Why are you here!"

Silas waited a moment before taking a step forward. "Because these are my friends. I've learned much from them that I need to make my life with Emily. They and my mother and my father have taught me about being a man. Not to be a killer, but to protect Emily and take care of her. So, I'm here with them. You stood with your friends. I'm standing with mine. Then I get to go home to Emily. If I turned my back on my friends, I wouldn't be the man Emily deserves."

The rage drained out of Vega. "What is your name?"

"Silas Grant."

Vega put his hand on Silas's shoulder. "Silas Grant, I think your Emily is very fortunate. Do you agree, Texians?"

"As lucky as Silas is to have Emily," Sam said, "Emily is even luckier to have Silas."

"Very well," Vega said. "I believe you are not going to hang me. How can I help you?"

Vega led the Texians into the shade of the jacal. There was a small fireplace in the back with a rudimentary stone chimney. The greasy ashes of last night's cookfire stirred in the breeze that came down the short chimney, and the room smelled of smoke. Next to the fireplace sat a cook pot and a tea pot. In a far corner a rusty axe was propped next to an even rustier machete with a cracked handle. On one wall hung bunches of red peppers, horsemint, and sage along with three rattlesnake hides and an armadillo carapace. On the other wall were at least a dozen rattlesnake tails. A simple bed of straw was on a low wooden frame, but it kept Vega off the floor and away from centipedes, scorpions, and snakes. Unless they decided to crawl up the frame.

Vega sat on his bed while the Texians arrayed themselves on the dirt floor. Vega offered what he had, which was some water, pulque, and a little dried meat. The Texians shared their provisions, and Vega came out the better for the exchange.

"Rafael, you said Captain Huerta was escorting the man who treated your leg," Juan said. "Did you hear the man's name?"

Vega nodded. "Dr. Thorn."

"You remember after all this time?" Jacob said.

Vega looked at Millsaps. "I remember the name of the man who saved my life."

"Do you know what happened to Dr. Thorn?" Juan said.

"We tried to find out who he was, but we never saw him again."

"You said 'we.' Who else was trying to find out?"

"Captain de la Peña. He told me to ask around about Dr. Thorn, but no one knew anything about him."

"Did you say de la Peña?" Horace asked. Vega nodded.

"That name mean something to you, Horace?" Juan said.

"I was with one of the groups that followed the retreating Mexican army. I was in the Mexican camp and had several conversations with an officer named José Enrique de la Peña."

"Yes, that is Captain de la Peña," Vega said. "He is a man of great honor and respect. One of the few officers I have ever known who cared for his men."

"Did Captain de la Peña talk to Huerta?" Horace asked.

"I don't think so. Huerta left soon after the battle."

"Just Huerta?" Juan said.

"Huerta and a squad, men loyal to him from the Tres Villas Battalion. And a wagon. One of the army ambulances went missing, and Captain de la Peña said Huerta took it."

"What did Huerta look like?" Juan said.

"Very tall. Taller than any of you. And he loved wearing his medals."

"And you think Huerta and his men rode south? To Mexico?"

"Possibly. But I believe they went to the coast. Captain de la Peña said there were ships bringing supplies from Mexico and taking messages back. They landed someplace on the Gulf Coast. We never saw the supplies. The officers kept them."

"So, you don't know what Huerta and his squad were transporting to the coast."

"No. We assumed it was a wounded officer. Captain de la Peña was trying to get answers, but he left when the rest of the army marched north. The wounded and a small garrison stayed at the Alamo. I didn't see the captain again."

"Any idea where we might find him?"

"The captain? I don't know."

"Do you think he would be involved in the rebellion in Mexico now?" Horace asked.

"Oh, yes. Captain de la Peña is a very passionate man," Vega said.

★

The Texians rode to Goliad and stayed the night.

"We need to split up," Horace said during dinner. "Some of us see what can be learned about the ambulance and Huerta going to the coast, others head to Mexico and see if we can find Captain de la Peña. We meet back here.

"I'll go to Mexico," Horace added. "I met de la Peña during the war. I think there's a good chance he would remember me."

"Where will you look?" J.C. asked.

"Start with Matamoros, I suppose. That's where the Mexican army headed after it left Texas. That's where the last of the Mexican forces under General Andrade marched. There's sure to be some veterans of the war there."

"I will go with you, Horace," Juan said. "Much of the rebellion is in northern Mexico, so perhaps we can find someone who knows de la Peña."

"I'll go, too," Henry said. "I been down there a few times, and I'm too slippery for the Mexicans to hold."

"I guess the rest of us will see what we can find out about this ambulance headed to the coast," J.C. said.

"Where on the coast?" Sam said. "It's a damned big coast."

"Could be almost anywhere," Jacob said.

"Galveston and Velasco are too far north," Silas said.

"And Port Isabel is a long way south, close to two hundred miles from Goliad," Jacob added. "But that still leaves Corpus Christi, Port Aransas, Linnville, Copano. Hell, they might've just used some empty stretch of beach. That's a lot of coastline if we're thinking of searching."

"I know how you can narrow it down," Henry said. "Ask the Horse Marines."

CHAPTER 18

"FELLAS," HENRY SAID, "I got a bad feelin' about this."

"Now, why would you say that?" Horace said, peering through Henry's spyglass. "Just because we're walking into a fortified city that was the headquarters of the Mexican army for the invasion of Texas?"

"Well, yeah."

"Yeah. May not be the best idea I ever had. But it's the only way I can think of to find de la Peña."

"We will avoid Casamata," Juan said, referring to the Mexican fortress that lay a few hundred feet from a bend in the Rio Grande that marked the river's furthest reach into Matamoros. The city was opposite the southernmost tip of Texas, on the Rio Grande.

"You don't think the folks in the fort would mind a few Texians droppin' in to ask where we can find a rebel sympathizer?" Henry said.

"They might get a bit ornery," Horace said.

Horace Alsbury, Henry Karnes, and Juan Seguin were perched on a slight rise in the middle of the river bend on the Texas side of the Rio Grande, though Mexicans contended that both sides of the river were Mexican sides. Mexico regarded the border between Texas and Mexico to be the Nueces River, 130 miles north.

Of course, Mexico had yet to give up on Texas being a part of Mexico.

"We'll cross upriver and head for the town plaza," Juan said.

Three miles from the Casamata fortress, the Rio Grande curved crazily as it rolled into Matamoros, in some places almost doubling back on itself. The Texians found a shallow spot in the river's twists and turns, waited until dark to push their way through the cane-brake on the bank without leaving a scar in the brush that evidenced their passing, and crossed into Mexico. They camped in the brush on the Mexican side of the river and moved at first light.

Traveling at a leisurely pace, the Texians reached the outskirts of Matamoros by mid-morning and weaved their way through busy streets until they reached the mercado, the city's central market a mile from Casamata.

Despite the hardships caused by the French blockade, the market was stirring with activity. The Mexican people still had their own goods to buy and sell, and a few black-market items made their way across the river, which was the cover story the Texians would use should Mexican authorities challenge them. They were just looking to do business.

The trio sipped coffee at a mercado outdoor café.

"We're here. Now what?" Henry said.

"We find some veterans of the war," Juan said. "Even better if they were with de la Peña's unit, the Toluca Battalion. Or with General Andrade. Since he was the last Mexican general to come through here from Texas, decent chance some of his men are still around."

"Ask some of these shopkeepers? They should know what's going on in town," Horace suggested.

With Juan in the lead, the Texians walked through the mercado's booths and stalls. Henry and Horace spent while Juan talked.

They surveyed bins of tomatoes, onions, squash, eggplant, braids of garlic bulbs, and heaps of red, yellow, and green peppers. Henry bought a straw sombrero from a stall laden with boots, brogans, shirts, and sashes; Horace purchased a bolt of red silk for Juana from a fabric booth; and Henry sampled ham and bought a string of sausages from a butcher's stand.

The Texians talked with one shopkeeper after another. Despite crossing palms with coin, they got no answers. No, they hadn't been in the army. Yes, there were veterans in town. The leads generated by these conversations amounted to nothing. None of the veterans knew about de la Peña. None of them knew about General Andrade. Or at least, none admitted to knowing.

Henry and Horace were munching on sausages while Juan spoke with a former Mexican army sergeant, who shook his head. Juan thanked the man, who walked quickly away.

"You get the feelin' these folks are uncomfortable talkin' about our man?" Henry said.

"I'm afraid so," Juan said. "The sergeant said de la Peña is earning a reputation as a troublemaker. He has written articles criticizing Santa Anna and the centralist government, and in support of General Urrea."

"Urrea?" Horace said. "He was the Mexicans' best general in Texas."

"This time he's not putting down a rebellion, he's stoking one," Juan said. "And de la Peña is a supporter of Urrea."

"You gentlemen are certainly drawing attention," a voice called in English to the Texians. "Best be careful who you talk to."

The Texians turned to face a tall, redheaded man with an Irish accent. "Hello, Henry," he said.

"If it ain't Francis Ryan," Henry said. "How's business?"

"Could be better," the Irishman said. "This damned blockade is bad for everyone."

"Horace, Juan, this Irish rogue is Francis Ryan. Francis, this is Juan Seguin…" Seguin and Ryan shook hands. "…and Horace Alsbury." Alsbury and Ryan greeted one another.

"A pleasure to meet you," Ryan said. He was handsome, wearing a tweed cap, a white shirt beneath a waist coat, breeches tucked into tall riding boots, and a green bandana tied loosely around his neck.

"Francis, last I seen, you was smugglin'…what was it?"

"Ladies' undergarments," Ryan said. "Ah, the market for such niceties dried up. People got no money for such things."

"What's your line now?" Horace said.

"Whatever I can sell."

"Haven't heard of you in Texas lately," Henry said.

"I've discovered I prefer the company of Catholics to Protestants. No offense, Henry. I run goods from your fine Texas sea ports to me adopted home. Mexico has welcomed me countrymen, and it's been profitable for all. You fellows, on the other hand, are not going to see a profit from this trip if you keep asking the wrong questions of the wrong people. You'll have the local constabulary down on all us foreigners."

"Mr. Ryan—" Juan said.

"Please, call me Francis."

"Fine, Francis. We're not looking for trouble," Juan said.

"You Texians are noted for causing trouble down here."

"True, but we're just looking for someone," Horace said. "Not for any trouble."

"We're simply trying to help a friend who got himself in a difficult situation." Juan said.

"And you'd know all about difficult situations, Francis," Henry said.

"That I do, Henry," Ryan said. "I know all sorts in Mexico. Who are you looking for?"

"A former Mexican army officer named de la Peña," Juan said.

"Oh, dear," Ryan said. "I can see why you lads are the talk of the mercado. You see, de la Peña is not terribly popular here, being there's an army fort in town and all. You're fortunate the soldados haven't already locked you up."

The Texians looked around the mercado, expecting bayonets to emerge from the crowd.

"You really don't know what's happening?" Ryan said. "A man named Antonio Canales is following the lead of you Texians to create his own republic. You're standing in the middle of a rebellion to create the Republic of the Rio Grande, so the soldiers are a little jumpy. If I were you, I'd get out of town."

"Francis, we just want to talk to de la Peña and get back across the river," Horace said. "Can you tell us where we might find him?"

Ryan considered the Texians for a moment. He paused while a pair of soldiers walked down the other side of the plaza, but they paid no notice of the Texians or Ryan.

"You're really not looking to make a mess of things and join in the troubles?"

"We don't want any part of anyone's war," Horace said.

"Because a lot of Texians are looking to do just that. Settle some scores. Or just spoiling for a fight."

"That's not us. We're just trying to help a friend," Juan said.

"I might know someone," Ryan said, "who knows someone, who knows your de la Peña. He's not here. He's just a little way south of here, a place called Villa de San Mateo del Pilón. Are you familiar with it?"

"Never heard of it," Horace said. "You know this place, Juan?"

"I have not been there, but I believe it is near Monterrey," Juan said, "which would be in the heart of the rebel faction."

"You work with the rebels?" Henry said.

"You see," Ryan said, "my line of work requires a certain, how should I say…"

"…moral flexibility?" Henry suggested.

"Yes, thank you, Henry," Ryan said. "I work with anyone and everyone, and I don't take sides. Francis Ryan is not a discriminating man."

"Unless someone can't pay," Henry said.

"Then I'm downright bigoted. But if you can pay, I'm your man."

"And how much do your services require?" Horace asked.

"For an old friend like Henry, the information is free. Though, if you'll be needing a guide…"

"How much, Francis?" Henry asked.

"Say, fifty American dollars? It's a five-day ride from here, so…"

"Thirty," Horace said.

"Hardly worth my time. But since time is all I have these days, I'll take it."

"Half now," Juan said, "and half when we arrive. Now, who are we going to meet?"

"Didn't I mention? General Andrade himself. He's up to his neck in the rebellion."

CHAPTER 19

"HENRY ASKED YOU to make our introduction to Mr. Burton, so, go ahead," J.C. said.

Silas looked across the hall of the Texas legislature at the man he was supposed to address. The man was tall, lean, distinguished, and was said to possess a sharp mind—a man of accomplishment and respect. A major with the Texas Rangers, a veteran of the Battle of San Jacinto, a senator in the Texas legislature, and a commissioner for Indian affairs in Sam Houston's government.

"Go on," J.C. said. Jacob and Sam nodded. Silas, however, was not reassured.

Silas walked toward Isaac Watts Burton while behind him Henry Karnes's co-conspirators edged to within earshot but out of direct of line of sight. But they definitely wanted to see Burton's face.

Burton was dressing down a government employee, one of the clerks who had involuntarily helped fund Silas's gift-giving largesse to Emily. The clerk retreated.

"Excuse me, Mr. Burton," Silas said. "I mean, Senator Burton."

Burton turned, looking annoyed. "Yes, young man. What do you want?"

"I was asked to deliver a message."

"Very well. Out with it."

Silas took a deep breath. "I was instructed…to say hello to Private Burton."

Burton glowered at Silas. "Were you?" Burton snarled. "And just who instructed you to be so insolent?"

"Henry Karnes."

Isaac Burton held his wrath for two more heartbeats before his bearded face erupted in laughter.

"I don't think anyone else in Texas would dare call me Private," Burton said. "How is Henry?"

"He's well, sir," Silas said, exhaling in relief. "He sends his regards."

"I doubt that, but it's kind of you to say," Burton said. He put his hand on Silas's shoulder. "If Henry sent you into the lion's den, my guess is some other dashed, no-account ne'er-do-wells are cavorting around these halls."

"Who you calling no-account?" J.C. said as he, Sam, and Jacob stepped forward.

"As I thought. Young man," Burton said to Silas, "you can learn much from these fellows. Just remember this: whatever they tell you, do the opposite."

"How are you, Isaac?" Sam said.

"Good," Burton said. "It's wonderful to see you. Been too long. What are you doing here? It must be something important to drag you to the state house."

"Is there someplace we can talk?" J.C. said.

"Of course," and Burton led the Texians through a maze of construction crews.

"If I may ask, sir," Silas said as they walked, "why did Henry want me to call you Private?"

"Because I was a private in Henry's cavalry company at San Jacinto," Burton said. "I may be a major and a senator, but Henry Karnes will always out-rank me. I'm older than Henry, but I learned as much from him as any man in Texas. You listen to what he has to say."

"Believe me, I do," Silas said.

They reached an area of finished offices and found one unoccupied. Burton invited the Texians in and closed the door.

"How can I help?" Burton said.

"We're tracking leads on a missing person, someone who disappeared after the Alamo," J.C. said. "His name is Dr. Thorn. We think he was captured by Urrea's troops and taken to the coast, possibly sailed to Mexico."

"And you've come to me because of the Horse Marines."

"No one knows the Gulf Coast during the war better," Sam said.

Isaac Burton held a unique position in Texas history. During the Texas Revolution, the Mexican army was being resupplied by merchant brigs sailing from Mexico to the Texas coast. The supplies were taken overland to Goliad or San Antonio, and those shipments continued even after San Jacinto, supplying the thousands of Mexican soldiers who remained in Texas after Santa Anna's capture.

Burton, by then a major in command of twenty Rangers, was charged with cutting the Mexican supply lines. Patrolling the Gulf Coast in June 1836, he spotted one of the brigs at anchor. With no artillery on hand, Burton hid most of his men while he and a few others signaled the merchant ship, convincing its crew that the men onshore were Mexican soldiers in need of help. A longboat was sent to the beach, and the Rangers quickly swarmed and overpowered its crew. They took the longboat out to the ship, disarmed the crew, and captured the brig.

They performed this bit of pirate theater on two more merchant brigs and sailed the prizes, loaded with supplies, to a friendly port.

Those actions earned Burton and his men the title of Horse Marines, a moniker they carried with pride.

As for J.C.'s cover story, every bit of it was true. They were tracking Dr. Thorn, who was captured by Urrea's troops, and did go missing, and may have boarded a ship to Mexico. J.C. could take comfort in not out-right lying to a senator, even if it wasn't the whole truth. It wasn't so much a half-truth, he reasoned, as a three-quarter truth.

"J.C., I don't know if I can tell you where it was," Burton said. "It was at Copano Bay, but there's got to be thirty, forty miles of coastline in the bay. I can show you, if you'd like."

"I hate to drag you down there," J.C. said.

"Please, drag me out of Houston for a few days. I could do with a break."

Burton led them from the state house. Being late in the day, they agreed the Texians would stay in a local inn, and the group would set out in the morning.

"Are those ships still around, sir?" Silas asked.

"I presume so. I never heard much about them after that. We brought them up the coast to Galveston and turned them over to the Texas Navy, though I doubt the Republic had the manpower or funds to operate them. They may have just been turned over to their crews, who were not all Mexican. The captains, at least, were not."

"They could still be operating as merchant brigs?" Silas said.

"Certainly possible."

"Do you remember the names of the ships?"

"I'll never forget," Burton said. "The first boat we captured was called *Watchman*. The other two were *Comanche* and *Fanny Butler*."

The journey to Copano Bay was one of the most interesting Silas had taken. Burton was every bit the storyteller that Sam, J.C., and Henry were, but now Silas got to hear new stories, including Burton's insights on Henry. The nightly campfires were a festival of tales of the Texas Revolution, and though Silas understood that most were exaggerated, he soaked them up.

He and Sam even got to tell Burton the story of the smugglers and the flour barrels at Corpus Christi Bay, though Sam gave all the credit to Silas. Burton seemed sincerely impressed.

On the fifth day, the Texians reached Copano Bay, which was a large, roughly rectangular inlet forty miles north of Corpus Christi and part of a system of bays. Copano was an extension of the wide Aransas Bay, and Copano had two smaller bays branching further inland, Mission Bay and Port Bay.

They arrived late and stayed the night in the town of Copano, which consisted of three piers and a dozen buildings unlike any Silas had ever seen. They looked like stone, with limestone walls studded with seashells.

The next morning, Burton led the search for Copano's rendezvous point with the Mexican-employed merchant brigs.

"I know there was a spot where we were able to hide most of the men," Burton said as the group walked along the beach. "A handful of us signaled the ships. I think it was…"

Burton slowed to a stop.

A small merchant brig was in the bay, anchored broadside to the shore. The Texians walked along the beach until they could see the ship's stern.

"That certainly looks like…good, Lord," Burton stammered. "I think it is. Gentlemen, tell me if I'm seeing things."

"Silas, you've got younger eyes," J.C. said. "Can you make out the name?"

Silas squinted at the ship through the sunlight reflecting off the bay. "*Watchman*."

Overcoming the shock of seeing a ghost from Burton's past, the Texians returned to the town and its piers, commandeered a longboat, and rowed toward the ship. J.C., in deference to his bad hip, handled the tiller while Jacob, Silas, Sam, and Senator Burton rowed. They saw no movement on the ship until the longboat bumped into *Watchman*'s hull, at which point a towheaded lookout, who had been sleeping on deck, appeared above the railing.

"Ahoy," Burton called. "May we come aboard? We'd like a word with your captain."

The lookout gawked at the newcomers. "Captain!" he shrieked.

A face with a scraggly beard and mustache emerged next to the lookout. "State your business!" he called.

"Is that you, Captain Jones? Captain Levi Jones?" Burton said.

"I'm Jones. Who are you?"

"I'm surprised you don't remember, Captain. I'm Isaac Burton. We met in this very bay two years ago."

"Oh, you! The bastard who tricked me and captured my ship! The war's finished. I have no business with you. Now get the hell away from my boat!"

"That's no way to speak to a Texas senator," J.C. said.

After a long pause, Jones looked down his nose at the men in the longboat, his mouth open and his mind turning. His eyes darted back and forth.

"Who…who's a senator?" Jones said.

"This gentleman," J.C. said, "who you knew as Major Burton is now Senator Isaac Burton of the Republic of Texas. You may feel you have no business with him, but if you would like to continue doing business at *any* Texas port, you'll watch your tongue."

"Or we'll cut it out," Jacob added. Millsaps was not the most talkative of the Texians, but he was the most persuasive.

"All right, all right, calm down," Jones said. "What do you want?"

"To talk, Captain Jones," Burton said. "Just to talk."

Jones disappeared while the lookout continued to stare at the longboat and its passengers. A few seconds later, a rope ladder descended over the side of the boat.

"Senator, allow Sam and me to go up, make sure there's no trouble," Jacob said. "We'll signal when it's safe to proceed. Sam?"

Sam nodded, checked the load in his pistol, and made sure his long knife was readily at hand. Jacob did the same. McCulloch took a strain on the rope ladder and Millsaps climbed up and was quickly over the rail. Sam followed. After a moment, Jacob waved to the boat. J.C. tied off the longboat to the ladder, and he, the senator, and finally Silas boarded *Watchman*.

"What do you want?" Jones barked.

"I'm curious, Captain," Burton said. "What are you doing here? You don't have any cargo. Are you waiting for a shipment?"

"How you know I got no cargo? You ain't searched the boat."

"You're riding high in the water, Captain. Your hold is empty."

Jones licked his lips nervously and fidgeted with a hole in his blue tailcoat.

"Why are you here?" Burton repeated.

"The French blockade," Jones said. "I can't get into Veracruz. My crew doesn't trust what that fella Brown said…" Jones swallowed his words. He saw that four of the Texians—everyone but Burton—had taken notice at the mention of Brown.

"Hiram Brown?" Jacob said.

Jones scratched his chin and realized he'd said too much. "Don't know," he said. "I mean, the damned French have the Mexican ports blockaded. I'm waiting for them to leave."

"How do you know Hiram Brown?" J.C. said.

"Don't know nobody by that name," Jones muttered.

"I see," Burton said. "Just some information, then, Captain. We're trying to learn the fate of a captive of the Mexican army back in 1836. He may have been brought to the coast and taken aboard one of the brigs bringing supplies to the Mexican army."

"I made a lot of those trips," Jones said. "Can't be expected to remember every passenger I took to Mexico. That was two years ago. Coulda been one of the other ships. There were three of us. You oughta know."

"I recall," Burton said. "Did any of you sail out of any other locations on the coast?"

"No, just here. The Mexican army had a small garrison to guard and offload supplies."

Burton looked to the Texians, and Silas took up the interrogation.

"Sometime in March or early April of 1836, there was a small detachment of Mexican soldiers. They had a wagon and a doctor. Do you recall them?"

"I don't remember much from that time. Too long ago. Could have been one of the other ships. I don't remember."

"A tall Mexican officer commanded this group. His name was Huerta. Someone described him as the tallest Mexican he'd ever seen."

That got Jones attention. His anger at the memory overcame his reticence to talk.

"By, God, I do remember him. Arrogant bastard. He bragged about the executions of Texian prisoners at Goliad. Showed me a watch, claimed he took it off the commander...what was his name?"

"Fannin," Jacob said.

"Yeah, Fannin," Jones said. "Said he took it from Fannin just before Fannin was, well, before he was shot." Jones looked sheepishly at the Texians. "Said Fannin asked to be shot in the chest, but Huerta ordered the firin' squad to shoot Fannin in the face. Bastard was proud of that. He demanded I take him and his men to Veracruz."

"Did you do so?" J.C. asked.

"Didn't have much choice. I was supposed to wait for one of the couriers who delivered messages back to Mexico. I tried to explain that, but Huerta said he'd shoot me and burn my boat. He wasn't jokin'."

"Captain, did Huerta have any civilians with him?" Silas said.

"There was a man with them, not in uniform. But he didn't come aboard. Refused to board the longboat, said there was nothin' more he could do."

The Texians looked at one another apprehensively. Had Dr. Thorn's patient died?

"Do you know what happened to him?" Silas said.

"Huerta thanked him for his help, and he and some of his men walked the man back up off the beach. A few minutes later, Huerta and the soldiers came back and got on the longboat, and we left. I figured they let the man go."

"This is very important," Silas said. "Could you please show us where that was?"

Jones sighed. "Oh, all right."

Jones and the Texians climbed into the longboat, and Jones directed the Texians to a stretch of beach two miles from the town, near an old lean-to of a shed set forty yards back from the beach. The longboat ground onto the shell-encrusted shingle.

After everyone splashed ashore, Jones looked around. "I'm pretty sure it was here. I seem to recall that shed."

"Where did the civilian go?" J.C. asked.

"Up around the shed and inland, I suppose. I figure he walked back to town."

The group followed the direction Jones indicated toward the lean-to. The ground transitioned from beach to sandy soil covered with grass. They circled around behind shed. Old trash, seashells, splintered timbers, and broken tools were piled at the back of the shed, which was near collapse. Another thirty yards inland the grass gave way to trees and brush. The group was headed that way when Silas stopped and looked at the ground. He knelt.

"What?" Jones said.

Silas turned his face and lowered his eyes to just above the surface of the ground.

"What are you listenin' for?" Jones said.

"I'm not listening," Silas said. "I'm looking." He stood, walked a few feet to his left, and knelt again. "The ground here, it's a little lower than everything around it. Settled."

Jacob and Sam knelt as well. "I'll be damned," Sam said.

Jacob returned to the shed, poked through the trash heap, and came away with a shovel, the handle of which was snapped off. He started digging at the indentation.

Silas, Sam, J.C., and Burton turned to the trash heap, looking for anything to use as a digging implement. They came away with a pair of graying, splintered boards, a length of pipe, and what was probably the snapped-off handle of the shovel with which Jacob was laboring.

The group began digging and scraping, everyone careful to avoid jabbing or hitting one another. The turf came away with some effort, and after several minutes Jacob's shovel scraped something beneath the loam.

"Hang on, boys," he called, and used his hand to brush away dirt from the object. Something white showed. Jacob continued to dig with his fingers and revealed bone with a round hole. An eye socket.

"A skull," Jacob said.

They kept excavating and more of the skeleton was revealed. Human. Taller than Silas, shorter than Burton. Bits of clothing remained, including a coat. Silas knelt at the edge of the grave and, trying not to disturb the corpse, examined the skeleton.

"You didn't hear anything, Captain?" Burton said. "No gunshot, no yelling?"

"No," Jones said.

Silas found holes in the coat, and pulled it back to reveal sharp cuts on the ribs.

"Bayonets, I'd bet," J.C. said. "Quick and quiet."

Silas searched the coat pockets. He came away with an empty bottle and a piece of wood. Silas scraped dirt off the bottle.

"Iodine," he said. He tossed the bottle to J.C.

Silas stood and brushed dirt off the wooden piece. It was a hollow tube. The sides were smooth, polished. One end widened out, like the bell of a trumpet. The other end had a flat, round piece, roughly the same diameter as the bell shape.

"Is that some kind of a child's toy?" Jacob asked.

"No," J.C. said. He took the tube from Silas and held one end to his ear. "It's used to listen to a patient's heart. A Frenchman invented it. Said he was embarrassed to press his ear against a female patient's chest. I think it's called a stethoscope."

The group looked at the skeletal remains.

"I think we found your Dr. Thorn," Burton said.

Everyone removed their hats, Jones doing so only after he noticed everyone else had.

Jacob nodded to Sam, and the two of them set to replacing the dirt over Dr. Thorn.

"Any idea if he has family?" Burton asked. J.C. shook his head. "I'll look into it. See if we can find his next of kin. They can collect the remains if they wish."

The group took two rough boards from the lean-to and fashioned a cross, and drove it in the ground above the dead man's head.

"Captain," Silas said forcefully and a little louder than intended. He was frustrated and angry at the apparent dead end their weeks of travel and questioning had come to. "Did anyone else come aboard. We must know. Anyone at all besides the soldiers?"

"No," Jones said. "I told you. Just the soldiers, Huerta, and one other officer."

"What other officer?" Silas said.

"How do I know?" Jones said, wanting to be done with this entire matter.

"This other officer, what did he look like?" Silas pressed, moving closer to Jones.

"I don't know," Jones said. "I couldn't see him."

"What? Why not?"

Jones sighed. "He was under a blanket, on a stretcher. Huerta said he was an officer. Said he'd been wounded."

"Wounded?"

"Yeah, poor fella," Jones said. "He lost a leg."

CHAPTER 20

FOR FIVE DAYS, Seguin, Alsbury, and Karnes followed Francis Ryan through a world of thornscrub.

They passed a few scattered villages and settlements that appeared on no map. Past a handful of hardscrabble goat ranches and subsistence farms which clung to scarce sources of water, existed beneath the concern of federalists or centralists, and were outside the interests of rebels or lawful authority.

But someone was interested. Everywhere were burned-out villages, ranches, and farms littered with corpses in varying degrees of decay.

"What's happened here?" Horace asked. "Is this the rebellion?"

Henry shook his head. "Comanches."

"Comanches? This far south?"

"Further," Henry said. "We hear they're raiding hundreds of miles into Mexico. Stealing horses and taking captives. And killing everyone else who gets in their way."

"What about the Mexican army? Where are they?"

"Fighting rebels," Ryan said.

"Leaving these people on their own," Juan said.

They traveled from Tamaulipas to Nuevo Leon without noticing they had moved from one state to the next. At Ryan's suggestion, they had purchased extra canteens in Matamoros and loaded up on water, as well as oats for the horses, which were loaded with other provisions onto Ryan's two pack mules. All along the route, they watered their horses and filled those canteens at every opportunity. Though it was Mexico's rainy season, the weather was clear throughout the trip, and temperatures remained high during the day before plunging in the dry night air.

The passage was across a flat landscape which rose imperceptibly from the sea level of the coast toward distant highlands. On the morning of the third day, the Sierra Madre Oriental mountains began to take shape on the horizon, and they knew they were half way to Villa de San Mateo del Pilón, which lay at the base of that range as it cut diagonally through northern Mexico.

On the fifth day, the terrain grew greener and the Rio Pilón appeared to the west. They broke from the path they had so relentlessly kept and rode to the river, indulged in its cool waters, and followed its flow toward the journey's end.

After crossing an arid, empty region, the land around the river exploded with life. They saw fields of maize, sorghum, and beans as well as orchards of oranges, grapefruits, and tangerines.

Fields were worked by a significant portion of Villa de San Mateo del Pilón's population, laboring for eight or nine hours a day, planting, tending, harvesting. An aguador, with leather straps holding a barrel on his back and a clay pitcher in front, walked through the fields providing water to the workers.

In the village, women mixed corn with lye, boiled it, washed it, and ground it on a metate to make tortillas. They would rise before dawn to make breakfast and lunch so the men could take food with them to work.

A handful of peasants gleaned leftover crops from harvested fields.

"Remind me to never complain about workin' hard," Henry said.

"Where do these folks stand on the rebellion?" Horace asked Ryan.

"They don't much care," the Irishman said. "Their only concerns are for their families. They leave it to the notables to worry about loyalties to the federalists or centralists."

"Notables?" Henry asked.

"Local landowners, merchants," Ryan said. "People like you, Señor Seguin."

Ryan led the Texians into town, which lay on a gradual slope rising west toward the mountains. A wide plaza lay in the middle of town, and on the north and south sides stood a general store, blacksmith, stable, cantina, and an inn. At the west end, the town's high point, was a church, and at its east end was a sheriff's office and jail. The Texians pulled up in front of the stable, where they paid for their horses to be watered and fed.

"All right, Francis, where's Andrade?" Henry said.

"Patience, lad," Ryan said. "Now, I didn't say I actually knew Andrade, and I may have slightly exaggerated that he absolutely is here, but I do believe he's here. It's just a matter of finding him."

"Ryan, where the hell—" Henry started.

"Now, just let me do a little checking around. I know these people. Why don't we go to the cantina and have a drink, and I'll talk to friends in town about your general."

"All right, Francis," Juan said, putting a restraining hand on Henry's shoulder. "You go to the cantina and we'll be there presently. I think we'd like to see the town."

"As you like," Ryan said. "The cantina is just there," he said and pointed to the opposite side of the plaza. "Drop by when you're ready and I'll buy you a drink." Ryan turned his horse and headed for the south side of town.

Once Ryan was well out of hearing distance, the Texians discussed their next move.

"Where do we start?" Horace said.

"We make our own investigation," Juan said. "I don't trust this Irishman."

"I'm not Catholic, but I say we try the church," Henry said.

"Sounds good," Juan said.

They walked slowly along the north side of Villa de San Mateo del Pilón's plaza, watching to be certain that Ryan had disappeared into the cantina before the Texians headed for the church.

The chapel, dedicated to St. Matthew, was smaller than the cathedral in San Antonio. They stepped through a tall, impressive entry with double doors, through a vestibule, and into the nave, which was empty. They were walking toward the chancel when a door behind the pulpit opened and a priest emerged. He was a very young Mestizo, with short hair parted on the right, clean shaven, and a pair of spectacles perched on his nose. He wore a simple black cassock with a white collar.

"I'm sorry, gentlemen," the priest said. "I didn't know anyone was here. Can I help you?"

"Good day, Father," Juan said. "We're looking for someone and thought perhaps you could help us. My name is Juan Seguin, and these are my friends, Henry Karnes and Horace Alsbury."

"Very nice to meet you. I'm Father Ortiz. Who are you looking for?"

"A friend of ours, a veteran of the Mexican army, has gone missing," Juan said. "We're trying to find an officer this friend served under, a captain named José Enrique de la Peña. We'd like to speak to him and see if he has any information regarding our friend."

"Ah, de la Peña," Ortiz said. "A controversial character. Does this have anything to do with the rebellion?"

"No, Father," Horace jumped in. "We're just trying to help a friend. It's possible he got caught up in the rebellion, but we really don't know. We believe our friend served with de la Peña in the Toluca Battalion."

"I see. I have heard of de la Peña, and someone in town may know of him. You gentlemen are not from Mexico, I suspect."

"No, we're from Texas. The friend we're trying to help is Mexican."

Ortiz seemed to think about this a moment. "Does this friend have a name?"

"Rafael Vega."

Ortiz beckoned the Texians to follow him, and the priest led the trio through the door behind the pulpit, into the chapel office, and out the back door. They were now behind the town, with a view to the mountains ten miles away.

"Wait here," Ortiz said. "I'll be back shortly."

Ortiz disappeared around the corner and headed into the town while the Texians stayed out of sight.

Sitting at a table by a window in the cantina, Francis Ryan watched Father Ortiz appear from the side of the church and walk briskly through the town plaza to the blacksmith.

"How much longer do we wait?" Horace asked. It had been an hour since Ortiz had left, and the sun was beginning to go down.

"I think we give we him a little more time," Juan said.

"No more than another half hour," Henry said. "I don't want to be out here at night."

Ortiz appeared from the door to his office. "I am sorry for the delay, gentlemen," he said breathlessly. "I just needed to discuss this with—"

At that moment, three men appeared at the north corner of the church. Three more came from the south side. All the Texians moved their hands to the guns in their belts.

"No, gentlemen, please," Ortiz said. "These men are here to help."

"They don't look helpful, and I ain't one for bein' surrounded," Henry said.

"Be at ease, gentlemen," said a tall, distinguished man who followed Ortiz to the back of the church. "I understand you are looking for de la Peña."

The six men—all armed—closed around the Texians.

"We just want to talk to him," Horace said.

"You are from Texas?" the tall man said. Juan nodded.

"Excellent. Allow me to introduce myself. I am Antonio Canales. Welcome to Mexico."

"You're Canales?" Henry said. "The leader of this rebellion?"

"That is correct," Canales said. "We have taken inspiration from your Republic of Texas, and soon we will declare the Republic of the Rio Grande. What a delight to have three genuine heroes of the Texas Revolution in our midst. Come, let me introduce you to General Andrade. He will be leading our army into battle against the centralist forces."

Ortiz led the Texians, Canales, and his men into the church, closing and locking the office door behind him. After making sure the nave was empty, he pushed his pulpit aside, revealing a hole in the floor with a ladder leading down. "This way, gentlemen," Ortiz said, and climbed down.

"Well?" Henry said.

"I guess we follow," Horace said, and they descended the ladder to a narrow passage under the church. From an alcove in the passage, Ortiz produced a pair of torches, lit them, and guided the group down a passage with dirt walls shored up with wood timbers.

The Texians could feel the floor descending under Villa de San Mateo del Pilón. A few minutes later, the passage ended in a room ten-feet wide and twenty-feet long which had been carefully excavated under the town. It had a dirt floor but wooden walls and ceiling, with heavy crossbeams and posts to prevent collapse. The walls of the room were lined with cases of muskets and bayonets and barrels of gun powder. In a corner was a ladder leading up to a hatch that was closed. Ortiz scaled the ladder and rapped on the hatch. His pattern was answered by another set of taps, and the door was unlocked from above and everyone climbed up.

They found themselves in a much larger room with a simple door on one side and a large, heavy sliding door on the opposite side. Tools hung on the walls, including bellows, hammers, and tongs, and a supply of metal ingots were stacked in a corner.

"We're in the storeroom of the blacksmith," Horace said.

On the opposite wall, a hidden door opened and a man in full military uniform entered the storeroom. He was gray-headed with a full mustache and sideburns, dressed in a blue double-breasted coat with blue lapels and gold cuffs and epaulettes, blue pants belted with a red sash, black shoes, white gloves, and a blue bicorn hat with white ruffles.

"General, I wish you would wait until I call for you," Canales said. "We can't be too careful."

"Nonsense, Antonio," the general said. "These are friends from Texas, come to our cause. Welcome, gentlemen, welcome. I am General Juan José Andrade."

"General, I think there's a little misunderstanding," Juan said. "We're looking for someone—"

"Yes, yes, de la Peña," Andrade said, unable to contain his excitement. "I expect him shortly. How wonderful to have you here. I remember you, Mr. Seguin. We met at the Alamo, did we not?"

"Yes, sir."

"When our forces surrendered the fort to you. All because of that coward Santa Anna. But from that disaster will come a new republic. Have you told them, Antonio?"

"Yes, General."

"It will be glorious. And with the help of General Urrea's forces in the south and men like you, we shall march on Mexico City and return Mexico to its federalist constitution. Now, tell me, how many more men can you bring to our cause?"

"General, you misunderstand us," Juan said. "We're not here to join you."

Then all hell broke loose.

The heavy sliding door at the back of the storeroom exploded, blasted apart by a round from a six-pound cannon. Two of Canales's men were killed instantly. A moment later, the door on the opposite wall, which led from the storeroom to the front of the blacksmith shop, was smashed open by a giant axe-wielding Mexican soldier, who made kindling of the door with one blow. Half a dozen soldiers poured into the room from the back and three more joined their towering friend from the front. All except the axe man had muskets with long sword bayonets. A captain followed the soldiers from the back.

The remainder of Canales's men, momentarily stunned by the explosion and disoriented by the smoke, drew their weapons, but the Mexican soldiers had one target in mind.

"Kill Andrade!" the captain yelled.

Half of the Mexican soldiers immediately fired at the old general, hitting him four times. Then they charged with bayonets and skewered the helpless general.

The soldiers lost their advantage by expending so much firepower on one target. They either hadn't expected so many rebels or just didn't notice them in the smoke, and now Canales's men opened fire, killing two soldiers. The room was filled with gunfire and clashing blades, lit only by the failing light of the sunset through the destroyed back door.

Henry, Horace, and Juan had not come to Mexico for a fight, but the fight had come to them and they dove into the battle. Henry shot the Mexican captain, dropped that spent pistol, drew a second and looked for another target. The giant with the axe had just cleaved open the head of one of Canales's men and was dislodging the blade from the victim's skull. Henry shot the tall Mexican between the eyes. His head snapped back, the axe slipped from his hands, and he fell backward.

Horace killed a soldier, then he was shot, spun, and fell. The soldier who shot Horace lunged with his bayonet to finish the Texian and Horace narrowly dodged the thrust. The soldier drew back to stab again when Henry seized the musket, pulled it away from the intended target, and drove his Bowie knife into the soldier's throat.

Across the room, one of Andrade's killers was trying to reload when Juan shot him. He fumbled his musket but didn't go down, and was drawing a knife when Juan picked up the Mexican captain's sword and slashed the soldier across the arm, sending the badly wounded man staggering out of the storeroom.

Another of Canales's men died beneath Mexican bayonets. The bodies were stacking up quickly, leaving little room to maneuver.

The last four soldiers squared off against Canales, his last two men, Henry, and Juan. There was no time for anyone to reload. From here on, it was a knife fight.

The soldiers charged and one of Canales's men was run through, screaming as the blade emerged from his back.

Henry parried a bayonet thrust with his knife and ripped the blade across his foe's face, who shrieked and reeled away. Juan dodged a bayonet and held the soldier's musket while Canales stabbed the attacker through the ribs.

Down to just two men and now outnumbered, the last soldiers fled.

"Gentlemen, I appreciate your help," a breathless Canales said. "I apologize for involving you in Mexico's troubles, but it's time now for a retreat." And with that, Canales and his last follower raced from the carnage.

Juan dropped the captain's sword, gathered pistols, and threw them into a burlap sack found on a blacksmith's bench while Henry helped Horace to his feet.

"Can you walk?" Henry asked.

"Yeah," Horace said. "Shot me in the shoulder but I'll make it. Where did..."

Horace spotted Father Ortiz crumpled against a wall. He had been butchered. Shot and bayoneted.

Darkness had fallen and confusion reigned all over town. People ran for cover when the combat commenced, and a few soldiers, stationed outside to deal with escaping rebels, fired at any target. Several townspeople, allied to Canales, returned fire. Flashes burst all over town.

"Where are the horses!" Horace yelled.

"Here!" someone called. It was Ryan. He had the Texians horses as well as his own and his pack mules. The Texians ran for the horses, mounted, and followed Ryan through the orchards and out of town.

★

They rode for an hour before they dared stop, not dismounting until they were sure they were not followed.

Juan helped Horace from his horse, then dug into his saddle bags for a roll of bandages.

"Henry, can you help me?" Juan called. He looked back, but Henry was still mounted.

"You gonna stay up there all night?" Horace called. "Henry?"

"Uh, fellas…"

A red stain was spreading on Henry's shirt.

"Oh, damn it, Henry," Horace called. "Damn it, no."

"I could use little help here," Henry said, and Juan and Ryan rushed to his side and eased Karnes from the saddle.

"When did that happen?"

"When we was runnin' from the blacksmith," Henry said. "Ain't sure who shot me. Don't guess it matters," he grunted as they helped him to the ground. Juan took the saddle from Henry's horse and set it so Henry could lean against it, and examined the wound.

"It's bad, Henry," Juan said.

"Yeah, kinda figured."

"I'll start a fire," Ryan said. "You'll want to keep warm."

"No fire," Henry said. "Could be soldiers still lookin' for us."

"They're miles away," Ryan said. "They won't be out here after dark. The Mexicans don't care for night fighting."

"Tell that to the defenders of the Alamo," Juan said. "Henry's right, no fire."

"Suit yourself."

Ryan set up camp, hauling out food and water while Juan bandaged the wounded. Horace's injury was serious but Henry's was the greater worry.

Juan and Ryan made the wounded as comfortable as possible, then pulled the pistols from the burlap bag and reloaded. There was decent light from a near-full moon, and Juan quickly had all the pistols ready. He handed Henry and Horace each a pistol, and tucked two into his belt.

Ryan, meanwhile, had unsaddled his horse and was brushing the animal down.

"Francis?"

"Yes, Henry," Ryan said without turning.

"What do you sell these days?"

"Whatever I can," he said. "Whatever people will buy."

"Hmm. Where do you get your merchandise?"

"Oh, from your ports along the Texas coast. Mexican ports are blockaded, you know. I don't understand why. Something about some damned-fool disagreement with the French."

Karnes nodded at Alsbury and Juan and tapped a finger on the butt of his pistol. Horace and Juan each drew a pistol in response.

"What ports do you use?" Henry asked.

Ryan shrugged, continuing to tend to his horse "Isabel, Linnville, Galveston."

"Seem far north," Henry said. "Long way to haul cargo. Ever do business around Corpus Christi Bay?"

Ryan stopped. He was in a bad way, his back to the Texians. He looked at his rifle, but it was in his saddle scabbard and impossible to draw. He eased his right hand toward the pistol in his belt.

"Maybe to pick up some flour?"

Ryan spun and tried to draw his pistol, but Karnes, Alsbury, and Seguin fired before the Irishman got his gun clear. All three shots were on target. Ryan was thrown back against his horse and collapsed on his face, dead.

"How did you know?" Horace asked.

"In the camp!" a voice yelled from the dark. "Lower your weapons."

With no idea of who or how many they were facing, the Texians complied.

A lone figure walked into the camp, carrying a pistol. He was attired in a white shirt, brown pants, leather boots, a striped sarape, and the white, wide-brimmed hat he wore as a captain of the Toluca Battalion delivering messages between General Castrillón and General Cós and Colonel Romero at the Alamo.

"Good evening, gentlemen," the newcomer said, looking at the dead Irishman and shoving his pistol into his belt. "Thank you for dealing with him."

"Well, I'll be," Horace said. "Good evening, José."

The newcomer peered into the moonlight. "Don Alsbury?"

"Henry, Juan," Horace said, "allow me to introduce José Enrique de la Peña."

"Would someone please explain to me what is going on?" Juan said. "Henry, how did you know about Ryan?"

"The brand on his horse. I seen that brand with the smugglers we chased off at Corpus Christi. Ryan was workin' for the centralists. That's why we got out of Matamoros so easy."

"We suspected Ryan might be an agent for the government," de la Peña said.

"Instead of soldiers arrestin' us in Matamoros, Francis used us for bait to find Andrade."

"They didn't realize they had Canales," de la Peña said. "He was the greater prize. I spoke with him before I followed you out of town. He is safe. The revolution is still alive."

"Right now, I want to keep these men alive," Juan said. "We must get help. Where can we find a doctor?"

"More soldiers will be pouring into the town. Antonio and his men have already pulled out. The nearest doctor is in Mier."

"We'll head there first thing in the morning," Juan said. "Henry, Horace, do you think you can travel?"

"Do we have a choice?" Henry said.

Juan and de la Peña searched Ryan's goods and found material to make poultices for the wounds. Horace's was to his left shoulder, beneath the collarbone. Henry's was much more concerning, located high on his abdomen.

"I have a suggestion," de la Peña said. "With their wounds, their pace of travel will be slow. I will ride ahead to Mier, find a doctor, and bring the doctor to you. You make what progress you can, and I will find you."

"Sounds good," Juan said.

"But be damned sure you come back," Henry said. "We come all this way to find you."

"Find me?"

"It's a long story, José," Horace said. "I'll explain later, but it's important that we talk."

"Of course," he said. "If you wish, I'll come to Texas with you."

The next morning, the Texians and de la Peña started north for Mier and Texas. Once they felt confident they were not being followed, de la Peña took his own mount and Francis Ryan's horse and pressed ahead, switching horses when one tired. Mier lay ninety miles north of Villa de San Mateo del Pilón, near the Rio Grande. Normally a three-day journey, it would take the wounded men at least five days to get there, but with two horses, de la Peña could make it in two and bring a doctor to Henry and Horace.

★

Seguin nursed his injured comrades north. Horace was in pain but holding up well. Henry was in agony and was in trouble, though he tried not to show it. His bleeding was difficult to stop and he undoubtedly had internal injuries. The evening after de la Peña went for a doctor, Juan rigged a travois so Henry no longer had to sit on his horse and he could be hauled behind one of the pack mules.

Three days later and still a good distance from Mier, de la Peña returned with the doctor.

"I tried to get a wagon but none was available," de la Peña said. "The army confiscated all of the wagons in Mier. They are searching everywhere for rebels and those who sympathize with them."

The doctor finished examining his patients and joined Juan and de la Peña.

"Your friend with the shoulder wound I think will recover. You did a good job bandaging his wound, and the poultice is working nicely. But your other friend is in very poor condition. I don't know how much more of this he can take. I've stopped the bleeding, but he needs better care than I can give him here. And he has a fever."

"What if we get him to your office in Mier?" Juan said.

"I am afraid that is impossible," the doctor said. "Mexican soldiers are in Mier, watching the border."

"We've got to get a wagon," Juan said. "Doctor, please give me a list of anything you need to help Henry. I will ride ahead to Texas and bring help. José, you keep going north, and I will meet you as soon as I can. Doctor, can you please stay with them? I will pay you well."

"Of course," the doctor said.

"If you must slow down for Henry's sake, do so," Juan told de la Peña.

"Fellas," Henry called from his travois, "if I'm gonna die, I want to die in Texas."

The caravan of wounded, now with de la Peña in the lead, inched its way north. Instead of thirty miles a day, they did well to travel fifteen, stopping occasionally to give Henry some water and a little to eat.

They stayed east of Mier and headed for the ford as agreed with Seguin. Finally, they could see Texas.

"Almost home, Henry," Horace said.

They topped a gently sloping hill and descended toward the Rio Grande. Dense thickets of mesquite surrounded the area, but this well-worn and heavily used road cut through to the ford. It was high risk to use such an open area but it was a risk they had to hazard. Henry wasn't up to a rough crossing or crashing through the scrub.

They were halfway down the hill, less than a hundred yards from the river, when a dozen Mexican soldiers rode out of the trees on their right. Another dozen broke through the brush on the left, and the two groups joined and arrayed in a line across the road. A young lieutenant, sword drawn, was at the center of the formation.

"Stop!" he called to the fugitives. "You are under arrest."

"Do we give or fight?" Henry said, raising on an elbow from his travois, a pistol in hand.

"We may as well fight, my friends," de la Peña said. "For they will surely execute us."

"We fight," Horace said, and started to draw his rifle from his saddle scabbard.

"Surrender now!" the lieutenant called. "You will lay down your weapons or you will be shot. And as a warning to the rest of your rabble in Texas to stay out of Mexico's affairs, we will cut off your heads and mount them on the border."

In the quiet moment before the fighting began, the hammer of a gun was heard, loudly and clearly, clicking back into full cock. The sound came not from the Mexicans or the outnumbered men before them, but from behind the soldiers.

Another click. And another. Four, five, six, seven more.

The lieutenant lost count.

"Lieutenant," a voice from the brush called in Spanish. "I don't know about the heads of those men in front of you, but I can guarantee what's going to happen to your head if you don't leave right now."

More clicks. More guns at full cock. There had to be at least a dozen, the lieutenant calculated. All with clear shots at the backs of his men, who made first-rate targets sitting high on horseback and completely stationary. Much to the lieutenant's horror, the sergeant beside him started to draw his pistol.

"Sergeant," another voice called from the brush. "That would be a poor choice."

"You play poker?" Henry whispered to de la Peña.

"What?" de la Peña said.

"Just watch."

The lieutenant struggled with what to do. He desperately wanted to turn, to see who this new enemy was, where it was, and how many.

"No need to turn around, Lieutenant," the first voice called. "If you want to keep your head and those of your men, ride out.

Turn your men down the path you came in on to your left. Ride out nice and easy. If I see one man go for his gun or move toward our friends, I promise all of you will die."

The lieutenant looked up. A horde of vultures swirled overhead.

"Ride out," the voice commanded. "Now."

Very slowly, the lieutenant sheathed his sword. "Platoon!" he called. He waved his arm and spurred his horse onto the path to his left, and his men followed. The gunmen hidden in the brush waited until the Mexican platoon was well out of sight.

"Hello, Henry," Silas said, easing his horse forward from cover. Silas had his Hawken rifle in one hand, a .50-caliber pistol in other.

Several feet to Silas's right, Sam McCulloch stepped out. He had a rifle and two pistols, and was busy uncocking them without accidentally shooting himself.

"Was you figurin' to burn all that powder yourself, Sam?"

"All at once, Henry. I'm a one-man volley."

J.C. limped out of the brush in a similar state of armament, followed by Juan Seguin and Jacob Millsaps.

"Five?" de la Peña said. "Just five?"

"I suggest we clear out before they figure out how few we are," Silas said. "We have a wagon for the wounded and the medical supplies the doctor requested."

"Captain de la Peña," Henry said, "if you play cards, do not play against Silas Grant."

"I understand," de la Peña said. "A very clever..." de la Peña looked closely at Silas. "How old is he?"

"Good to see you, Jacob, J.C.," Horace said. "Where'd you boys come from?"

"We finished on the coast and rode to Goliad when Juan showed up," J.C. said. "Then we hurried down here."

"What about Senator Burton? Did you find him?"

"We did," J.C. said. "He sailed back to Houston."

"Sailed?"

"Long story. I'll explain later. Now let's get you home."

CHAPTER 21

DURING THE TEXAS Revolution, Goliad was a strategic crossroad. The Atascosito Road ran from Matamoros along the Gulf Coast to Goliad, where it divided, one path heading east toward Galveston Bay, the other northeast into the heart of Texas. El Camino Real de los Tejas led from Goliad to San Antonio. The town possessed a strong fortress, the Presidio of La Bahia, which lay in a bend in the San Antonio River. Texians captured the fortress early in the war, and Colonel James Fannin held it until his ill-fated attempt to retreat north led to his men's capture and eventual execution.

Now, Goliad was again at the center of the Texians' world. Because word had spread, northwest to San Antonio, south down the Gulf Coast, and east to Houston and Nacogdoches.

Henry Wax Karnes was dying.

The Texians and de la Peña arrived in Goliad six days after crossing the Rio Grande. Even with the doctor from Mier on hand, Henry was slipping away.

By the time the Texians reached Goliad, Erasmo Seguin had assembled a medical team—including Dr. Nicholas Labadie, who had removed bullets from numerous Texians during the Revolution—and ensconced them at the Dimmitt House, an inn and trading post in Goliad. They immediately went to work on Henry, who objected to their prodding and poking but was too weak to do anything about it.

"I've seen this before," de la Peña said. "We lost many men at the Alamo, dying slowly. But we had no doctors, no surgeons, so, perhaps…"

"Dr. Labadie says he should be dead already," J.C. said. "He's strong, so, maybe…"

The Texians and de la Peña had gathered in the Dimmitt House's sitting room.

"I wish we could do something," Silas said.

"We can," J.C. said. "We do what Henry wants. We keep going. We've come too far to stop now."

On the ride north from the Rio Grande, the Texians had caught up with one another on their activities since speaking with Rafael Vega on the road to Goliad.

Horace and Juan were told of Senator Burton leading the Texians to Copano Bay, discovering *Watchman*, locating Dr. Thorn's remains, and the testimony of Levi Jones about a wounded man missing a leg who was put aboard *Watchman* and sailed to Mexico.

"What happened to Senator Burton?" Juan asked. "You didn't make him ride back to Houston alone?"

"He sailed to Houston on *Watchman*," J.C. said. "I think Captain Jones wanted to get in the Senator's good graces after Jones made some pretty insulting comments."

Horace and Juan related their journey from Matamoros to Villa de San Mateo del Pilón to Mier.

Finally, the Texians described the entire Crockett affair to de la Peña, who sat quietly, digesting the story, and remained silent when it was finished.

"It doesn't appear the Mexicans know anything about our investigations, about us chasing Crockett?" Silas asked.

"It doesn't sound like it," Juan said.

"What happened in Villa de San Mateo del Pilón has nothing to do with Crockett," de la Peña finally spoke. "It's about the rebellion in Mexico. I don't think the Mexican government knows anything about Crockett. Tell me, gentlemen, do you now believe Crockett is alive?"

It was the first time the question had been posed directly since the investigation began, though every one of the Texians had considered it again and again.

"Just a few weeks ago, I would have said no," J.C. said. "But now, with everything we've seen. Yes. I think he's alive."

Juan, Horace, Silas, and Sam nodded in agreement.

Jacob hesitated. "Even with his leg blown off," he said, "I'm surprised he gave up. Maybe he didn't have a choice. Maybe he couldn't fight. Or maybe he did surrender."

"I do not believe David Crockett surrendered," de la Peña said, rising to his feet and pacing the room. "My friends, everything you have seen and told me all makes sense. Finally, after two years of being haunted by the thought that there might have been a competent doctor who could have saved my men. What happened to him? Where did he come from and why did he disappear? I understand now.

"During the battle, my battalion's commanding officers were wounded and I was tasked with relaying messages between General Castrillón and General Cós and Colonel Romero. The man you spoke with, Vega, saw Dr. Thorn escorted into the fort by Captain Huerta. Vega told me this at the time, and I followed Huerta into the fort. When I arrived, I saw a stretcher being taken out through the south gate, and Huerta followed the stretcher. And I saw who was directing it all. General Joaquin Ramirez y Sesma.

"I do not exaggerate when I say that I despise Ramirez. He made a profit on the army's march north, keeping money intended to buy provisions for the troops. When he arrived in San Antonio, he failed to seize the bridge between with city and the Alamo, which would have prevented the defenders from taking refuge in the Alamo. He is a timid, irresolute commander, but he is also a cruel and opportunistic man.

"You said one of your witnesses saw a tall general among the Texian dead, near the palisade. I believe he was standing over your Crockett until Huerta could carry him off and Dr. Thorn could keep him alive."

"General Ramirez saw Crockett, wounded and helpless, recognized him, and took him prisoner," Silas said.

"In case the need of such a hostage should ever arise," de la Peña said. "All of Mexico knows of the Americans' desire for the lands from here to the Pacific Ocean. Ramirez ordered Huerta to commandeer the doctor, who was being held away from the rest of the army in case a senior officer needed help. Huerta grabbed a wagon. I learned later that an ambulance went missing after the battle. Huerta and his hand-picked men took Crockett to Copano, boarded one of the brigs shuttling supplies north and messages south, and sailed him to Mexico."

De la Peña stared off into the distance, putting the final pieces together. "This is all about Santa Anna. Ramirez is utterly loyal to him, and Huerta is completely loyal to Ramirez. They would have put Crockett someplace under Santa Anna's control. And he was born in Veracruz."

"Maybe he's there, in Veracruz?" Horace said.

"I don't think they would keep him in a city," de la Peña said. "Too many people, too many eyes, too likely to be discovered. They'd want someplace private, secluded."

"A farm or ranch?" Silas suggested.

"Santa Anna has two haciendas in the Veracruz region," de la Peña said.

J.C. looked around the room. "We have to figure out which one."

★

The death watch was drawing to a close.

The doctors' best efforts had slowed his descent but could not stop it, and finally Henry had had enough. He thanked them for their efforts but asked them to leave him in peace.

"It's my time," was the last thing he said to Dr. Labadie.

Labadie nodded, conceding the inevitable. He shook Henry's hand and left.

At Henry's request, each of the Texians paid a final visit. Erasmo, who Henry thanked for his hospitality and kindness. Then Juan Seguin, Horace Alsbury, J.C. Neill, and Sam McCulloch. He thanked each of them for their friendship and companionship through times good and bad, for their courage, for their determination, and for allowing him on this final adventure.

"Wouldn't have missed it for the world," he said.

Sam, like everyone else, emerged from Henry's room cuffing his eyes. He composed himself and went looking for Silas. He found him in the Dimmitt House's sitting room, in silence. Silas looked up at Sam's approach.

"Do you know," Sam said, taking a chair opposite Silas, "what Henry's biggest contribution to the victory at San Jacinto was?"

Silas was a little surprised at the question and took a moment to respond. "He was second in command for Lamar's cavalry and he routed the—"

"No," Sam interrupted. "I mean, yes, he did that. But earlier than that. Three days before the battle, Henry and Deaf Smith were scouting when they captured a Mexican courier carrying documents that revealed the location and disposition of Santa Anna's forces and his battle plans. That's when Sam Houston learned that Santa Anna had moved too far away from the rest of his army. Left himself vulnerable. So, Sam Houston moved the army to Buffalo Bayou, and we attacked at San Jacinto and won the war. That doesn't happen if not for Henry."

"I didn't know," Silas said.

"Yeah. Not enough folks do. That's a good and great man dying in that room."

"I won't forget him."

"I know you won't. You get in there now. He wants to see you."

Silas wasn't sure he was up to this. In his short life, he'd never had anyone dear to him die. His parents and siblings were alive and well, he respected but was not close to his uncle who was killed in the war, and he had never met his grandparents, alive or dead in some far-flung land. Silas Grant had never dealt with death.

He walked into Henry's room. Jacob was seated in a corner, and that was fine with Henry. Jacob was staying to the end.

Henry was pale as the sheets around him. His eyes were sunken, his face gaunt. Beads of sweat lined his face from the fever, but the medical devices and pills and ointments were gone.

"You're gonna have to come closer," Henry rasped.

Silas strode across the room and fell to his knees at Henry's bedside, barely holding himself together. He had no idea what to say and managed to choke off asking Henry how he was doing. Henry lifted his hand and Silas took it.

"Henry," was all that came out of his quivering lips.

"I need you to do me a favor. It's important."

"Anything. Anything."

"This is gonna sound easy, but it ain't. It's hard. I'm askin' you to make a promise for the rest of your life." Henry looked into Silas's eyes. "Marry that girl."

Henry laid back, and for a moment Silas thought he was asleep, but his eyes fluttered open again.

"I never had anybody like Emily," Henry said, staring up at the ceiling. "I've had my share of women. Probably more than my share," and he smiled at the thought of the Powell sisters in a tent not long ago. "But no one...no one like that. Nothin' like you and she got. That's about the only thing I regret."

Henry turned to Silas again. "I want you to hear me now. You hold on to Emily. Hold on to that woman. I know you want to take care of her, and it's good you feel that way. But you let her take care of you, too. You hear me?" his voice cracked.

"I hear you, Henry." Silas's eyes filled with tears. "I promise. I'll never let Emily go."

"Good. That's good."

No one in the Dimmitt House slept that night. By morning it was over. Henry Karnes passed away just before dawn.

Jacob finally emerged from the death watch to a hall filled with Texians, who peeked through the door. Henry was covered with a sheet.

Jacob looked near as ghastly as Henry had. He hadn't slept or eaten in days, forgoing himself to sit with his friend and make sure he was not alone for even a moment of his last days. That had been accomplished.

"He had one last message for us," Jacob said, and looked at each Texian in turn, just as he had weeks ago when the Texians viewed the sketch and began this quest. Jacob's eyes challenged every Texian. None flinched. None looked away.

"Bring Crockett home."

Riders from Goliad spread the word throughout Texas. One of the Republic's legends was gone.

Erasmo brought an undertaker of great skill and respect to handle the final arrangements, and by the next day, Henry was ready for his last journey.

Henry was placed not in a plain pine box but a coffin of polished oak with a padded interior and a pillow for his head. On the coffin's lid was a silver star of Texas.

For his trip to San Antonio, where the funeral was to be held, he rode in a black hearse with glass sides, brass lanterns at the corners, drawn by four horses, and accompanied by Sam, Jacob, J.C., and Horace out front, and Juan, Erasmo, and Silas behind the hearse. They invited de la Peña to join them. He said he'd be honored, and rode alongside Silas.

The procession swelled along the route, attracting veterans of the Revolution, Henry's friends, and people who had never met Henry Karnes but knew of him and greatly admired him.

When the hearse reached San Antonio, it felt as though half of Texas had turned out for the funeral. The onlookers included much of the Republic of Texas government, including Mirabeau B. Lamar, David G. Burnett, Anson Jones, and Edward Burleson, as well as a crowd of Texas Rangers, including Robert McAlpin Williamson, John Coffee Hays, and William Wallace. Sam Houston was to give the eulogy, and Isaac Burton was to speak as well.

Horace was able to convince Juana to make a rare appearance in San Antonio, and afterward she was glad she came.

Elizabeth Powell, her two sons, and her two grieving daughters were there.

Also in attendance was a crowd from the Brazos Valley, including Sam's wife and siblings, as well as Silas's parents, brother, and sister. Silas introduced twelve-year-old Thomas Grant to several legendary Texians while three-year-old Katie Grant just wanted to be held by her big brother.

And Emily was there, having traveled with the Grants. Silas felt certain she would attend, but his relief at seeing Emily so overwhelmed him that he rushed into her arms the instant he saw her and broke down in tears. She held him without saying a word.

Finding a place for everyone to stay was a monumental challenge, especially when so many dignitaries were able to wheedle more than their fair share of the limited space in town. Fortunately, Erasmo Seguin had sent word days earlier of the impending funeral and urged the city fathers to prepare, and a tent city sprouted on the southside of town next to the San Antonio River. Erasmo, however, provided space for the Texians who had been with Henry at the end, as well as their families.

There were some raised eyebrows when it was revealed that Jacob, Horace, J.C., Sam, Juan, and Silas were to be the pallbearers, especially when so many figures of great stature were available. But Sam Houston, who was to oversee the ceremony, would brook no objections. Horace, to compensate for his wounded left shoulder, was assigned to the left side of the casket.

Everywhere in the city was great anticipation of the funeral.

Almost everywhere.

In 1838, there were three great landmarks in San Antonio: the Alamo, the San Antonio River, and the Cathedral de San Fernando on the west side of the city's central plaza. Much of San Antonio's cultural history centered around the Cathedral, construction of which began in 1731, just thirteen years after the town's founding. San Fernando was host to one of the city's most memorable social occasions a few years earlier, when lovely San Antonio native Maria Ursula Veramendi married future hero of the Texas Revolution Jim Bowie.

But now the Cathedral turned its back on another hero of Texas.

Henry Wax Karnes, veteran of the battles of Concepcion, Béxar, and San Jacinto, who went to Matamoros to negotiate the release of Texas prisoners from the Mexican Army only to be imprisoned before affecting his own escape, and who raised eight companies of Texas Rangers to defend the frontier, was refused a funeral in the Cathedral de San Fernando and denied burial in the Campo Santos Cemetery on the west edge of town.

Because, although Henry was a beloved hero, he was not Catholic.

So, when more than a thousand Texians gathered in the plaza to say farewell to Henry, if the Cathedral had been on fire, it is doubtful that any in attendance would have attempted to dissuade the blaze. Given the situation, San Fernando's priests wisely kept out of sight.

On a sunny morning, Texas said farewell to Henry Wax Karnes as he would have preferred: out of doors, under God's one true church. A platform was set at the opposite end of the plaza, away from the cathedral, and Sam Houston and Isaac Burton spoke eloquently.

Then the casket was carried from town by Henry's friends, with President Houston leading the way. The procession walked past the cemetery to a quiet, shady spot behind the graveyard, where the mourners laid Henry to rest.

Later that afternoon, an enormous festival was held in the plaza to celebrate Henry's life. Señora Candelaria made the arrangements. There was dance and music, tables were filled with food, beer and whiskey flowed, and the stories of Henry's exploits filled the night. Everyone agreed that Henry would have approved.

CHAPTER 22

SAN AGUSTIN WAS five miles south of the heart of Mexico City, in the shadow of the snow-covered volcano of Ajusco, surrounded by orchards of apricot, pear, and plum trees, and dotted with gardens of all manner of flowers.

It was a beautiful setting for blood sport.

For three days each year, this sleepy village erupted in festivities surrounding cockfights and associated gambling. It was difficult to tell what gleamed more under the Mexican sun—the coins being wagered, the blades of the victors, or the blood of the defeated.

The fête of San Agustin was an occasion that crossed all lines of culture and class. Rich or poor, Mexico came to San Agustin to gamble on chickens with knives strapped to their legs and sent into a ring to slaughter one another in an explosion of feathers and gore. Mexico's president, much of his cabinet, and many foreign dignitaries bet gold from boxes and seats around the cock square, their coachmen and servants bet silver in the arena's doorways, and peasants bet copper on the streets.

Surrounding the stadium in which these fowl fights took place were the real winners of the fête—the gambling houses. As long as they kept their books balanced, the bookmakers won no matter which cocks survived.

And for the fête of San Agustin, even the churches were open to sanctify the sin.

On the last day of the fête, Powhatan Ellis endured a traffic jam through constricted roads into San Agustin, his coach mired in the crowd of gamblers arriving via cart or carriage, on horse or mule or foot.

Once in the arena, Ellis jostled his way to his seat. Surrounded by gaily dressed men and women in the gallery, Ellis recognized a number of foreign ministers enthusiastically betting on the outcomes. The American sat patiently through bout after bout of crowing combatants.

Ellis did not want to be here. He wanted to continue the pursuit of information from Mrs. Ward regarding the sketch. Ellis had waited impatiently for some word from Mrs. Ward, who had told Hiram Brown at Real del Monte that she would review Fanny Calderón de la Barca's journals to determine where she had made the sketch that had set off this chain of events. Ellis had attempted to insinuate himself inconspicuously into the path of the travels of the Spanish minister, his wife, and their companion but had so far been unsuccessful.

Instead, he was sitting here watching chickens turning one another into cutlets.

"Good afternoon, Powhatan," Luis Cuevas said, taking a seat to Ellis's left. "I'm delighted you could come. Have you had many winners?"

"I'm not much of a gambler," the American minister told the Mexican secretary of foreign affairs.

"Have you never attended a cockfight?"

"I've seen my share. Cockfights are not quite so elegant in the United States."

"But you do not have bullfighting, am I correct?"

"No bullfights, Luis. Americans don't appreciate men with swords fighting a bull. But they enjoy pitting animals against one another. Dogfights, dogs killing rats, bulls fighting bears, that sort of thing."

"But bullfighting is an art, Powhatan," Luis said. "These other fights you describe, they have very little style."

"No, Luis, they have absolutely no style, but people like them."

"You mean, people like to wager on them."

"Precisely."

"But attending events such as this is part of our duties, is it not?" Cuevas said. "No matter how distasteful we may find them."

"You don't care for the cockfights?"

"Actually, I never miss the fête," Cuevas said. "I made a tidy profit the last two years."

"Congratulations," Ellis said.

"Cheer up, Powhatan. I believe you will be pleased by the other guests I've invited," Cuevas said, and departed to place more bets.

Ellis sighed and thought of being someplace else. Any place else.

"Good afternoon, Mr. Ellis," a soft voice called from his right.

Ellis turned to see Fanny Calderón de la Barca, stunning in a rather low-cut floral print dress, take the seat next to him. Beside her was her husband, the Spanish minister Ángel Calderón de la Barca. And opposite him was a woman Ellis had not met but Hiram Brown had described.

Ellis belatedly stood to greet the Spanish minister's party and was introduced to Mrs. Ward, who curtsied in greeting.

"It's very nice to meet you, Mrs. Ward," Ellis said. "I admire your sketches," he said, hoping to ignite the conversation he so desperately needed to have with this lady. Instead, Mrs. Ward nodded politely, smiled, and took her seat. The minister and Fanny sat, and, finally, Ellis resumed his seat.

"It's so nice to see you again Mr. Ellis," Fanny said.

"A delight to see you Madame Calderón de la Barca."

"Are you winning today? Your bets, I mean, on the cockfights."

"I'm not much of a gambler."

"That is very wise, Mr. Ellis," Ángel said. "Gambling and drink, two sins a man should avoid."

"Yes. Fortunately, I'm not a man," Fanny said. "I'll place a bet or two today."

"Good luck to you," Ellis said.

"It's not quite the glory of a bullfight, is it?" Ángel said. "No riders, no matador. I do miss the magnificence of the great bullrings in Spain. I will show you someday, my dear."

"That would be wonderful," Fanny said.

She watched two gamecocks hurl themselves at one another, wings flapping, kicking their feet at the opponent. Blood and plumage flew. She sighed. "Just two birds in a knife fight."

"You disapprove?" The tone of Ellis's voice told Fanny he did not enjoy the fights.

"Not if the bird I bet on wins," she said. She glanced at her husband, put her hand on Ángel's thigh. "Besides, I appreciate a strong cock."

Ellis cleared his throat and glanced to his right. Ángel glanced at Fanny and at Ellis, and offered a small, embarrassed smile.

"Ángel," Fanny said, "would you get me something to drink? Something sinful."

The minister rose, bowed, and went in search of refreshment.

"Now, Mr. Ellis, may I ask you a question?"

"Of course. How can I be of help?"

Fanny moved closer, her lips next to Ellis's face. That beautiful face, those sensational lips. He could smell her perfume. This woman was so alluring—

"You can tell me what this bullshit is about this sketch," Fanny said.

Ellis almost choked. "I'm not sure—"

"An old friend in Mexico? What old friends do you have in the hinterlands of Mexico?"

"I, uh—"

"Especially an old friend who just happens to look like Davy Crockett."

Ellis was suddenly reminded of the evening had seen the sketch, the sight of which caused his head to spin, his heartbeat to quicken, and his mouth go dry. That was the picture of health compared to this.

As the fabulous Fanny Calderón de la Barca seized him with her eyes, every drop of blood drained from Powhatan Ellis's face. He forgot how to breathe. He actually forgot how to breathe. His lungs had apparently seized up, and he wondered if his heart would be next. He very nearly fainted, and he could tell from the wry, satisfied smile that crossed Fanny's amazing face that he had gone pale, white as a bed sheet. His oxygen-deprived brain reeled.

He tried to respond but was dismayed to discover that he had lost the power of speech.

"Come, now, Mr. Ellis," Fanny cooed. "What is this about?"

"It's just…"

"Just what, Powhatan?" She leaned closer. Stunning cleavage peeked out from the top of Fanny's dress.

Unbelievable! Ellis thought. *I'm fantasizing about this woman while she's dissecting me and turning my world upside down!*

"I don't know what this is about, Mr. Ellis," Fanny said. "I don't know what you and the American government are up to. I doubt this is about an old friend. Frankly, I don't care what this is about. But I do insist you not involve Mrs. Ward in your intrigues. She is a lovely person who is far too trusting to be involved in political games. And she knows nothing of the matters into which you are inquiring. You *are* inquiring, are you not? Or was it just coincidence that you took that sketch from the Prussian ministry and sent Mr. Brown to Real del Monte?"

Ellis remained silent, staring impassively at Fanny.

"I will make a deal with you," she said, just as her husband returned with a glass of tequila, which he handed to his wife. She drained it in one gulp. "Mrs. Ward has tired of Mexico and wishes to return to the United States. You have a ship that can move freely through the French blockade. Correct?"

"Correct," Ellis said.

"Good. Will you be so kind as to provide passage for Mrs. Ward to America? Perhaps your Mr. Brown could escort her to New Orleans. From there she can make her own travel arrangements home. Would that be agreeable?"

"Completely," Ellis said.

"I thought as much. Have Mr. Brown meet her at the port of Veracruz in eight days. Will your ship be available at that time?"

"I will see to it," Ellis said, the color returning to his face.

"Thank you, Mr. Ellis. Now we should be going. We are dining shortly before attending a ball at Calvario. I wish you could join us at General Moran's home tonight. He has a splendid house and garden, and we are told the president may attend."

"That should be very pleasant." The early exit took him by surprise. But why not? Everything about this meeting had been an ambush.

"I regret that you have matters to which you must attend," and Fanny rose and nodded to her husband, who also stood.

Ellis stood, trying to think what to do. This entire business was definitely outside his portfolio, and he still didn't have the answers he needed regarding the sketch.

Fanny smiled and extended her hand, and Ellis bowed and took the delicate hand of Madame Calderón de la Barca.

"Goodbye, Mr. Ellis. And good luck." Fanny whirled and walked away. Mrs. Ward fell in behind her, and the Spanish minister, after nodding a farewell to Ellis, brought up the rear of the three-person formation. They vanished into the crowd.

Ellis sat back down, dumbfounded. *Now what?*

When he regained his senses, he realized Fanny had pressed a folded piece of paper into his hand. A road-worn bit of drawing paper. He unfolded it, not bothering to shield it from those around him. Fortunately, the crowd was intent on the next cockfight.

He opened the paper. It was the sketch of Crockett. But something new was at the bottom of the page. On the right side of the page was a vertical line that curved down off the bottom of the page. The letter V was written next to the line. From the V, a double line stretched to the left, crossed a thin line marked "Medio," and meandered its way across the width of the page.

A third of the way from the right side of the page was written "Sante Fe." A third of the way from the left side of the page was another double line, headed up and running into a final notation. Three words. Circled.

"Manga de Clavo."

★

"How much do you think she knows?" Brown said when he and Ellis were alone in the legation that night.

"I don't know," Ellis said. He tapped his fingers nervously on his desk. "She recognized Crockett, but I suppose that shouldn't be too surprising since she lived near Washington. She's one of the few people in Mexico who could recognize the face in the sketch."

Ellis laid the sketch flat on his desk.

"What do you make of this? It's a map, I'm sure of that," Ellis said.

"That line on the right, with a V next to it," Brown said. "That must be the coast. The V must be Veracruz."

"Medio is the Rio Medio, which is just outside town, is it not?"

"About five miles from the docks. There's a bridge across the river on the road heading west."

"And Sante Fe?"

"A small village outside of Veracruz. This double line across the page must be the road out of Veracruz."

Ellis studied the map. "The double line branching off that road is, what, a side road? And Manga de Clavo?"

"Santa Anna has two haciendas in the hills outside of Veracruz. Hacienda del Lencero is southeast of the city of Xalapa, about fifty miles from Veracruz. The other is Manga de Clavo, about fifteen miles from the port."

"Manga de Clavo," Ellis said. "I believe the minister, his wife, and Mrs. Ward toured that area after they docked at Veracruz when they arrived in Mexico. I know she met Santa Anna. God, if only I had the first batch of letters she sent home. Every one of them reads like a travelogue. Who she met, where she met them, what she saw. She probably talked about meeting Santa Anna. That must be it. That must be where Mrs. Ward saw Crockett."

"I'll try to confirm that with Mrs. Ward at the ship," Brown said. "I'll deliver the map and information to the Texians. The question remains, however, how much did de la Barca tell Ward? Do you think she told Mrs. Ward the name of the subject of her drawing?"

That very disturbing thought had not crossed Ellis's mind.

"It's one thing to have Fanny in Mexico with that information," Ellis said. "I don't think she would say anything to the Mexicans. I don't know if she's said anything to her husband. But Mrs. Ward, well, I don't know. You spoke to her. Is she likely to say something once she's back in the United States?"

"Unlikely, I think," Brown said. He thought for a moment. "I do not believe she would deliberately reveal the secret, but could she accidentally say something? Perhaps telling of her travels in Mexico, and the name just come out? Possibly."

"Could we detain her? Hold her somewhere until this mess is resolved?"

"Problematic. Where would we hold her? For what reason? We'd have to depend on the cooperation of additional people who know nothing about the matter. The more people involved, the more risk of exposure, of publicity."

"What do we do?"

"I think we have to trust her. I'll talk to her. Try to find out what she knows about the sketch and its subject. If she knows nothing, we have no problem. If she does know the identity of the sketch's subject, I'll impress the need to absolute secrecy. After I show the map to the Texians, I'll destroy the sketch. Then any talk is just wild rumor without evidence, same as the business with the prisoner in the mine."

"Very well," Ellis said. "That sounds like our best course. I don't see an alternative."

Brown did see an alternative but said nothing to Ellis.

There were so many loose ends. Loose ends were never good. They had a tendency to stay loose. Fray. Unravel. Entangle. And lead back.

And Brown didn't want anything leading back to Ellis. Or himself.

But perhaps he could assuage his anxiety. Tie up those loose ends. He would talk to Mrs. Ward and learn what she knew, and if she was as ignorant of this matter as Madame Calderón de la Barca would have Ellis believe, they would have no problems. No loose ends.

The next morning, Brown headed for Veracruz to await Mrs. Ward, escort her onto *Woodbury*, and sail to New Orleans. Then he would return to Texas.

CHAPTER 23

SANTA ANNA SULKED.

Antonio de Padua María Severino López de Santa Anna y Pérez de Lebrón dreamed of resurrecting a career so dreadfully damaged by his thrashing at the hands of nine hundred out-numbered, tired, but vengeful Texians in eighteen minutes at San Jacinto. After his capture a day after the battle, when he was found in a private's uniform, Santa Anna spent a year in captivity in Texas and United States before being returned to Mexico. Now he was a man in exile at his hacienda in the hills in his home state of Veracruz.

Once he ruled a nation that stretched more than twenty-five hundred miles—from Central America to the Pacific Northwest.

Now he was reduced to twelve leagues of land.

Once he lived in the National Palace, home of Mexico's rulers since the days of the Aztecs.

Now he resided in a hacienda with a lovely stone house that stayed cool in summer and warm and dry in winter, a stable for his treasured white destrier, a blacksmith's shop, a coop for his collection of gamecocks, a cock square for their battles with rival landowners' gamecocks, a kitchen, a smokehouse, and apartments for staff and guards.

Once he lived in opulence.

Now he paced wood floors adorned with colorful wool rugs from Alpujarras, along walls hung with paintings in rococo, gold-leaf frames, in rooms with hand-carved, painted benches depicting Mexican birds and flowers.

Once he worked from an office where once sat the conqueror Cortés.

Now he made do with a sunny study with a spectacular vargueno writing cabinet.

Once he slept in a palatial bedroom.

Now he slept in a large bed with a hand-carved headboard, surrounded by armoires of inlaid marquetry, all made of golden brown, burled parota wood.

Once he feasted in an opulent dining room with heads of state.

Now he dined on venison, cabrito, beef, chicken, fish, vegetables, fruits, and cheeses from farms around his hacienda, served on French white and gold porcelain in a dining room with a large parota wood table.

Once he lived in one of the most polluted cities in the world.

Now he dwelled in a green, verdant, tree- and flower-filled land.

As places of exile went, a disgraced president could do a lot worse than Manga de Clavo.

The ridiculous thing about Santa Anna's exile was that being at Manga de Clavo was exactly what he wanted.

After coming to power in 1833, his first term as president lasted nineteen days. He wasn't chased from office, was not victim of a scandal or coup or assassination attempt. He simply wasn't interested in the job's day-to-day duties, so he turned things over to his vice president and retired to Manga de Clavo.

After two weeks off, he returned to office—for eighteen days. Over the course of twenty-two years, Santa Anna would eventually hold the office of president eleven times for a grand total of six years. Nine of his terms would last less than a year, three less than a month, and his total time in office through his first ten terms as president would add up to less than a single four-year term of an American president.

Santa Anna very much wanted the title of president, but he found the job tiresome. His interests—besides feeding his ego—were elsewhere.

He enjoyed blood sports and indulged in cockfights and bull-fights, which perhaps accounted for his eagerness to lead armies into battle. Those campaigns, which had the side benefit of removing him from the presidential desk that he found so confining, satisfied his bloodlust, evidenced by his conduct against his enemies. Prior to his order of no quarter at the Alamo and to execute Texian prisoners at Goliad, Santa Anna, after defeating Mexican rebels at Zacatecas, turned the city over to his troops for two days of rape, murder, and looting.

His other great passion was women, though not necessarily for those to whom he was wed. He was married twice to wealthy young women but didn't bother to attend either wedding, allowing surrogates—first his bride's father and second a friend—to handle the vows. Both unions brought Santa Anna considerable wealth, some of which he used to buy Manga de Clavo.

Though married, his appetite for women was unrestrained. Over his lifetime, Santa Anna had more than four hundred mistresses and incalculable one-night stands. He was certainly a lady's man: tall and handsome with black hair atop a high forehead. He was polished, educated, intelligent, well-dressed, and fluent in Spanish, English, and French.

So in 1838, even though in disgrace, Santa Anna had all he truly wanted. He lived where he wished, did what he wished, and slept with whom he wished.

But his ambitions would not permit him to enjoy his wealth and holdings. From this luxurious garden spot fifteen miles from the port of Veracruz, Santa Anna plotted redeeming his name, returning to power, and punishing his enemies.

Those enemies were numerous, and counted among them was José Enrique de la Peña, a captain of the Toluca Battalion in Santa Anna's army who was held in high regard by his men.

"Who is this upstart!" Santa Anna railed, rising from behind his desk and throwing a weeks-old copy of the newspaper *El Cosmopolita* across his study. "How dare he criticize me! He'd be nothing without me! I approved his promotion to captain!"

"My general—" Santa Anna's tall, clean-shaven aide-de-camp tried to calm the tirade.

"He's calling for others to join Urrea! Against me! Me!" Santa Anna was red in the face. "Who is he to question the Napoleon of the West?"

José Enrique de la Peña had become the most vocal critic of Santa Anna.

Though de la Peña felt the army's invasion of Texas justified and believed in maintaining the integrity of Mexican territory, he criticized the handling of the campaign by Santa Anna and members of his senior staff. He criticized the "ignorance, stupidity, and cruelty" of the commander-in-chief. He felt Santa Anna's "interests were in war, for war would increase his fame." He believed Santa Anna ignored the advice of advisors, and felt Santa Anna pushed for battle rather than allowing the enemy to surrender because Santa Anna felt there was no glory without bloodshed.

He was outraged and astonished that Santa Anna, who knew the Texians were nearby at San Jacinto, could be taken by surprise in the middle of the afternoon. And he seethed that Santa Anna, in an act of supreme cowardice, signed away Texas in exchange for his own life.

"My general," the aide-de-camp said, calmly remaining at attention. "De la Peña is of no consequence. No one pays him any attention."

"Someone is paying him attention! He speaks against me at every opportunity. He incites rebellion and he supports enemies like that traitor Urrea. His articles are in newspapers, and now I'm told he plans to publish a memoir with a diary of his time on the campaign! What does he know? Ramirez, find this man and put an end to him. I will not tolerate such insolence!"

Sometimes, Ramirez thought, *Santa Anna forgets he is no longer president.*

Joaquin Ramirez y Sesma was of Spanish descent. He had dark hair and a long nose, cast a lean figure, and looked formidable with sword in hand, though his performance on the battlefield had been lackluster. He failed to take action when opportunities presented themselves, such as when he refused to seize the bridge across the San Antonio River, a move that could have prevented many of the Texians from taking shelter in the Alamo.

He was, however, skilled at slaughter. On the morning of the final assault on the Alamo, his lancers operated outside the walls of the fort, chasing down and butchering the handful of defenders who tried to flee when the battle was hopeless.

But what Ramirez offered, and what Santa Anna most valued, was unwavering loyalty.

After Santa Anna's defeat and exile to Manga de Clavo, Ramirez remained steadfast. Both Ramirez and his right-hand man, Captain

Carolino Huerta, never gave thought to abandoning the former president. That devotion was rewarded by Santa Anna, who made Ramirez his aide-de-camp and put Huerta in charge of Manga de Clavo's small staff of guards, which consisted of a handful of Huerta's soldiers from the campaign in Texas.

From Ramirez and Huerta, Santa Anna would build a new army, return to power, and crush his enemies like Urrea, Antonio Canales, and de la Peña.

Still, the general fought his own battles with paranoia born of making so many enemies, and the public criticisms of de la Peña exacerbated his anxiety.

"Ramirez, I want you to prepare for an evacuation," Santa Anna said, pacing his study in a nervous frenzy.

"Evacuation, my general? From Manga de Clavo?"

"Urrea's forces cannot be far. That traitor will come for me. It's not enough he stole my glory in Texas. He wants me dead or in prison."

"As you wish, my general," Ramirez said. "To where should we go if the need arises? Not Mexico City?"

"No, I have far too many enemies there," Santa Anna said, continuing to patrol his study and peeking out windows. "No, we will move operations to Xalapa, to my hacienda at Lencero. We should move immediately. We will take everything."

"My general, may I suggest we consider staying here, at least for the moment," Ramirez said. "I believe the presence of the French forces off our shores will keep the rebels away. And the French could present an opportunity for you if foreign troops land in Veracruz."

Santa Anna stopped his pacing and considered Ramirez's suggestion. "Do we know how many troops the French have?"

"They cannot have more than a few thousand."

"And they will need most of those to occupy the fort and the city," Santa Anna said.

"Any units moving away from the city will be only a few companies," Ramirez said.

"But if we strike at those troops outside of the city and score a quick victory…"

"You will be seen has having driven off the invaders."

"Excellent! I will lead our troops into battle again. I shall turn back the foreigners and regain my honor and my rightful place in Mexico. How many men can you raise?"

"I believe we can reach near-battalion strength in a few weeks. They will be mostly conscripts, but we can recruit several nearby veterans. I will have Huerta start organizing immediately. We will need to outfit them with weapons and uniforms."

"Never mind the battalion, Ramirez. We won't need that many. A company will do."

"One company?"

"A battalion of conscripts would be useless against French regulars," Santa Anna explained. He had transformed from anxious exile to the leader he had once been. His pacing had stopped, his nervous glances were gone. He was focused, mind clear, thoughts sharp.

"Untrained men would break and run at the first shot. But if we can field a company, even though untrained, we can be seen putting men that I raised and outfitted in the field against the invader. The government is already panicking. When French troops land and I volunteer my own troops to scout and harass the enemy without being asked to do so, Mexico City will commit to me the troops we need. President Bustamante will have no choice. I know him. He is in over his head. Urrea is leading an insurrection, the ports are closed, and his government is swimming in debt. We do not need to raise battalions, Ramirez, nor ask for support from the army. No, Bustamante will come to me for help."

Ramirez smiled and nodded. "I will see to raising a company. We will keep them here at the hacienda until they are needed, which will provide extra protection for you."

"Yes," Santa Anna said, his eyes gleaming. "And if the French set one foot on Mexican soil, I will strike them." He paused. "Still, be prepared to retreat to Lencero if either Urrea or the French reach us before we are ready."

"Very good, sir," Ramirez said, started to leave but stopped at the door. "What do we do with the prisoner?"

Santa Anna waived his hand dismissively.

"If anyone attacks Manga de Clavo," Santa Anna said, "kill him."

CHAPTER 24

BROWN REACHED VERACRUZ well ahead of Mrs. Ward. *Woodbury*, anchored at the edge of the blockade since Brown's return to Mexico, sent a longboat to the dock every other day to check for messages, and Brown requested the ship put in to port in two days in anticipation of Mrs. Ward's arrival.

Mrs. Ward reached the dock a few hours before the ship, but she was amiable as they waited, and she and Brown chatted pleasantly.

Yes, she and Fanny had figured out where Mrs. Ward saw the subject of the sketch.

Yes, she remembered Manga de Clavo and meeting Santa Anna.

"How did you come to meet him?" Brown said, "I mean, the man in the sketch?"

"Fanny and Ángel were speaking with Santa Anna and his aide-de-camp, and I asked if I could take a walk around the grounds, perhaps make a drawing or two. And I met this gentleman sitting at a table. You know, I remember this now. Isn't that funny? I didn't remember it when you and I spoke, or when Fanny and I spoke. She figured out where we were. But now, talking to you, I remember."

"That is funny, isn't it?" Brown said. "What was the man doing?"

"He was making something. A round piece of wood with big posts, uh, teeth, he said. He said it was used in a mill."

"A pit wheel?" Brown suggested.

"No, I don't think that was it," Mrs. Ward said. "Oh, I just can't remember sometimes."

"A spur…" Brown hinted.

"Yes, a spur wheel! That was it! I have no idea what it's for, but he said he once owned a mill. You know, his face was just so interesting, I just had to draw him. Very handsome but a little sad. He mentioned Tennessee. I think he was sad about being such a long way from home."

"Did he mention his name?"

"I don't think he did. You would think he must have, but I don't believe he did."

"It is odd," Brown said.

No, she didn't know the name of the man in the sketch. Hiram Brown really wanted to believe her. And he did believe her. He believed she was absolutely sincere. At that moment, she did not know the name of the man in the sketch. Yet these shards of memory kept floating in her mind, drifting away and coming back. A word here. A suggestion there. And an entire picture sketched itself together. Like filling in the details of a portrait, stroke by stroke by stroke.

Loose ends.

Woodbury arrived an hour later. Brown stowed Mrs. Ward's things on board and showed her around the ship. Just before sundown, while there was still enough light to navigate the harbor's tricky waters, *Woodbury* slid past San Juan de Ulna and set sail for the United States.

★

Two days later, *Woodbury* was 150 miles off the coast of Mexico. It was late in the evening, and the winds were mild and the Gulf was calm.

Mrs. Ward was standing at *Woodbury's* rail, listening to the gentle creaking of the ship's timbers and ropes and to the sound of the ocean breaking on the ship's bow. She leaned on the rail and watched the moonlight shimmer off the waves. It had been a smooth voyage.

"Beautiful, isn't it?" Mrs. Ward said.

"Yes," Brown agreed.

"The sea can be so peaceful, so tranquil."

Brown's knife thrust was quick, accurate, and as painless as such things are possible. He drove a long dagger between Mrs. Ward's sixth and seventh ribs, under her left arm, up at a twenty-degree angle. The blade sliced deeply into her heart and she died almost instantly, eyes wide in surprise, emitting only a brief gasp inaudible to anyone other than her killer.

Her body didn't fall to the deck. Brown caught Mrs. Ward with his right arm, still grasped with his left hand the knife which was now a convenient handle, and flipped her over the side of the ship, pulling the knife free as she dropped. He released the dagger, and corpse and murder weapon disappeared into the Gulf of Mexico.

He made a quick examination of the deck, his hand, and his clothes. No blood anywhere.

Per a previous arrangement with the ship's first mate, no one was on deck.

When Mrs. Ward didn't rise for breakfast, her absence was attributed to seasickness. Happened all the time. Early in the afternoon, her cabin was found empty and her disappearance discovered. It was assumed she accidentally fell overboard the previous night. It must have happened at watch change, so no one heard her call for help. She would have been in the ocean for fourteen hours by now and could have drifted anywhere in a hundred-mile radius. There was no point in going back, Brown, the captain, and the first mate agreed.

Woodbury sailed on, not to New Orleans, but to Houston.

A week after Henry's funeral the Texians gathered for what they believed and ardently hoped was the start of the final act of the drama. After nearly three months, thousands of miles back and forth across Texas, and one tragic trip to Mexico, they were ready to make an end.

They gathered in the Brazos Valley, this time in San Felipe de Austin, half a day's ride south of Groce's Landing.

Known simply as San Felipe by its residents, prior to the Texas Revolution the town was the center of the area's culture and trade. In addition to administrative and land offices, San Felipe boasted general stores and taverns, a blacksmith, hotel, post office, newspaper, school, and more than six hundred residents.

But the Alamo fell, the Texian army retreated, and to deny the town to the Mexican army, San Felipe met the same fate as Gonzales. It was burned.

After the Revolution, the town began to recover but never reached its pre-war levels. A courthouse had been built, as had several log cabins, an inn and tavern, and a general store. But Texas's government and society had gone elsewhere.

Which made it a perfect location for the Texians. They were able to rest and plan out of sight, yet they were within easy reach of Houston, where Alcée la Branche awaited word from Hiram Brown. La Branche had been informed of the Texians' location and that they were preparing for the voyage to Veracruz. They just needed a ship and to know their destination.

The Texians waited in San Felipe's inn. The innkeeper, a gruff, mustachioed fellow named Pardue, was delighted at their arrival since every room was available and he'd had few patrons in weeks.

"Dead town," he muttered. "Don't know why I came back."

"Faith, brother," Jacob said. "We have to have faith in one another. I'm trying to rebuild Gonzales. We just keep working."

"Faith don't pay the bills," Pardue said.

"No, it does not," Jacob said. "But seven of us are here now with a few more coming. We'll be here several days, so maybe that'll help. And we'd appreciate some privacy."

"Friend, I'll cut you a deal. You and your friends can have the whole place for a week."

"That'll fix us up fine."

Pardue was smiling so broadly he couldn't say another word.

"I'm pretty sure I know the answer to this," Horace said, "but is there any way we can hit both haciendas?" Horace was healing nicely, had been resting extensively, and had already informed the rest of the group that the only way they could keep him from going was to shoot him again.

"I cannot see how," de la Peña said. "I believe one of the haciendas is close to Veracruz, fifteen to twenty miles away. The other is near Xalapa. That's fifty miles away."

"We'd need horses to get there and back," Jacob said.

The Texians and de la Peña were gathered in one of the inn's empty rooms. They had shoved the bed aside, set a small table in the middle of the room, pulled a chair from each of their rooms, and created a meeting area. Jacob took a seat at the door, listening for anyone in the hall nosing about, which was likely to be extremely detrimental to that person's health.

The room had blank walls of unpainted timber, though some-one had nailed an old horseshoe—heel up—above the door.

Juan had a map of Mexico spread on the table. J.C. was hovering over the map, attempting to measure distances from Veracruz to various locations. He looked glum.

"If we're going to Xalapa, what if we landed further up the coast?" Silas said. "Is Xalapa fifty miles inland from Veracruz or fifty miles up the coast?"

"It's up the coast," de la Peña said, moving to the map and pointing out Xalapa. "It's up the coast, perhaps twenty-five miles from the gulf."

"We couldn't dock the ship there," Jacob said. "But if we can figure out where to land, we could reach the beach by longboat. No matter how we do this, we've got to be in and out of there quick. In Mexico no more than two days. Disembark the ship at night and reach the hacienda late that first day. Enter the hacienda just before dawn the next day. Get out of there and make it back to the ship by the end of the second day."

"Fifteen miles each way to the hacienda nearer Veracruz, that should be no problem as long as we don't get lost," Horace said. "Twenty-five miles to Xalapa, well, we just have to move fast. I'm a little worried about getting back to the coast and finding that longboat."

"If we don't know which hacienda is the target, what do we do?" Sam said. "Split up? I agree with Jacob, we have to be out in two days. I can't see going to one place, finding out he's not there, and getting to the other before we're caught."

"That would mean just three of us to each hacienda," Jacob said. "Without knowing how many we're up against."

"Gentlemen," de la Peña said. "I know you have known me for only a few days, and while I deeply appreciate the kindness and hospitality you have shown, I know I am not a part of your fellowship. But if you'll allow, I would like to accompany you to do this thing. I believe I can be of help. I know the area and its people. And, I will admit, when I stood outside the Alamo after that terrible battle and witnessed the bloodshed that Santa Anna caused, I promised to seek revenge against him. I would very much like a chance to help you, and in doing so, hurt him."

The Texians looked around the room at one another.

"Just so you know," Horace said, "we're not going down there for revenge."

"I understand."

"I think we need all the help we can get," Silas said. "And he's seen a lot more fighting than I have."

"I'm for him," Jacob said, and that was that. José was now one of the Texians.

J.C. had yet to say a word and everyone knew why. As long as they'd been traveling by horse, he was a fully capable participant. But a journey of fifteen to twenty-five miles—each way—on foot was another matter. Not with his bad hip injured at San Jacinto.

"Boys, I…" J.C. tried to say. "I…"

"We know, J.C.," Horace said. "We understand."

"I can't stand the thought of staying behind! It's just, well, damn it, it's just not right." J.C. grasped the edge of the table, his knuckles white. "To have come this far…"

"I've been thinking about that," Silas said. "I think you should come with us."

"Silas, I don't think I can walk fifteen miles, much less twenty-five."

"You don't have to. Jacob, Sam, did you notice what the captain of *Watchman* said?"

"About Brown?" Jacob said.

"Yeah," Silas said. "He mentioned Brown and went quiet. Hard to imagine he was talking about someone other than our Hiram Brown."

"I don't trust Brown," Jacob said.

"Me neither," Silas said. "And I'd feel a lot better not having him at our back, in control of our only way out of Mexico. That's where you come in, J.C."

"You can make sure we got a ride home," Sam said.

"All right," J.C. brightened. "I'll watch him and his crew. But how do we explain why I'm staying on the boat? Do we make up some story?"

"No," Silas said. "Keep it simple. When we get down there, we tell them your hip has seized up and you can't walk."

"You can even show 'em your scar if you want to, J.C." Horace said.

"I'll try to avoid dropping my breeches."

"But watch them, and watch them careful," Sam warned. "Don't turn your back on Brown. Keep your knife and gun close all the time."

"Speaking of guns, how's everybody heeled?" J.C. said. "Everyone should have two pistols and good knife. You got a good knife, Silas?"

"Yes, sir. But I only have one pistol."

"We'll get you another," J.C. said.

They ran through their armament. Horace had a German Wisthaler double-barreled shotgun, Juan had an English Allen scatter-gun, and Sam, Jacob, and de la Peña had long rifles.

"You got a long rifle, Silas?" J.C. said.

"Oh," Sam said, "he's got us all beat."

"What are you carrying?" Juan said.

"Hawken .50-caliber," Silas said. Everyone whistled. "My father got it in St. Louis."

"I hear those Hawkens are good up to four-hundred yards," Horace said.

The Texians spent the rest of the evening checking their firearms. They found another pistol for Silas and confirmed that his knife was up to the task. Silas had a Bowie knife with a ten-inch blade, which curled below the spine of the blade to a sharp stabbing point. The grip was of maple, fastened to the tang by steel pins. The base of the blade had a silver coin cross-guard.

"I bought this after hearing of Jim Bowie in the Vidalia Sandbar fight," Silas said. "Will it do?"

"Yeah," J.C. said, "that'll settle somebody's hash."

They called it an early night and used the next day to again check weapons and every other piece of equipment they would take. They sharpened knives and tested the efficacy of their gunpowder, confirmed their supply of bullets, powder, patches, and percussion caps, and packed bandages, canteens, and dried meat.

And they waited for Hiram Brown.

There was still no sign of him the next morning, and no one felt like checking equipment again, so they decided to relax for a day. None of them remembered the last time they had truly just relaxed for a day, much of which was devoted to the inn's small billiard hall.

"Silas, is your room sufficient?" Horace asked, acting as spokesperson for the rest of the Texians.

"Yes, sir," Silas said, furrowing his brow at the question. "It's a fine room."

"Comfortable?"

"Yes, sir."

"Not too small for you?"

"No, sir."

"You think maybe your room could accommodate one more?"

The confusion on his face quickly disappeared.

"What are you waiting for?" Horace said and nodded to the north.

Silas was mounted and gone within two minutes, leaving his guns and knife in his room and barely remembering to grab his hat. He was back in the afternoon with Emily.

José grinned at Horace, who shrugged in response.

"We mean to bring that boy home," Horace said. "It's just…" He watched Emily and Silas. The way they smiled and looked at each other. "They haven't had much time together, and we thought they should have a little more time before we go." He looked at the lovers, arm in arm, surrounded by the other Texians.

"Just in case."

✯

Hiram Brown and Alcée la Branche arrived from Houston the next day and were given rooms in Pardue's inn. La Branche wanted to freshen up a bit but Brown was having none of it. He dumped his gear and called the Texians together.

The Texians gave Brown and la Branche a rundown of everything they'd learned since their last meeting in San Antonio. Brown listened without looking up. He seemed haggard, worn, his complexion sallow. The circles under his eyes were not there a few months ago, and he didn't meet the Texians' gaze.

There was something else, Silas thought. He looked in anguish.

"I am sorry to hear of Henry," Brown said. "I truly am. But I agree with your conclusions. It sounds like Ramirez and Huerta spirited Crockett out and down to Mexico. The only question left is where Crockett is now. I think I have the answer.

"You are correct," he said to de la Peña. "Santa Anna has two haciendas. El Lencero on the outskirts of Xalapa and Manga de Clavo nearer to Veracruz. I have people in that region who've been looking around. They tell me Lencero is largely vacant, just a couple of caretakers in residence. Santa Anna is at Manga de Clavo and has been since he returned to Mexico last year. That confirms the information from the…sketch's artist…" Brown trailed off for a moment, "…that the, uh, drawing was made at Manga de Clavo."

"Our destination is Manga de Clavo?" Juan said.

"Yes," Brown said, pulled the sketch from his saddlebags, and spread it on the table. He pointed to a crude drawing at the bottom of the sketch. "This map, which Mr. Ellis obtained, shows the location where the sketch was made. The hacienda is a little more than fifteen miles from the docks in Veracruz. The main house is on a small hill, surrounded by a handful of outbuildings. On one side is a kitchen and a smokehouse. On the other side are quarters for staff, a smithy, and a stable. Further out is a coop for gamecocks and a pit for cockfights. A well sits near the kitchen. They're building a mill but that's about half a mile east of the hacienda on a stream that runs north and south.

"I could not determine where Crockett is held," Brown added. "My guess is somewhere in the house. He may be working on the mill, but I doubt they would keep him there."

"Any idea as to how many guards?" Jacob asked.

"The last information I have is probably ten, plus the two officers you mentioned. My sources didn't know their names, but from the descriptions, I'd bet they're Ramirez and Huerta. And

Santa Anna. Plus, assorted household staff. Cooks, groundskeeper, carpenter, blacksmith. They may not be eager to die for Santa Anna but take no chances."

The room fell silent. The Texians would be out-numbered more than two to one.

I will have to kill someone, Silas thought.

Brown stood and drew a small knife from a scabbard at his hip, and carefully cut away the bottom portion of the drawing paper, separating map from sketch. He handed the map to Jacob. He pulled a box of matches from his saddlebags, ignited one, and set fire to the sketch. He held it while the flame crept up the paper and consumed the face, and dropped it to the table and allowed it to be completely incinerated.

"Seven of you?" Brown said.

"Seven," Jacob answered.

Brown packed up his saddlebags, ignoring the ash dancing on the table. "We leave at dawn."

Emily knew that wherever Silas was headed, it was dangerous. She could sense it from Silas and his comrades. She allowed herself a tear in private but did her best not to show how frightened she was.

But Silas knew.

He was scared, too. Terrified, in fact. Although frightened of serious injury or death, his much greater fear was letting the others down. That was the worst fate he could imagine—doing something wrong or foolish and getting someone else hurt. Or killed.

These men were warriors, veterans of gun fights and hand-to-hand combat when no quarter was given or expected. The closest Silas had been to battle was play-acting a French officer at Corpus

Christi Bay and bluffing Mexican soldiers on the border. He had never drawn a weapon with the intent of taking another man's life, and chances were good that he would do so in the next few days. That would make him a killer, Rafael Vega said.

"Blood does not wash away," Vega had said.

Dinner on their last night in San Felipe was tense and conversation minimal. Silas and Emily spent most of the meal holding hands tightly under the table and showing thin, insincere smiles.

Since the Texians were leaving at first light, dinner broke up early. Emily said goodbye to each member of the expedition and accompanied Silas upstairs to their room while the rest of the group sipped whiskey.

"Señorita Perry is a very strong young woman," José said after the couple was gone. "This must be difficult for her."

"More than you know," Sam said. "Her parents are dead. Only family is a brother who returned home, two thousand miles away back east."

"She stayed here for her young man?" José said.

Sam nodded.

The room fell silent. Pensive stares into shot glasses of dark brown whiskey.

"She is very brave," José said.

"Mm," everyone agreed.

"Gentlemen, let's try not to put her bravery to the test," Brown said. He raised his glass. "Everybody comes home."

"Everybody comes home," the Texians echoed and drank against the regretful chill.

"And she's beautiful," J.C. said after the whiskey disappeared.

"Wouldn't you agree, Juan?" Horace said.

"Si, very beautiful," Juan conceded. "Chica preciosa. I don't know if she's the prettiest girl in Texas…" and he paused and reconsidered the young woman who had chanced being alone on the Texas frontier in pursuit of her dream. "But I certainly understand why young Silas is so in love with her."

★

Silas and Emily sat on their bed and held each other. Emily tried but couldn't keep from crying a little. For a long time, they remained in embrace. Emily's arms around his shoulders, her head on his chest. Silas's arms around her, one hand slowly stroking her red hair. Then, struck by the possibility that this could be their last night, they undressed one another and made love intensely, fueled not by lust or passion but by a longing to be one.

Silas and Emily didn't normally speak much after making love. They simply cuddled and fell asleep in each other's arms.

"Emily, can I ask you something?"

"Of course."

"About our first night together."

"That was so wonderful."

"It was wonderful. Incredible. I can't think of words to describe how wonderful."

"But…"

"But it was also…surprising."

"Ah."

"I mean, you showing up like that. It was a dream come true. I was never so happy to see anyone in my life."

"I noticed."

"But…"

Emily sat up on an elbow. "How did I know to show up at your cabin with a pitcher of water and a washcloth when you'd be naked?"

"Yeah. It just seemed like such an incredible, fantastic… coincidence."

Emily grinned. "Silas, you are so sweet and handsome, and such a caring man and such a caring lover. But, sometimes, you're a little slow."

"…huh?"

"I went to your cabin while you were with the work crew. I tossed out the water from your washstand."

Silas couldn't muster a response.

"You are such a gentleman, which I dearly love about you. But you weren't going to take me to bed until we were married. I didn't want to wait."

There followed several heartbeats of silence.

"So…you seduced me?"

Emily laid her head on Silas's chest. "Yep."

Silas smiled deeply, contentedly, and kissed Emily's forehead. "God, I love you, Emily."

"I love you, Silas."

They dozed a little, drifting in and out of sleep. Watching each other, listening to each other breathe, catching each other awake, losing themselves in a touch, a caress, a smile.

About three hours before dawn, as Emily slept in his arms, Silas found himself wide awake, and the doubt he had held at bay all day surged over him. What business did a sixteen-year-old have going off like this? Did he think he was this heroic warrior? Who was he fooling?

Or he could stay here. Stay right here, safe. Safe and holding Emily. Don't get up, just stay in this room and they'll be gone and be fine, better off without him.

He remembered hearing his father's news that the family was moving to Texas. Silas had been so excited by the idea until the night before they left, when he was seized by a terrible fear because the great adventure looming upon him seemed overwhelming.

He closed his eyes and tried forcing himself to sleep, but his mind betrayed him and the doubt reared up and everything seemed so big and so crushing—

"Silas." Emily's voice reached through his apprehension. "Silas, my love, I believe in you. Go and do this thing that you must do. Then come home to me."

The tension in his chest eased and he looked at Emily. In the dark could just make out her smile. They kissed.

"Sleep now."

As was his custom, Jacob Millsaps rose an hour before dawn into early-morning dark. He had checked everything more times than he could remember. Now he was going to check everything once more.

As he approached the stable, he saw light bleeding out from under the door. He opened the door and found Silas standing next to his horse. Checking everything once more.

"Morning," Jacob said.

"Um, good morning," Silas said.

"How is Emily getting home?" Jacob asked. "Not by herself, I hope."

"My father is on the way. He'll be here this morning to escort her back. I asked him to wait a couple of days and come down."

"Were you going to send her back even if we weren't ready?"

Silas hesitated. "No." He shrugged. "My father would have understood."

"I have no doubt he would. He wants to protect his future daughter-in-law. What did you tell your folks about where we're going?"

"I talked to my father. He…kind of figured something was going on. I mean, with all of us. Me and you and the others. He didn't press for details. Just asked if it was important. I said it was. He said he'd talk to my mother and told me to be careful. I think he understands."

"Sure," Jacob said. "He went off to war himself."

Silas swallowed. "Is that what we're doing?"

"I hope not. But it's likely there will be some fighting."

"I know. I mean, I guess I've known all along."

"But it's different, now that it's close."

"Yeah."

Jacob said no more and began running through his mental checklist. Silas turned to inspect his own gear.

"Jacob?"

Jacob turned. Silas did not face him.

"I wanted to tell you…at dinner…last night…I…" Silas lost the words.

"You're scared."

Silas looked over his shoulder toward Jacob. "You know? Do the others—"

"We all know."

Silas sighed and laid his forehead on his saddle. "You must think I'm a coward."

Jacob walked across the stable and put his hand on Silas's shoulder.

"You know how we know? Because we're scared." That surprised Silas. "We just hide it better. Sometimes. We're about to sail hundreds of miles to a place none of us have ever been. Go on foot and attack a place maybe filled with enemies. You'd have to be a damned fool not to be scared. Silas, every man I've ever known was scared before going into a fight. We were all scared at San Jacinto. But being afraid does not make you a coward. Giving in to your fear does. You're standing here now, so you're no coward.

"There is not one man in Texas, and I mean not one, who has a better reason than you to stay home. You're risking..." Jacob shook his head and looked toward the inn where Emily lay sleeping. "Damn, son, you're risking more than any of us. For a man you've never met.

"If that's not brave, I truly do not know what is."

CHAPTER 25

SILAS GRANT FOUND himself out of sight of land for the first time in his life.

The trip aboard the smugglers' brig captured at Corpus Christi Bay had been within a few miles of the Gulf Coast. Now he was aboard a US navy schooner, a fast-fighting ship that was bigger than the brig with twice its crew. It had four twelve-pound cannon and one six-pounder, and although it couldn't challenge the big French ships of the line, it felt like a real warship.

Woodbury plowed and rolled its way through five- to seven-foot seas. During the day, Silas found the waves exhilarating, and at night they rocked him to sleep.

"You're a natural, lad," said *Woodbury*'s captain, H.D. Hunter.

"You think so?"

"You haven't thrown up yet, and you walk this pitching deck like you're right at home."

"Don't mind him, Captain," Horace muttered. "He's too young and stupid to know when he's miserable."

J.C., Horace, Sam, and Jacob were suffering from varying levels of seasickness, as well as heightened anxiety as the last view of land slipped away aft. Juan was enduring but not enjoying while José, who had seafaring experience, was unaffected.

Captain Hunter had been gracious, though Silas wondered if this veteran sailor, who had overseen *Woodbury*'s construction, was tired of running a passenger service for Brown.

Late on the second day, the seas calmed and they entered the outer edge of the French blockade zone below the Rio Grande that was approximately 150 miles to starboard.

They had gone over the plan for the landing and the march to Manga de Clavo multiple times, and for the first time in days, Silas felt confident about the upcoming rescue raid. He missed Emily terribly, but he was glad he was here and could not imagine that he had actually entertained the thought of staying home.

Now if he could just get through this alive.

Woodbury approached Veracruz to the sound of artillery. The blockade of the port had turned into an assault, and the French were now intent on capturing the city.

The massive French ships battered San Juan de Ulna, the island fort that guarded the entrance to the port. Its defenders returned fire but were badly outmatched.

"The fire from the town is weakening!" a lookout on *Woodbury*'s mainmast called.

The Texians and Brown crowded the railing and watched great clouds of smoke erupt from the deafening guns of the French ships. Even at a mile distance, every man on *Woodbury* could feel the shock of the French ordnance.

"Lord," Jacob said. "I saw all those cannon firing at the Alamo, but I've never seen anything like this."

"We had one eighteen-pounder at the Alamo," J.C. said. "How many you figure the French have?"

"The big ship there, *Montebello*," Brown said, "has seventeen eighteen-pounders, seventeen twenty-four-pounders, and sixteen thirty-six-pounders." He paused. "That's on each side of the ship."

"On each side?" J.C. said. "Thirty-two of those giant guns on one ship? I've never seen a thirty-six-pound cannon."

J.C. rubbed his jaw as he watched the bombardment. Other than Millsaps, the Texians normally kept clean-shaven chins but now sported a few days growth of whiskers, electing not to drag a razor across their face while onboard ship. Beardless Silas, to his chagrin, was the only member of the group not in need of a barber.

Another broadside tore chunks of stone from San Juan de Ulua's walls.

"We'll wait until the French silence the Mexican artillery, which should not be long from the look of things," Hunter said. "My guess is, the French will land troops this afternoon. We'll dock tomorrow or the next day, after they get things under control and the shooting calms."

"Captain—" Brown started to say but thought better of it.

"I'm not taking the ship in under fire, Mr. Brown." The captain walked away.

As Hunter predicted, the Mexican cannon were finished a short time later, and the French began landing soldiers. They met light resistance, casualties were few in desultory fighting, and they cleared the Mexican troops from the docks. The combat was more intense in the fort, where the Mexicans put up a spirited resistance.

The sound of gunfire lasted through the night.

The next morning, *Woodbury* headed to the dock. The Texians rose to find the crew focused on the ship's port bow.

"Is there a problem, Captain?" Silas asked.

"During the night, we collided with one of the French ships," Hunter said.

"Is the ship damaged? I didn't feel anything."

"That's because we didn't actually collide with anything."

"What?"

"It's the excuse we're using for docking an American ship in the middle of a French attack on a Mexican city," Brown said.

"We eased a couple of sailors with hammers over the side, and they did a little damage to the bow," Hunter explained. "The damage is superficial but will be quite visible. We'll dock to make repairs. And tonight, we'll slip you Texians into the city."

Silas's pulse quickened. He was invading a foreign country and going into combat. It was impossible to imagine that the Texians could avoid a fight before this was finished. In the next forty-eight hours, men would try to kill him and he would try to kill them. He had known this for weeks, that this quest meant risking his life. But there was knowing it and there was coming face to face with the reality of it.

And reality was pulling into port.

★

Three hours later, *Woodbury* docked. Everyone remained on board, awaiting the arrival of the French demanding to know their business. Although the Americans and French were cooperating, the officers on the ground were not interested in political arrangements. They wanted to know what a foreign ship was doing in their landing zone.

French officers boarded *Woodbury* and interrogated Captain Hunter, who explained their need to make repairs. Brown, too, spoke with the French, who eventually were satisfied with the answers and gave permission for crew members to disembark, search the dockside warehouses for supplies, and to hire a local carpenter. *Woodbury* had a perfectly qualified carpenter who would oversee repairs, but it didn't hurt appearances to make a show of needing help.

The search for supplies the ship didn't need and a carpenter it already had also served to delay their time in dock without raising suspicions among any onlooking Mexican officials.

Two hours after sundown, Brown led the six-man rescue squad ashore. He had accepted Neill's excuse for remaining on the ship and seemed pleased, as J.C.'s presence would allow Brown to interact more freely off the ship with the French.

Brown and the Texians made their way to a warehouse two blocks from the docks and ducked inside, where they found a grim-faced Mexican, a mule, and a cart.

"Everything ready, Salvator?" Brown asked the Mexican.

"Everything you asked for," Salvator said. "Now can I get back to my tavern? I hate Veracruz."

"Yeah, you can get going," Brown said. "And thank you."

"Good luck to you all," Salvator said to the Texians and exited through a side door.

The cart was loaded with blankets, bundles of wood, and a heap of clothes.

"Change into those," Brown said. "Stow your weapons in the bundles and your clothes under the blankets. You need anything else?"

"No, I think we're good," Jacob said.

"I'll see you in two days," Brown said. "Good luck." To the Texians' surprise, he shook the hand of each man before returning to the ship.

The Texians changed into the simple shirts, pants, boots, and sombreros of the local peasantry. Each man hid his weapons and supplies inside one of the cart's bundles of firewood, which were just stacks of oak branches tied together. An hour later, in the full dark of night and with de la Peña in the lead, they stepped outside, steered the mule and cart northwest, joined a procession of refugees fleeing the fighting, and headed out of Veracruz.

Three hours later, they were across the bridge over the Rio Medio into the Mexican countryside.

CHAPTER 26

THE ROAD WAS clear and the Texians made good time, even in the darkness of a thin crescent moon and with a disagreeable mule dragging the cart. They marched through terrain with sparse vegetation over sandy, rolling hills, and mixed with the parade of refugees.

After a few miles, the land began to turn lush and green, and by dawn they had left behind the wastes around Veracruz.

"I had no idea what a rough place Veracruz is," Silas said.

"I'll be happy to see it tomorrow, if only to sail away from it forever," Horace said.

Shortly after dawn, they no longer felt safe on the road. They had seen no military activity but couldn't believe the situation would hold. At some point, the Mexican army would be moving down that road to Veracruz, and the Texians wanted no chance encounters. Yet they had seen no army presence in response to the French incursion.

After an hour of urging and pulling the mule to drag the cart through the increasingly hilly ground, they led the cart off the road and hid it behind a large ceiba tree with an enormous sprawling trunk. They unloaded the wood bundles containing their weapons and ammunition, covered the wagon with branches, and untethered the mule, which suddenly felt like walking and moved away. Each man claimed the bundle with his gear, slung it on his back, and the Texians set out.

"I was thinking," Silas said as they passed a grove of banana trees. "If Colonel Crockett lost a leg, how are we going to get him to Veracruz? Can he walk fifteen miles?"

"It's a different situation than J.C.," Horace said. "J.C. has a bad hip and that's hard to overcome. It's painful with every step he takes. But a man with a peg leg can get around pretty good. You ever meet Three-Legged Willie?"

"Robert Williamson? The Ranger?" Silas said. "I've heard of him."

"Willie's right leg is permanently bent at the knee, straight back. Caused by a disorder when he was about your age. Willie has a wooden leg that he fastens to his knee. He has no problem walking. He's even a fine dancer."

"Oh, that's why he…has that nickname," Silas said. "I thought maybe…it was…"

Which set the Texians to chortling.

"Does Emily have a nickname for you?" Sam asked.

"What," Silas continued, ignoring the comment, "if Colonel Crockett doesn't have a peg leg?"

"We'll steal him a horse," Jacob said.

"Or you can carry him," Horace said.

"I'd rather find him a horse," Silas said.

Two hours later, they skirted a village of bamboo huts with roofs of palm leaves. The settlement, which the Texians believed was the Sante Fe indicated on the map, was occupied by a handful of villagers, a herd of goats, and a chorus of half-naked children playing happily in the shade of palm trees.

In mid-afternoon, they located the road which the map indicated led north to Manga de Clavo. They paralleled the road, careful to stay hidden in the trees two hundred yards off the path. When the road curved left away from a hill, the Texians stayed right, climbed a long, slow rise, and cautiously crawled to its summit.

Below was Manga de Clavo, just as described. The house, the outbuildings. On one side, kitchen, well, and smokehouse. On the other, staff quarters, blacksmith, and stable. A half mile away they could see a mill under construction on a stream. Everything as Brown had indicated.

Except for row after row of white canvas tents housing a company of Mexican soldiers in the hacienda's courtyard.

One platoon was going through drills conducted by a sergeant who, even from this distance, appeared thoroughly disgusted with his charges. He wasn't half so disappointed in the soldiers as were the Texians.

"Where in hell did they come from?" Sam said.

"This," Horace said, "is a problem."

The Texians could also see two small cannon, probably six-pounders, alongside a caisson of cannon balls and powder in the middle of the camp.

"They must not have been here when Brown and his spies came through a couple of weeks ago," Jacob said, and dug into his gear and found the spyglass which had been bequeathed to him by Henry. He trained it on the camp. "Got to be near a hundred men. I can see one of the tall officers."

Jacob handed the glass to de la Peña, who took a long look at the troops below.

"That is Huerta," José said. "I recognize the man next to him," and indicated a soldier wearing an eyepatch and barking at a squad struggling to attach bayonets to muskets. "One of Huerta's chosen men. Fierro, I think is his name. A brute. He took pleasure in cruelty at Zacatecas.

"I do not see Ramirez, but he rarely mixes with the soldiers." De la Peña continued to survey the scene. "Most of these men are not very good soldiers," he finally said.

"How so?" Jacob asked.

"Even during our march to Texas, the men looked better than this. None of these men have proper shoes. We had that problem at times, but I don't see any of these men with soldier's boots. All are wearing sandals. They're wearing peasant pants, not uniform pants. Many of them seem to have difficulty with their cross belts, as if they've never worn them before. They have other problems as well." Groups of soldiers were trying to stack their muskets, but the stacks kept toppling over. "These men appear to be raw, untrained. I think they were grabbed from their farms in the last few days, handed jackets, muskets, and shakos and told they were soldiers. The Mexican army in Texas had many such men but they at least had some training."

Huerta and the one-eyed man continued to berate the soldiers. Away from their view, two men tossed down their muskets, threw off their army jackets, and ran with one soldier shouting at them to come back.

"There are only a handful of trained soldiers down there," José said. "Huerta's men. They must be the guards Brown mentioned."

After sunset, the Texians crawled closer to the hacienda's courtyard. They could see three guards, who appeared to be newly conscripted, patrolling the perimeter of the camp. Another guard, who looked to be one of Huerta's professionals, was atop the house.

They could see no sign of Crockett or a holding area. The house still seemed the most likely location.

The reconnaissance completed, the Texians crawled back to their vantage point on the hill.

"Maybe we don't have to fight a whole company," Sam said, and grinned at Silas. "We bluff 'em."

CHAPTER 27

THE TEXIANS HAD a little to eat and tried to get some sleep, one man keeping watch on one-hour shifts. Battle veterans Jacob, Sam, Juan, Horace, and José grabbed scraps of sleep, but Silas was restless and spent the night staring at the battlefield to be.

At three o'clock in the morning, they made final preparations. They went over the plan again. Everyone's assignments. Everyone's targets. The outbuildings, the house, the courtyard. Discussed options when circumstances changed. What they would do if one of them was wounded.

Or killed.

"When José gets things started," Jacob said, "Juan and Horace, you let loose with those shotguns. Fire one barrel, wait a second, and fire again. Fire into the thick of them. I hate to do it, but we got no choice. While you're reloading, the rest of us will try to pick off Huerta's guards. Choose your targets well. Take out the professional soldiers and leave these other poor bastards if you can."

"How can I tell the difference?" Silas said.

"The professionals' uniforms are in order, the conscripts aren't," Sam explained.

"You expect me to tell the difference in the middle of a fight? At night?"

"I take your point," Sam said. "If he looks like he wants to fight, shoot him. If he's running away, let him go."

Silas's left hand trembled slightly as he looked down the hill. "We're really doing this."

Sam put his hand on Silas's shoulder. "Stay calm and stay close. You'll be fine."

Silas nodded. "Anyone know what day it is?" he said.

"What day?" Horace said.

"I think today is Sunday," Jacob said.

"Just…wondered," Silas said.

"Sunday, before dawn," José whispered. "That's when the final attack on the Alamo came."

Jacob looked at José and nodded. "Time to finish this."

Jacob took off his sombrero and motioned for the others to do the same. No need to have a large white shape catch the meager moonlight and give away their approach.

The Texians crawled to the foot of the hill, hidden by tall grass forty yards from the conscripts' camp. Then they waited.

A few campfires burned but only the night watch was visible: three plodding conscripts walking the camp perimeter and one of Huerta's men on the roof of the hacienda's house. It was more likely he was watching the camp than the perimeter. The rest of the company was bedded down in the tents.

In a few minutes, one of the patrolling conscripts walked within a few yards of the Texians' position. As the guard passed, Sam silently rose, stepped forward, and cracked him in the back of the head with a pistol butt. The guard crumpled and Sam dragged him to the Texians. José took off the unconscious man's blue jacket and put it on over his peasant attire, donned the guard's shako, picked up the guard's musket, and calmly walked into the camp.

José had taken several steps when another of the conscript guards approached. The guard spotted de la Peña, who he presumed was a fellow conscript, but paused in confusion. As much as the man wanted to crawl into his tent and bed, it wasn't time to change the guard. He started to call to de la Peña.

Silas was at the man's back before he could utter a word and slammed the butt of his Hawken into the base of the man's skull. There was a sickening crunch that Silas was certain must have awakened the entire camp, but the only movement was the guard, who collapsed onto his face. Silas left the man where he lay and crawled back to his position.

"Good work," one of the Texians whispered. Silas couldn't tell who.

Silas felt a warm, wet smear on the Hawken's iron butt plate. Blood. Silas could just make out the motionless form of the conscript several yards away.

Am I a killer now?

De la Peña had not noticed the removal of the second guard and continued into the camp. He crouched by one of the fires and checked that he was unobserved. The guard atop the house had nodded off, his head drooping on his chest. José grabbed a burning piece of firewood, and, staying low, moved to the caisson. He peeked into the caisson, dropped the burning wood among the powder barrels, and retreated to the Texians' position. He slid to a stop next to Sam, removed the blue jacket and shako, took up his rifle, and waited with the rest of the Texians.

"Heads down," Sam said, and the six-man squad hunkered.

It took a couple of minutes for the fire to reach the powder. Silas felt his heart thump and thunder through the interminable delay, and he was beginning to doubt the plan and desperately wanted to lift his head and risk a peek at the caisson.

Then night turned to day.

The detonation was much larger than anticipated. The cannon were tossed aside, careening over tents and crushing occupants. A large wood fragment from the caisson struck the third conscript guard and killed him instantly. Several tents were thrown across the camp, the men inside dead or badly injured. Other tents were on fire. The camp was chaos.

The Texians, with their heads down, had suffered neither injury nor loss of night vision from the flash of the blast, though their ears were ringing.

Stunned conscripts tumbled out into a fire-flickered darkness of burning tents and smoldering bodies. Men were yelling and confusion reigned, but the sergeant's brief drills had some impact. A few were putting on shakos, a few more blue jackets. Most were picking up muskets from the stacks that had been scattered by the explosion, and they looked about for an officer, for some instruction as to what to do.

Juan fired his first shotgun barrel and three men went down. Next came Horace's first barrel, Juan's second, and Horace's second. Confusion gave way to terror, yells to screams. The thunderous reports shattered the soldiers' tenuous grasp on good military order, drove them into full panic, and sent them scrambling away from the source of the blasts, away from the hacienda, and toward the Veracruz road.

The guard on the roof stood, lit by the fires in the camp, and Jacob shot him through the chest.

Huerta, his jacket on but not buttoned and his sword drawn, rushed out of the hacienda looking for an enemy, thinking Manga de Clavo was under attack from the French or Urrea's troops. He saw nothing but his fleeing company. The sergeant and two of Huerta's chosen men appeared from one of the staff outbuildings and tried to stop the fear-driven exodus to no avail, and the sergeant, Huerta, and the two chosen men pursued the conscripts. In the light of the burning camp, Silas could see that one of the men following was the one-eyed Fierro that José had identified the previous afternoon, and Silas was relieved to see him go.

Three more guards took up position on top of the hacienda buildings. Sam shot the man atop the blacksmith's building and de la Peña dropped the man over the kitchen.

Silas took aim at the third guard, on the roof of the house. He fired. When the smoke from his Hawken cleared, the man was gone.

The Texians reloaded as quickly as possible, though it occurred to Silas that he had never loaded a gun in the dark. He hoped he did so correctly.

"Let's go!" Jacob shouted, and the six sprang from their position and ran into the mangled camp.

Silas felt a surge of fear and excitement overwhelm his senses as he plunged into the smoking courtyard. A shotgun blast sounded somewhere but he couldn't see who fired or the target, and all around him was yelling and confusion. Shapes poured out of the staff quarters, appearing in the glimmering light of the fires before disappearing into the smoke, fading in and out of view. Silas realized he was standing still, flat-footed still out in the open in the middle of combat. No one had warned him of such a condition, but it seemed a really bad idea.

Move, his mind said.

He was struggling to tell friend from foe, straining through the battle fog, when one of the shapes materialized into one of Huerta's guards.

Move.

The man spotted Silas. The guard was about fifty yards away, well within the effective range of the musket that he snapped to his shoulder. He fired. Silas sensed the bullet zip past his left ear and felt his left shoulder flinch away from the attack. The guard didn't bother to reload. He simply charged with his bayonet, the reflection of the courtyard's flames dancing on seventeen inches of steel blade.

Silas had seconds to live or die with a bayonet in his belly.

Move!

He raised the Hawken, aimed, prayed it was properly loaded, and pulled the trigger. A reassuring flash, bang, and kick told Silas his reload was good. Through the rifle smoke, he saw the guard shot in the chest. The man's body folded around the impact and the bullet tore out his back.

Someone—a tall man Silas thought was Jacob—ran into the house. Two guards fired at him, then pursued the Texian. Silas, his eyes stinging from the smoke, followed.

He burst through the front door.

Horace, Sam, and José searched the outbuildings but found no opposition. The hacienda staff had fled into the countryside, wanting no part of the skirmish.

Behind Horace, the stable doors flew open and a rider galloped away on a huge white horse and vanished down the same path the panicked conscripts had followed.

Fires still crackled from the conflagration of the caisson. Otherwise, the battlefield had gone quiet. Horace crouched behind the well, giving him cover and a view of the hacienda courtyard, while Sam guarded the house's front door. Sam had lost track of Juan and Jacob. He had last seen Silas run into the house and desperately wanted to follow, but he knew he had to cover the entrance. Discipline got the better of him and he stayed at his post, cursing under his breath and praying for his friends.

Wherever they were.

★

Silas found himself in the large, empty entryway of a house that was eerily still. Lamps were lit in a large room beyond the entry, and other lamps must have been elsewhere because he could see light oozing from other rooms. To his right, the nearest looked like a dining area. Further away, maybe a study. To his left was a hall. Silas went left.

The hall was deceptively short and led into a sitting room with ornately carved benches of a beautiful, rich wood Silas had never seen. With rifle at the ready, Silas stepped into the sitting room before he realized his rifle was empty. He paused to reload. That's when he felt it.

His left shoulder was wet. And hurt. A lot.

I'm shot.

The guard in the courtyard had not missed. Silas craned his head over to try to look at the wound, but all he could see was blood spreading at the top of his white shirt. He could move his left arm but, damn, it hurt. With his right hand, he carefully felt his collarbone which seemed intact. His fingers probed further and a painful rebuke told him he had found the bullet hole in the meat above his collarbone, close by his neck. Had the bullet struck a few inches to the right...

He finished reloading the Hawken, though it was difficult because his left arm's movement and strength were diminished.

He heard footsteps behind him. More than one person. No time to worry about his shoulder now.

Silas darted through the room and into another hall. This one was longer. From somewhere ahead came a noise, a crash. Silas moved toward the sound, down the hall which ran about twenty feet and turned right. He peeked around the corner while listening for the footsteps behind. Not running but coming on steadily. Were they following him? How? He looked back and saw his own blood trail on the wood floor.

Around the corner, the hall remained empty, illuminated by a lamp in a wall sconce. Two doors faced each other halfway down on either side, and a third door sat at the end of the hall. The door to his left was open, the room within dark. Silas crept forward, gripping the Hawken and trying to steady himself. He wondered which of these rooms the crashing noise had come from. He heard the footsteps again, getting closer.

With no alternative but to get out of the hall, he opened the door to his right, guessing—hoping—that everyone had emptied their rooms when the battle began. It was a bedroom, empty. Silas stepped in, making sure he dripped blood across the threshold, and quickly doubled back to the opposing room and ducked inside. He pressed himself against the wall inside the doorway, gritting his teeth against the angry protest of his bullet hole.

The room was dark and unoccupied. It was elaborately decorated and contained a large bed, a dressing table, armoire, and writing desk. The bedsheets showed that the occupant had just risen, but an officer's jacket hanging in the open armoire suggested he had not finished dressing. An officer's bicorne hat sat on the dressing table.

The footsteps in the hall grew louder, and Silas could hear voices whispering in Spanish. Two men, he thought. Silas realized he was cut off. In the close confines of the hall and with only one shot, his rifle would be of limited use. He leaned it against the dressing table. Pistols. His two pistols. One shot for each guard. He had little experience firing a pistol with his left hand, but maybe at close quarters he wouldn't need to be too accurate. He worried about the tingling in that left arm that must be a result of the bullet wound. He pulled one of the pistols from his belt with his right hand, reached for the other with his left.

The second pistol. It wasn't there. He felt around his waist but the gun was gone. His breathing quickened and he fought off panic. It must have fallen out of his belt somewhere outside.

I didn't feel that? Three pounds and more than a foot long and I didn't feel it tumble out?

He shifted the remaining pistol to his left hand and drew his Bowie knife with his right. Both hands were trembling.

Silas could see the men's shadows now. The shadows of their shakos. Of their muskets. Of their bayonets.

Something about a bayonet terrified Silas. Something about being run through with a long steel blade was more dreadful than a bullet, and well-trained professional soldiers with bayonets were coming for him.

The footsteps stopped. Maybe studying the blood trail.

"Miguel," one of the guards whispered. "Dónde esta el—"

"Cállate!" A deeper voice. Telling the first man to shut up. Further away, Silas thought. Far side of the hall.

His heart hammering in his chest and his mouth dry, Silas waited for the guards to reach the door. They stopped, peering into Silas's darkened hiding place. Another noise, a heavy thud, came from the end of the hall.

"La celda!" the deeper voice said, and the guards moved past Silas's door.

Silas pushed aside the pain in his shoulder, took a deep breath, and stepped into the hall.

The guards turned at Silas's sudden presence. The man nearer to the door from which Silas emerged was tall, of slight build, with a thin mustache, and long, dark hair hanging out the back of his shako. The second man was shorter, broader in the chest and shoulders, and clean shaven. Must be Miguel. Neither were conscripts. They looked like veterans. Probably served on the Zacatecas and Texas campaigns. Men who had taken Mexican and Texian lives. Huerta's chosen men.

Calm and focus descended on Silas. He allowed himself a fraction of a second to locate his target and slashed his knife at the nearer man's neck. No hesitation. A determined, full-force swing.

The Bowie's edge caught the tall guard two inches under the chin on his left side, slicing through skin, muscle, left carotid artery, jugular vein, and windpipe. The tall guard dropped his musket and clasped his hands to his neck, blood spewing between his fingers, down his blue jacket, down his white trousers, on the walls, on Silas's arm and chest and hair and face. The tall guard coughed blood, his eyes went wide, and he staggered but kept his feet.

Silas brought the pistol to bear on the second man, but the guard desperately swung his musket and the bayonet struck the pistol's barrel. With the grip in Silas's left hand weakened by the bullet wound, the impact sent the pistol flying down the hall.

Miguel faced the attacker, a blond-haired Anglo-looking youth in peasant clothing, and snarled and began to swing his musket and bayonet toward the blood-stained boy. He would pin him to the wall, twist the blade in the boy's gut, pull the bayonet free, and stab him again and again and again and again. It would not be a quick, painless death.

The hall restricted Miguel's attack and the butt of the musket slammed into the wall, but Silas could see the gleaming bayonet coming at him. No time to think.

With his now-empty left hand and ignoring the pain in his shoulder, Silas grabbed the tall, throat-slit guard by his bloody cross belts and hurled him into the second guard, parrying the bayonet thrust.

Miguel was knocked back by the tall guard's body, which collapsed across Miguel's musket, dragging down the point of his bayonet. As Miguel frantically wrenched the weapon free, Silas lunged forward, putting all his weight behind the attack, pinning the second guard against the wall and driving the Bowie knife into the man's chest.

Silas Grant didn't know his way around human anatomy as did Hiram Brown, so his strike was not so clean. But what Silas lacked in precision, he made up for in single-minded savagery. His jaw set, he pushed and twisted and relentlessly drove the Bowie cracking and carving its way through the bone and muscle of Miguel's chest wall before the blade plunged into the heart beneath, not stopping until the knife's point emerged from the guard's back. Miguel tried to form a protest, an objection, a curse against this boy, but all he managed was an airless choke. He looked down at the steel buried in his torso up to the knife's silver coin cross-guard. The choking finally stopped and Miguel dropped his musket.

Even as Miguel slid to the floor, Silas kept up the pressure of his attack, causing the tip of Bowie to scrape a blood-smeared gouge down the wall behind the body. He kept up his attack until he was certain the enemy was dead, until he no longer smelled the enemy's breath, until he saw the life go out of the enemy's eyes. Only then did his wrath relent, and he slumped against the corpse.

Silas, gulping air and his hands again shaking, felt a fresh torment. Far greater than before. He looked to his right at Miguel's fallen musket. There was blood on bayonet.

He drew back and saw he had only partially parried the Mexican's thrust. The bayonet had carved a gash several inches long below the ribs on Silas's right side, and blood coursed down his hip to drench his pant leg. His breath caught in his throat. Silas pushed himself off the dead man, sagged back against opposite the wall, and tried to calm the intense pain that seized his entire body.

It took a moment for Silas to absorb the pain and fight off its grip, and his breathing, though still too fast, finally began to settle. He leaned over the second guard, whose dead eyes stared back. The hate in Miguel's eyes had survived his death.

Silas tried to pull the knife from the man's chest but the effort detonated a new wave of agony from the bayonet wound, and he fell onto his butt and swallowed a scream.

Maybe just leave the knife. Except the way this day was going, he might need it again.

He struggled off his backside and made it to his knees in front of the corpse, grabbed the knife handle with both hands, and tried to drag it free without further inflaming his side or shoulder, but the knife was wedged between the dead man's ribs and angled beneath his breastbone. The blade snapped off. Silas tumbled backward, stoking the fire in his wounds, the Bowie's useless maple grip in his hand.

His teeth clenched and breathing labored, Silas glared at the broken Bowie and drew back to throw it away, but he paused, calmed, and instead shoved the remnant into his ammunition pouch. He steadied himself against the wall, scaled its rough surface to make it to his feet, and stood.

Stood over two dead bodies.

Stood over his kills.

And felt...satisfaction. These men were going to kill him. But he killed them.

The throat-cut guard's right foot was twitching, its toe tapping the floor.

Now, Silas thought, *I am a killer*. Satisfaction and sorrow tangled together.

How many? Three, four? No, five. Five men dead by his hand. Two men shot. One man's throat cut. One man stabbed. One man's skull bashed in.

No time for this.

Silas's whole body was shaking.

No time for this!

Silas closed his eyes and tried to still his tremors. He opened his eyes and took a slow breath but almost gagged from a metallic, salty taste in his mouth and realized it was an enemy's blood, and he spat but the repulsive flavor remained. He wiped his face with a sleeve.

Move!

He ducked back into the bedroom from which he'd sprung his attack and collected his Hawken rifle, returned to the hall, stepped over the dead bodies, and found his pistol. He advanced to the last door.

La celda, Miguel said. *The cell.*

Silas was greeted with silence and a foul smell from the other side of the door.

The door was not locked, and Silas threw it open and found a small bedroom transformed into a slaughterhouse, slick with blood and offal and filled with a stomach-churning stench.

On the floor was a man lying on his back. His abdomen has been scythed open and his guts spilled out between his hands. The instrument of the disembowelment was a sword, a Mexican Cuirassier saber, a straight, heavy blade with a handle wrapped in hardened brown leather and protected by an ornate knuckle guard. Silas knew this because the sword was sticking out of the dead man's chest.

Blood and entrails were everywhere, on the floor, on an overturned chair, on the body, on the man's face which was a contorted mask of pure horror, eyes and mouth wide open.

Silas could see the man was tall. Broad shoulders. Dark hair. A long nose. Silas hesitantly took a step forward for a closer examination the corpse's face when he noticed the man's legs. His left leg.

His left leg was missing below the knee.

Silas gasped and fell back against the wall, his left shoulder burning and right side stinging, his pistol hanging limp in his right hand and his Hawken rifle in his left. His mind boiled with rage, sorrow, and frustration.

All this. Everything that had happened. Henry's death. The men slaughtered this morning. The lives Silas took.

All for this.

He lowered his head and squeezed his eyes shut, and the muscles in his neck and jaw tensed.

Then all he could think of was finding Crockett's killer. Finding him and butchering him with his own sword.

Silas carefully slung his Hawken rifle over his right shoulder, stuck his pistol in his belt, stepped forward through the corpse's bowels, and yanked the sword from the dead man's chest. Again, Silas's wounds objected, but his anger was stronger than his pain.

What was he going to tell the others? We were too late? Minutes too late?

A splashing noise. Through his fury and grief, Silas heard a splashing noise. From a small room through a doorless entry at the back of the bedroom that was Crockett's death chamber.

Was this the killer cleaning up?

Silas stepped back from the body and leveled the bloody blade at the doorless entry.

From the back room, a man stepped into the bedroom where the gutted corpse lay. The man, wiping his hands on a towel, was dressed in red-spattered peasant clothing. He was tall. Dark hair, though with wisps of gray, parted down the middle. Thin but with broad shoulders. A long nose. Sparkling eyes.

And a peg leg below the knee in place of his left calf and foot. Silas's mouth fell open and his rage vanished.

"I thought…" Silas began, lowered the sword, and gawked at the tall man. "I thought he was… He's missing a leg."

The tall man crossed the room and stood next to the dead man, seemingly oblivious of the heaps of intestines.

"Naw," the tall man drawled. "He ain't missin' a leg." The tall man extended his wooden leg and jabbed the corpse hard in the side, and Silas heard a rib crack. The impact caused the corpse to shift slightly and the missing leg, sloshing through the pooled gore, sprang from beneath the body where the limb had folded back and been pinned when the man fell.

Silas exhaled and looked away from the corpse to the tall man. Whose face Silas recognized. A face that slowly grinned.

The face from the sketch.

"Colonel Crockett?"

The grin grew. "Call me David."

Silas beamed and laughed and didn't know what to do with himself. His injuries forgotten, replaced by relief and surprise and pure joy, he grabbed Crockett by the arm.

"It's very nice to meet you, sir," Silas smiled. "So very nice to meet you." His brow suddenly furrowed and he pointed to the corpse. "Who's he?"

"This?" David Crockett said. "This is General Joaquin Ramirez y Sesma of the Mexican army and aide-de-camp to Santa Anna. I've wanted to kill this son of a bitch ever since he hit me on the head at the Alamo with the hilt of the very sword you're holding. He run in here to kill me. I reckon all that ruckus outside was you? I'm guessin' you're not alone."

Silas just nodded.

"I figured he'd show up to finish me. Ramirez was a tough-soundin' fella, but didn't have much gravel in his gizzard. Talked a better fight than he fit. Shoulda seen the look on his face when I whacked him with my chair. But I made sure he was awake before I killed him. I wanted him to see it comin'. I ain't much for killin' folk, but this time, God help me, I enjoyed it."

Silas didn't know how to respond.

"Sorry," Crockett said. "I shouldn't say that."

"Colonel Crockett, I can't begin to imagine what you've been through," Silas said. "And I've killed men today."

"From the look of you, I'd say you only did what you had to."

Silas glanced over his shoulder toward the dead men in the hall. "So, why do I feel like there's a hand twisting my guts?" He immediately snapped his head back around. "No time for this. We'd best be going. Is there anything here you need?"

Crockett didn't bother to look around the room. "Naw. Nothing here I ever want to see again."

Silas tossed the sword away. "Follow me."

CHAPTER 28

"GIVE ME A moment," Crockett said as he and Silas left the room that had been Crockett's prison cell for two years. He stepped into the room from which Silas had ambushed the guards and emerged carrying a rifle, powder horn, and ammunition pouch.

"That's Ramirez's quarters," Crockett said. "He used to gloat that he took a few trinkets from the Alamo, including this fine Kentucky long rifle. Time to liberate it, too."

"You may need it," Silas said. "Can you walk fifteen miles?"

Crockett grinned again. "Watch me."

Silas backtracked through the house while doing math in his head. Their information was that the hacienda probably had ten guards, soldiers who had served with Huerta. Capable fighting men. He had seen two follow Huerta in pursuit of the conscripts. Jacob and Sam and José each shot one. Silas shot two outside, one on the roof and the man in the courtyard who shot Silas, and he killed two in the knife fight in the hall.

That left one. Someplace.

As Silas edged into the sitting room, two gunshots sounded from the short hall at the opposite side of the room. A moment later, a guard appeared, red stains spreading from bullet holes in his chest and forehead. He took one more step and pitched forward.

Jacob and Juan emerged from the short hall, keeping an eye on the fallen guard, smoke curling from the barrels of their pistols.

"Jacob," Silas called, and he and Crockett stepped into the sitting room.

Jacob Millsaps and Juan Seguin looked up and saw the ghost, and their jaws dropped. The Texians had come to accept the possibility that Crockett was alive, a possibility that grew to probability, probable enough to send them on this expedition. But despite the evidence, there was still that shred of doubt.

"Well, I'll be," Jacob said, smiling more broadly than Silas thought possible, and rushed toward Crockett. Jacob, Juan, and Crockett embraced.

"Dang, it's good to see you, David!" Jacob said.

"Good to see you, Jacob, Juan," Crockett said.

"Are you hurt?" Juan asked Crockett, whose clothes were stained with Ramirez's blood.

"Considering everything, I am blessed. And uninjured."

"We should get you out of here," Jacob said. "There are two more of Huerta's men someplace."

"No need to concern yourself," Crockett said. "This young man took care of them."

Jacob and Juan had been so focused on Crockett that they hadn't even noticed the blood-covered Silas.

"My God, Silas," Juan said.

"Some of this is other people's blood," Silas said.

"You're shot," Juan said. "Let me look."

Silas flinched and hissed as Juan peeled the shirt away from the bullet hole.

"Bullet went clear through, just above the collarbone. That needs to be bandaged."

"When did you get shot?" Crockett asked.

"In the courtyard. I'm all right. Let's get moving."

"We also need to see about that gash," Jacob said, and frowned as he examined the grisly cut. "Sorry. That probably hurts. Bayonet?"

"Mm-hmm," Silas groaned. "I'm all right," he said unconvincingly. "I just want to get away from this place."

"All right," Jacob said. "But you're bleeding pretty good. Horace is going to look at those wounds when we get clear."

"Before we take another step," Crockett said, "what is your name, young man?"

"Sorry, sir, I forgot my manners. My name is Silas Grant."

"Silas Grant, I cannot tell you what a pleasure it is to meet you. If you hadn't dealt with Diego and Miguel—they were the guards in the hall—I have no doubt they'd have killed me. I owe you my life. Thank you, Silas."

"You're welcome, sir."

"Jacob, Juan, you think I can get this young fella to stop callin' me sir?"

"Probably not," Jacob said.

"I'm afraid he's naturally polite," Juan said.

Everyone made sure all their guns were loaded, and the three Texians escorted David Crockett out of Santa Anna's home.

They found Sam watching the front door, and another back-slapping greeting ensued. They stepped out of the house and found Horace crouching by the hacienda well, and another reunion resulted.

"Horace, when you get a chance, would you tend to Silas?" Juan said. "He's wounded."

"Silas?" Sam gaped at the ghastly sight of his young friend. "Oh, God, are you—"

"I look worse than I am," Silas said, swallowing his words and trying to move his lungs as little as possible. "At least, I hope. But damn it, this hurts like hell."

Sam tried to flash a reassuring smile but it came out a tight-lipped grimace. "I think that's the first time I've ever heard you cuss."

"Seemed like the time to start."

"Shot and bayoneted on the same day and lived to tell of it!" Crockett said.

"Ohhhh," Sam groaned and slowly shook his head. "Emily Perry is going to kick my ass." That made Silas smile.

"Come here, Silas, let me take a look at you," Horace said.

"Where's José?" Jacob asked.

"Up here," de la Peña called from the roof of the house where he was keeping watch.

"I brought some bandages," Horace said. "Let's get you fixed up." He dressed the bullet hole and turned his attention to Silas's slashed side. "You got carved pretty good." He probed the wound, and Silas flinched away slightly from the exam but did his best to muffle a groan. "The bayonet missed your liver, otherwise you probably wouldn't be standing here. The fellow who did this, did he get away?"

"No," Silas murmured. "No, he didn't."

Horace wrapped Silas's side. "That'll have to do until we get to the ship." He looked at Silas's face. The boy was exhausted. Hurting, and not just physically. Horace lowered his voice. "You all right?"

Silas just nodded and put a hand to the bayonet wound. *Bayonet wound.* The words seemed surreal. Horrifying. "Thank you, Horace."

Horace drew a bucket of water from the well and helped Silas wash blood from his hair and face. Silas rinsed blood from his mouth, then gulped down water, unable to quench a sudden, overwhelming thirst. But he felt human again.

The sun was beginning to rise and an orange glow infused the battleground. From the roof, de la Peña watched Silas step onto the corpse-strewn field and stand among shattered bodies. Through the water dripping from his sandy-blond hair, Silas could see at least a dozen dead men. More. He paused by a dead guard, the man who had shot Silas. The man Silas had shot and killed. It was that close. Silas was just that close to lying there. But he was alive, and this man was dead.

Now I am a killer. Emily, I am a killer.

"Did anyone see Santa Anna?" José said.

"No, no sign of him," Juan said. "We searched the whole house."

"I saw a rider leave after you entered the house," Horace said.

"White horse?" José asked.

"Yeah."

"That was probably him. He rides a white charger."

"Can you see anything up there? Anyone coming?" Jacob said.

"Nothing," José said.

"Come on down and let's get started for Veracruz. We got a long walk."

Seven men left blood-soaked Manga de Clavo.

The Texians reached the edge of the hacienda courtyard where they had started the attack. Silas stopped next to the body of a conscript, face down, the back of his head a thick mass of bloody hair where his skull had been crushed.

"I'm sorry."

Sam waited a moment before putting a hand on Silas's back. "We have to go."

Silas nodded, and the Texians began hiking up the hill where they camped the previous night, aiming for the brush from which they'd come.

"I'm afraid I don't know you, sir," Crockett said to José. "I'm David Crockett."

"A very great pleasure, sir. I am José Enrique de la Peña."

"Oh, I've heard your name."

"My name?"

"Not spoken of well. Loudly, but not well. You really got under Santa Anna's skin."

"Good to hear."

"We get over this hill, we keep going east," Jacob said. "We're a little north of the road to Veracruz, so we'll just angle to the south."

The Texians topped the hill.

At the base of the hill's long back slope, forming up in two lines, was a portion of the conscripted company that the Texians had sent in flight earlier that morning. A few with blue jackets, most with heads uncovered, but every man had a musket affixed with a bayonet.

Long, lethal, steel bayonets.

Huerta, his jacket now buttoned, was there with his two remaining chosen men at his side. And in front of the formation was Santa Anna on his white charger.

"Boys, I've seen this show before," Crockett said. "And I didn't much care for the ending."

"They recovered faster than I imagined," Horace said.

"Looks like about forty…fifty…sixty of them," Jacob said. "We could fall back to the hacienda but we'd be trapped."

"I don't see anyone behind us," Horace said. "We need to keep watch for them trying to flank us."

"Thank goodness they're untrained," Sam said. "Maneuvering them would be difficult."

"And we can't run because of me," Crockett said, and tapped his rifle on his wooden leg.

Silas stared at Crockett.

"Don't even think about us leaving you," Silas said. "That is not happening. We've been through too much for that. We're all getting out of here. We made a promise to Henry."

"Henry?" Crockett said, a look of concern on his face. "Henry Karnes?"

"Henry was wounded when we were looking for José," Horace explained. "Henry's dead."

Crockett closed his eyes and lowered his head. "Oh, God," he said. "Henry was a good friend."

"So," Silas said, "I'm taking you out of here if I have to throw you over my shoulder."

The Gentleman from the Cane lifted his head. He grinned. "I believe you would. Don't worry. I ain't ready to hang up my fiddle." Crockett considered the Mexican infantry arrayed at the base of the hill. "If I heard correct, you got these boys to panic and run earlier. Think they're any more peart for a fight now?"

"How do we send them running?" Horace said. "I don't see how we fool them again."

"No more bluffs," Silas said with a shake of his head. "Decapitate them. Shoot the leaders. Starting with him," and he jabbed a finger at Santa Anna on his horse.

"They're a little out of range, even for our Kentucky long rifles," Sam said. "Make it about four hundred yards."

"Let them come on a little," Jacob said. "Make the first shots count. Take out the officers and maybe the rest will break. If they get close, Horace and Juan can open up with the shotguns."

Crockett ran his hand over the rippled grain in his rifle's fiddleback maple stock. Here he was, face to face with Santa Anna, rifle in hand. For two years, he had dreamed of this moment. But McCulloch was right. The Mexicans were out of range.

Crockett glanced to his left at the young man who had found him in the hacienda. Silas was looking at him.

"This," Silas said, and lifted his Hawken rifle, "might get there. Care to borrow it?"

A hint of a smile crossed Crockett's lips. He exchanged rifles with Silas, admiring the Hawken's craftsmanship. He ran his finger along the barrel with its octagonal exterior shape.

Crockett put the Hawken to his shoulder. Felt good.

"Rear trigger sets the front?" he asked.

"Yes, sir. Then that front is a hair trigger."

Sergeant Manuel Loranca had also seen this show before and he was none too happy to again march into Texian rifles.

Loranca participated in the attack at the Alamo and saw the range and effectiveness of the Texian long guns, which had taken such a terrible toll on the Mexican assault troops. At this distance, he thought—or hoped—they were out of range.

He knew the Texians were well out of range of the Mexicans' muskets. Loranca's Brown Bess could be effective at one hundred yards, but the rest of the company was armed with India Pattern muskets, a cheaper version of the Brown Bess. There would be no point in opening fire until the Texians were within eighty yards. Assuming these untrained men could hit a target at eighty yards.

And their bayonets would be useless until the last few yards. Assuming these untrained men could hold together long enough to take steel to the Texians.

Three hundred yards of walking into the Texians' fire. As men began to drop—and the officers would be targeted first—Loranca feared these inexperienced men would break.

✯

The Texians could see a soldier, probably the sergeant they had seen attempting to whip the conscripts into shape yesterday in the hacienda camp, pacing back and forth and getting the raw, press-ganged men to dress their lines.

Huerta was at the center of the formation, and his last two guards moved to either end of the front line of soldiers. Santa Anna nudged his horse forward a step and drew his sword.

Crockett sighted on the preening peacock atop his destrier.

Huerta looked up at Santa Anna. Appeared to say something. Probably warning him that, sitting up high, he was making himself an inviting target.

Crockett fired. In the same instant, Santa Anna began to dismount.

The bullet struck the horn of Santa Anna's saddle, smashing his hand before deflecting into the general's left leg. Even from four hundred yards, the Texians could hear his shriek as he toppled from the destrier and crumpled to the ground.

Huerta immediately moved to take the horse's reins to prevent the destrier from stepping on its injured master, and Huerta's last two guards rushed to Santa Anna's side. Huerta led the horse away and handed the reins to a conscript, returned to Santa Anna, and motioned for four of the conscripts to assist his chosen men in carrying the general back to the hacienda.

✯

"Thank you." Crockett handed the Hawken back to Silas. "Thank you very much."

The Mexican company was disoriented but that condition was dissipating as Huerta motivated them to attack the Texians, and his men were responding. The sun was catching on that swarm of bayonets, and the sight of all that deadly steel again chilled Silas.

The bullet wound in his shoulder throbbed, the gash in his side was sharp and screaming and surging with every breath, and he could feel blood seeping through the bandage and dripping down his side. But a single thought overpowered the pain.

Keep those bayonets away.

Even if it meant killing again.

Silas's father had taught him to load rifle and pistol again and again and again until each step was muscle memory. He did not think. He acted. Those lessons served him well this morning when he reloaded in the dark. Now he employed them again.

Silas set the hammer to half cock and put the rifle's butt on the ground, steadying it against the inside of his left foot. He charged the barrel with black powder, 140 grains for this extreme range. He centered a patch atop the barrel, pushed a .50-caliber ball into the patch, and rammed the load home, making sure the ball was secure against the powder. Silas replaced the ramrod beneath the barrel, lifted the Hawken to his chest, and placed a cap on the percussion lock's nipple. He set the hammer to full cock.

I am not dying here.

He looked for a target.

I am going home.

★

The company was shaken by Santa Anna's agonized screams, but Huerta seized command and exhorted them to action. He did not threaten or curse. He called on their patriotism to rise against these enemies of Mexico, invaders who had struck down their leader. To kill the defilers of their country, enemies who had come for their wives and children.

It was working. The conscripts began to cheer and raised their muskets. Bayonets clanged and scraped against one another.

"Viva Mexico! Viva Mexico!"

The rabble were turning into soldiers.

Sergeant Loranca, however, was unmoved. And unconvinced. A disciplined, experienced company could take the casualties necessary to close within musket range, fire a volley, and make a bayonet charge. They would take casualties, but sixty against seven would carry the day.

However, he doubted these untrained men would reach the top of the hill. Not after their leaders were shot.

But if they withdrew into the woods, they could close on the Texians without offering themselves up for target practice on this hillside gallery.

Huerta drew his sword and raised it over his head, his face a mask of maniacal delight. Finally, he would lead an attack against an enemy, and he would personally cut the head off Crockett as should have been done two years ago.

"Captain, wait—" Loranca shouted.

"Company!" Huerta bellowed. "Forward!"

Four hundred yards up the slope, Silas ignored the fire in his side as he lifted the Hawken. He rested the blood-stained butt plate against his right shoulder, laid his cheek against the curved walnut stock, and took aim down the iron blade sight at the end of the thirty-six-inch barrel. He let out half a breath, steadied himself. The pain in his wounds faded.

No more hesitation, no qualms, no fears, no anxiety over taking a life. This man was an enemy coming to kill him. Bringing bayonets to slaughter Silas and his friends.

Silas pulled the rear trigger, setting the front trigger and allowing the Hawken to be fired with a slight pressure, and carefully laid his finger on the front trigger as the soldiers took their first steps up the hill.

✯

Sergeant Loranca observed what transpired in the next second as discernible, distinct events.

A puff of dirty white smoke blossomed in front of the men at the top of the rise, emanating from the short Texian in the middle of their line.

It took one second for the .50-caliber ball to cover four hundred yards.

For the report of the gunshot to reach the conscripts.

For the bullet to impact Huerta's face just below the nose, rip through his head, detonate the back of his skull, and explode a cloud of blood, bone, teeth, and brains into the faces of his soldiers, who instinctively flinched and stopped their march.

It took another moment for Huerta to realize he was dead. He teetered on his heels just long enough for the men at the front of the formation to look into the jagged hole in the back of their captain's head.

Huerta toppled back at the feet of Sergeant Loranca, who was now speckled with the insides of Huerta's brainpan and promoted to command of the conscripts.

Loranca could see the short Texian who had just killed Huerta. The short Texian's next move, Loranca knew, would be to reload and take aim.

At him.

Keeping the barrel of his musket lowered, Loranca slowly raised an empty hand to the Texians and turned to the soldiers he had inherited, who were again on the edge of panic, ready to run and never look back. Their faces turned to the sergeant.

"It's all right, men," Loranca said. "Let's go home."

Loranca took one look at Huerta's dead body, the excited anticipation of the attack still on what was left of his face. He glanced at the great white destrier, which had wandered a few feet away and was grazing on a tussock of feathergrass.

Then he led the conscripts south toward the Veracruz road, a trail of jackets and shakos and muskets marking their passage through the woods outside of Manga de Clavo.

CHAPTER 29

THE TEXIANS SAW the Mexican soldiers move off, but their attention was on the corpse lying four hundred yards away at the base of the long, grassy hill. Slowly, they glanced at Silas.

"I never seen the like," Horace whispered.

Silas took no notice of their stares and began reloading the Hawken.

"That's the finest shot I ever seen," Crockett breathed. "Not Daniel Boone nor Timothy Murphy could match it."

The only sound Silas made was the scrape of a ramrod being withdrawn from the Hawken before plunging down the rifle's barrel to secure a new .50-caliber ball onto fresh gunpowder. He relaxed his jaw, slowly exhaled, and winced as the pain returned.

Jacob and José followed the Mexicans from a discreet distance for a few hundred yards to confirm the retreat was sincere and not a ruse to draw the Texians in a wooded ambush.

The morning sun felt warm on Silas's face. It was going to be a hot day. A long walk. He looked around the campsite, spotted his abandoned sombrero, and stepped toward the hat but couldn't bend to pick it up because of the bayonet wound.

Crockett walked past Silas and retrieved the sombrero. He started to put it on the boy's head, thought better, and instead handed the hat to the young man.

Then the Texians set out for Veracruz.

☆

There was nothing else to be done for Silas. The bleeding had slowed but the wound in his side still leaked. Deep breaths were far too painful, so Silas took short sips of air, followed by quick exhales. He found himself counting his breaths, something to occupy his mind and not think about his pain and about the blood he was losing and the possibility of losing enough blood to go into shock in the Mexican countryside miles from Veracruz and the ship and proper medical care. He counted to a hundred and started again, trying to measure the distance by the number of breaths he took but his mind kept losing track of the tally.

I used to be good at math.

He tried to find a comfortable position to carry his rifle, but in his left hand the Hawken tugged on his bullet-wounded shoulder, in his right it weighed his arm down against his bayonet-wounded side. The left arm could deal with it better.

Why does the hike back seem so much longer than the march in?

He damned sure wasn't going to ask one of the others to carry the Hawken.

After a few hours, they reached the hidden cart and retrieved their clothes. Silas was anxious to be rid of his bloody outfit but needed help stripping off the ruined rags. Horace reexamined Silas and found the dressing on the bayonet slash soaked through, so he added more bandages and checked for signs of shock. Fortunately, the boy wasn't dizzy, his lips weren't turning blue, and he didn't seem confused. Not that it mattered. If Silas went into shock out here, the Texians couldn't do much for him.

"Why don't you let me carry that Hawken?" Sam said.

"I can manage," Silas said.

"I know you can manage. Let me carry it. Please."

Silas looked at Sam, hesitated, started to object, but handed him the ten-pound rifle. Losing the weight did feel better.

"Thanks, Sam."

"We'll get you stitched up when we get to the ship," Horace said.

How far to the ship? Don't ask. The answer would be depressing. Stitched? That's gonna hurt. Don't think about it. Think about Emily. Think about going home and seeing Emily. Yeah, think about Emily.

The other Texians returned to their normal attire as well, pulled the cart from its hiding place, and left it by the road for some locals to find and put to good use.

An hour later, Silas approached Crockett. "Colonel," he said, barely above a whisper, "what did you say were the names of the guards in the hall?"

The question took Crockett by surprise and he didn't answer immediately. He looked at Silas, who had his eyes down. "Diego and Miguel."

"One was taller," Silas said.

"That was Diego."

Diego. The man whose throat I cut was named Diego.

"The other was kind of barrel chested."

"Miguel."

Miguel. The man I stabbed through the heart was Miguel.

"What were they like?"

"We didn't have long conversations," Crockett said. "They were in the army for years and had seen a lot of fighting. Hard men. Miguel had a mean streak. Diego wasn't a bad sort."

"Did they have wives, children?"

"Miguel never mentioned anyone. Diego had a family."

Silas nodded and drifted back a few steps.

Sam sidled up to Crockett. "What was that about?"

"A troubled young man trying to understand who he just killed."

As they neared Veracruz, the Texians and Crockett discussed one other matter that required attention—Crockett's name.

Crockett's return to America was supposed to be anonymous so the Texians couldn't very well call him by his given name. The Texians went through a variety of options with Crockett, none of which he found appealing. Finally, it was decided to leave the choice to him at a later time so that none of the Texians would know his name and he could truly vanish. For now, the Texians would call him Mr. Greene, adopting as a temporary moniker the name of the county in which he was born.

By late afternoon, they reached the outskirts of Veracruz. J.C. Neill and Hiram Brown were waiting to escort them to the ship, along with a detachment of French troops, who by that time had complete control of the city and the fort of San Juan de Ulna.

"Hello, David," a smiling J.C. said, shaking Crockett's hand. "Can't tell you how happy I am to see you again."

"Good to see you, too, J.C."

"And this is Hiram Brown," J.C. said. "He helped us find you."

"Thank you, sir," Crockett said.

"I am very pleased to meet you…" Brown said.

"…Mr. Greene," Horace said.

"Mr. Greene," Brown said. He shook Crockett's hand.

"Gentlemen," José said, "thank you for allowing me to be a part of this. I'm very proud of the blow we struck against Santa Anna today. However, I think this is where we part company. I still have work to do in Mexico."

"We understand," Jacob said.

"Captain de la Peña, I feel the same of Mexico as you," Brown said. "But right now, we need to get all of you away from Veracruz. We don't know if Santa Anna or the Mexican army have additional forces nearby, and the French want us out. Immediately."

"Yes, return to Mexico later," Horace said. "For now, come with us. My wife and I would like you to be a guest at our home."

José nodded. "Very well, Horace. I would like that."

"Besides," Jacob said, "we've earned us a little celebration."

"Indeed, you have," Brown said. "All of you. I am so delighted that everyone made it back in one piece." He paused and looked at Silas. Blood had again seeped through his bandages. "Are you all right, Silas?"

Silas, whose side was making breathing awful, offered a thin but unconvincing smile.

"He's wounded," Sam said.

"There's a doctor on the ship. We'll get you fixed up as soon as possible. Now, let's get you home."

"I haven't been liquored in more than ten years, but I could do with a horn now," Crockett said from the deck of the repaired *Woodbury* as the schooner slid north across the calm, moon-lit gulf toward New Orleans.

"What's next?" asked Silas, his wounds cleaned, stitched, re-bandaged, and still aching but feeling better.

"Haven't given it much thought," Crockett said. "Never figured to leave Mexico alive."

"What about returning to politics?" Brown said, causing the Texians to glance warily at Brown.

"Naw. World figures me dead. Oughta leave it that way. Besides, I was finished with Washington."

"What about your family?" Jacob asked.

"Elizabeth was done with me long ago. I reckon they're fine without me droppin' back into their lives."

"Your boy John won your seat in Congress," Jacob said.

"You don't say. I hope he's better at politics than his father."

"What next?" Silas repeated, concerned that Crockett could be rescued only to find himself abandoned. "You've got no money."

"Mr. la Branche is waiting for us in New Orleans," Brown said. "He's arranged a small stake to get you started."

"That's very kind," Crockett said. "At my age, you don't get many more chances. You fellas have given me one more to find my place. I'd love to stay in Texas. Some of the richest country I've ever seen. Plenty of lumber, mill streams. But I don't see how that's possible. Too many folks know me.

"There was a spot. Western Tennessee, up on the Obion. Good huntin'. Bear, deer, elk. A man could build, live. Maybe I can find someplace like that. Out west.

"So, I'll do what I've always done," David Crockett said. "Begin again."

EPILOGUE 1

THE TEXIANS LAST saw David Crockett in New Orleans. He was attired in new clothes, his face sported a growth of beard, he was well-funded courtesy of the US government, and still carried the rifle he liberated from Manga de Clavo. Crockett boarded a steamboat headed up the Mississippi for St. Louis, from there to begin again somewhere out west.

The Texians spent a few days enjoying the pleasures of New Orleans while Silas received medical attention and rested until a doctor cleared him for the journey to Texas. The group reboarded *Woodbury* and sailed to Houston, where Dr. Ashbel Smith followed up with Silas and agreed to his fitness for the last leg of the journey.

Horace Alsbury would return to his ranch outside Goliad, J.C. Neill to Harrisburg, Jacob Millsaps to Gonzales, Juan Seguin to his senatorial duties, José Enrique de la Peña to Mexico, and Sam McCulloch to the Brazos Valley. But before the Texians headed to their respective destinations, they escorted Silas home.

Though he was recovering and improving, Silas still looked like someone who had recently been shot and bayoneted and bled all over Mexico when he arrived at his parents' home, where Emily had been staying in anxious anticipation.

"He's all right, Emily," Sam said before he and Jacob helped Silas from the wagon which had transported him from coast. "He got a little…hurt. But he's fine. He's going to be fine. Doctors said he needs to take it easy awhile. And I know you'll take good care of him."

"Shot in the shoulder, son?" Duncan Grant said as Silas, his arm in a sling, made it to his feet.

"A Brazos Valley tradition," Sam said.

Duncan forced a smile and stepped forward to help Silas. He wanted to leap to the side of his wounded son but staved off the impulse and tried—unsuccessfully—to hide his concern. Behind Duncan, Alice Grant swallowed hard and muffled her own urge to burst into tears at the sight of her injured child.

"Is Silas hurt?" Katie asked, clutching her mother's skirt.

"I'm all right, Katie," Silas said.

"He just got a little…cut…in his side," Sam sputtered, "…from a…" and he cleared his throat, "…bayonet."

"You got bayonetted?" Thomas Grant asked his older brother. "Wow! Bet that hurt."

The medical report complete, Sam braced for Emily's wrath he'd been dreading since the Texians began their march from Manga de Clavo.

There was no angry outburst, no cry or gasp or reprimand. Instead, Emily stepped forward, hugged Sam, and kissed his cheek. "Thank you," she said.

Sam, lost in those green eyes, could only smile in response and felt himself fall a little bit in love with Emily. She hugged each of Silas's comrades and thanked them, leaving each man wearing a broad, sappy grin.

Emily moved to Silas, gently took his face in her hands, and gave him a long, deep kiss that buckled the knees of every man present, Silas's father and brother included.

"Mm," one of the Texians let slip.

When the kiss finally ended, Silas said farewell to his friends and Emily helped him into the house.

The Texians watched the young lovers depart.

Sam, J.C., Jacob, Horace, and José slowly turned to Juan.

Seguin took a deep breath, raised an eyebrow, then exhaled slowly. "Yeah," he conceded. "Prettiest girl in Texas."

EPILOGUE 2

THE JOURNEY TOOK forty days. Crossing rivers. Navigating forests. Avoiding slave-hunting patrols.

He traveled mostly at night, parallel to but well off the roads.

The horse Sam provided had been good for the initial escape. He'd walked it until dawn and ridden hard to the east. Beyond that, a horse would attract attention. Joe couldn't sell the beast as that would raise suspicion, so he simply left it near a farm.

He lived off the land, rarely stopping to spend his precious money, and only for a few essentials at out-of-the-way posts, never any towns. Fortunately, McCulloch had supplied him well for the start of the quest. The bag Sam provided contained dried meat, dried fruit, nuts, pemmican, a canteen, and a knife, but Joe lost the bag crossing the Mississippi River.

When Joe finally reached Alabama, he found a carter who provided directions to Concecuh County. Once there, a field hand pointed him to Sparta, Alabama, and the Nicholas Travis farm.

Joe—ragged, emaciated, and exhausted—stumbled onto the farm and slowly walked toward the master of the property, William Barrett Travis's younger brother, Nicholas.

Nicholas Travis approached this scarecrow of a man cautiously and asked his business. Joe explained that he was the man servant of Nicholas's brother, William, in Texas. Joe told Nicholas of his brother, of his bravery, of his honor, how he lived and how he died.

Travis welcomed Joe into his home, fed and clothed him, introduced him to his wife and children, and reintroduced him to William's orphaned children, Charlie and Susan Isabella.

Nicholas Travis's family later paid $650 to the William Barret Travis estate, forever severing Joe from that bond. Joe remained with the family the rest of his life, caring for Charlie and Susan Isabella. Though he never saw his mother, brothers, or sister again, Joe later fathered his own family in Alabama. Decades later, he accompanied William Barret Travis's youngest brother, James, on a pilgrimage to San Antonio to see the place where his brother died.

But when Joe returned to the Alamo, he did so a freeman.

HISTORICAL NOTES

FIRST THINGS FIRST: David Crockett died March 6, 1836, at the Alamo.

His survival and subsequent captivity depicted in the novel are purely fictional. Not long after the Alamo, a White prisoner doing hard labor in a mine in Mexico allegedly claimed to be Crockett, but this story was not believed to be true.

I call him David throughout the novel because he preferred David to Davy, which, personally, I can understand.

Was Crockett killed in battle or captured and executed? We will never know for certain. The death of David Crockett is a case study in the fallibility of witness testimony. In the novel, I describe the wildly different versions of his final moments.

The locations in the novel are based on historical places, though some no longer exist. I tried to make each as authentic as the historic record—and the needs of my story—allowed.

Manga de Clavo was Santa Anna's hacienda located approximately fifteen miles from Veracruz. It was visited by Fanny Calderón de la Barca, and her description in her letters was the basis of my fictional version. The layout of the house and its furnishings are fictional. Manga de Clavo no longer exists. The nearby hill from which the Texians launched their raid is fictional.

Casa Blanca was Erasmo Seguin's hacienda. It no longer exists.

Bernardo Plantation no longer exists, although there have been archaeological digs at the site. It had two chimneys in 1838, and two more were later added.

Groce's Landing did exist, but the course of the Brazos River has changed so much that the location is no longer on the river.

Villa de San Mateo del Pilón is now known as Montemorelos. The description of the town is fictional.

The Pastry War took place in 1838-39. France took and held Veracruz until Mexico agreed to pay 600,000 pesos. There were approximately 280 casualties between the two sides, including Santa Anna, who was wounded in the leg which had to be amputated. His action in the Pastry War propelled him back into the good graces of the Mexican public, and Santa Anna again became president in 1839.

The American schooner *Woodbury* was present during the blockade and siege. H.D. Hunter was a US Navy officer who over-saw *Woodbury*'s construction. I found no record of who was in command when the ship was in the Gulf of Mexico.

The féte of San Agustin was described by Fanny Calderón de la Barca.

About the biggest change I made for the novel was the timing of Fanny and Ángel's tour of Mexico, which actually took place after the Pastry War.

The incident with smugglers on Corpus Christi Bay is based on a historic event, and the location of that incident—in which smugglers were driven away and left behind barrels of flour—is today a section of the city of Corpus Christi known as Flour Bluff. I could find no other historical details of the incident.

There was rebellion in Mexico in the time of the novel, and General Urrea and Antonio Canales were participants. General Andrade was the commander of the Alamo when it was surrendered after San Jacinto. His role in the rebellion and his fate in the novel are fictional.

The origin of the phrase "Immortal 32," which refers to the thirty-two men from Gonzales who rode to San Antonio in response William Barrett Travis's call for help, is unclear, though it may have been the 1911 movie *The Immortal Alamo*. It probably did not exist in 1838.

Of the named characters in the novel, approximately 80 percent are based upon historic figures.

Of the Texians, Horace Alsbury, Henry Wax Karnes, Samuel McCulloch Jr., James Clinton Neill, and Juan Seguin were significant figures from the Texas Revolution, as was Juan's father, Erasmo Seguin. I hope I have done them justice.

Henry was wounded in a fight with Comanches in 1839 and never fully recovered. He died of yellow fever in 1840.

As to Henry's funeral in the novel, the priests of Cathedral de San Fernando denied Henry burial in the Campo Santos cemetery because he was Protestant. There is a monument to Henry in Milam Park, near where he is believed to have been buried. Cathedral de San Fernando still stands in San Antonio.

Sam McCulloch is recognized as the first Texian casualty in the Texas Revolution, shot in the shoulder during the capture of the fort at Goliad in 1835. He was a free Black man, and he married Mary Lorena Vess, a White woman, in 1837. There is a bronze statue of Sam by sculptor Craig Campobella in Montgomery, Texas.

Sam's sisters, Harriet, Jane, and Mahaly, were free Black women, born into slavery in Alabama but emancipated by their White father. Harriet and Jane were twins who later became ranchers and owners of land, horses, and cattle in Texas. The McCulloch family took in a young man named Uldy, who was a slave until Sam's father emancipated him.

José Enrique de la Peña was an officer with Santa Anna's army in Texas and authored a memoir/diary which gained notoriety upon its translation and publication in 1975 because it described Crockett being captured and executed at the Alamo. More important to me is de la Peña's vivid descriptions of the suffering of Mexican troops on the march north into Texas and in the aftermath of the Alamo as well as his criticism of Santa Anna and some of his senior officers. The tragic story of José's young friend, Lieutenant José Maria Heredia, was described in de la Peña's book. De la Peña was a lieutenant at the time of the storming of the Alamo and was promoted to captain a short time later. I moved up his promotion to refer to him by the same rank throughout the book.

Fanny Calderón de la Barca was a historic character. Her letters from Mexico, published as the book *Life in Mexico*, provided background material for this novel. As to my descriptions of Fanny's appearance, a painting of Fanny shows her to have been a remarkable beauty.

Fanny's husband, Ángel, was the first Spanish ambassador to independent Mexico.

Mrs. Ward was real. She accompanied Fanny on her travels in Mexico and made sketches such as the described drawings of the Puente Nacional Bridge and the interior of an Indian hut. That is all history seems to know of her. Her fate in the novel is purely fictional.

Luis Cuevas was Mexican minister of foreign affairs in 1838.

Powhatan Ellis was an American judge and politician who was US Envoy Extraordinary and Minister Plenipotentiary to Mexico in 1838. He served in Congress at the same time as Crockett.

Alcée la Branche was US ambassador to the Republic of Texas in 1838.

Jean Pierre Isidore Alphonse Dubois de Saligny was French ambassador to Texas.

Dr. Nicholas Labadie was a physician and pharmacist. Originally from Louisiana, he joined Sam Houston's army after the Alamo, fought at San Jacinto, and treated the wounded. He continued to practice medicine in Texas after the war.

Isaac Burton and his Rangers, who were dubbed the Horse Marines, captured three merchant brigs delivering supplies to the Mexican army at Copano Bay in 1836. The ships were *Watchman, Comanche,* and *Fanny Butler.* Little is known of the ultimate fates of those ships.

Joaquin Ramirez y Sesma and Carolino Huerta were officers in Santa Anna's army and were described in de la Peña's diary/memoir.

Sergeant Manuel Loranca was a Mexican solder in the attack on the Alamo.

Joe was the slave of William Barret Travis. Some of the details of Joe in the novel are thanks to the wonderful book *Joe—The Slave Who Became an Alamo Legend,* by Ron J. Jackson Jr. and Lee Spencer White. I also want to credit that book for the phrase "living dead" in relation to slavery, referring to family members torn from one another, alive but never seen again. The bits in the novel about Joe being on a crew clearing land for the building of Austin and about Sam helping him escape are fictional. One of Joe's brothers, William, escaped from slavery and became author, lecturer, playwright, historian, and abolitionist William Wells Brown, who wrote *Clotel; or, The President's Daughter,* published in 1853 and the first novel by an African American author.

Susanna Dickinson was the source of the allegations against Juana Alsbury, but her portrayal in the novel is largely fictional. The Alamo House is fictional.

Of the witnesses interviewed by the Texians, only farmer Sotero, *Watchman* Captain Levi Jones, and former Mexican soldier Rafael Vega are fictional.

Madam Powell's boarding house was burned by the Mexican army as it began its long retreat from Texas. She rebuilt it, but it no longer exists.

Dr. William Thorn was captured by Urrea's forces at Copano Bay. There is no record of him being at the Alamo, nor is there any record I could find of his ultimate fate.

Dr. Ashbel Smith was a Yale-educated physician, came to Texas in 1837, was surgeon general of the Republic of Texas, and established the first hospital in Houston.

Algernon Thompson fought in the Texas Revolution and later worked in Texas government.

The tavern operator, Salvator, is described in Fanny Calderón de la Barca's letters.

In chapter 29, Crockett comments that Silas's shot that killed Huerta could not be matched by Daniel Boone or Timothy Murphy. Murphy was a legendary sniper in the American Revolution who killed two senior British officers with shots from three hundred yards.

Hiram Brown, Father Ortiz, Coyotl and Yaretzi, and Frank Ogden are fictional. Patrick Ryan is fictional although there were a large number of Irish immigrants in Mexico.

Jacob Millsaps is a fictional brother of Isaac Millsaps, who was one of the Immortal 32 and left behind a blind wife and seven children when he rode to the Alamo.

As for Silas and Emily, they are fictional and not based upon or inspired by any person. Rather than create them out of whole cloth, I gave them ties to figures from Texas history. Silas is the fictional nephew of Dr. James Grant, a significant figure in the Texas Revolution who was killed in combat with Mexican troops. Emily is the fictional sister of James Perry, who fought in the Revolution and was a staunch critic of Sam Houston.

Silas and Emily live on in my imagination, and their story will continue.

ACKNOWLEDGMENTS

I WANT TO acknowledge those who helped make the publication of this novel a reality:

My thanks to Amanda Brown, my editor. It's a traumatic thing to hand a piece of your soul over to a stranger for examination and critique. Fortunately, Amanda mitigates an author's anxiety with a wonderful combination of professionalism and friendliness. She meticulously edited the manuscript, insured continuity throughout, and provided valuable feedback, advice, and encouragement. Amanda is a delight to work with, and *Rescuing Crockett* is better for her work. If you are a writer in need of an editor, I wholeheartedly recommend Amanda (amandabrownedits.com).

My thanks to Damon Freeman and his team at Damonza for creating the cover for *Rescuing Crockett* and formatting the novel's pages for print and eBook.

My thanks to Carol Narsutis, my high school journalism teacher who made me a better writer and got me to seriously pursue writing as a career.

My thanks to all the authors who have inspired me in a lifetime of reading.

Most of all, my thanks to Suzanne, my wife, partner, lover, and best friend. From the moment I cooked up the idea of this novel, she patiently listened to me talk about the research, characters, and plot as the novel took shape, acting as sounding board and prime reader. I know an author shouldn't use a relative as a reader, but most relatives do not possess Suzanne's thirty years' experience evaluating writing as a literature teacher. As she read *Rescuing Crockett*, we discussed the questions she had and what she was experiencing and feeling. I cannot thank her enough. Suzanne is the best person I have ever known.

Finally, to the historians of Texas and Mexico. Historical accuracy in a novel is nice but not essential, and it took a backseat to my story. Authenticity, however, is important, and the following authors and works provided inspiration, background, and details that added to the authenticity of this novel. Anything in this novel that is not historically authentic or accurate is purely due to me. My thanks to:

- *Alamo Traces, New Evidence and New Conclusions* by Thomas Ricks Lindley
- *A Narrative of the Life of David Crockett, of the State of Tennessee,* by David Crockett
- *Anglos and Mexicans in the Making of Texas, 1836–1986,* by David Montejano
- *A Revolution Remembered: The Memoirs and Selected Correspondence of Juan N. Seguín,* edited by Jesús F. de la Teja
- *Black Texans,* by Alwyn Barr

- *Built in Texas*, edited by Francis Edward Abernethy, line drawings by Reese Kennedy
- *David Crockett: Hero of the Common Man*, by William Groneman III
- *David Crockett: The Lion of the West*, by Michael Wallis
- *Early Texas Architecture*, by Gordon Echols
- *Eighteen Minutes: The Battle of San Jacinto and the Texas Independence Campaign*, by Stephen L. Moore
- *Elite Series: The Texas Rangers*, by Dr. Stephen Hardin and Richard Hook
- *Everyday Life and Politics in Nineteenth Century Mexico*, by Mark Wasserman
- *Faces of Béxar: Early San Antonio & Texas*, by Jesús F. de la Teja
- *Handbook of Texas*, online from the Texas State Historical Association
- *Historical Atlas of Texas*, by A. Ray Stephens and Dr. William M. Holmes
- *Horses*, by Elwyn Hartley Edwards
- *Joe, the Slave Who Became an Alamo Legend*, by Ron J. Jackson Jr. and Lee Spencer White
- *Life in Mexico*, by Madame Calderón de la Barca
- *Lone Star: A History of Texas and the Texans*, by T.R. Fehrenbach
- *Men-At-Arms Series: The Alamo and the War of Texan Independence 1835–36*, by Philip Haythornthwaite and Paul Hannon
- *Men-At-Arms Series: The Mexican-American War 1946–48*, by Philip Katcher and G.A. Embleton
- *Sea of Mud*, by Gregg J. Dimmick
- *Sleuthing the Alamo*, by James E. Crisp

- *The Alamo Remembered: Tejano Accounts and Perspectives*, by Timothy M. Matovina
- *The Immortal 32*, by Rita Kerr
- *The Peacemakers: Arms and Adventure in the American West*, by R.L. Wilson
- *The Tejano Community, 1836–1900*, by Arnoldo De León
- *Texian Iliad: A Military History of the Texas Revolution*, by Stephen L. Hardin
- *The Texas Republic: A Social & Economic History*, by William Ransom Hogan
- *Three Roads to the Alamo*, by William C. Davis
- *What It Is Like to Go to War*, by Karl Marlantes
- *With Santa Anna in Texas*, by José Enrique de la Peña

ABOUT THE AUTHOR

 David Z. Pyke has always been a writer. His relationship with words began in elementary school, where he read *Beowulf* and *Dracula* by the time he was 10 years old. He wrote his first stories for newspapers when he was 15 and has written professionally for 47 years.

His passion stems from his heritage: Pyke is a native Texan related to one of the Alamo defenders. His great-great-great-great-great-granduncle, Isaac Millsaps, was one of the Immortal 32, the reinforcements from Gonzales who answered William Barret Travis's call for help, rode to San Antonio, and died in the Alamo on March 6, 1836.

In 1991, a mutual friend introduced David to Suzanne, an English literature teacher from Missouri. Their first date was on a Friday the 13th. She later confessed that before that first date, she read some of his stories to make sure he could write. Apparently, he received a passing grade. They were engaged five months later, married four months after that, and in 2022 celebrated their 30th anniversary.

davidzpyke.com

Made in the USA
Coppell, TX
02 February 2025

45293413R20213